GREAT ILLUSTRATED CLASSICS

A List of the Principal Works by ALEXANDRE DUMAS (Père) and their Dates

The Conspirators or Chevalier d'Harmental—1843

Ascanio—1843–44

The Three Musketeers—1844

The Regent's Daughter—1844

The Count of Monte Cristo—1844–45

Twenty Years After—1845

Marguerite de Valois—1845

The Chevalier de Maison-Rouge—1846

Chicot, The Jester—1846

Memoirs of a Physician—1846–48

The Forty-five Guardsmen—1848

Vicomte de Bragelonne or Twenty Years Later—1848–50
  (includes The Man in the Iron Mask)

The Queen's Necklace—1849–50

The Black Tulip—1850

The Taking of the Bastile—1853

The Countess de Charny—1853–55

The Page of the Duke of Savoy—1855

The Company of Jehu—1857

Neapolitan Lovers—1864

Love and Liberty—1864

The Prussian Terror—1867

The Whites and the Blues—1867–68

D'Artagnan

THE MAN IN THE
IRON MASK

BY *ALEXANDRE DUMAS*

With illustrations by J. A. Beaucé
Philippoteaux and others, and a
foreword by Emile Van Vliet

NEW YORK · DODD, MEAD & COMPANY

THE MAN IN THE IRON MASK

PUBLISHED IN THE UNITED
STATES OF AMERICA, 1944
BY DODD, MEAD & COMPANY, INC.

PREFACE

FOR THE READER

THE identity of the famous prisoner of the Bastille who wore the mask is one of the mysteries which history has not finally solved. At least three different explanations have been advanced, with plausibility and considerable proof; but obviously two of these, and perhaps all three, are wrong. The episode has long been a favorite of the novelists, to whom it offers the opportunity for invention and drama without end; but no one has woven a more thrilling tale about this historic incident than Dumas, in the final section of the great three musketeers cycle.

Strictly speaking, the Dumas story of the man in the iron mask is not a separate novel in itself, but is part of that epic which begins with the appearance of D'Artagnan and his yellow-coated pony in the streets of Meung and ends with this same D'Artagnan receiving, at the last moment of his life, the fleur-de-lised baton of *Maréchal* of France. The iron mask episode is found toward the end of this long and renowned chronicle and may be judiciously sorted out from a wealth of plot and sub-plot in the text of the third volume of "The Vicomte de Bragelonne."

In order to make the story more readily available to the reader, the present editor has succeeded, it is hoped, in taking from the original novel those incidents and episodes which relate particularly to the man in the iron mask and which in themselves comprise a completely integrated story. That story is presented under the appropriate title, as nearly as possible in the very words of Dumas himself, with only here and there, at considerable intervals, a connecting phrase or two added to bridge the gap where some unrelated episode is omitted.

But, when all is said, the present volume remains essentially the story of the adventurous closing years of those four men who had performed such prodigies—attacking armies, assaulting castles, terrifying death itself—Athos, Porthos, Aramis, and their captain, D'Artagnan. Although in spirit these four are still guardsmen, as

Preface

we first knew them, in these latter pages they are somewhat changed in outward appearance. Aramis has long since become a Jesuit and risen to the highest eminence of the Society, yet still plays his secret part in affairs of state. Porthos, wealthy and retired from active service, is now M. le Baron du Vallon. The indefatigable D'Artagnan is captain of the King's own guard and personal confidant of the King, subject to his orders alone. It is he who has been pleading with Louis, as the story opens, for the freedom of Athos, whose arrest the King has just ordered. Athos, Comte de la Fère, is the father of Raoul, Vicomte de Bragelonne, whom Louise de la Vallière, favorite of Louis, has just renounced, breaking their betrothal. Athos has put his head in the lion's mouth by going directly to the King to plead for his desperately unhappy son and has not only failed but has aroused all the fury of the King's jealousy and anger. Only the calmness and intrepidity of D'Artagnan have saved the old musketeer's head. As it is, the opening pages reveal Athos being conducted to the Bastille by D'Artagnan as a prisoner of the King, neither of them realizing that Aramis has already preceded them there on his secret mission to the mysterious prisoner hidden within the grim walls. There the reader will find his erstwhile friends gathered as he begins the story.

EMILE VAN VLIET.

NEW YORK, JUNE 1939.

CONTENTS

Contents

ILLUSTRATIONS

THE MAN IN THE IRON MASK

CHAPTER I

THREE GUESTS ASTONISHED TO FIND THEMSELVES AT SUPPER TOGETHER

A CARRIAGE arrived at the outside gate of the Bastille. A soldier on guard stopped it; but D'Artagnan had only to utter a single word to procure admittance, and the carriage passed on. While they were proceeding along the covered way which led to the courtyard of the governor's residence, D'Artagnan, whose lynx eye saw everything, even through the walls, suddenly cried out, "What is that out yonder?"

"Well," said Athos, quietly, "what is it?"—"Look yonder, Athos!" —"In the courtyard?"—"Yes, yes; make haste!"—"Well, a carriage; very likely conveying a prisoner like myself."—"That would be too droll."—"I do not understand you."—"Make haste and look again, and look at the man who is just getting out of that carriage."

At that very moment a second sentinel stopped D'Artagnan; and while the formalities were gone through, Athos could see at a hundred paces from him the man whom his friend had pointed out to him. He was, in fact, getting out of the carriage at the door of the governor's house. "Well," inquired D'Artagnan, "do you see him?"— "Yes; he is a man in a grey suit."—"What do you say of him?"—"I cannot very well tell. He is, as I have just now told you, a man in a grey suit, who is getting out of a carriage; that is all."— "Athos, I will wager anything it is he."—"He?—who?"—"Aramis."

"Aramis arrested? Impossible!"—"I do not say he is arrested, since we see him alone in his carriage."—"Well, then, what is he doing here?"—"Oh, he knows Baisemeaux, the governor!" replied the musketeer, slyly. "My faith! we have arrived just in time."— "What for?"—"In order to see what we can see."

"I regret this meeting exceedingly. When Aramis sees me, he will be very much annoyed,—in the first place at seeing me, and in the

1

next at being seen."—"Very well reasoned."—"Unfortunately, there is no remedy for it. Whenever any one meets another in the Bastille, even if he wished to draw back to avoid him, it would be impossible."

"Athos, I have an idea: the question is, to spare Aramis the annoyance you were speaking of, is it not?"—"What is to be done?"—"I will tell you; or, in order better to explain myself, let me relate the affair in my own manner. I will not recommend you to tell a falsehood, for that would be impossible for you to do."—"Well, what is it?"—"Well, I will lie for both of us; it is so easy to do that, with the nature and habits of a Gascon."

Athos smiled. The carriage stopped where the one we have just now pointed out had stopped; namely, at the door of the governor's house. "It is understood, then?" said D'Artagnan, in a low voice to his friend. Athos consented by a gesture.

They ascended the staircase. There will be no occasion for surprise at the facility with which they had entered into the Bastille, if it be understood that before passing the first gate—in fact, the most difficult of all—D'Artagnan had announced that he had brought a prisoner of State. At the third gate, on the contrary,—that is to say, when he had once fairly entered the prison,—he merely said to the sentinel, "To M. Baisemeaux;" and they both passed on. In a few minutes they were in the governor's dining-room; and the first face which attracted D'Artagnan's observation was that of Aramis, who was seated side by side with Baisemeaux, and awaited the announcement of a good meal, whose odour impregnated the whole apartment. If D'Artagnan pretended surprise, Aramis did not pretend at all; he started when he saw his two friends, and his emotion was very apparent. Athos and D'Artagnan, however, made their salutations; and Baisemeaux, amazed, completely stupefied by the presence of those three guests, began to perform a few evolutions around them.

"Ah, there!" said Aramis, "by what chance—"—"We were just going to ask you," retorted D'Artagnan.—"Are we going to give ourselves up as prisoners?" cried Aramis, with an affectation of hilarity.—"Ah! ah!" said D'Artagnan; "it is true the walls smell deucedly like a prison. M. de Baisemeaux, you know you invited me to sup with you the other day."—"I?" cried Baisemeaux.—"Ah! one would say you had fallen from the clouds. You have no recollection of it?"

The Three Astonished Guests

Baisemeaux turned pale and then red; looked at Aramis, who looked at him; and finally stammered, "Certainly—I am delighted —but—upon my honour—I have not the slightest—Ah! I have such a wretched memory."—"Well, I am wrong, I see," said D'Artagnan, as if he were offended.—"Wrong, how?"—"Wrong to remember, it seems."

Baisemeaux hurried towards him. "Do not stand on ceremony, my dear captain," he said. "I have the poorest head in the kingdom. Take me from my pigeons and their pigeon-house, and I am no better than the rawest recruit."—"At all events, you remember it now," said D'Artagnan, boldly.—"Yes, yes," replied the governor, hesitating; "I think I remember."

"It was when you came to the palace to see me; you told me some story or other about your accounts with M. de Louvière and M. de Tremblay."—"Oh, yes! perfectly."—"And about M. d'Herblay's kindness to you."—"Ah!" exclaimed Aramis, looking the unhappy governor full in the face; "and yet you just now said you had no memory, M. de Baisemeaux."

Baisemeaux interrupted the musketeer in the midst of his revelations. "Yes, yes, you're quite right; it seems to me that I am still there. I beg a thousand pardons. But now, once for all, my dear M. d'Artagnan, be sure that at this present time, as at any other, whether invited or not, you are master here,—you and M. d'Herblay, your friend," he said, turning towards Aramis; "and this gentleman too," he added, bowing to Athos.

"Well, I thought it would be sure to turn out so," replied d'Artagnan. "This is the occasion of my coming: Having nothing to do this evening at the Palais-Royal, I wished to judge for myself what your ordinary style of living was like; and as I was coming along I met Monsieur the Count." Athos bowed. "The count, who had just left his Majesty, handed me an order which required immediate attention. We were close by here; I wished to call in, even if it were for no other object than that of shaking hands with you and of presenting the count to you, of whom you spoke so highly in the king's presence that very evening when—"

"Certainly, certainly—M. le Comte de la Fère, is it not?"—"Precisely."—"Monsieur the Count is welcome."—"And he will sup with you two, I suppose; while I, unfortunate dog that I am, must run off on a matter of duty. Oh, what happy beings you are, compared to myself!" D'Artagnan added, sighing as loud as Porthos might have done.

"And so you are going away?" said Aramis and Baisemeaux together, with the same expression of delighted surprise, the tone of which was immediately noticed by D'Artagnan. "I leave you in my place," he said, "a noble and excellent guest;" and he touched Athos gently on the shoulder, who, astonished also, could not help exhibiting his surprise a little,—which was noticed by Aramis only, for M. de Baisemeaux was not quite equal to the three friends in point of intelligence.

"What! are you going to leave us?" resumed the governor.—"I shall be away only about an hour or an hour and a half. I will return in time for dessert."—"Oh, we will wait for you!" said Baisemeaux.—"No, no; that would be really disobliging me."—"You will be sure to return, though?" said Athos, with an expression of doubt. —"Most certainly," he said, pressing his friend's hand confidentially; and he added in a low voice, "Wait for me, Athos; be cheerful and lively as possible, and above all, don't allude to business affairs, for Heaven's sake!" and a renewed pressure of the hand impressed upon the count the necessity of being discreet and impenetrable.

Baisemeaux led D'Artagnan to the gate. Aramis, with many friendly protestations of delight, sat down by Athos, determined to make him speak; but Athos possessed all the virtues in their highest excellence. If necessity had required it, he would have been the finest orator in the world; but when there was need of silence he would die rather than utter a syllable.

Ten minutes after D'Artagnan's departure, the three gentlemen sat down to table, which was covered with the most substantial display of gastronomic luxury. Large joints, exquisite dishes, preserves, the greatest variety of wines, appeared successively upon the table, which was served at the king's expense, and of which expense M. Colbert would have no difficulty in saving two-thirds, without any one in the Bastille being the worse for it.

Aramis was incessantly asking himself by what extraordinary chance Athos was at Baisemeaux's when D'Artagnan was no longer there, and why D'Artagnan did not remain when Athos was there. Athos sounded all the depths of the mind of Aramis, who lived in the midst of subterfuge, evasion, and intrigue; he studied his man well and thoroughly, and felt convinced that he was engaged upon

4

some important project. And then he too began to think of his own personal affair, and to lose himself in conjectures as to D'Artagnan's reason for having left the Bastille so abruptly, and for leaving behind him a prisoner so badly introduced and so badly looked after by the prison authorities. But we shall not pause to examine into the thoughts and feelings of these personages; we will leave them to themselves, surrounded by the remains of poultry, game, and fish, mutiliated by the generous knife of Baisemeaux. We are going to follow D'Artagnan instead, who, getting into the carriage which had brought him, cried out to the coachman, "To the king! and burn the pavement!"

CHAPTER II

WHAT TOOK PLACE AT THE LOUVRE DURING THE SUPPER AT THE BASTILLE

M DE SAINT-AIGNAN, the courtier, had executed the commission with which the king had entrusted him for his favorite, La Vallière; but whatever his eloquence might have been, he did not succeed in persuading the young girl that she had in the king a protector powerful enough for her under any combination of circumstances, and that she had no need of any one else in the world when the king was on her side. In point of fact, at the very first word, Louise, in a passion of tears, abandoned herself in utter despair to a sorrow which would have been far from flattering for the king, if he had been a witness of it from a corner of the room. De Saint-Aignan, in his character of ambassador, felt greatly offended at it, as his master himself would have been, and returned to announce to the king what he had seen and heard. It is there that we now find him, in a state of great agitation, in the presence of the king, still more agitated than he.

"But," said the king to the courtier, when the latter had finished his report, "what did she decide to do? Shall I, at least, see her presently before supper? Will she come to me, or shall I be obliged to go to her room?"—"I believe, Sire, that if your Majesty wishes to see her, you will not only have to take the first step in advance, but will have to go the whole way."

5

The Man in the Iron Mask

"Nothing for me! Does that Bragelonne still possess her heart?" muttered the king between his teeth.—"Oh, Sire, that is not possible; for it is you alone whom Mademoiselle de la Vallière loves, and that, too, with all her heart. But you know that De Bragelonne belongs to that proud race who play the part of Roman heroes." The king smiled feebly; he knew how true the illustration was, for Athos had just left him. "As for Mademoiselle de la Vallière," De Saint-Aignan continued, "she was brought up under the care of the Dowager Madame; that is to say, in austere retirement. This engaged young couple coldly exchanged their little vows in the presence of the moon and the stars; and now, when they find they have to break those vows, it plays the very deuce with them."

De Saint-Aignan thought he should have made the king laugh; but on the contrary, from a mere smile Louis passed to the greatest seriousness of manner. He already began to experience a remorse which the count had promised D'Artagnan he would inflict upon him. He reflected that, in fact, these young persons had loved and sworn fidelity to each other; that one of the two had kept his word, and that the other was too conscientious not to feel her perjury most bitterly; and with remorse, jealousy sharply pricked the king's heart. He did not say another word; and instead of going to pay a visit to his mother or the queen or Madame, in order to amuse himself a little and make the ladies laugh, as he himself used to say, he threw himself into the huge arm-chair in which his august father, Louis XIII., had passed so many weary days and years in company with Baradas and Cinq-Mars.

De Saint-Aignan perceived that the king was not to be amused at that moment; he tried a last resource, and pronounced Louise's name, which made the king look up immediately. "What does your Majesty intend to do this evening? Shall Mademoiselle de la Vallière be informed of your intention to see her?"—"It seems she is already aware of that," replied the king. "No, no, Saint-Aignan," he continued, after a moment's pause; "we will both of us pass our time in dreaming. When Mademoiselle de la Vallière shall have sufficiently regretted what she now regrets, she will deign, perhaps, to give us some news of herself."—"Ah, Sire, is it possible you can so misunderstand that devoted heart?"

The king rose, flushed with vexation; he was a prey to jealousy in its turn. De Saint-Aignan was just beginning to feel that his position

6

was becoming awkward, when the curtain before the door was raised. The king turned hastily round. His first idea was that a letter from Louise had arrived; but instead of a letter of love, he saw only his captain of musketeers standing upright and silent in the doorway. "M. d'Artagnan!" he said. "Ah! well, Monsieur?"

D'Artagnan looked at De Saint-Aignan; Louis's eyes took the same direction as those of his captain. These looks would have been clear to any one, and they were especially so to De Saint-Aignan. The courtier bowed and quitted the room, leaving the king and D'Artagnan alone. "Is it done?" inquired the king.—"Yes, Sire," replied the captain of the musketeers, in a grave voice, "it is done!"

The king was unable to say another word. Pride, however, obliged him not to pause there. Whenever a sovereign has adopted a decisive course, even though it be unjust, he is compelled to prove to all witnesses, and particularly to himself, that he was quite right in so adopting it. A good means for effecting that—an almost infallible means, indeed—is to try to prove his victim to be in the wrong. Louis, brought up by Mazarin and Anne of Austria, knew better than any one else his vocation as a monarch; he therefore endeavoured to prove it on the present occasion. After a few moment's pause, which he had employed in making silently to himself the same reflections which we have just expressed aloud, he said in an indifferent tone, "What did the count say?"—"Nothing at all, Sire."—"Surely he did not allow himself to be arrested without saying something?"—"He said he expected to be arrested, Sire."

The king raised his head haughtily. "I presume," he said, "that M. le Comte de la Fère has not continued to play his obstinate and rebellious part?"—"In the first place, Sire, what do you term rebellious?" quietly asked the musketeer. "Is that man a rebel, in the eyes of the king, who not only allows himself to be shut up in the Bastille, but who even opposes those who do not wish to take him there?"

"Who do not wish to take him there!" exclaimed the king. "What do you say, Captain? Are you mad?"—"I believe not, Sire."—"You speak of persons who did not wish to arrest M. de la Fère?"—"Yes, Sire."—"And who are they?"—"Those whom your Majesty intrusted with that duty, apparently."—"But it is you whom I entrusted with it," exclaimed the king.—"Yes, Sire; it is I."

"And you say that, despite my orders, you had the intention of not arresting the man who had insulted me!"—"Yes, Sire, that was really my intention. I even proposed to the count to mount a horse that I had had prepared for him at the Barrière de la Conférence." —"And what was your object in getting this horse ready?"—"Why, Sire, in order that M. le Comte de la Fère might be able to reach Havre, and from that place make his escape to England."

"You betrayed me then, Monsieur?" cried the king, kindling with a wild pride.—"Exactly so."

There was nothing to say in answer to statements made in such a tone; the king was astounded at such an obstinate and open resistance on the part of D'Artagnan. "At least you had a reason, M. d'Artagnan, for acting as you did?" said the king, proudly.—"I have always a reason, Sire."—"Your reason cannot be your friendship for the count, at all events,—the only one that can be of any avail, the only one that could possibly excuse you,—for I placed you entirely at your ease in that respect."

"Me, Sire?"—"Did I not give you the choice to arrest or not to arrest M. le Comte de la Fère?"—"Yes, Sire; but—"—"But what?" exclaimed the king, impatiently.—"But you warned me, Sire, that if I did not arrest him, your captain of the guards should do so."

"Was I not considerate enough towards you when I did not compel you to obey me?"—"To me, Sire, you were, but not to my friend; for my friend would be arrested all the same, whether by myself or by the captain of the guards."—"And this is your devotion, Monsieur,—a devotion which argues and reasons! You are no soldier, Monsieur!"—"I wait for your Majesty to tell me what I am."— "Well, then,—you are a Frondeur."—"And since there is no longer any Fronde, Sire, in that case—"

"But if what you say is true—"—"What I say is always true, Sire."—"What have you come to say to me, Monsieur?"—"I have come to say to your Majesty: Sire, M. de la Fère is in the Bastille." —"That is not your fault, it would seem."—"That is true, Sire. But, at all events, he is there; and since he is there, it is important that your Majesty should know it."

"Ah, M. d'Artagnan, so you set your king at defiance!"—"Sire—" —"M. d'Artagnan, I warn you that you are abusing my patience."— "On the contrary, Sire."—"What do you mean by 'on the contrary'?" —"I have come to get myself arrested too."

"To get yourself arrested,—you!"—"Of course. My friend will

be lonely down there; and I have come to propose to your Majesty to permit me to bear him company. If your Majesty will but give the word, I will arrest myself; I shall not need the captain of the guards for that, I assure you."

The king darted towards the table and seized a pen to write the order for D'Artagnan's imprisonment. "Pay attention, Monsieur, that this is for ever!" cried the king, in a tone of stern menace.— "I can quite believe that," returned the musketeer; "for when you have once done such an act as that, you will never be able to look me in the face again." The king dashed down his pen violently. "Leave the room, Monsieur!" he said.

"Oh, not so, Sire, if it please your Majesty!"—"How not so?"— "Sire, I came to speak temperately to your Majesty. Your Majesty got into a passion with me: that is a misfortune; but I shall not the less on that account say what I had to say to you."—"Your resignation, Monsieur,—your resignation!" cried the king.

"Sire, you know whether I care about my resignation or not, since at Blois, on the day when you refused King Charles the million which my friend the Comte de la Fère gave him, I tendered my resignation to your Majesty."—"Very well, then, do it at once!"— "No, Sire; for there is no question of my resignation at the present moment. Your Majesty took up your pen just now to send me to the Bastille,—why should you change your intention?"

"D'Artagnan! Gascon that you are! who is the king, allow me to ask,—you or myself?"—"You, Sire, unfortunately."—"What do you mean by 'unfortunately'?"—"Yes, Sire; for if it were I—"—"If it were you, you would approve of M. d'Artagnan's rebellious conduct, I suppose?"—"Certainly."

"Really?" said the king, shrugging his shoulders.—"And I should tell my captain of the musketeers," continued D'Artagnan,—"I should tell him, looking at him all the while with human eyes and not with eyes like coals of fire, 'M. d'Artagnan, I have forgotten that I am king; I have descended from my throne to insult a gentleman.' "

"Monsieur!" cried the king, "do you think you can excuse your friend by exceeding him in insolence?"—"Oh, Sire! I shall go much further that he did," said D'Artagnan; "and it will be your own fault. I shall tell you what he, a man full of delicacy, did not tell you; I shall say: 'Sire, you sacrificed his son, and he defended his son; you sacrificed him; he addressed you in the name of honour, of religion, of virtue,—you repulsed, pursued, imprisoned him.' I shall be harder than he was, for I shall say to you: 'Sire, choose! Do you wish to have friends or lackeys, soldiers or slaves, great men or puppets? Do you wish men to serve you or to crouch before you? Do you wish men to love you or to fear you? If you prefer baseness, intrigue, cowardice,—oh! say it, Sire! We will leave you,—we who are the only surviving illustrations, nay, I will say more, the only models of the valour of former times; we who have done our duty, and have exceeded, perhaps, in courage and in merit the men already great for posterity. Choose, Sire, and without delay! Whatever remains to you of the grand nobility, guard it with a jealous eye; of courtiers you will always have enough. Delay not—and send me to the Bastille with my friend; for if you have not known how to listen to the Comte de la Fère, that is to say, to the most sweet and noble voice of honour; if you do not know how to listen to D'Artagnan, that is to say, to the most candid and rough voice of sincerity,—you are a bad king, and to-morrow will be a poor king. Now, bad kings are hated; poor kings are driven away.' That is what I had to say to you, Sire; you are wrong to have driven me to it."

The king threw himself back in his chair cold and livid. Had a thunderbolt fallen at his feet, he could not have been more astonished; he appeared as if his respiration had ceased, and as if he were at the point of death. That rough voice of sincerity, as D'Artagnan had called it, had pierced through his heart like a sword-blade. D'Artagnan had said all that he had to say. Comprehending the king's anger, he drew his sword, and approaching Louis XIV. respectfully, placed it on the table. But the king, with a furious gesture, thrust aside the sword, which fell on the ground and rolled to D'Artagnan's feet. Notwithstanding his mastery over himself, D'Artagnan too, in his turn, became pale and trembled with indignation. "A king," he said, "may disgrace a soldier,—he may exile him, and may even condemn him to death; but were he a hundred times a king, he has no right to insult him by casting dishonour on his sword! Sire, a king of France has never repulsed with contempt the sword of a man such as I am! Stained with disgrace as this sword now is, it has henceforth no other sheath than either your heart or my own. I choose my own, Sire; give thanks for it to God, and my patience." Then snatching up his sword, he cried, "My blood be upon your head!" and with a rapid gesture he placed the hilt upon the floor and directed the point of the blade towards his breast. The king, however, with a movement still more rapid than that of D'Artagnan, threw his right arm round the musketeer's neck, and with his left hand seized hold of the blade by the middle, and returned it silently to the scabbard. D'Artagnan, upright, pale, and still trembling, suffered the king to do all, without aiding him, to the very end. Then Louis, overcome, returned to the table, took a pen, wrote a few lines, signed them, and offered the paper to D'Artagnan.

"What is this paper, Sire?" inquired the captain.—"An order for M. d'Artagnan to set the Comte de la Fère at liberty immediately."

D'Artagnan seized the king's hand and kissed it; he then folded the order, placed it in his belt, and quitted the room. Neither the king nor the captain spoke a word. "Oh, human heart, director of kings!" murmured Louis, when alone; "when shall I learn to read in your recesses, as in the leaves of a book? No, I am not a bad king, nor am I a poor king; but I am still a child."

CHAPTER III

POLITICAL RIVALS

D'ARTAGNAN had promised M. de Baisemeaux to return in time for dessert, and he kept his word. They had just reached the finer and more delicate class of wines and liqueurs with which the governor's cellar had the reputation of being most admirably stocked, when the spurs of the captain resounded in the corridor, and he himself appeared at the threshold. Athos and Aramis had played a close game; neither had been able to gain the slightest advantage over the other. They had supped, talked a good deal about the Bastille, of the last journey to Fontainebleau, of the intended *fête* that M. Fouquet was about to give at Vaux; they had generalised on every possible subject, and no one, excepting Baisemeaux, had alluded to private matters.

D'Artagnan arrived in the very midst of the conversation, still pale and disturbed by his interview with the king. Baisemeaux hastened to give him a chair; D'Artagnan accepted a glass of wine,

and set it down empty. Athos and Aramis both remarked his emotion; as for Baisemeaux, he saw nothing more than the captain of
the king's musketeers, to whom he endeavoured to show every attention. To be near the king entitled any one to all privileges, in the
eyes of M. de Blaisemeaux.

But although Aramis had remarked that emotion, he had not been
able to guess the cause of it. Athos alone believed that he had detected it. To him D'Artagnan's return, and particularly the manner
in which he, usually so impassive, seemed overcome, signified, "I
have just asked the king something which he has refused me." Thoroughly convinced that his conjecture was correct, Athos smiled, rose
from the table, and made a sign to D'Artagnan, as if to remind him
that they had something else to do than to sup together. D'Artagnan immediately understood him, and replied by another sign.
Aramis and Baisemeaux watched this silent dialogue, and looked
inquiringly at each other. Athos felt that he was called upon to give
an explanation of what was passing. "The truth is, my friends,"
said the Comte de la Fère, with a smile, "that you, Aramis, have been
supping with a State criminal, and you, M. de Baisemeaux, with your
prisoner."

Baisemeaux uttered an exclamation of surprise and almost of delight. That worthy man took pride in his fortress. Profit aside, the
more prisoners he had, the happier he was; and the higher the prisoners were in rank, the prouder he felt. Aramis assumed an expression which he thought the situation required, and said: "Well, dear
Athos, forgive me; but I almost suspected what has happened. Some
prank of Raoul or La Vallière, is it not?"—"Alas!" said Baisemeaux.
—"And," continued Aramis, "you, a high and powerful nobleman
as you are, forgetful that there are now only courtiers,—you have
been to the king, and told him what you thought of his conduct?"—
"Yes, you have guessed right."

"So that," said Baisemeaux, trembling at having supped so fa-
miliarly with a man who had fallen into disgrace with the king,—"so
that, Monsieur the Count—"—"So that, my dear governor," said
Athos, "my friend D'Artagnan will communicate to you the contents
of the paper which I perceive just peeping out of his belt, and which
assuredly can be nothing else than the order for my incarceration."

Baisemeaux held out his hand with his accustomed eagerness.
D'Artagnan drew two papers from his belt, and presented one of

them to the governor, who unfolded it, and then read, in a low tone of voice, looking at Athos over the paper, as he did so, and pausing from time to time: " 'Order to detain in my château of the Bastille M. le Comte de la Fère.' Oh, Monsieur! this is indeed a very melancholy honour for me."

"You will have a patient prisoner, Monsieur," said Athos, in his calm, soft voice.—"A prisoner, too, who will not remain a month with you, my dear governor," said Aramis; while Baisemeaux, still holding the order in his hand, transcribed it upon the prison registry. —"Not a day, or rather not even a night," said D'Artagnan, displaying the second order of the king; "for now, dear M. de Baisemeaux, you will have the goodness to transcribe also this order for setting the count immediately at liberty."

"Ah!" said Aramis, "it is a labour that you have spared me, D'Artagnan;" and he pressed the musketeer's hand in a significant manner, and that of Athos at the same time.

"What!" said the latter, in astonishment, "the king sets me at liberty!"—"Read, my dear friend!" returned D'Artagnan. Athos took the order and read it. "It is quite true," he said.

"Are you sorry for it?" asked D'Artagnan.—"Oh, no, on the contrary! I wish the king no harm; and the greatest evil or misfortune that any one can wish kings is that they should commit an act of injustice. But you have had a difficult and painful task, I know. Tell me, have you not, D'Artagnan?"—"I? Not at all," said the musketeer, laughing; "the king does everything I wish him to do."

Aramis looked fixedly at D'Artagnan, and saw that he was not speaking the truth. But Baisemeaux had eyes for nothing but D'Artagnan, so great was his admiration for a man who could make the king do all he wished.

"And does the king exile Athos?" inquired Aramis.—"No, not precisely. The king did not explain himself upon that subject," replied D'Artagnan; "but I think the count could not do better, unless indeed he wishes particularly to thank the king—"—"No, indeed," replied Athos, smiling.

"Well, then, I think," resumed D'Artagnan, "that the count cannot do better than to retire to his own château. However, my dear Athos, you have only to speak, to tell me what you want. If any particular place of residence is more agreeable to you than another, I can obtain it for you."—"No, thank you," said Athos; "nothing can be more agreeable to me, my dear friend, than to return to the solitude beneath my noble trees on the banks of the Loire. If Heaven be the overruling physician of the evils of the mind, Nature is a sovereign remedy. And so, Monsieur," continued Athos, turning again towards Baisemeaux, "I am now free, I suppose?"

"Yes, Monsieur the Count, I think so,—at least, I hope so," said the governor, turning over and over the two papers in question; "unless, however, M. d'Artagnan has a third order to give me."— "No, my dear M. Baisemeaux, no," said the musketeer; "the second is quite enough. We can stop there."

"Ah! Monsieur the Count," said Baisemeaux, addressing Athos, "you do not know what you are losing. I should have placed you at thirty livres, like the generals—what am I saying?—I mean at fifty livres, like the princes; and you would have supped every evening as you have supped to-night."—"Allow me, Monsieur," said Athos, "to prefer my mediocrity;" and then, turning to D'Artagnan, he said, "Let us go, my friend."—"Let us go," said D'Artagnan.

"Shall I have the happiness of having you as my companion?"— "To the city gate only," replied D'Artagnan; "after which I will tell you what I told the king: 'I am on duty.' "—"And you, dear Aramis," said Athos, smiling; "will you accompany me? La Fère is on the road to Vannes."—"Thank you, my dear friend," said Aramis; "but I have an appointment in Paris this evening, and I cannot leave without very serious interests suffering by my absence."

"In that case," said Athos, "I must say adieu, and take my leave of you. My dear M. de Baisemeaux, I have to thank you exceedingly for your good will, and particularly for the specimen you have given me of the Bastille fare;" and having embraced Aramis, and shaken hands with M. de Baisemeaux, and having received their wishes for an agreeable journey from them both, Athos set off with D'Artagnan.

When once these two guests had departed, Baisemeaux did not in the least perceive that the conversation suffered by their absence. He thought that wine after supper, and that of the Bastille in particular, was excellent; and that it was a stimulant quite sufficient to make an honest man talk. But he little knew his greatness, who was never more impenetrable than at dessert. His greatness, however, perfectly understood M. de Baisemeaux, when he reckoned on making the governor discourse by the means which the latter regarded as efficacious. The conversation, therefore, without flagging in appearance, flagged in reality; for Baisemeaux not only had it nearly all to himself, but further kept speaking only of that singular event,—the incarceration of Athos, followed by so prompt an order to set him again at liberty. Nor, moreover, had Baisemeaux failed to observe that the order of arrest and that of liberation were both in the king's hand. But the king would not take the trouble to write such orders except under pressing circumstances. All this was very interesting, and, above all, very puzzling to Baisemeaux; but as, on the other hand, all this was very clear to Aramis, the latter did not attach to the occurrence the same importance as did the worthy governor. Besides, Aramis rarely put himself out of the way for anything, and he had not yet told M. de Baisemeaux for what reason he had now done so; and so, at the very climax of Baisemeaux's dissertation, Aramis suddenly interrupted him. "Tell me, my dear M. Baisemeaux," said he, "have you never any other diversions at the Bastille than those at which I have assisted during the two or three visits I have had the honour to pay you?"

This address was so unexpected that the governor, like a vane which suddenly receives an impulsion opposed to that of the wind, was quite dumfounded at it. "Diversions!" said he; "but I take them continually, Monseigneur."—"Oh, to be sure! And these diversions—"—"Are of every kind."—"Visits, no doubt?"—"No, not visits. Visits are not frequent at the Bastille."

"What! are visits rare, then?"—"Very rare."—"Even on the part of your society?"—"What do you mean by my 'society,'—the prisoners?"—"Oh, no! Your prisoners, indeed! I know well it is you who visit them, and not they you. By your society I mean, my dear M. Baisemeaux, the society of which you are a member."

Baisemeaux looked fixedly at Aramis, and then, as if the idea which had flashed across his mind were impossible, "Oh!" he said, "I have very little society at present. If I must own it to you, my dear M. d'Herblay, the fact is, to stay at the Bastille appears for the most part distressing and distasteful to persons of the gay world. As for the ladies, it is never without a dread, which costs me inflnite trouble to allay, that they come to my quarters. And, indeed, how should they avoid trembling a little, poor things, when they see those gloomy dungeons, and reflect that they are inhabited by prisoners who—" In proportion as the eyes of Baisemeaux concentrated their gaze on the face of Aramis, the worthy governor's tongue faltered more and more, until finally it stopped altogether.

"No, you don't understand me, my dear M. Baisemeaux,—you don't understand me. I do not at all mean to speak of society in general, but of a particular society,—of the society, in a word, to which you are affiliated." Baisemeaux nearly dropped the glass of muscat which he was in the act of raising to his lips. "Affiliated!" cried he, "affiliated!"

"Yes, affiliated, undoubtedly," repeated Aramis, with the greatest self-possession. "Are you not a member of a secret society, my dear M. Baisemeaux?"—"Secret?"—"Secret or mysterious."—"Oh, M. d'Herblay!"—"See! you don't deny it."—"But, believe me—"—"I believe what I know."—"I swear to you."

"Listen to me, my dear M. Baisemeaux! I say 'yes,' you say 'no.' One of us two necessarily says what is true; and the other, it inevitably follows, what is false."—"Well, and then?"—"Well, we shall come to an understanding presently."—"Let us see," said Baisemeaux; "let us see,"—"Now drink your glass of muscat, dear M. Baisemeaux," said Aramis. "What the devil! you look quite scared." —"No, no, not the least in the world; no."—"Drink, then."

Baisemeaux drank, but he swallowed the wrong way. "Well," resumed Aramis, "if, I say, you are not a member of a society, secret or mysterious, whichever you like to call it,—the epithet is of no consequence,—if, I say, you are not a member of a society similar to that I wish to designate, well, then, you will not understand a word of what I am going to say, that is all."—"Oh! be sure beforehand that I shall not understand anything."—"Well, well!"—"Try now; let us see."

"That is what I am going to do. If, on the contrary, you are one of the members of this society, you will immediately answer me, 'yes' or 'no.' "—"Begin your questions, then," continued Baisemeaux, trembling.

"You will agree, dear M. de Baisemeaux," continued Aramis, with the same impassiveness, "that it is evident a man cannot be a member of a society, it is evident that he cannot enjoy the advantages it offers to the affiliated, without being himself bound to certain little services."—"In short," stammered Baisemeaux, "that would be intelligible if—"—"Well," resumed Aramis, "there is in the society of which I speak, and of which, as it seems, you are not a member—"— "Allow me," said Baisemeaux; "I should not like to say absolutely."

"There is an engagement entered into by all the governors and captains of fortresses affiliated to the order." Baisemeaux grew pale. "Now the engagement," continued Aramis, firmly, "is of this nature." Baisemeaux rose, manifesting unspeakable emotion. "Go on, dear M. d'Herblay; go on!" said he. Aramis then spoke, or rather recited, the following sentence, in the same tone as if he had been reading it from a book: "The aforesaid captain or governor of a fortress shall allow to enter, when need shall arise, and on demand of the prisoner, a confessor affiliated to the order." He stopped. Baisemeaux was quite distressing to look at, being so wretchedly pale and trembling. "Is not that the text of the agreement?" quietly asked Aramis.

"Monseigneur!" began Baisemeaux.—"Ah, well, you begin to understand, I think."—"Monseigneur," cried Baisemeaux, "do not trifle so with my unhappy mind! I find myself nothing in your hands, if you have the malignant desire to draw from me the little secrets of my administration."—"Oh, by no means! Pray undeceive yourself, dear M. Baisemeaux; it is not the little secrets of your administration that I aim at, but those of your conscience."

"Well, then, my conscience be it, my dear M. d'Herblay! But have some consideration for the situation I am in, which is no ordinary one."—"It is no ordinary one, my dear Monsieur," continued the inflexible Aramis, "if you are a member of this society; but it is quite a natural one if, free from all engagements, you are answerable only to the king."—"Well, Monsieur, well! I obey only the king. Good God! whom else would you have a French gentleman obey?"

Aramis did not yield an inch; but with that silvery voice of his continued: "It is very pleasant for a French gentleman, for a prelate of France, to hear a man of your mark express himself so loyally, dear De Baisemeaux, and having heard you, to believe no more than you do."—"Have you doubted, Monsieur?"—"I? Oh, no!"—"And so you doubt no longer?"—"I have no longer any doubt that such a man as you, Monsieur," said Aramis, gravely, "does not faithfully serve the masters whom he voluntarily chose for himself."

"Masters!" cried Baisemeaux.—"Yes, masters, I said."—"M. d'Herblay, you are still jesting, are you not?"—"Oh, yes! I understand that it is a more difficult position to have several masters than one; but the embarrassment is owing to you, my dear Baisemeaux, and I am not the cause of it."

"Certainly not," returned the unfortunate governor, more embarrassed than ever; "but what are you doing? You are leaving the table?"—"Assuredly."—"Are you going?"—"Yes, I am going."— "But you are behaving very strangely towards me, Monseigneur."

"I am behaving strangely,—in what respect?"—"Have you sworn, then, to put me to the torture?"—"No, I should be sorry to do so."— "Remain, then."—"I cannot."—"And why?"—"Because I have no longer anything to do here; and, indeed, I have duties to fulfil elsewhere."

"Duties so late as this?"—"Yes; understand me now, my dear M. de Baisemeaux. They told me at the place whence I came, 'The aforesaid governor or captain will allow to enter, as need shall arise, on the prisoner's demand, a confessor affiliated with the order.' I came; you do not know what I mean, and so I shall return to tell them that they are mistaken, and that they must send me elsewhere." —"What! you are—" cried Baisemeaux, looking at Aramis almost in terror.—"The confessor affiliated to the order," said Aramis, without changing his voice.

But, gentle as the words were, they had the same effect on the unhappy governor as a clap of thunder. Baisemeaux became livid, and it seemed to him as if Aramis's beaming eyes were two forks of flame, piercing to the very bottom of his soul. "The confessor!" murmured he; "you, Monseigneur, the confessor of the order!"—"Yes, I; but we have nothing to unravel together, seeing that you are not one of the affiliated."—"Monseigneur!"—"And I understand that, not being so, you refuse to comply with its commands."

"Monseigneur, I beseech you, condescend to hear me."—"And wherefore?"—"Monseigneur, I do not say that I have nothing to do with the society."—"Ah! ah!"—"I say not that I refuse to obey."— "Nevertheless, M. de Baisemeaux, what has passed wears very much the air of resistance."—"Oh, no. Monseigneur, no! I only wished to be certain."—"To be certain of what?" said Aramis, in a tone of supreme contempt.—"Of nothing at all, Monseigneur." Baisemeaux lowered his voice, and bending before the prelate said, "I am at all times and in all places at the disposal of my masters, but—"

"Very good. I like you better thus, Monsieur," said Aramis, as he resumed his seat, and put out his glass to Baisemeaux, whose hand trembled so that he could not fill it. "You were saying 'but'—" continued Aramis.—"But," replied the unhappy man, "having no notice, I was far from expecting."—"Does not the Gospel say, 'Watch, for the moment is known only of God'? Do not the rules of the order say, 'Watch; for that which I will, you ought always to will also'? And on what pretext is it that you did not expect the confessor, M. de Baisemeaux?"—"Because, Monseigneur, there is at present in the Bastille no prisoner ill."

Aramis shrugged his shoulders. "What do you know about that?" said he.—"But nevertheless, it appears to me—"—"M. de Baisemeaux," said Aramis, turning round in his chair, "here is your servant, who wishes to speak with you;" and at this moment Baisemeaux's servant appeared at the threshold of the door.

"What is it?" asked Baisemeaux, sharply.—"Monsieur," said the man, "they are bringing you the doctor's return." Aramis looked at Baisemeaux with a calm and confident eye. "Well," said Baisemeaux, "let the messenger enter."

The messenger entered, saluted, and handed in the report. Baisemeaux ran his eye over it, and raising his head said, in surprise, "No. 2 Bertaudière is ill."—"How was it, then," said Aramis, carelessly, "that you told me everybody was well in your hotel, M. de Baisemeaux?" and he emptied his glass without removing his eyes from Baisemeaux.

The governor then made a sign to the messenger, and when he had quitted the room said, still trembling, "I think that there is in the article, 'on the prisoner's demand.'"—"Yes, it is so;" answered Aramis. "But see what it is they want with you now."

At that moment a sergeant put his head in at the door. "What do you want now?" cried Baisemeaux. "Can you not leave me in peace for ten minutes?"—"Monsieur," said the sergeant, "the sick man, No. 2 Bertaudière, has commissioned the turnkey to request you to send him a confessor."

Baisemeaux very nearly sank on the floor; but Aramis disdained to reassure him, just as he had disdained to terrify him. "What must I answer?" inquired Baisemeaux.—"Just what you please," replied Aramis, compressing his lips; "that is your business. *I* am not governor of the Bastille."—"Tell the prisoner," cried Baisemeaux, quickly,—"tell the prisoner that his request is granted." The sergeant left the room. "Oh, Monseigneur, Monseigneur," murmured

Baisemeaux, "how could I have suspected?—how could I have fore-seen this?"—"Who told you to suspect, and who asked you to fore-see?" contemptuously answered Aramis. "The order suspects, the order knows, the order foresees,—is not that enough?"

"What do you command?" added Baisemeaux.—"I?—nothing at all. I am nothing but a poor priest, a simple confessor. Have I your orders to go and see the sufferer?"—"Oh, Monseigneur, I do not or-der; I pray you to go."—" 'Tis well; then conduct me to him."

CHAPTER IV

THE PRISONER

SINCE Aramis's singular transformation into a confessor of the order, Baisemeaux was no longer the same man. Up to that period the place which Aramis had held in the worthy gover-nor's estimation was that of a prelate whom he respected and a friend to whom he owed a debt of gratitude; but after that revelation which had upset all his ideas, he felt himself an inferior, and that Aramis was his master. He himself lighted a lantern, summoned a turnkey, and said, returning to Aramis, "I am at your orders, Monseigneur." Aramis merely nodded his head, as much as to say, "Very good;" and signed to him with his hand to lead the way. Baisemeaux ad-vanced, and Aramis followed him.

It was a beautiful starry night; the steps of the three men re-sounded on the flags of the terraces, and the clinking of the keys hanging from the jailer's girdle made itself heard up to the stories of the towers, as if to remind the prisoners that liberty was out of their reach. It might have been said that the alteration effected in Baise-meaux had extended itself even to the prisoners. The turnkey, the same who on Aramis's first arrival had shown himself so inquisitive and curious, had now become not only silent, but even impassible. He held his head down, and seemed afraid to keep his ears open. In this wise they reached the basement of the Bertaudière, the first two stories of which were mounted silently and somewhat slowly; for Baisemeaux, though far from disobeying, was far from exhibiting any eagerness to obey. Finally, they arrived at the door. The jailer

The Prisoner

had the key ready, and opened the door. Baisemeaux showed a disposition to enter the prisoner's chamber; but Aramis, stopping him on the threshold, said, "The rules do not allow the governor to hear the prisoner's confession."

Baisemeaux bowed, and made way for Aramis, who took the lantern and entered, and then signed to them to close the door behind him. For an instant he remained standing, listening to learn whether Baisemeaux and the turnkey had retired; but as soon as he was assured by the dying sound of their footsteps that they had left the tower, he put the lantern on the table and gazed around. On a bed of green serge, similar in all respects to the other beds in the Bastille, save that it was newer, under ample curtains half drawn, reposed a young man to whom we have once before introduced Aramis. According to custom, the prisoner was without a light. At the hour of curfew he was bound to extinguish his lamp; it may be seen how much he was favoured in being allowed to keep it burning until that hour. Near the bed a large leathern arm-chair, with twisted legs, held his clothes. A little table—without pens, books, paper, or ink—stood deserted near the window; while several plates, still unemptied, showed that the prisoner had scarcely touched his recent repast. Aramis saw that the young man was stretched upon his bed, his face half concealed by his arms. The arrival of a visitor did not cause any change of position; either he was waiting in expectation or he was asleep. Aramis lighted the candle from the lantern, pushed back the arm-chair, and approached the bed with an appearance of mingled interest and respect.

The young man raised his head. "What is it?" said he.—"Have you not desired a confessor?" replied Aramis.—"Yes."—"Because you are ill?"—"Yes."—"Very ill?" The young man gave Aramis a piercing glance, and answered, "I thank you." After a moment's silence, "I have seen you before," he continued.

Aramis bowed. Doubtless the scrutiny which the prisoner had just made of the cold, crafty, and imperious character stamped upon the features of the Bishop of Vannes was little reassuring to one in his situation, for he added, "I am better."—"And then?" said Aramis.—"Why, then, being better, I have no longer the same need of a confessor, I think."

"Not even of the haircloth, of which the note you found in your bread informed you?" The young man started; but before he had

21

either assented or denied, Aramis continued, "Not even of the ecclesiastic from whom you were to hear an important revelation?"—"If it be so," said the young man, sinking again on his pillow, "it is different; I listen."

Aramis then looked at him more closely, and was struck with the easy majesty of his mien,—one which can never be acquired unless Heaven has implanted it in the blood or in the heart. "Sit down, Monsieur!" said the prisoner. Aramis bowed and obeyed.

"How does the Bastille agree with you?" asked the bishop.— "Very well."—"You do not suffer?"—"No."—"You have nothing to regret?"—"Nothing."—"Not even your liberty?"—"What do you call liberty, Monsieur?" asked the prisoner, with the tone of a man who is preparing for a struggle.—"I call liberty the flowers, the air, light, the stars, the happiness of going whithersoever the nervous limbs of twenty years of age may wish to carry you."

The young man smiled,—whether in resignation or contempt, it would have been difficult to tell. "Look!" said he; "I have in that Japanese vase two roses gathered yesterday evening in the bud from the governor's garden. This morning they have blown and spread their vermilion chalices beneath my gaze; with every opening petal they unfold the treasures of their perfume, filling my chamber with fragrance. Look now on these two roses; even among roses these are beautiful, and the rose is the most beautiful of flowers. Why, then, do you bid me desire other flowers when I possess the loveliest of all?"

Aramis gazed at the young man in surprise. "If *flowers* constitute liberty," sadly resumed the captive, "I am free, for I possess them." —"But the air!" cried Aramis,—"air so necessary to life!"— "Well, Monsieur," returned the prisoner, "draw near to the window; it is open. Between heaven and earth the wind whirls its storms of hail and lightning, wafts its warm mists, or breathes in gentle breezes. It caresses my face. When mounted on the back of this arm-chair, with my arms around the bars of the window to sustain myself, I fancy I am swimming in the wide expanse."

The countenance of Aramis darkened while the young man was speaking. "Light!" continued the prisoner,—"I have what is better than light! I have the sun,—a friend who comes to visit me every day without the permission of the governor or the jailer's company. He comes in at the window, and traces in my room a quadrilateral which starts from the window and reaches to the hangings of my bed. This luminous figure increases from ten o'clock till mid-day, and decreases from one till three slowly, as if, having hastened to come, it sorrowed at leaving me. When its last ray disappears, I have enjoyed its presence for four hours. Is not that sufficient? I have been told that there are unhappy beings who dig in quarries, and labourers who toil in mines, who never behold the sun at all." Aramis wiped the drops from his brow. "As to the stars which are so delightful to view," continued the young man, "they all resemble one another save in size and brilliancy. I am a favoured mortal; for if you had not lighted that candle, you would have been able to see the beautiful star which I was gazing at from my couch before your arrival, and whose rays were playing over my eyes."

Aramis lowered his head; he felt himself overwhelmed by the bitter flow of that sinister philosophy which is the religion of the captive. "So much, then, for the flowers, the air, the daylight, and the stars," tranquilly continued the young man; "there remains freedom of movement. Do I not walk all day in the governor's garden if it is fine; here, if it rains; in the fresh air, if it is warm; in the warm, thanks to my fireplace, if it be cold? Ah, Monsieur, do you fancy," continued the prisoner, not without bitterness, "that men have not done everything for me that a man can hope for or desire?"

"Men!" said Aramis, raising his head; "be it so! But it seems to me you forget Heaven."—"Indeed, I have forgotten Heaven," murmured the prisoner, without emotion; "but why do you mention it? Of what use is it to talk to a prisoner of Heaven?" Aramis looked steadily at this singular youth, who possessed the resignation of a martyr with the smile of an atheist. "Is not God in everything?" he murmured in a reproachful tone.—"Say rather, at the end of everything," answered the prisoner, firmly.

"Be it so," said Aramis; "but let us return to our starting-point." —"I desire nothing better," returned the young man.—"I am your confessor."—"Yes."—"Well, then, you ought, as a penitent, to tell me the truth."—"All that I wish is to tell it to you."

"Every prisoner has committed some crime for which he has been imprisoned. What crime, then, have you committed?"—"You asked me the same question the first time you saw me," returned the prisoner.—"And then, as now, you evaded giving me an answer."—"And

what reason have you for thinking that I shall now reply to you?"—
"Because this time I am your confessor."

"Then, if you wish me to tell what crime I have committed, explain to me in what a crime consists; for as my conscience does not accuse me, I aver that I am not a criminal."—"We are often criminals in the sight of the great of the earth, not alone for having ourselves committed crimes, but because we know that crimes have been committed." The prisoner manifested the deepest attention. "Yes, I understand you," he said, after a pause; "yes, you are right, Monsieur. It is very possible that in that light I am a criminal in the eyes of the great."—"Ah! then you know something," said Aramis, who thought he had pierced not merely through a defect in the harness, but through the joints of it.

"No, I am not aware of anything," replied the young man; "but sometimes I think, and I say to myself in those moments—"—"What do you say to yourself?"—"That if I were to think any further, I should either go mad or I should divine a great deal."—"And then—and then—" said Aramis, impatiently.—"Then I leave off."

"You leave off?"—"Yes; my head becomes confused, and my ideas melancholy. I feel ennui overtaking me; I wish—"—"What?"
—"I don't know; but I do not like to give myself up to longing for things which I do not possess, when I am so happy with what I have."

"You are afraid of death?" said Aramis, with a slight uneasiness.
—"Yes," said the young man, smiling. Aramis felt the chill of that smile, and shuddered. "Oh, as you fear death, you know more than you admit!" he cried.—"And you," returned the prisoner, "who bade me to ask to see you,—you, who when I did ask for you came here promising a world of confidence,—how is it that, nevertheless, it is you who are silent, and 'tis I who speak? Since, then, we both wear masks, either let us both retain them or put them aside together."

Aramis felt the force and justice of the remark, saying to himself, "This is no ordinary man." "Are you ambitious?" said he suddenly to the prisoner, aloud, without preparing him for the alteration.—
"What do you mean by ambition?" replied the youth.—"It is," replied Aramis, "a feeling which prompts a man to desire more than he has."

"I said that I was contented, Monsieur; but perhaps I deceive

D'Artagnan drew his sword, and approaching Louis XIV respectfully, placed it on the table

myself. I am ignorant of the nature of ambition; but it is not impossible I may have some. Come, open my mind; I ask nothing better."—"An ambitious man," said Aramis, "is one who covets what is beyond his station."—"I covet nothing beyond my station," said the young man, with an assurance of manner which yet again made the Bishop of Vannes tremble.

Aramis was silent. But to look at the kindling eye, the knitted brow, and the reflective attitude of the captive, it was evident that he expected something more than silence. That silence Aramis now broke. "You lied the first time I saw you," said he.—"Lied!" cried the young man, starting up on his couch, with such a tone in his voice and such lightning in his eyes that Aramis recoiled in spite of himself.—"I should say," returned Aramis, bowing, "you concealed from me what you knew of your infancy."—"A man's secrets are his own, Monsieur," retorted the prisoner, "and not at the mercy of the first chance-comer."

"True," said Aramis, bowing still lower than before, " 'tis true; pardon me, but to-day do I still occupy the place of a chance-comer? I beseech you to reply, Monseigneur." This title slightly disturbed the prisoner; but nevertheless he did not appear astonished that it was given to him. "I do not know you, Monsieur," said he.—"Oh, if I but dared, I would take your hand and would kiss it!"

The young man seemed as if he were going to give Aramis his hand; but the light which beamed in his eyes faded away, and he coldly and distrustfully withdrew his hand. "Kiss the hand of a prisoner!" he said, shaking his head; "to what purpose?"—"Why did you tell me," said Aramis, "that you were happy here? Why, that you aspired to nothing? Why, in a word, by thus speaking, do you prevent me from being frank in my turn?"

The same light shone a third time in the young man's eyes, but died as before, without leading to anything. "You distrust me," said Aramis.—"And why say you so, Monsieur?"—"Oh, for a very simple reason! If you know what you ought to know, you ought to mistrust everybody."—"Then be not astonished that I am mistrustful, since you suspect me of knowing what I know not."

Aramis was struck with admiration at this energetic resistance. "Oh, Monseigneur, you drive me to despair!" said he, striking the arm-chair with his fist.—"And on my part I do not comprehend you, Monsieur."—"Well, then, try to understand me." The prisoner looked fixedly at Aramis. "Sometimes it seems to me," said the latter, "that I have before me the man whom I seek, and then—"—"And then your man disappears,—is it not so?" said the prisoner, smiling. "So much the better."

Aramis rose. "Certainly," said he; "I have nothing further to say to a man who mistrusts me as you do."—"And I, Monsieur," said the prisoner, in the same tone, "have nothing to say to a man who will not understand that a prisoner ought to be mistrustful of everybody."—"Even of his old friends?" said Aramis. "Oh, Monseigneur, you are too cautious!"

"Of my old friends?—you one of my old friends,—you?"—"Do you no longer remember," said Aramis, "that you once saw in the village where your early years were spent—"

"Do you know the name of the village?" asked the prisoner.—"Noisy-le-Sec, Monseigneur," answered Aramis, firmly.—"Go on!" said the young man, without expression of assent or denial on his countenance.

"Stay, Monseigneur!" said Aramis; "if you are positively resolved to carry on this game, let us break off. I am here to tell you many things, 'tis true; but you must allow me to see that, on your side, you have a desire to know them. Before revealing the important matters I conceal, be assured that I am in need of some encouragement, if not candour; a little sympathy, if not confidence. But you keep yourself entrenched in a pretended ignorance which paralyses me. Oh, not for the reason you think; for ignorant as you may be, or indifferent as you feign to be, you are none the less what you are, Monseigneur, and there is nothing—nothing, mark me!—which can cause you not to be so."

"I promise you," replied the prisoner, "to hear you without impatience. Only, it appears to me that I have a right to repeat the question I have already asked,—'Who are you?'"—"Do you remember, fifteen or eighteen years ago, seeing at Noisy-le-Sec a cavalier, accompanied by a lady plainly dressed in black silk, with flame-coloured ribbons in her hair?"

"Yes," said the young man; "I once asked the name of this cavalier, and was told that he called himself the Abbé d'Herblay. I was astonished that the abbé had so warlike an air, and was told that there was nothing singular in that, seeing that he was one of Louis XIII.'s musketeers."—"Well," said Aramis, "that musketeer of other times, that abbé afterwards, then Bishop of Vannes, is to-day your confessor."—"I know it; I recognised you."

"Then, Monseigneur, if you know that, I must add a fact of which you are ignorant,—that if the king were to know this evening of the presence here of this musketeer, this abbé, this bishop, this confessor, he who has risked everything to visit you would to-morrow see glitter the executioner's axe at the bottom of a dungeon more gloomy and more obscure than yours."

While hearing these words, delivered with emphasis, the young man had raised himself on his couch and gazed more and more eagerly at Aramis. The result of this scrutiny was that he appeared to derive some confidence from it. "Yes," he murmured, "I remember perfectly. The woman of whom you speak came once with you, and twice afterwards with the woman—" He hesitated.—"With another woman who came to see you every month,—is it not so, Monseigneur?"—"Yes."—"Do you know who this lady was?" The light seemed ready to flash from the prisoner's eyes. "I am aware that she was one of the ladies of the court," he said.

"You remember that lady well, do you not?"—"Oh, my recollection can hardly be very confused on this head!" said the young prisoner. "I saw that lady once with a gentleman about forty-five years old. I saw her once with you, and with the lady dressed in black with flame-coloured ribbons. I have seen her twice since with the same person. These four persons, with my tutor and old Perronnette, my jailer and the governor of the prison, are the only persons with whom I have ever spoken, and, indeed, almost the only persons I have ever seen."

"Then, you were in prison?"—"If I am a prisoner here, there I was comparatively free, although in a very narrow sense. A house which I never quitted, a garden surrounded with walls I could not clear,—these constituted my residence; but you know it, as you have been there. In a word, being accustomed to live within these bounds, I never cared to leave them. And so you will understand, Monsieur, that not having seen anything of the world, I can desire nothing; and therefore, if you relate anything, you will be obliged to explain everything to me."—"And I will do so," said Aramis, bowing; "for it is my duty, Monseigneur."

"Well, then, begin by telling me who was my tutor."—"A worthy and above all an honourable gentleman, Monseigneur; fit guide both

The Man in the Iron Mask

for body and soul. Had you ever any reason to complain of him?"—
"Oh, no; quite the contrary. But this gentleman of yours often
used to tell me that my father and mother were dead. Did he deceive me, or did he speak the truth?"—"He was compelled to comply
with the orders given him."

"Then he lied?"—"In one respect. Your father is dead."—"And
my mother?"—"She is dead for you."—"But then she lives for
others, does she not?"—"Yes."

"And I—and I, then [the young man looked sharply at Aramis],
am compelled to live in the obscurity of a prison?"—"Alas! I fear
so."—"And that because my presence in the world would lead to the
revelation of a great secret?"—"Certainly, a very great secret."

"My enemy must indeed be powerful, to be able to shut up in the
Bastille a child such as I then was."—"He is."—"More powerful
than my mother, then?"—"And why do you ask that?"—"Because
my mother would have taken my part." Aramis hesitated. "Yes,
Monseigneur; more powerful than your mother."

"Seeing, then, that my nurse and preceptor were carried off, and
that I also was separated from them,—either they were, or I am,
very dangerous to my enemy?"—"Yes; a peril from which he freed
himself by causing the nurse and preceptor to disappear," answered
Aramis, quietly.—"Disappear!" cried the prisoner; "but how did
they disappear?"—"In the surest possible way," answered Aramis:
"they are dead." The young man turned visibly pale, and passed
his hand tremblingly over his face. "From poison?" he asked.—
"From poison."

The prisoner reflected a moment. "My enemy must indeed have
been very cruel, or hard beset by necessity, to assassinate those two
innocent persons, my sole support; for that worthy gentleman and
that poor woman had never harmed a living being."—"In your family, Monseigneur, necessity is stern. And so it is necessity which
compels me, to my great regret, to tell you that this gentleman and
the unhappy lady were assassinated."

"Oh, you tell me nothing I am not aware of!" said the prisoner,
knitting his brows.—"How?"—"I suspected it."—"Why?"—"I will
tell you."

At this moment the young man, supporting himself on his elbows,
drew close to Aramis's face, with such an expression of dignity, of
self-command, and of defiance even, that the bishop felt the elec-

28

tricity of enthusiasm strike in devouring flashes from that seared heart of his into his brain of adamant.

"Speak, Monseigneur! I have already told you that by conversing with you I endanger my life. Little value as it has, I implore you to accept it as the ransom of your own."—"Well," resumed the young man, "this is why I suspected that they had killed my nurse and my preceptor—"—"Whom you used to call your father."— "Yes! whom I called my father, but whose son I well knew I was not."

"Who caused you to suppose so?"—"Just as you, Monsieur, are too respectful for a friend, he was also too respectful for a father." —"I, however," said Aramis, "have no intention to disguise myself."

The young man nodded assent, and continued: "Undoubtedly, I was not destined to perpetual seclusion," said the prisoner; "and that which makes me believe so now, above all, is the care that was taken to render me as accomplished a cavalier as possible. The gentleman attached to my person taught me everything he knew himself, —mathematics, a little geometry, astronomy, fencing, and riding. Every morning I went through military exercises, and practised on horseback. Well, one morning during summer, it being very hot, I went to sleep in the hall. Nothing up to that period, except the respect paid me by my tutor, had enlightened me, or even roused my suspicions. I lived as children, as birds, as plants, as the air and the sun do. I had just turned my fifteenth year—"—"This, then, was eight years ago?"—"Yes, nearly; but I have ceased to reckon time."

"Excuse me; but what did your tutor tell you, to encourage you to work?"—"He used to say that a man was bound to make for himself in the world that fortune which Heaven had refused him at his birth. He added, that, being a poor obscure orphan, I had no one but myself to look to; and that nobody either did or ever would take any interest in me. I was, then, in the hall I have spoken of, asleep from fatigue in fencing. My tutor was in his room on the first floor, just over me. Suddenly I heard him exclaim; and then he called, 'Perronnette! Perronnette!' It was my nurse whom he called."— "Yes! I know it," said Aramis. "Continue, Monseigneur!"

"Very likely she was in the garden; for my tutor came hastily downstairs. I rose, anxious at seeing him anxious. He opened the garden door, still crying out, 'Perronnette! Perronnette!' The win-

The Man in the Iron Mask

dows of the hall looked into the court. The shutters were closed; but through a chink in them I saw my tutor draw near a large well, which was almost directly under the windows of his study. He stooped over the brim, looked into the well, again cried out, and made wild and affrighted gestures. Where I was, I could not only see, but hear; and see and hear I did."

"Go on, I pray you!" said Aramis.—"Dame Perronnette came running up, hearing the governor's cries. He went to meet her, took her by the arm, and drew her quickly towards the edge; after which, as they both bent over it together, 'Look, look!' cried he; 'what a misfortune!' 'Calm yourself, calm yourself,' said Perronnette; 'what is the matter?' 'The letter!' he exclaimed; 'do you see that letter?' pointing to the bottom of the well. 'What letter?' she cried. 'The letter you see down there,—the last letter from the queen.' At this word I trembled. My tutor—he who passed for my father, he who was continually recommending to me modesty and humility—in correspondence with the queen! 'The queen's last letter!' cried Perronnette, without showing other astonishment than at seeing this letter at the bottom of the well; 'but how came it there?' 'A chance, Dame Perronnette,—a singular chance. I was entering my room; and on opening the door, the window too being open, a puff of air came suddenly and carried off this paper,—this letter from the queen; I darted after it, and gained the window just in time to see it flutter a moment in the breeze and disappear down the well.' 'Well,' said Dame Perronnette; 'and if the letter has fallen into the well, 'tis all the same as if it were burned; and as the queen burns all her letters every time she comes—' 'Every time she comes!' So this lady who came every month was the queen," said the prisoner.—"Yes," nodded Aramis.

" 'Doubtless, doubtless,' continued the old gentleman; 'but this letter contained instructions,—how can I follow them?' 'Write immediately to her; give her a plain account of the accident, and the queen will no doubt write you another letter in place of this.' 'Oh! the queen would never believe the story,' said the good gentleman, shaking his head; 'she will imagine that I want to keep this letter instead of giving it up like the rest, so as to have a hold over her. She is so distrustful, and M. de Mazarin so— This devil of an Italian is capable of having us poisoned at the first breath of suspicion.' " Aramis almost imperceptibly smiled.

The Prisoner

" 'You know, Dame Perronnette, they are both so suspicious in all that concerns Philippe.' 'Philippe' was the name they gave me," said the prisoner. 'Well, 'tis no use hesitating,' said Dame Perronnette; 'somebody must go down the well.' 'Of course; so that the person who goes down may read the paper as he is coming up.' 'But let us choose some villager who cannot read, and then you will be at ease.' 'Granted; but will not any one who descends guess that a paper must be important for which we risk a man's life? However, you have given me an idea, Dame Perronnette; somebody shall go down the well, but that somebody shall be myself.' But at this notion Dame Perronnette lamented and cried in such a manner, and so implored the old nobleman, with tears in her eyes, that he promised her to obtain a ladder long enough to reach down, while she went in search of some stout-hearted youth, whom she was to persuade that a jewel had fallen into the well, and that this jewel was wrapped in a paper. 'And as paper,' remarked my perceptor, 'naturally unfolds in water, the young man would not be surprised at finding nothing, after all, but the letter wide open.' 'But perhaps the writing will be already effaced by that time,' said Dame Perronnette. 'No consequence, provided we secure the letter. On returning it to the queen, she will see at once that we have not betrayed her; and consequently, as we shall not rouse the distrust of Mazarin, we shall have nothing to fear from him.' Having come to this resolution, they parted. I pushed back the shutter, and seeing that my tutor was about to re-enter, threw myself on my couch, in a confusion of brain caused by all I had just heard. My tutor opened the door a few moments after, and thinking I was asleep, gently closed it again. As soon as ever it was shut, I rose, and listening heard the sound of retiring footsteps. Then I returned to the shutter, and saw my tutor and Dame Perronnette go out together. I was alone in the house. They had hardly closed the gate before I sprang from the window and ran to the well. Then, just as my tutor had leaned over, so leaned I. Something white and luminous glistened in the green and quivering ripples of the water. The brilliant disk fascinated and allured me; my eyes became fixed, and I could hardly breathe. The well seemed to draw me in with its large mouth and icy breath; and I thought I read, at the bottom of the water, characters of fire traced upon the letter the queen had touched. Then, scarcely knowing what I was about, and urged on by one of those instinctive impulses which drive men upon their destruction, I made fast one end of the rope to the bottom of the well-curb; I left the bucket hanging about three feet under water,—at the same time taking infinite pains not to disturb that coveted letter, which was beginning to change its white tint for a greenish hue,—proof enough that it was sinking,—and then, with a piece of wet canvas protecting my hands, slid down into the abyss. When I saw myself hanging over the dark pool, when I saw the sky lessening above my head, a cold shudder came over me, I was seized with giddiness, and the hair rose on my head; but my strong will mastered all. I gained the water, and at once plunged into it, holding on by one hand, while I immersed the other and seized the precious paper, which, alas! came in two in my grasp. I concealed the two fragments in my coat, and helping myself with my feet against the side of the pit, and clinging on with my hands, agile and vigorous as I was, and above all pressed for time, I regained the brink, drenching it as I touched it with the water that streamed from all the lower part of my body. Once out of the well with my prize I rushed into the sunlight, and took refuge in a kind of shrubbery at the bottom of the garden. As I entered my hiding-place, the bell which resounded when the great gate was opened, rang. It was my tutor returning. I had but just time. I calculated that it would take ten minutes before he would gain my place of concealment, even if, guessing where I was, he came straight to it; and twenty if he were obliged to look for me. But this was time enough to allow me to read the cherished letter, whose fragments I hastened to unite again. The writing was already fading, but I managed to decipher it all."

"And what read you there, Monseigneur?" asked Aramis, deeply interested.—"Quite enough, Monsieur, to see that my tutor was a man of noble rank, and that Perronnette, without being a lady of quality, was far better than a servant; and also to perceive that I must myself be high-born, since the queen, Anne of Austria, and Mazarin, the prime minister, commended me so earnestly to their care."

Here the young man paused, quite overcome. "And what happened?" asked Aramis.—"It happened, Monsieur," answered he, "that the workmen they had summoned found nothing in the well, after the closest search; that my tutor perceived that the brink was watery; that I was not so well dried by the sun as to escape Dame

The Prisoner

Perronnette's observing that my garments were moist; and, lastly, that I was seized with a violent fever, owing to the chill and the excitement of my discovery, an attack of delirium supervening, during which I related the whole adventure; so that, guided by my avowal, my tutor found under the bolster the two pieces of the queen's letter."—"Ah!" said Aramis, "now I understand."

"Beyond this, all is conjecture. Doubtless the unfortunate lady and gentleman, not daring to keep the occurrence secret, wrote all to the queen, and sent back to her the torn letter."—"After which," said Aramis, "you were arrested and removed to the Bastille?"—"As you see."—"Then your two attendants disappeared?"—"Alas!"

"Let us not take up our time with the dead, but see what can be done with the living. You told me you were resigned?"—"I repeat it."—"Without any desire for freedom?"—"As I told you."—"Without ambition, sorrow, or thought?" The young man made no answer. "Well," asked Aramis, "why are you silent?"—"I think that I have spoken enough," answered the prisoner, "and that now it is your turn. I am weary."

Aramis gathered himself up, and a shade of deep solemnity spread itself over his countenance. It was evident that he had reached the crisis in the part he had come to the prison to play. "One question," said Aramis.—"What is it? Speak!"—"In the house you inhabited there were neither looking-glasses nor mirrors, were there?"

"What are those two words, and what is their meaning?" asked the young man; "I do not even know them."—"They designate two pieces of furniture which reflect objects; so that, for instance, you may see in them your own lineaments as you see mine now, with the naked eye."—"No; there was neither a glass nor a mirror in the house," answered the young man.

Aramis looked round him. "Nor is there here, either," he said; "they have taken the same precaution."—"To what end?"—"You will know directly. Now, you have told me that you were instructed in mathematics, astronomy, fencing, and riding; but you have not said a word about history."—"My tutor sometimes related to me the principal deeds of the King Saint Louis, King Francis I., and King Henry IV."

"Is that all?"—"That is about all."—"This also was done by design; just as you were deprived of mirrors, which reflect the present, so you were left in ignorance of history, which reflects the past. Since your imprisonment books have been forbidden you; so that you are unacquainted with a number of facts by means of which you would be able to reconstruct the shattered edifice of your recollections and your interests."—"It is true," said the young man.

"Listen, then: I will in a few words tell you what has passed in France during the last twenty-three or twenty-four years,—that is, from the probable date of your birth; in a word, from the time that interests you."—"Say on!" and the young man resumed his serious and attentive attitude.

"Do you know who was the son of Henry IV.?"—"At least I know who his successor was."—"How?"—"By means of a coin dated 1610, which bears the effigy of Henry IV.; and another of 1612, bearing that of Louis XIII. So I presumed that, there being only two years between the two dates, Louis was Henry's successor."— "Then," said Aramis, "you know that the last reigning monarch was Louis XIII.?"—"I do," answered the youth, slightly reddening.

"Well, he was a prince full of noble ideas and great projects, always, alas! deferred by the troubles of the times and the struggle that his minister Richelieu had to maintain against the great nobles of France. The king himself was of a feeble character, and died young and unhappy."—"I know it."—"He had been long anxious about having an heir,—a care which weighs heavily on princes, who desire to leave behind them more than one pledge that they will be remembered and their work will be continued."

"Did King Louis XIII. die without children?" asked the prisoner, smiling.—"No; but he was long without one, and for a long while thought he should be the last of his race. This idea had reduced him to the depths of despair, when suddenly his wife, Anne of Austria—" The prisoner trembled. "Did you know," said Aramis, "that Louis XIII.'s wife was called Anne of Austria?"—"Continue!" said the young man, without replying to the question.

"When suddenly," resumed Aramis, "the queen announced an interesting event. There was great joy at the intelligence, and all prayed for her happy delivery. On the 5th of September, 1638, she gave birth to a son." Here Aramis looked at his companion, and thought he observed him turning pale. "You are about to hear," said Aramis, "an account which few could now give; for it refers to a secret which is thought to be buried with the dead or entombed in the abyss of the confessional."

The prisoner of the Bastille

The Prisoner

"And you will tell me this secret?" broke in the youth.—"Oh!" said Aramis, with unmistakable emphasis, "I do not know that I ought to risk this secret by entrusting it to one who has no desire to quit the Bastille."—"I listen, Monsieur."

"The queen, then, gave birth to a son. But while the court was rejoicing over the event, when the king had shown the newborn child to the nobility and people, and was sitting gaily down to table to celebrate the event, the queen, who was alone in her room, was again taken ill, and gave birth to a second son."—"Oh!" said the prisoner, betraying a better acquaintance with affairs than he had admitted, "I thought that Monsieur was only born in—" Aramis raised his finger. "Let me continue," he said.

The prisoner sighed impatiently, and paused. "Yes," said Aramis, "the queen had a second son, whom Dame Perronnette, the midwife, received in her arms."—"Dame Perronnette!" murmured the young man.

"They ran at once to the banqueting-room, and whispered to the king what had happened; he rose and quitted the table. But this time it was no longer happiness that his face expressed, but something akin to terror. The birth of twins changed into bitterness the joy to which that of an only son had given rise, seeing that in France (a fact of which you are assuredly ignorant) it is the oldest of the king's sons who succeeds his father—"—"I know it."—"And that the doctors and jurists assert that there is ground for doubting whether he who first makes his appearance is the elder by the law of Heaven and of Nature."

The prisoner uttered a smothered cry, and became whiter than the coverlet under which he hid himself. "Now you understand," pursued Aramis, "that the king, who with so much pleasure saw himself repeated in one, was in despair about two; fearing that the second might dispute the claim of the first to seniority, which had been recognised only two hours before, and so this second son, relying on party interests and caprices, might one day sow discord and engender civil war in the kingdom,— by these means destroying the very dynasty he should have strengthened."—"Oh, I understand, I understand!" murmured the young man.

"Well," continued Aramis, "this is what is related; this is why one of the queen's two sons, shamefully parted from his brother, shamefully sequestered, is buried in the profoundest obscurity; this is why

35

The Man in the Iron Mask

that second son has disappeared, and so completely that not a soul in France, save his mother, is aware of his existence."—"Yes; his mother, who has cast him off!" cried the prisoner, in a tone of despair.—"Except also," Aramis went on, "the lady in the black dress; and, finally, excepting—"

"Excepting yourself, is it not,—you, who come and relate all this, —you, who come to rouse in my soul curiosity, hatred, ambition, and perhaps even the thirst of vengeance;—except you, Monsieur, who, if you are the man whom I expect, to whom the note I have received applies, whom, in short, Heaven ought to send me, must possess about you—"—"What?" asked Aramis.—"A portrait of the king, Louis XIV., who at this moment reigns upon the throne of France."

"Here is a portrait," replied the bishop, handing the prisoner a miniature in enamel, on which Louis was depicted life-like, with a handsome, lofty mien. The prisoner eagerly seized the portrait, and gazed at it with devouring eyes. "And now, Monseigneur," said Aramis, "here is a mirror."

Aramis left the prisoner time to recover his ideas. "So high, so high!" murmured the young man, eagerly comparing the likeness of Louis with his own countenance reflected in the glass. "What do you think of it?" at length said Aramis.—"I think that I am lost," replied the captive; "the king will never set me free."

"And I—I demand," added the bishop, fixing his piercing eyes significantly upon the prisoner,—"I demand which of the two is the king,—the one whom this miniature portrays, or the one whom the glass reflects?"—"The king, Monsieur," sadly replied the young man, "is he who is on the throne, who is not in prison, and who, on the other hand, can cause others to be entombed there. Royalty is power; and you see well how powerless I am."—"Monseigneur," answered Aramis, with a respect he had not yet manifested, "the king, mark me, will, if you desire it, be he who quitting his dungeon shall maintain himself upon the throne on which his friends will place him."

"Tempt me not, Monsieur!" broke in the prisoner, bitterly.—"Be not weak, Monseigneur," persisted Aramis. "I have brought all the proofs of your birth: consult them; satisfy yourself that you are a king's son; and then let us act."—"No, no; it is impossible."

"Unless, indeed," resumed the bishop, ironically, "it be the destiny of your race that the brothers excluded from the throne shall be always princes without valour and without honour, as was your uncle M. Gaston d'Orléans, who ten times conspired against his brother Louis XIII."

"What!" cried the prince, astonished; "my uncle Gaston 'conspired against his brother,'—conspired to dethrone him?"—"Exactly, Monseigneur; for no other reason."—"What are you telling me, Monsieur?"—"I tell you the truth."—"And he had friends,—devoted ones?"—"As much so as I am to you."—"And, after all, what did he do?—Failed!"

"He failed, I admit, but always through his own fault; and for the sake of purchasing, not his life (for the life of the king's brother is sacred and inviolable), but his liberty, he sacrificed the lives of all his friends one after another; and so at this day he is the very shame of history, and the detestation of a hundred noble families in this kingdom."

"I understand, Monsieur; either by weakness or treachery, my uncle slew his friends."—"By weakness; which in princes is always treachery."—"And cannot a man fail, then, from incapacity and ignorance? Do you really believe it possible that a poor captive such as I, brought up not only at a distance from the court, but even from the world,—do you believe it possible that such a one could assist those of his friends who should attempt to serve him?" And as Aramis was about to reply, the young man suddenly cried out, with a violence which betrayed the temper of his blood: "We are speaking of friends; but how can *I* have any friends,—I, whom no one knows, and who have neither liberty, money, nor influence to gain any?"

"I fancy I had the honour to offer myself to your royal Highness." —"Oh, do not style me so, Monsieur; 'tis either irony or cruelty! Do not lead me to think of aught else than these prison walls which confine me; let me again love, or at least submit to, my slavery and my obscurity."—"Monseigneur, Monseigneur! if you again utter these desperate words, if after having received proof of your high birth you still remain poor-spirited and of feeble purpose, I will comply with your desire,—I will depart, and renounce for ever the service of a master to whom so eagerly I came to devote my assistance and my life!"

"Monsieur," cried the prince, "would it not have been better for you to have reflected, before telling me all that you have done, that you would break my heart for ever?"—"And so I desired to do, Monseigneur."

"Is a prison the fitting place to talk to me about power, grandeur, and even royalty? You wish to make me believe in splendour, and we are lying hidden in night; you boast of glory, and we are smothering our words in the curtains of this miserable bed; you give me glimpses of absolute power, and I hear the step of the jailer in the corridor,—that step which, after all, makes you tremble more than it does me. To render me somewhat less incredulous, free me from the Bastille; give air to my lungs, spurs to my feet, a sword to my arm, and we shall begin to understand each other."—"It is precisely my intention to give you all this, Monseigneur, and more; only, do you desire it?"

"A word more," said the prince. "I know there are guards in every gallery, bolts to every door, cannon and soldiery at every barrier. How will you overcome the sentries, spike the guns? How will you break through the bolts and bars?"—"Monseigneur, how did you get the note which announced my arrival to you?"—"You can bribe a jailer for such a thing as a note."—"If we can corrupt one turnkey, we can corrupt ten."

"Well, I admit that it may be possible to release a poor captive from the Bastille; possible so to conceal him that the king's people shall not again ensnare him; possible, in some unknown retreat, to sustain the unhappy wretch in some suitable manner."—"Monseigneur!" said Aramis, smiling.—"I admit that whoever would do thus much for me would seem more than mortal in my eyes; but as you tell me I am a prince, brother of a king, how can you restore me the rank and power of which my mother and my brother have deprived me? And as I must pass a life of war and hatred, how will you make me conqueror in those combats, and invulnerable to my enemies? Ah, Monsieur, reflect upon this! Place me, to-morrow, in some dark cavern in a mountain's base; yield me the delight of hearing in freedom the sounds of river and plain, of beholding in freedom the sun of the blue heavens, or the stormy sky,—and it is enough. Promise me no more than this,—for, indeed, more you cannot give; and it would be a crime to deceive me, since you call yourself my friend."

Aramis waited in silence. "Monseigneur," he resumed after a moment's reflection, "I admire the firm, sound sense which dictates your words; I am happy to have discovered my monarch's mind."

The Prisoner

"Again, again! oh, for mercy's sake," cried the prince, pressing his icy hands upon his clammy brow, "do not play with me! I have no need to be a king to be the happiest of men."—"But I, Monseigneur, wish you to be a king for the good of humanity."—"Ah!" said the prince, with fresh distrust inspired by the word,—"ah! with what, then, has humanity to reproach my brother?"

"I forgot to say, Monseigneur, that if you condescend to allow me to guide you, and if you consent to become the most powerful monarch on earth, you will have promoted the interests of all the friends whom I devote to the success of your cause; and these friends are numerous."—"Numerous?"—"Still less numerous than powerful, Monseigneur."—"Explain yourself."—"It is impossible. I will explain, I swear before Heaven, on that day when I see you sitting on the throne of France."

"But my brother?"—"You shall decree his fate. Do you pity him?"—"Him who leaves me to perish in a dungeon? No! I do not pity him."—"So much the better."

"He might have himself come to this prison, have taken me by the hand, and have said, 'My brother, Heaven created us to love, not to contend with each other. I come to you. A barbarous prejudice has condemned you to pass your days in obscurity, far from all men and deprived of every joy. I will make you sit down beside me; I will buckle round your waist our father's sword. Will you take advantage of this reconciliation to put down or to restrain me? Will you employ that sword to spill my blood?' 'Oh, never!' I would have replied to him; 'I look on you as my preserver, and will respect you as my master. You give me far more than Heaven bestowed; for through you I possess liberty and the privilege of loving and being loved in this world.' "

"And you would have kept your word, Monseigneur?"—"Oh, on my life!"—"While now?"—"While now I perceive that I have guilty ones to punish."—"In what manner, Monseigneur?"

"What do you say as to the resemblance that Heaven has given me to my brother?"—"I say that there was in that likeness a providential instruction which the king ought to have heeded; I say that your mother committed a crime in rendering those different in happiness and fortune whom Nature created so similar in her womb; and I conclude that the object of punishment should be only to restore the

39

equilibrium."—"By which you mean—"—"That if I restore you to your place on your brother's throne, he shall take yours in prison."

"Alas! there is so much suffering in prison, especially to a man who has drunk so deeply of the cup of enjoyment."—"Your royal Highness will always be free to act as you may desire; and if it seems good to you, after punishment, may pardon."

"Good! And now, are you aware of one thing, Monsieur?"—"Tell me, my Prince."—"It is that I will hear nothing further from you till I am clear of the Bastille."—"I was going to say to your Highness that I should only have the pleasure of seeing you once again."—"And when?"—"The day when my Prince leaves these gloomy walls."

"Heavens! how will you give me notice?"—"By coming here to seek you."—"Yourself?"—"My Prince, do not leave this chamber save with me; or if in my absence you are compelled to do so, remember that I am not concerned in it."—"And so, I am not to speak a word of this to any one whatever, save to you?"—"Save only to me." Aramis bowed very low.

The prince offered his hand. "Monsieur," he said, in a tone that issued from his heart, "one word more,—my last. If you have sought me for my destruction; if you are only a tool in the hands of my enemies; if from our conference, in which you have sounded the depths of my mind, anything worse than captivity result,—that is to say, if death befall me,—still receive my blessing, for you will have ended my troubles and given me repose from the tormenting fever that has preyed upon me these eight years."—"Monseigneur, wait the result ere you judge me," said Aramis.

"I say that in such a case I should bless and forgive you. If, on the other hand, you are come to restore me to that position in the sunshine of fortune and glory to which I was destined by Heaven; if by your aid I am enabled to live in the memory of man, and confer lustre on my race by deeds of valour or by solid benefits bestowed upon my people; if from my present depths of sorrow, aided by your generous hand, I raise myself to the very height of honour,—then to you, whom I thank with blessings, to you will I offer half my power and my glory; though you would still be but partly recompensed, and your share must always remain incomplete, since I could not divide with you the happiness received at your hands."

"Monseigneur," replied Aramis, moved by the pallor and excitement of the young man, "the nobleness of your heart fills me with joy and admiration. It is not you who will have to thank me, but rather the nation whom you will render happy, the posterity whose name you will make glorious. Yes; I shall have bestowed upon you more than life,—I shall give you immortality."

The prince offered his hand to Aramis, who sank upon his knee and kissed it. "Oh!" cried the prince, with a charming modesty.— "It is the first act of homage paid to our future king," said Aramis. "When I see you again, I shall say, 'Good-day, Sire.' "

"Till then," said the young man, pressing his wan and wasted fingers over his heart,—"till then, no more dreams, no more strain upon my life,—it would break! Oh, Monsieur, how small is my prison,—how low the window,—how narrow are the doors! To think that so much pride, splendour, and happiness should be able to enter in and remain here!"—"Your royal Highness makes me proud," said Aramis, "since you imply it is I who brought all this;" and he rapped immediately on the door.

The jailer came to open it with Baisemeaux, who devoured by fear and uneasiness was beginning, in spite of himself, to listen at the door. Happily, neither of the speakers had forgotten to smother his voice, even in the most passionate outbreaks.

"What a confession!" said the governor, forcing a laugh; "who would believe that a mere recluse, a man almost dead, could have committed crimes so numerous, and taking so long to tell of?" Aramis made no reply. He was eager to leave the Bastille, where the secret which overwhelmed him seemed to double the weight of the walls.

As soon as they reached Baisemeaux's quarters, "Let us proceed to business, my dear governor," said Aramis.—"Alas!" replied Baisemeaux.—"You have to ask me for my receipt for one hundred and fifty thousand livres," said the bishop.—"And to pay over the first third of the sum," added the poor governor, with a sigh, taking three steps towards his iron strong-box.

"Here is the receipt," said Aramis.—"And here is the money," returned Baisemeaux, with a threefold sigh.—"The order instructed me only to give a receipt; it said nothing about receiving the money," rejoined Aramis. "Adieu, Monsieur the Governor!" And he departed, leaving Baisemeaux stifled with joy and surprise at this regal gift so grandly given by the Confessor Extraordinary to the Bastille.

The Man in the Iron Mask

CHAPTER V

HOW MOUSTON HAD BECOME FATTER WITHOUT GIVING PORTHOS NOTICE THEREOF, AND OF THE TROUBLES WHICH CONSEQUENTLY BEFELL THAT WORTHY GENTLEMAN

PORTHOS and D'Artagnan had recently been seldom together. One was occupied with harassing duties for the king; the other had been making many purchases of furniture, which he intended to forward to his estate, and by aid of which he hoped to establish in his various residences something of that court luxury which he had witnessed in all its dazzling brightness in his Majesty's society.

D'Artagnan, ever faithful, one morning during an interval of service thought about Porthos, and being uneasy at not having heard anything of him for a fortnight, directed his steps towards his hotel, and pounced upon him just as he was getting up. The worthy baron had a pensive,—nay, more, a melancholy air. He was sitting on his bed, only half dressed, and with legs dangling over the edge, contemplating a great number of garments, which with their fringes, lace, embroidery, and slashes of ill-assorted hues were strewed all over the floor. Porthos, sad and reflective as La Fontaine's hare, did not observe D'Artagnan's entrance, which was moreover screened at this moment by M. Mouston, whose personal corpulence, quite enough at any time to hide one man from another, was for the moment doubled by a scarlet coat which the intendant was holding up by the sleeves for his master's inspection, that he might the better see it all over. D'Artagnan stopped at the threshold, and looked at the pensive Porthos; and then, as the sight of the innumerable garments strewing the floor caused mighty sighs to heave from the bosom of that excellent gentleman, D'Artagnan thought it time to put an end to these dismal reflections, and coughed by way of announcing himself.

"Ah!" exclaimed Porthos, whose countenance brightened with joy, "ah! ah! Here is D'Artagnan. I shall, then, get hold of an idea!" At these words Mouston, doubting what was going on behind him, got out of the way, smiling kindly at the friend of his master, who thus found himself freed from the material obstacle which had prevented his reaching D'Artagnan. Porthos made his sturdy knees crack again in rising, and crossing the room in two strides found himself face to face with his friend, whom he folded to his breast with a force of affection that seemed to increase with every day. "Ah!" he repeated, "you are always welcome, dear friend; but just now you are more welcome than ever."

"But you seem in the dumps here?" exclaimed D'Artagnan. Porthos replied by a look expressive of dejection. "Well then, tell me all about it, Porthos, my friend, unless it is a secret."—"In the first place," returned Porthos, "you know I have no secrets from you. This, then, is what saddens me."

"Wait a minute, Porthos; let me first get rid of all this litter of satin and velvet."—"Oh, never mind!" said Porthos, contemptuously; "it is all trash."—"Trash, Porthos! Cloth at twenty livres an ell, gorgeous satin, regal velvet!"—"Then you think these clothes are—"—"Splendid, Porthos, splendid. I'll wager that you alone in France have so many; and suppose you never had any more made, and were to live a hundred years, which wouldn't astonish me, you could still wear a new dress the day of your death without being obliged to see the nose of a single tailor from now till then."

Porthos shook his head. "Come, my friend," said D'Artagnan, "this unnatural melancholy in you frightens me. My dear Porthos, pray get out of it, then; and the sooner the better."—"Yes, my friend, so I will; if indeed it is possible."—"Perhaps you have received bad news from Bracieux?"—"No; they have felled the wood, and it has yielded a third more than the estimate."—"Then has there been a falling off in the pools of Pierrefonds?"—"No, my friend; they have been fished, and there is enough left to stock all the pools in the neighbourhood."

"Perhaps your estate at Vallon has been destroyed by an earthquake?"—"No, my friend; on the contrary, the ground was struck by lightning a hundred paces from the château, and a fountain sprung up in a place entirely destitute of water."—"What in the world is the matter, then?"—"The fact is, I have received an invitation for the *fête* at Vaux," said Porthos, with a lugubrious expression.

"Well, do you complain of that? The king has caused a hundred mortal heart-burnings among the courtiers by refusing invitations.

And so, my dear friend, you are of the party for Vaux? Bless my soul!"—"Indeed, I am!"—"You will see a magnificent sight."—"Alas! I doubt it, though."—"Everything that is grand in France will be brought together there!"—"Ah!" cried Porthos, tearing out a lock of his hair in despair.—"Eh! Good heavens! are you ill?" cried D'Artagnan.—"I am as strong as the Pont-Neuf! It isn't that."—"But what is it, then?"—"It is that I have no clothes!"

D'Artagnan stood petrified. "No clothes, Porthos! no clothes," he cried, "when I see more than fifty suits on the floor!"—"Fifty, yes; but not one that fits me!"—"What! not one that fits you? But are you not measured, then, when you give an order?"—"To be sure, he is," answered Mouston; "but unfortunately I have grown stouter."

"What! you stouter?"—"So much so that I am now bigger than the baron. Would you believe it, Monsieur?"—"*Parbleu!* it seems to me that is quite evident."—"Do you see, stupid?" said Porthos; "that is quite evident!"—"Be still, my dear Porthos!" resumed D'Artagnan, becoming slightly impatient. "I don't understand why your clothes should not fit you because Mouston has grown stouter."

"I am going to explain it," said Porthos. "You remember having related to me the story of the Roman general Antony, who had always seven wild boars, kept roasting, cooked to different degrees, so that he might be able to have his dinner at any time of the day he chose to ask for it? Well, then, I resolved, as at any time I might be invited to court to spend a week,—I resolved to have always seven suits ready for the occasion."—"Capitally reasoned, Porthos! Only, a man must have a fortune like yours to gratify such whims. Without counting the time lost in being measured, the fashions are always changing."—"That is exactly the point," said Porthos, "in regard to which I flattered myself I had hit on a very ingenious device."

"Tell me what it is; for I don't doubt your genius."—"You remember that Mouston once was thin?"—"Yes; when he was called Mousqueton."—"And you remember, too, the period when he began to grow fatter?"—"No, not exactly. I beg your pardon, my good Mouston."—"Oh, you are not in fault, Monsieur!" said Mouston, graciously. "You were in Paris; and as for us, we were in Pierrefonds."

How Mouston Became Fatter

"Well, well, my dear Porthos; there was a time when Mouston began to grow fat. Is that what you wished to say?"—"Yes, my friend; and I greatly rejoiced over it at that time."—"Indeed, I believe you did," exclaimed D'Artagnan.—"You understand," continued Porthos, "what a world of trouble it spared me."—"No, my dear friend, I do not yet understand; but perhaps with the help of explanation—"—"Here it is, my friend. In the first place, as you have said, to be measured is a loss of time, even though it occur only once a fortnight. And then, one may be travelling, and may wish to have seven suits always ready. In short, I have a horror of letting any one take my measure. Confound it! either one is a gentleman or he is not. To be scrutinised and scanned by a fellow who completely analyses you by inch and line,—'tis degrading. Here, they find you too hollow; there, too prominent. They recognize your strong and weak points. See, now, when we leave the measurer's hands, we are like those strongholds whose angles and different thicknesses have been ascertained by a spy."

"In truth, my dear Porthos, you possess ideas entirely your own." —"Ah! you see, when a man is an engineer—"—"And has fortified Belle-Isle,—'tis natural, my friend."—"Well, I had an idea, which would doubtless have proved a good one but for Mouston's carelessness." D'Artagnan glanced at Mouston, who replied by a slight movement of his body, as if to say, "You will see whether I am at all to blame in all this."

"I congratulated myself, then," resumed Porthos, "at seeing Mouston get fat; and I did all I could, by means of substantial feeding, to make him stout,—always in the hope that he would come to equal myself in girth, and could then be measured in my stead."— "Ah," cried D'Artagnan, "I see! That spared you both time and humiliation."

"Consider my joy when after a year and a half's judicious feeding, —for I used to feed him myself,—the fellow—"—"Oh, I lent a good hand myself, Monsieur!" said Mouston, humbly.—"That's true. Consider my joy when one morning I perceived Mouston was obliged, like myself, to compress himself to get through the little secret door that those fools of architects had made in the chamber of the late Madame du Vallon, in the château of Pierrefonds. And, by the way, about that door, my friend, I should like to ask you, who know everything, why these wretches of architects, who ought by

45

rights to have the compasses in their eye, came to make doorways through which nobody but thin people could pass?"

"Oh! those doors," answered D'Artagnan, "were meant for gallants, and they have generally slight and slender figures."—"Madame du Vallon had no gallant!" answered Porthos, majestically. —"Perfectly true, my friend," resumed D'Artagnan; "but the architects were imagining the possibility of your marrying again."

"Ah, that is possible!" said Porthos. "And now that I have received an explanation why doorways are made too narrow, let us return to the subject of Mouston's fatness. But see how the two things fit each other! I have always noticed that ideas run parallel. And so, observe this phenomenon, D'Artagnan! I was talking to you of Mouston, who is fat, and it led us on to Madame du Vallon —"—"Who was thin?"—"Hum! is it not marvelous?"—"My dear friend, a *savant* of my acquaintance, M. Costar, has made the same observation as you have; and he calls the process by some Greek name, which I forget."—"What! my remark is not then original?" cried Porthos, astounded. "I thought I was the discoverer."

"My friend, the fact was known before Aristotle's days,—that is to say, about two thousand years ago."—"Well, well, 'tis no less true," remarked Porthos, delighted at the idea of having concurred with the sages of antiquity.—"Wonderfully. But suppose we return to Mouston. It seems to me, we have left him fattening under our very eyes."—"Yes, Monsieur," said Mouston.

"Well," said Porthos, "Mouston fattened so well that he gratified all my hopes by reaching my standard; a fact of which I was well able to convince myself, by seeing the rascal one day in a waistcoat of mine, which he had turned into a coat,—a waistcoat the mere embroidery of which was worth a hundred pistoles."—" 'Twas only to try it on, Monsieur," said Mouston.

"From that moment I determined to put Mouston in communication with my tailors, and to have him measured instead of myself." —"A capital idea, Porthos; but Mouston is a foot and a half shorter than you."

"Exactly! They measured him down to the ground, and the end of the skirt came just below my knee."—"What a wonder you are, Porthos! Such a thing could happen only to you."—"Ah, yes, pay your compliments; there is something upon which to base them! It was exactly at that time—that is to say, nearly two years and a half

How Mouston Became Fatter

ago—that I set out for Belle-Isle, instructing Mouston (so as always to have, in every event, a pattern of every fashion) to have a coat made for himself every month."—"And did Mouston neglect to comply with your instructions? Ah, that would not be right, Mouston!" —"No, Monsieur, quite the contrary, quite the contrary!"—"No, he never forgot to have his coats made; but he forgot to inform me that he had grown stouter!"

"But it was not my fault, Monsieur! Your tailor never told me." —"And this to such an extent, Monsieur," continued Porthos, "that the fellow in two years has gained eighteen inches in girth, and so my last dozen coats are all too large in progressive measure from a foot to a foot and a half!"—"But the rest,—those which were made when you were of the same size?"—"They are no longer the fashion, my dear friend. Were I to put them on, I should look like a fresh arrival from Siam, and as though I had been two years away from court."

"I understand your difficulty. You have how many new suits?— thirty-six, and yet not one to wear. Well, you must have a thirty-seventh made, and give the thirty-six to Mouston."—"Ah, Monsieur!" said Mouston, with a gratified air. "The truth is, that Monsieur has always been very generous to me."—"Do you mean to think that I hadn't that idea, or that I was deterred by the expense? But it wants only two days to the *fête*. I received the invitation yesterday; made Mouston post hither with my wardrobe, and only this morning discovered my misfortune; and from now till the day after to-morrow, there isn't a single fashionable tailor who will undertake to make me a suit."—"That is to say, one covered with gold, isn't it?"—"I especially wish it so!"

"Oh, we shall manage it! You won't leave for three days. The invitations are for Wednesday, and this is only Sunday morning."— " 'Tis true; but Aramis has strongly advised me to be at Vaux twenty-four hours beforehand."—"How! Aramis?"—"Yes, it was Aramis who brought me the invitation."—"Ah, to be sure, I see! You are invited on the part of M. Fouquet?"—"By no means,—by the king, dear friend. The letter bears the following as large as life: 'M. le Baron du Vallon is informed that the king has condescended to place him on the invitation list—' "—"Very good; but you leave with M. Fouquet?"

"And when I think," cried Porthos, stamping on the floor,—

47

"when I think I shall have no clothes, I am ready to burst with rage! I should like to strangle somebody or destroy something!" —"Neither strangle anybody nor destroy anything, Porthos; I will manage it all. Put on one of your thirty-six suits, and come with me to a tailor."—"Pooh! my agent has seen them all this morning." —"Even M. Percerin?"—"Who is M. Percerin?"—"He is the king's tailor, *parbleu!*"

"Oh! ah, yes!" said Porthos, who wished to appear to know the king's tailor, but now heard his name mentioned for the first time; "to M. Percerin's, by Jove! I thought he would be too much engaged."—"Doubtless he will be; but be at ease, Porthos! He will do for me what he won't do for another. Only, you must allow yourself to be measured!"—"Ah!" said Porthos, with a sigh, " 'tis vexatious, but what would you have me do?"—"Do? As others do,— as the king does."—"What! Do they measure the king too? Does *he* put up with it?"—"The king is a beau, my good friend; and so are you, too, whatever you may say about it." Porthos smiled triumphantly. "Let us go to the king's tailor," he said; "and since he measures the king, I think, by my faith, I may well allow him to measure me!"

CHAPTER VI

WHO MESSIRE JEAN PERCERIN WAS

THE king's tailor, Messire Jean Percerin, occupied a rather large house in the Rue St. Honoré, near the Rue de l'Arbre-Sec. He was a man of great taste in elegant stuffs, embroideries, and velvet, being hereditary tailor to the king. The preferment of his house reached as far back as the time of Charles IX.; from whose reign dated, as we know, fancies in *bravery* difficult enough to gratify. The Percerin of that period was a Huguenot, like Ambroise Paré, and had been spared by the Queen of Navarre,—the beautiful Margot, as they used to write and say too in those days,—because, in sooth, he was the only one who could make for her those wonderful riding-habits which she preferred to wear, seeing that they were marvellously well suited to hide certain anatomical defects which the Queen of Navarre used very studiously

to conceal. Percerin being saved made, out of gratitude, some beautiful black bodices, very inexpensive indeed, for Queen Catherine,
who ended by being pleased at the preservation of a Huguenot on
whom she had long looked with aversion. But Percerin was a prudent man; and having heard it said that there was no more dangerous sign for a Huguenot than to be smiled upon by Catherine,
and having observed that her smiles were more frequent than usual,
he speedily turned Catholic, with all his family; and having thus
become irreproachable, attained the lofty position of master tailor to
the crown of France. Under Henry III., gay king as he was, this
position was as high as one of the loftiest peaks of the Cordilleras.
Now, Percerin had been a clever man all his life, and by way of
keeping up his reputation beyond the grave, took very good care
not to make a bad death of it; and so contrived to die very season-
ably,—at the very moment he felt his powers of invention declining.
He left a son and daughter, both worthy of the name they were
called upon to bear,—the son a cutter as unerring and exact as the
square rule, the daughter apt at embroidery and at designing ornaments. The marriage of Henry IV. and Marie de Médicis, and the
exquisite court mourning for the aforementioned queen, together
with a few words let fall by M. de Bassompierre, king of the beaux
of that period, made the fortune of the second generation of Percerins. M. Concino Concini, and his wife Galigaï, who subsequently
shone at the French court, sought to Italianise the fashion, and introduced some Florentine tailors; but Percerin, touched to the quick
in his patriotism and his self-esteem, entirely defeated these foreign-
ers by his designs in brocatelle,—so effectually that Concino was the
first to give up his compatriots, and held the French tailor in such
esteem that he would never employ any other; and thus wore a
doublet of his on the very day that Vitry blew out his brains with his
pistol at the Pont du Louvre.

It was that doublet, issuing from M. Percerin's workshop, which
the Parisians rejoiced in hacking into so many pieces with the human flesh it covered. Notwithstanding the favour Concino Concini
had shown Percerin, the king Louis XIII. had the generosity to bear
no malice to his tailor and to retain him in his service. At the time
when Louis the Just afforded this great example of equity, Percerin
had brought up two sons, one of whom made his début at the marriage of Anne of Austria, invented that admirable Spanish costume

The Man in the Iron Mask

in which Richelieu danced a saraband, made the costumes for the tragedy of *Mirame*, and stitched on to Buckingham's mantle those famous pearls which were destined to be scattered on the floors of the Louvre. A man becomes easily illustrious who has made the dresses of M. de Buckingham, M. de Cinq-Mars, Mademoiselle Ninon, M. de Beaufort, and Marion de Lorme. And thus Percerin III. had attained the summit of his glory when his father died. This same Percerin III., old, famous, and wealthy, yet further dressed Louis XIV.; and having no son, which was a great cause of sorrow to him, seeing that with himself his dynasty would end, he had brought up several hopeful pupils. He possessed a carriage, a country-house, lackeys the tallest in Paris; and by special authority from Louis XIV., a pack of hounds. He worked for Messieurs de Lyonne and Letellier, under a sort of patronage; but, politic man as he was, and versed in State secrets, he never succeeded in fitting M. Colbert. This is beyond explanation; it is matter for intuition. Great geniuses of every kind live upon unseen, intangible ideas; they act without themselves knowing why. The great Percerin (for, contrary to the rule of dynasties, it was, above all, the last of the Percerins who deserved the name of Great),—the great Percerin was inspired when he cut a robe for the queen or a coat for the king; he could invent a mantle for Monsieur, a clock for Madame's stocking; but in spite of his supreme genius, he could never hit the measure of M. Colbert. "That man," he used often to say, "is beyond my art; my needle never can hit him off." We need scarcely say that Percerin was M. Fouquet's tailor, and that the superintendent highly esteemed him.

M. Percerin was nearly eighty years old,—nevertheless, still fresh, and at the same time so dry, the courtiers used to say, that he was positively brittle. His renown and his fortune were great enough for Monsieur the Prince, that king of fops, to take his arm when talking over the fashions; and for those least eager to pay never to dare to leave their accounts in arrear with him,—for M. Percerin would for the first time make clothes upon credit, but the second never, unless paid for the former order. It is easy to see that a tailor of such standing, instead of running after customers, would make difficulties about receiving new ones. And so Percerin declined to fit *bourgeois*, or those who had but recently obtained patents of nobility. It was stated, even, that M. de Mazarin, in return

50

Marie-Thérèse

Who Messire Jean Percerin Was

for a full suit of ceremonial vestments as cardinal, one fine day slipped letters of nobility into his pocket. Percerin was endowed with intelligence and wit. He might be called very lively. At eighty years of age he still took with a steady hand the measure of women's waists.

It was to the house of this great lord of tailors that D'Artagnan took the despairing Porthos; who, as they were going along, said to his friend: "Take care, my good D'Artagnan, not to compromise the dignity of a man such as I am with the arrogance of this Percerin, who will, I expect, be very impertinent; for I give you notice, my friend, that if he is wanting in respect to me I will chastise him."—"Presented by me," replied D'Artagnan, "you have nothing to fear, even though you were—what you are not."—"Ah! 'tis because—"

"What! Have you anything against Percerin, Porthos?"—"I think that I once sent Mouston to a fellow of that name."—"And then?"—"The fellow refused to supply me."—"Oh, a misunderstanding, no doubt, which 'tis pressing to set right! Mouston must have made a mistake."—"Perhaps."—"He has confused the names." —"Possibly. That rascal Mouston never can remember names."— "I will take it all upon myself."—"Very good."

"Stop the carriage, Porthos; here we are!"—"Here! how here? We are at the Halles; and you told me the house was at the corner of the Rue de l'Arbre-Sec."—" 'Tis true; but look!"—"Well, I do look, and I see—"—"What?"—*"Pardieu!* that we are at the Halles!"

"You do not, I suppose, want our horses to clamber up on the top of the carriage in front of us?"—"No."—"Nor the carriage in front of us to mount on the one in front of it?"—"Still less."—"Nor that the second should be driven over the roofs of the thirty or forty others which have arrived before us?"—"No; you are right, indeed. What a number of people! And what are they all about?"—" 'Tis very simple,—they are waiting their turn."

"Bah! Have the comedians of the Hôtel de Bourgogne shifted their quarters?"—"No; their turn to obtain an entrance to M. Percerin's house."—"And we are going to wait too?"—"Oh, we shall show ourselves more ready and less proud than they!"—"What are we to do, then?"—"Get down, pass through the footmen and lackeys, and enter the tailor's house, which I will answer for our doing, especially if you go first."—"Come, then," said Porthos.

The Man in the Iron Mask

They both alighted, and made their way on foot towards the establishment. The cause of the confusion was that M. Percerin's doors were closed, while a servant standing before them was explaining to the illustrious customers of the illustrious tailor that just then M. Percerin could not receive anybody. It was bruited about outside still, on the authority of what the great lackey had said confidentially to some great noble whom he favoured, that M. Percerin was engaged upon five dresses for the king, and that, owing to the urgency of the case, he was meditating in his office on the ornaments, colours, and cut of these five suits. Some, contented with this reason, went away again, happy to repeat it to others; but others, more tenacious, insisted on having the doors opened,—and among these last, three Blue Ribbons, intended to take part in a ballet which would inevitably fail unless the said three had their costumes shaped by the very hand of the great Percerin himself.

D'Artagnan, pushing on Porthos, who scattered the groups of people right and left, succeeded in gaining the counter behind which the journeymen tailors were doing their best to answer questions. We forgot to mention that at the door they wanted to put off Porthos, like the rest; but D'Artagnan, showing himself, pronounced merely these words, "The king's order," and was let in with his friend. Those poor devils had enough to do, and did their best, to reply to the demands of the customers in the absence of their master, leaving off drawing a stitch to turn a sentence; and when wounded pride or disappointed expectation brought down upon them too cutting rebukes, he who was attacked made a dive and disappeared under the counter.

The line of discontented lords formed a picture full of curious details. Our captain of musketeers, a man of sure and rapid observation, took it all in at a glance; but having run over the groups, his eye rested on a man in front of him. This man, seated upon a stool, scarcely showed his head above the counter which sheltered him. He was about forty years of age, with a melancholy aspect, pale face, and soft luminous eyes. He was looking at D'Artagnan and the rest, with his chin resting upon his hand, like a calm and inquiring spectator. Only, on perceiving and doubtless recognising our captain, he pulled his hat down over his eyes. It was this action, perhaps, that attracted D'Artagnan's attention. If so, the gentleman who had pulled down his hat produced an effect entirely dif-

Who Messire Jean Percerin Was

ferent from what he had desired. In other respects, his costume was plain, and his hair evenly cut enough for customers who were not close observers to take him for a mere tailor's apprentice perched behind the board and carefully stitching cloth or velvet. Nevertheless, this man held up his head too often to be very productively employed with his fingers. D'Artagnan was not deceived,— not he; and he saw at once that if this man was working on anything, it certainly was not on cloth.

"Eh!" said he, addressing this man, "and so you have become a tailor's boy, M. Molière?"—"Hush, M. d'Artagnan!" replied the man, softly; "in Heaven's name! you will make them recognise me."—"Well, and what harm?"—"The fact is, there is no harm; but—"—"You were going to say there is no good in doing it, either, is it not so?"—"Alas! no; for I was occupied in looking at some excellent figures."

"Go on, go on, M. Molière! I quite understand the interest you take in it. I will not disturb your study."—"Thank you."—"But on one condition,—that you tell me where M. Percerin really is."— "Oh, willingly! in his own room. Only—"—"Only that one can't enter it?"—"Unapproachable."—"For everybody?"—"For everybody. He brought me here, so that I might be at my ease to make my observations, and then he went away."

"Well, my dear M. Molière, but you will go and tell him I am here."—"I!" exclaimed Molière, in the tone of a courageous dog from which you snatch the bone it has legitimately gained; "I disturb myself! Ah, M. d'Artagnan, how hard you are upon me!"— "If you don't go directly and tell M. Percerin that I am here, my dear Molière," said D'Artagnan, in a low tone, "I warn you of one thing,—that I won't exhibit to you the friend I have brought with me."

Molière indicated Porthos by an imperceptible gesture. "This gentleman, is it not?"—"Yes." Molière fixed upon Porthos one of those looks which penetrate the minds and hearts of men. The subject doubtless appeared very promising to him, for he immediately rose and led the way into the adjoining chamber.

CHAPTER VII

THE SAMPLES

DURING all this time the crowd was slowly rolling on, leaving at every angle of the counter either a murmur or a menace, as the waves leave foam or scattered seaweed on the sands, when they retire with the ebbing tide. In about ten minutes Molière reappeared, making another sign to D'Artagnan from under the hangings. The latter hurried after him, with Porthos in the rear, and after threading a labyrinth of corridors, introduced him to M. Percerin's room. The old man, with his sleeves turned up, was gathering up in folds a piece of gold-flowered brocade, so as the better to exhibit its lustre. Perceiving D'Artagnan, he put the silk aside, and came to meet him, by no means radiant and by no means courteous, but on the whole in a tolerably civil manner. "The captain of the musketeers will excuse me, I am sure, for I am engaged."

"Eh! yes, on the king's costumes; I know that, my dear M. Percerin. You are making three, they tell me."—"Five, my dear Monsieur,—five!"—"Three or five, 'tis all the same to me, my dear Monsieur; and I know that you will make them most exquisitely." —"Yes, I know. Once made, they will be the most beautiful in the world, I do not deny it; but that they may be the most beautiful in the world, they must first be made; and to do this, Captain, I am pressed for time."—"Oh, bah! there are two days yet; 'tis much more than you require, M. Percerin," said D'Artagnan, in the coolest possible manner.

Percerin raised his head with the air of a man little accustomed to be contradicted, even in his whims; but D'Artagnan did not pay the least attention to the airs which the illustrious tailor began to assume. "My dear M. Percerin," he continued, "I bring you a customer."—"Ah! ah!" exclaimed Percerin, crossly.—"M. le Baron du Vallon de Bracieux de Pierrefonds," continued D'Artagnan.

Percerin attempted a bow, which found no favour in the eyes of the terrible Porthos, who from his first entry into the room had been regarding the tailor askance. "A very good friend of mine," concluded D'Artagnan.—"I will attend to Monsieur," said Percerin, "but later."—"Later? but when?"—"Why, when I have time."

The Samples

"You have already told my valet as much," broke in Porthos, discontentedly.—"Very likely," said Percerin; "I am nearly always pushed for time."—"My friend," returned Porthos, sententiously, "there is always time when one chooses to find it." Percerin turned crimson,—a very ominous sign indeed in old men blanched by age. "Monsieur," said he, "is very free to confer his custom elsewhere."

"Come, come, Percerin," interposed D'Artagnan, "you are not in a good temper to-day. Well, I will say one more word to you, which will bring you on your knees: Monsieur is not only a friend of mine, but more,—a friend of M. Fouquet."—"Ah! ah!" exclaimed the tailor, "that is another thing." Then turning to Porthos, "Monsieur the Baron is attached to the superintendent?" he inquired.—"I am attached to myself," shouted Porthos, at the very moment when the tapestry was raised to introduce a new speaker in the dialogue. Molière was all observation; D'Artagnan laughed; Porthos swore.

"My dear Percerin," said D'Artagnan, "you will make a dress for the baron? 'Tis I who ask you."—"To you I will not say nay, Captain."—"But that is not all; you will make it for him at once."— " 'Tis impossible before eight days."—"That, then, is as much as to refuse, because the dress is wanted for the *fête* at Vaux."—"I repeat that it is impossible," returned the obstinate old man.

"By no means, dear M. Percerin, above all if *I* ask you," said a mild voice at the door,—a silvery voice which made D'Artagnan prick up his ears. It was the voice of Aramis. "M. de Herblay!" cried the tailor.—"Aramis!" murmured D'Artagnan.—"Ah, our bishop!" said Porthos.

"Good-morning, D'Artagnan! good-morning, Porthos; good-morning, my dear friends," said Aramis. "Come, come, M. Percerin, make the baron's dress, and I will answer for it you will gratify M. Fouquet;" and he accompanied the words with a sign which seemed to say, "Agree, and dismiss them." It appeared that Aramis had over M. Percerin an influence superior even to D'Artagnan's; for the tailor bowed in assent, and turning round upon Porthos, "Go and get measured on the other side," said he, rudely. Porthos coloured in a formidable manner. D'Artagnan saw the storm coming, and addressing Molière said to him in an undertone, "You see before you, by dear Monsieur, a man who considers himself disgraced if you measure the flesh and bones that Heaven has given him; study this type for me, Aristophanes, and profit by it."

The Man in the Iron Mask

Molière had no need of encouragement, and his gaze dwelt upon the baron Porthos. "Monsieur," he said, "if you will come with me, I will make them take your measure without the measurer touching you."—"Oh!" said Porthos, "how do you make that out, my friend?"—"I say that they shall apply neither line nor rule to the seams of your dress. It is a new method we have invented for measuring people of quality, who are too sensitive to allow low-born fellows to touch them. We know some susceptible persons who will not put up with being measured,—a process which, as I think, wounds the natural dignity of man; and if perchance Monsieur should be one of these—"—"*Corbœuf!* I believe I am one of them." —"Well, that is a capital coincidence, and you will have the benefit of our invention."

"But how in the devil can it be done?" asked Porthos, delighted. —"Monsieur," said Molière, bowing, "if you will deign to follow me, you will see."

Aramis observed this scene with all his eyes. Perhaps he fancied from D'Artagnan's liveliness that he would leave with Porthos, so as not to lose the conclusion of a scene so well begun. But, clear-sighted as he was, Aramis deceived himself. Porthos and Molière left together. D'Artagnan remained with Percerin.

Why? From curiosity, doubtless; probably to enjoy a little longer the society of his good friend Aramis. As Molière and Porthos disappeared, D'Artagnan drew near the Bishop of Vannes,—a proceeding which appeared particularly to disconcert him. "A dress for you also, is it not, my friend?" Aramis smiled. "No," said he.— "You will go to Vaux, however?"—"I shall go, but without a new dress. You forget, dear D'Artagnan, that a poor bishop of Vannes is not rich enough to have new dresses for every *fête*."

"Bah!" said the musketeer, laughing; "and do we write no more poems now, either?"—"Oh, D'Artagnan," exclaimed Aramis, "I have long given over all these follies!"—"True," repeated D'Artagnan, only half convinced. As for Percerin, he had relapsed into his contemplation of the brocades.

"Don't you perceive," said Aramis, smiling, "that we are greatly boring this good gentleman, my dear D'Artagnan?"—"Ah! ah!" murmured the musketeer, aside; "that is, I am boring you, my friend." Then aloud, "Well, then, let us leave. I have no further

56

business here; and if you are as disengaged as I, Aramis—"—"No; not I—I wished—"

"Ah! you had something private to say to M. Percerin? Why did you not tell me so at once?"—"Something private, certainly," repeated Aramis, "but not from you, D'Artagnan. I hope you will believe that I can never have anything so private to say that a friend like you may not hear it."—"Oh, no, no! I am going," said D'Artagnan, but imparting to his voice an evident tone of curiosity; for Aramis's annoyance, well dissembled as it was, had not escaped him, and he knew that in that impenetrable mind even the most apparently trivial thing was designed to some end,—an unknown one, but one which from the knowledge he had of his friend's character the musketeer felt must be important.

On his part, Aramis saw that D'Artagnan was not without suspicion, and pressed him. "Stay, by all means!" he said; "this is what it is." Then turning towards the tailor, "My dear Percerin," said he.—"I am even very happy that you are here, D'Artagnan."—"Oh, indeed!" exclaimed the Gascon, for the third time, even less deceived this time than before. Percerin never moved. Aramis roused him violently, by snatching from his hands the stuff upon which he was engaged. "My dear Percerin," said he, "I have near at hand M. Lebrun, one of M. Fouquet's painters."—"Ah, very good!" thought D'Artagnan; "but why Lebrun?"

Aramis looked at D'Artagnan, who seemed to be occupied with an engraving of Mark Antony. "And you wish to have made for him a dress similar to those of the Epicureans?" answered Percerin; and while saying this in an absent manner, the worthy tailor endeavoured to recapture his piece of brocade. "An Epicurean's dress?" asked D'Artagnan, in a tone of inquiry.

"I see," said Aramis, with a most engaging smile; "it is written that our dear D'Artagnan shall know all our secrets this evening. Yes, my friend, you have surely heard speak of M. Fouquet's Epicureans, have you not?"—"Undoubtedly. Is it not a kind of poetical society, of which La Fontaine Loret, Pellisson, and Molière are members, and which holds its sittings at St. Mandé?"—"Exactly so. Well, we are going to put our poets in uniform, and enroll them in the service of the king."

"Oh, very well; I understand,—a surprise M. Fouquet is getting up for the king. Be at ease; if that is the secret about M. Lebrun, I will not mention it."—"Always agreeable, my friend! No, M. Lebrun has nothing to do with this part of it; the secret which concerns him is far more important than the other."—"Then, if it is so important as all that, I prefer not to know it," said D'Artagnan, making a show of departure.

"Come in, M. Lebrun, come in!" said Aramis, opening a side-door with his right hand and holding back D'Artagnan with his left. —"I' faith, I too am quite in the dark," quoth Percerin.

Aramis took an "opportunity," as is said in theatrical matters. "My dear M. Percerin," he continued, "you are making five dresses for the king, are you not?—one in brocade, one in hunting-cloth, one in velvet, one in satin, and one in Florentine stuffs?"—"Yes; but how do you know all that, Monseigneur?" said Percerin, astounded.— "It is all very simple, my dear Monsieur. There will be a hunt, a banquet, a concert, a promenade, and a reception; these five kinds of dress are required by etiquette."—"You know everything, Monseigneur!"—"And a great many more things too," murmured D'Artagnan.

"But," cried the tailor, in triumph, "what you do not know, Monseigneur, prince of the church though you are; what nobody will know; what only the king, Mademoiselle de la Vallière, and myself do know,—is the colour of the materials, the nature of the ornaments, and the cut, the *ensemble*, the finish of it all!"—"Well," said Aramis, "that is precisely what I have come to ask you, dear Percerin."—"Ah, bah!" exclaimed the tailor, terrified, though Aramis had pronounced these words in his sweetest and most honeyed voice. The request appeared, on reflection, so exaggerated, so ridiculous, so monstrous to M. Percerin that first he laughed to himself, then aloud, and finished with a shout. D'Artagnan followed his example, not because he found the matter so "very funny," but in order not to allow Aramis to cool.

Aramis suffered them to laugh, and then, when they had become quiet, "At first view," said he, "I appear to be hazarding an absurd question, do I not? But D'Artagnan, who is incarnate wisdom itself, will tell you that I could not do otherwise than ask you this."— "Let us see," said the attentive musketeer, perceiving with his wonderful instinct that they had only been skirmishing till now, and that the moment of battle was approaching.—"Let us see," said Percerin, incredulously.

Baisemeaux, governor of the Bastille

The Samples

"Why, now," continued Aramis, "does M. Fouquet give the king a *fête?* Is it not to please him?"—"Assuredly," said Percerin. D'Artagnan nodded assent. "By delicate attentions, by some happy device, by a succession of surprises, like that of which we were talking, —the enrolment of our Epicureans?"—"Admirable."

"Well, then, this is the surprise we intend, my good friend. M. Lebrun, here, is a man who draws most exactly."—"Yes," said Percerin; "I have seen his pictures, and observed that the dresses were highly elaborated. That is why I at once agreed to make him a costume,—whether one to agree with those of the Epicureans, or an original one."—"My dear Monsieur, we accept your offer, and shall presently avail ourselves of it; but just now M. Lebrun is not in want of the dresses you will make for himself, but of those you are making for the king."

Percerin made a bound backwards, which D'Artagnan, calmest and most appreciative of men, did not consider overdone,—so many strange and startling aspects wore the proposal which Aramis had just hazarded. "The king's dresses! Give the king's dresses to any mortal whatever! Oh, for once, Monseigneur, your Grace is mad!" cried the poor tailor, in extremity.

"Help me now, D'Artagnan," said Aramis, more and more calm and smiling. "Help me now to persuade Monsieur; for *you* understand, do you not?"—"Eh! eh!—not exactly, I declare."—"What! you do not understand that M. Fouquet wishes to afford the king the surprise of finding his portrait on his arrival at Vaux; and that the portrait, which will be a striking resemblance, ought to be dressed exactly as the king will be on the day it is shown?"—"Oh, yes, yes!" said the musketeer, nearly convinced, so plausible was this reasoning. "Yes, my dear Aramis, you are right; it is a happy idea. I will wager it is one of your own, Aramis."

"Well, I don't know," replied the bishop; "either mine or M. Fouquet's." Then scanning Percerin, after noticing D'Artagnan's hesitation, "Well, M. Percerin," he asked, "what do you say to this?"—"I say that—"—"That you are, doubtless, free to refuse. I know well,—and I by no means count upon compelling you, my dear Monsieur. I will say more; I even understand all the delicacy you feel in taking up with M. Fouquet's idea,—you dread appearing to flatter the king. A noble spirit, M. Percerin, a noble spirit!" The tailor stammered. "It would indeed be a very pretty compliment to pay the young prince," continued Aramis; "but as the superintendent told me, 'If Percerin refuse, tell him that it will not at all lower him in my opinion, and I shall always esteem him; only —' "—"Only?" repeated Percerin, rather troubled.—" 'Only,' " continued Aramis, " 'I shall be compelled to say to the king,'—you understand, my dear M. Percerin, that these are M. Fouquet's words,—'I shall be constrained to say to the king, "Sire, I had intended to present your Majesty with your portrait; but owing to a feeling of delicacy, exaggerated perhaps, but creditable, M. Percerin opposed the project." ' "

"Opposed!" cried the tailor, terrified at the responsibility which would weigh upon him; "I to oppose the desire, the will of M. Fouquet when he is seeking to please the king! Oh, what a hateful word you have uttered, Monseigneur! Oppose! Oh, 'tis not I who said it, thank God! I call the captain of the musketeers to witness it! Is it not true, M. d'Artagnan, that I have opposed nothing?"

D'Artagnan made a sign indicating that he wished to remain neutral. He felt that there was an intrigue at the bottom of it, whether comedy or tragedy; he was disgusted at not being able to fathom it, but in the meanwhile wished to keep clear. But already Percerin, goaded by the idea that the king should be told he had stood in the way of a pleasant surprise, had offered Lebrun a chair, and proceeded to bring from a wardrobe four magnificent dresses, the fifth being still in the workmen's hands; and these masterpieces he successively fitted upon four lay figures, which imported into France in the time of Concini had been given to Percerin II. by Maréchal d'Ancre after the discomfiture of the Italian tailors ruined in their competition. The painter set to work to draw and then to paint the dresses. But Aramis, who was closely watching all the phases of his toil, suddenly stopped him.

"I think you have not quite got it, my dear Lebrun," he said; "your colours will deceive you, and on canvas we shall lack that exact resemblance which is absolutely requisite. Time is necessary for attentively observing the finer shades."—"Quite true," said Percerin; "but time is wanting, and on that head you will agree with me, Monseigneur, I can do nothing."—"Then the affair will fail," said Aramis, quietly, "and that because of a want of precision in the colours."

Nevertheless, Lebrun went on copying the materials and ornaments with the closest fidelity,—a process which Aramis watched with ill-concealed impatience. "What in the devil, now, is the meaning of this imbroglio?" the musketeer kept saying to himself.—"That will certainly never do," said Aramis. "M. Lebrun, close your box, and roll up your canvas."—"But, Monsieur," cried the vexed painter, "the light is abominable here."

"An idea, M. Lebrun, an idea! If we had a sample of the materials, for example, and with time and a better light—"—"Oh, then," cried Lebrun, "I would answer for the effect!"—"Good!" said D'Artagnan, "this ought to be the knot of the whole thing; they want a sample of each of the materials. *Mordioux!* will this Percerin give it now?" Percerin, beaten in his last retreat, and duped moreover by the feigned good-nature of Aramis, cut out five samples and handed them to the Bishop of Vannes.

"I like this better. That is your opinion, is it not?" said Aramis to D'Artagnan.—"My dear Aramis," said D'Artagnan, "my opinion is that you are always the same."—"And, consequently always your friend," said the bishop, in a charming tone.

"Yes, yes," said D'Artagnan, aloud; then, in a low voice, "If I am your dupe, double Jesuit that you are, I will not be your accomplice; and to prevent it, 'tis time I left this place. Adieu, Aramis," he added, aloud, "adieu; I am going to rejoin Porthos."—"Then wait for me," said Aramis, pocketing the samples; "for I have done, and shall not be sorry to say a parting word to our friend." Lebrun packed up, Percerin put back the dresses into the closet, Aramis put his hand on his pocket to assure himself that the samples were seure, and they all left the study.

CHAPTER VIII

WHERE, PROBABLY, MOLIÈRE FORMED HIS FIRST IDEA OF THE "BOURGEOIS GENTILHOMME"

D'ARTAGNAN found Porthos in the adjoining chamber; but no longer an irritated Porthos, or a disappointed Porthos, but Porthos radiant, blooming, fascinating, and chatting with Molière, who was looking upon him with a species of idolatry, and as a man would who had not only never seen anything better, but not even ever anything so good. Aramis went straight up to Porthos and offered him his delicate white hand, which lost itself in the gigantic hand of his old friend,—an operation which Aramis never hazarded without a certain uneasiness. But the friendly pressure having been performed not too painfully for him, the Bishop of Vannes passed over to Molière. "Well, Monsieur," said he, "will you come with me to St. Mandé?"—"I will go anywhere you like, Monseigneur," answered Molière.

"To St. Mandé!" cried Porthos, surprised at seeing the proud bishop of Vannes fraternising with a journeyman tailor. "What! Aramis, are you going to take this gentleman to St. Mandé?"— "Yes," said Aramis, smiling; "our work is pressing."—"Besides, my dear Porthos," continued D'Artagnan, "M. Molière is not altogether what he seems."—"In what way?" asked Porthos.—"Why, this gentleman is one of M. Percerin's chief clerks, and he is expected at St. Mandé to try on the dresses which M. Fouquet has ordered for the Epicureans."—" 'Tis precisely so," said Molière; "yes, Monsieur."

"Come, then, my dear M. Molière," said Aramis; "that is, if you have done with M. du Vallon?"—"We have finished," replied Porthos.—"And you are satisfied?" asked D'Artagnan.—"Completely so," replied Porthos.

Molière took his leave of Porthos with much ceremony, and grasped the hand which the captain of the musketeers furtively offered him. "Pray, Monsieur," concluded Porthos, mincingly, "above all, be exact."—"You will have your dress after to-morrow, Monsieur the Baron," answered Molière; and he left with Aramis.

D'Artagnan, taking Porthos's arm, inquired, "What has this tailor done for you, my dear Porthos, that you are so pleased with him?" —"What has he done for me, my friend,—done for me!" cried Porthos, enthusiastically.—"Yes, I ask you, what has he done for you?" —"My friend, he has done that which no tailor ever yet accomplished,—he has taken my measure without touching me!"

"Ah, bah! tell me how he did it!"—"First, then, they went, I don't know where, for a number of lay figures, of all heights and sizes, hoping there would be one to suit mine; but the largest—that of the drum-major of the Swiss Guard—was two inches too short, and half a foot too slender."—"Indeed!"—"It is exactly as I tell you, D'Artagnan; but he is a great man, or at the very least a great

Molière Has an Idea

tailor, is this M. Molière. He was not at all put at fault by the circumstance."

"What did he do, then?"—"Oh, it is a very simple matter! I' faith, 'tis an unheard-of thing that people should have been so stupid as not to have discovered this method from the first. What annoyance and humiliation they would have spared me!"—"Not to speak of the dresses, my dear Porthos."—"Yes, thirty dresses."—"Well, my dear Porthos, tell me M. Molière's plan."

"Molière? You call him so, do you? I shall make a point of recollecting his name."—"Yes; or Poquelin, if you prefer that."—"No; I like Molière best. When I wish to recollect his name, I shall think of *volière* [an aviary]; and as I have one at Pierrefonds—"—"Capital!" returned D'Artagnan; "and M. Molière's plan?"

" 'Tis this: instead of pulling me to pieces, as all these rascals do, making me bend in my back, and double my joints,—all of them low and dishonourable practices—" D'Artagnan made a sign of approbation with his head. " 'Monsieur,' he said to me," continued Porthos, " 'a gentleman ought to measure himself. Do me the pleasure to draw near this glass;' and I drew near the glass. I must own I did not exactly understand what this good M. Volière wanted with me —"—"Molière."—"Ah, yes; Molière, Molière. And as the fear of being measured still possessed me, 'Take care,' said I to him, 'what you are going to do with me; I am very ticklish, I warn you!' But he, with his soft voice (for he is a courteous fellow, we must admit, my friend),—he, with his soft voice, said: 'Monsieur, that your dress may fit you well, it must be made according to your figure. Your figure is exactly reflected in this mirror. We shall take the measure of this reflection.' "

"In fact," said D'Artagnan, "you saw yourself in the glass; but where did they find one in which you could see your whole figure?" —"My good friend, it is the very glass in which the king sees himself."—"Yes; but the king is a foot and a half shorter than you are."

"Ah! well, I know not how that may be,—it would no doubt be a way of flattering the king,—but the looking-glass was too large for me. 'Tis true that its height was made up of three Venetian plates of glass, placed one above another, and its breadth of the three similar pieces in juxtaposition."—"Oh, Porthos, what excellent words you have at your command! Where in the world did you make the collection?"—"At Belle-Isle. Aramis explained them to the architect."

"Ah, very good! Let us return to the glass, my friend."—"Then this good M. Volière—"—"Molière."—"Yes, Molière,—you are right. You will see now, my dear friend, that I shall recollect his name too well. This excellent M. Molière set to work tracing out lines on the mirror with a piece of Spanish chalk, following throughout the shape of my arms and my shoulders, all the while expounding this maxim, which I thought admirable,—'It is necessary that a dress should not incommode its wearer.' "

"In reality," said D'Artagnan, "that is an excellent maxim, which is, unfortunately, seldom carried out in practice."—"That is why I found it all the more astonishing when he expatiated upon it."—"Ah! he expatiated?"—*"Parbleu!"*—"Let me hear his theory."

" 'Seeing that,' he continued, 'one may in awkward circumstances or in a troublesome position have one's doublet on one's shoulder, and not desire to take it off—' "—"True," said D'Artagnan.—" 'And so,' continued M. Volière—"—"Molière."—"Molière; yes. 'And so,' went on M. Molière, 'you want to draw your sword, Monsieur, and you have your doublet on your back. What do you do?' 'I take it off,' I answered. 'Well, no,' he replied. 'How "no"?' 'I say that the dress should be so well made that it can in no way encumber you, even in drawing your sword.' 'Ah, ah! Put yourself on guard!' pursued he. I did it with such wondrous firmness that two panes of glass burst out of the window. ' 'Tis nothing, nothing,' said he; 'keep your position.' I raised my left arm in the air, the fore-arm gracefully bent, the ruffle drooping, and my wrist curbed, while my right arm, half extended, securely covered my waist with the elbow, and my breast with the wrist."

"Yes," said D'Artagnan, " 'tis the true guard,—the academic guard."—"You have said the very word, dear friend. In the meanwhile Volière—"—"Molière."—"Hold! I should certainly, after all, prefer to call him— What did you say his other name was?"—"Poquelin."—"I prefer to call him Poquelin."

"And how will you remember this name better than the other?"—"You understand— He call himself Poquelin, does he not?"—"Yes."—"I shall recall to mind Madame Coquenard."—"Good!"—"I shall change *Coq* into *Poq, nard* into *lin;* and instead of *Coquenard* I shall have *Poquelin*."—" 'Tis wonderful!" cried D'Artagnan,

Molière Has an Idea

astounded. "Go on, my friend! I am listening to you with admiration."

"This Coquelin sketched my arm on the glass—"—"I beg your pardon,—Poquelin."—"What did I say, then?"—"You said 'Coquelin.' "—"Ah, true! This Poquelin, then, sketched my arm on the glass; but he took his time over it,—he kept looking at me a good deal. The fact is, that I was very handsome. 'Does it weary you?' he asked. 'A little,' I replied, bending a little in my hands; 'but I could yet hold out an hour.' 'No, no; I will not allow it. We have here some willing fellows who will make it a duty to support your arms, as, of old, men supported those of the prophet.' 'Very good,' I answered. 'That will not be humiliating to you?' 'My friend,' said I, 'there is, I think, a great difference between being supported and being measured.' "

"The distinction is full of sense," interrupted the captain.— "Then," continued Porthos, "he made a sign. Two lads approached: one supported my left arm; while the other, with infinite address, supported my right arm. 'Another man!' cried he. A third approached. 'Support Monsieur by the waist,' said he. The *garçon* complied."—"So that you were at rest?" asked D'Artagnan.—"Perfectly; and Poquenard drew me on the glass."

"Poquelin, my friend."—"Poquelin,—you are right. Stay! decidedly I prefer calling him Volière."—"Yes; and then it was over, wasn't it?"—"During that time Volière drew me on the mirror."— " 'Twas delicate in him."—"I much like the plan: it is respectful, and keeps every one in his place."

"And there it ended?"—"Without a soul having touched me, my friend."—"Except the three *garçons* who supported you."—"Doubtless; but I have, I think, already explained to you the difference there is between supporting and measuring."—" 'Tis true," answered D'Artagnan, who said afterwards to himself, "I' faith, I greatly deceive myself, or I have been the means of a good windfall to that rascal Molière, and we shall assuredly see the scene hit off to the life in some comedy or other."

Porthos smiled. "What are you laughing at?" asked D'Artagnan. —"Must I confess it? Well, I was laughing over my good fortune." —"Oh, that is true; I don't know a happier man than you. But what is this last piece of luck that has befallen you?"—"Well, my dear fellow, congratulate me."—"I desire nothing better."—"It

65

seems I am the first who has had his measure taken in that manner."
"Are you sure of it?"—"Nearly so. Certain signs of intelligence
which passd between Volière and the other *garçons* showed me the
fact."—"Well, my friend, that does not surprise me from Molière,"
said D'Artagnan.—"Volière, my friend."—"Oh, no, no, indeed! I
am very willing to leave you to say Volière; but I myself shall continue to say Molière. Well, this, I was saying, does not surprise me,
coming from Molière, who is a very ingenious fellow, and whom you
inspired with this grand idea."

"It will be of great use to him by and by, I am sure."—"Won't it
be of use to him, indeed! I believe you, it will, and not a little so;
for you see my friend Molière is of all known tailors the man who
best clothes our barons, counts, and marquises—according to their
measure." On this observation, neither the application nor the
depth of which shall we discuss, D'Artagnan and Porthos quitted M.
Percerin's house and rejoined their carriage, wherein we will leave
them in order to look after Molière and Aramis at St. Mandé.

CHAPTER IX

THE BEEHIVE, THE BEES, AND THE HONEY

THE Bishop of Vannes, much annoyed at having met D'Artagnan at M. Percerin's, returned to St. Mandé in no very
good humour. Molière, on the other hand, quite delighted at
having made such a capital rough sketch, and at knowing where to
find its original again whenever he should desire to convert his sketch
into a picture, arrived in the merriest of moods. All the first story of
the left wing was occupied by the most celebrated Epicureans in
Paris, and those on the freest footing in the house,—every one in his
compartment, like the bees in their cells, employed in producing the
honey intended for that royal cake which M. Fouquet proposed to
offer his Majesty Louis XIV. during the *fête* at Vaux. Pellisson, his
head leaning on his hand, was engaged in drawing out the plan of the
prologue to "Les Fâcheux," a comedy in three acts, which was to be
put on the stage by Poquelin de Molière, as D'Artagnan called him,
or Coquelin de Volière, as Porthos styled him. Loret, with all the
charming innocence of a journalist,—the journalists of all ages have

The Beehive, the Bees, and the Honey

always been so artless!—Loret was composing an account of the
fêtes of Vaux, before those *fêtes* had taken place. La Fontaine
sauntered about among them,—a wandering, absent-minded, boring,
unbearable shade, buzzing and humming at everybody's shoulder a
thousand poetic inanities.

Molière burst out laughing; Pellisson and Loret followed his example. At this juncture the Bishop of Vannes appeared, with a roll
of plans and parchments under his arm. As if the angel of death had
chilled all gay and sprightly fancies, as if that wan form had scared
away the Graces to whom Xenocrates sacrificed, silence immediately
reigned through the study, and every one resumed his self-possession
and his pen.

Aramis distributed the notes of invitation, and thanked them in
the name of M. Fouquet. "The superintendent," he said, "being
kept to his room by business, could not come to see them, but begged
them to send him some of the fruits of their day's work, to enable
him to forget the fatigue of his labour in the night." At these words,
all settled to work. La Fontaine placed himself at a table, and set
his rapid pen running over the vellum; Pellisson made a fair copy of
his prologue; Molière gave fifty fresh verses, with which his visit to
Percerin had inspired him; Loret, his article on the marvellous *fêtes*
he predicted; and Aramis, laden with booty like the king of the bees,
—that great black drone, decked with purple and gold,—re-entered
his apartment, silent and busy. But before departing, "Remember,
gentlemen," said he, "we all leave to-morrow evening."

Aramis re-entered, after a brief disappearance. "Will any one go
with me?" he asked. "I am going by way of Paris, after having
passed a quarter of an hour with M. Fouquet. I offer my carriage."
—"Good!" said Molière. "I accept it; I am in a hurry."—"I shall
dine here," said Loret. "M. de Gourville has promised me some
crawfish,—

> Il m'a promis des écrevisses—

Find a rhyme for that, La Fontaine."

Aramis went out laughing, as only he could laugh, and Molière followed him. They were at the bottom of the stairs, when La Fontaine opened the door and shouted out,—

> "Moyennant que tu l'écrivisses,
> Il t'a promis des écrevisses."

The Man in the Iron Mask

The shouts of laughter reached the ears of Fouquet at the moment Aramis opened the door of the study. As to Molière, he had undertaken to order the horses, while Aramis went to exchange a parting word with the superintendent. "Oh, how they are laughing there!" said Fouquet, with a sigh.—"And do you not laugh, Monseigneur?" —"I laugh no longer now, M. d'Herblay. The *fête* is approaching; money is departing."—"Have I not told you that was my business?" —"Yes; you promised me millions."—"You shall have them the day after the king's *entrée* into Vaux."

Fouquet looked closely at Aramis, and passed his icy hand across his moistened brow. Aramis perceived that the superintendent either doubted him, or felt that he was powerless to obtain the money. How could Fouquet suppose that a poor bishop, ex-abbé, ex-musketeer, could procure it? "Why doubt me?" said Aramis. Fouquet smiled and shook his head. "Man of little faith!" added the bishop.

"My dear M. d'Herblay," answer Fouquet, "if I fall—"—"Well, if you 'fall'—"—"I shall at least fall from such a height that I shall shatter myself in falling." Then giving himself a shake, as though to escape from himself, "Whence come you," said he, "my friend?" —"From Paris,—from Percerin."

"And what have you been doing at Percerin's,—for I suppose you attach no great importance to our poets' dresses?"—"No; I went to prepare a surprise."—"Surprise?"—"Yes; which you are to give to the king."—"And it will cost much?"—"Oh, a hundred pistoles you will give Lebrun!"

"A painting? Ah, all the better! And what is this painting to represent?"—"I will tell you. Then at the same time, whatever you may say of it, I went to see the dresses for our poets."—"Bah! and they will be rich and elegant?"—"Splendid! There will be few great monseigneurs with dresses so good. People will see the difference between the courtiers of wealth and those of friendship." —"Ever generous and graceful, dear prelate!"—"In your school."

Fouquet grasped his hand. "And where are you going?" he said. —"I am off to Paris, when you shall have given me a certain letter." —"For whom?"—"M. de Lyonne."—"And what do you want with Lyonne?"—"I wish to make him sign a *lettre de cachet*."—"*Lettre de cachet!* Do you desire to put somebody in the Bastille?"—"On the contrary,—to let somebody out."

Another Supper at the Bastille

"And who?"—"A poor devil,—a youth, a lad who has been imprisoned these ten years for two Latin verses he made against the Jesuits."—" 'Two Latin verses!' and for 'two Latin verses' the miserable being has been in prison for ten years?"—"Yes."—"And has committed no other crime?"—"Beyond this, he is as innocent as you or I."—"On your word?"—"On my honour!"—"And his name is—"—"Seldon."

"Oh, that is too cruel! You knew this, and you never told me!" —" 'Twas only yesterday his mother applied to me, Monseigneur." —"And the woman is poor?"—"In the deepest misery."—"Oh, God!" said Fouquet, "thou dost sometimes bear with such injustice on earth that I understand why there are wretches who doubt thy existence! Stay, M. d'Herblay!" and Fouquet, taking a pen, wrote a few rapid lines to his colleague Lyonne.

Aramis took the letter, and made ready to go. "Wait!" said Fouquet. He opened his drawer, and took out ten government notes which were there, each for a thousand livres. "Stay!" he said. "Set the son at liberty, and give this to the mother; but, above all, tell her not—"—"What, Monseigneur?"—"That she is ten thousand livres richer than I. She would say I am a poor superintendent! Go; and I hope that God will bless those who are mindful of his poor!"—"So also do I hope," replied Aramis, kissing Fouquet's hand. And he went out quickly, carrying off the letter for Lyonne and the notes for Seldon's mother, and taking up Molière, who was beginning to lose patience.

CHAPTER X

ANOTHER SUPPER AT THE BASTILLE

SEVEN o'clock sounded from the great clock of the Bastille,— that famous clock which, like all the accessories of the State prison, the very use of which is a torture, brought to the prisoners' notice the lapse of every hour of their suffering. The timepiece of the Bastille, adorned with figures, like most of the clocks of the period, represented Saint Peter in bonds. It was the supper hour of the unfortunate captives. The doors, grating on their enormous

The Man in the Iron Mask

hinges, opened for the passage of the baskets and trays of provisions, the delicacy of which, as M. de Baisemeaux has himself taught us, was regulated by the condition in life of the prisoner. We understand on this head the theories of M. de Baisemeaux, sovereign dispenser of gastronomic delicacies, head cook of the royal fortress, whose trays, full laden, were ascending the steep staircases, carrying some consolation to the prisoners in the bottom of honestly filled bottles. This same hour was that of the governor's supper also. He had a guest to-day, and the spit turned more heavily than usual. Roast partridges flanked with quails and flanking a larded leveret; boiled fowls; ham, fried and sprinkled with white wine; *cardons* of Guipuzcoa and *la bisque d'écrevisses,*—these together with the soups and *hors d'œuvres,* constituted the governor's bill of fare.

Baisemeaux, seated at table, was rubbing his hands and looking at the Bishop of Vannes, who, booted like a cavalier, dressed in gray, with a sword at his side, kept talking of his hunger and testifying the liveliest impatience. M. de Baisemeaux de Montlezun was not accustomed to the unbending movement of his greatness my Lord of Vannes; and this evening Aramis, becoming quite sprightly, volunteered confidence on confidence. The prelate had again a little touch of the musketeer about him. The bishop just trenched on the borders only of licence in his style of conversation. As for M. de Baisemeaux, with the facility of vulgar people, he gave himself loose rein, on this touch of *abandon* on the part of his guest. "Monsieur," said he, —"for indeed to-night I don't like to call you Monseigneur—"—"By no means," said Aramis; "call me Monsieur,—I am booted."

"Do you know, Monsieur, of whom you remind me this evening?" —"No! faith," said Aramis, taking up his glass; "but I hope I remind you of a good companion."—"You remind me of two, Monsieur. François, shut the window; the wind may annoy his greatness."—"And let him go," added Aramis. "The supper is completely served, and we shall eat it very well without waiters. I like extremely to be *tête-à-tête* when I am with a friend." Baisemeaux bowed respectfully. "I like extremely," continued Aramis, "to help myself."

"Retire, François!" cried Baisemeaux. "I was saying that your Greatness puts me in mind of two persons,—one very illustrious, the late cardinal, the great cardinal of La Rochelle, who wore boots like

Another Supper at the Bastille

you."—"Indeed," said Aramis; "and the other?"—"The other was a certain musketeer, very handsome, very brave, very adventurous, very fortunate, who from being abbé turned musketeer, and from musketeer turned abbé." Aramis condescended to smile. "From abbé," continued Baisemeaux, encouraged by Aramis's smile,—"from abbé, bishop, and from bishop—"—"Ah, stay there, I beg!" exclaimed Aramis.—"I say, Monsieur, that you give me the idea of a cardinal."

"Enough, dear M. Baisemeaux! As you said, I have on the boots of a cavalier; but I do not intend, for all that, to embroil myself with the church this evening."—"You have wicked intentions, however, Monseigneur."—"Oh, yes; wicked I own, as everything mundane is."—"You traverse the town and the streets in disguise?"—"In disguise, as you say."—"And do you still make use of your sword?"—"Yes, I should think so; but only when I am compelled. Do me the pleasure to summon François."

"Have you no wine there?"—" 'Tis not for wine, but because it is hot here and the window is shut."—"I shut the windows at supper-time so as not to hear the sounds or the arrival of couriers."—"Ah, yes! You hear them when the window is open?"—"But too well, and that disturbs me. You understand!"—"Nevertheless, I am suffocated. François!" François entered. "Open the windows, I pray you, François! You will allow him, dear M. Baisemeaux?"—"You are at home here," answered the governor. The window was opened.

"Do you not think," said M. de Baisemeaux, "that you will find yourself very lonely, now that M. de la Fère has returned to his household gods at Blois? He is a very old friend, is he not?"—"You know it as I do, Baisemeaux, seeing that you were in the musketeers with us."—"Bah! with my friends I reckon neither bottles nor years."—"And you are right. But I do more than love M. de la Fère, dear Baisemeaux; I venerate him."—"Well, for my part, though 'tis singular," said the governor, "I prefer M. d'Artagnan to the count. There is a man for you, who drinks long and well! That kind of people allow you at least to penetrate their thoughts."

"Baisemeaux, make me tipsy to-night! Let us have a debauch as of old; and if I have a trouble at the bottom of my heart, I promise you, you shall see it as you would a diamond at the bottom of your glass."—"Bravo!" said Baisemeaux; and he poured out a great glass of wine and drank it off at a draught, trembling with joy at the idea

71

of being, by hook or by crook, in the secret of some high archi-episcopal misdemeanour. While he was drinking he did not see with what attention Aramis was noting the sounds in the great court. A courier arrived about eight o'clock, as François brought in the fifth bottle; and although the courier made a great noise, Baise-meaux heard nothing.

"The devil take him!" said Aramis.—"What? who?" asked Baise-meaux. "I hope 'tis neither the wine you drink nor he who is the cause of your drinking it."—"No; it is a horse, who is making noise enough in the court for a whole squadron."—"Pooh! some courier or other," replied the governor, redoubling his numerous bumpers. "Yes, the devil take him, and so quickly that we shall never hear him speak more! Hurrah! hurrah!"

"You forget me, Baisemeaux! my glass is empty," said Aramis, showing his dazzling goblet.—"Upon honour, you delight me. François, wine!" François entered. "Wine, fellow! and better."—"Yes, Monsieur, yes; but a courier has just arrived."—"Let him go to the devil, I say."—"Yes, Monsieur, but—"—"Let him leave his news at the office; we will see to it to-morrow. To-morrow,—there will be time to-morrow; there will be daylight," said Baisemeaux, chanting the words.

"Ah, Monsieur," grumbled the soldier François, in spite of him-self,—"Monsieur!"—"Take care," said Aramis, "take care!"—"Of what, dear M. d'Herblay?" said Baisemeaux, half intoxicated.

"The letter which the courier brings to the governor of a fortress is sometimes an order."—"Nearly always."—"Do not orders issue from the ministers?"—"Yes, undoubtedly; but—"—"And what do these ministers do but countersign the signature of the king?"—"Perhaps you are right. Nevertheless, 'tis very tiresome when you are sitting before a good table, tête-à-tête with a friend— Ah! I beg your pardon, Monsieur; I forgot that it is I who invite you to supper, and that I speak to a future cardinal."

"Let us pass over that, dear Baisemeaux, and return to our soldier, —to François."—"Well, and what has François done?"—"He has demurred!"—"He was wrong, then."—"However, he *has* demurred, you see; 'tis because there is something extraordinary in this matter. It is very possible that it was not François who was wrong in de-murring, but you, who will be wrong in not listening to him."—"Wrong! I to be wrong before François!—that seems rather hard."

Another Supper at the Bastille

—"Pardon me, merely an irregularity. But I thought it my duty to make an observation which I deem important."

"Oh, perhaps you are right!" stammered Baisemeaux. "The king's order is sacred; but as to orders that arrive when one is at supper, I repeat, may the devil—"—"If you had said as much to the great cardinal, eh! my dear Baisemeaux, and if his order had been important—"—"I do it that I may not disturb a bishop. *Morbleu!* Am I not, then, excusable?"

"Do not forget, Baisemeaux, that I have worn the uniform, and am accustomed to see everywhere obedience."—"You wish, then—" —"I wish that you should do your duty, my friend; yes, at least before this soldier."—" 'Tis mathematically true," exclaimed Baisemeaux. François still waited. "Let them send this order of the king up to me," he said, recovering himself. And he added in a low tone: "Do you know what it is? I will tell you; it is something about as interesting as this: 'Beware of fire near the powder-magazine,' or 'Look close after such a one, who is clever at escaping.' Ah! if you only knew, Monseigneur, how many times I have been suddenly awakened from the very sweetest and deepest slumber by messengers arriving at full gallop to tell me, or rather bring me a slip of paper containing these words: 'M. de Baisemeaux, what news?' 'Tis clear enough that those who waste their time writing such orders have never slept in the Bastille. They would know better the thickness of my walls, the vigilance of my officers, the number of my rounds. But, indeed, what can you expect, Monseigneur? It is their business to write and torment me when I am at rest, and to trouble me when I am happy," added Baisemeaux, bowing to Aramis. "Then let us leave them to their business."—"And do you do yours," added the bishop, smiling, but with command in his expression notwithstanding.

François re-entered. Baisemeaux took from his hands the minister's order. He slowly undid it, and as slowly read it. Aramis pretended to be drinking, so as to be able to watch his host through the glass. Then, having read it, "What was I just saying?" Baisemeaux exclaimed.

"What is it?" asked the bishop.—"An order of release! There, now; excellent news, indeed, to disturb us!"—"Excellent news for him whom it concerns, you will at least agree, my dear governor!" —"And at eight o'clock in the evening!"—"It is charitable!"—"Oh!

charity is all very well; but it is for that fellow who is low-spirited, and not for me who am amusing myself," said Baisemeaux, exasperated.

"Will you lose by him, then? And is the prisoner who is to be set at liberty a high payer?"—"Oh yes, indeed! a miserable, five-livre rat!"—"Let me see it," asked M. d'Herblay. "It is no indiscretion?" —"By no means; read it."

"There is 'Urgent' on the paper; you noticed that, I suppose?"— "Oh, admirable! 'Urgent!'—a man who has been there ten years! It is *urgent* to set him free to-day, this very evening at eight o'clock! —*urgent!*" and Baisemeaux, shrugging his shoulders with an air of supreme disdain, flung the order on the table and began eating again. "They are fond of these dodges," he said, with his mouth full; "they seize a man, some fine day, maintain him for ten years, and write to you, 'Watch this fellow well,' or 'Keep him very strictly.' And then, as soon as you are accustomed to look upon the prisoner as a dangerous man, all of a sudden, without cause or precedent, they write, 'Set him at liberty;' and add to their missive, 'Urgent.' You will own, my Lord, 'tis enough to make one shrug his shoulders!"

"What do you expect? It is they who write," said Aramis, "and it is for you to execute the order."—"Good! good! execute it! Oh, patience! You must not imagine that I am a slave."—"Gracious Heaven! my very good M. Baisemeaux, who ever said so? Your independence is known."—"Thank Heaven!"—"But your good heart also is known."—"Ah, don't speak of it!"—"And your obedience to your superiors. Once a soldier, you see, Baisemeaux, always a soldier."

"And so I shall strictly obey; and to-morrow morning, at daybreak, the prisoner referred to shall be set free."—"To-morrow?"— "At dawn."—"Why not this evening, seeing that the *lettre de cachet* bears, both on the direction and inside, 'Urgent'?"—"Because this evening we are at supper, and our affairs are urgent, too!"—"Dear Baisemeaux, booted though I be, I feel myself a priest; and charity has higher claims upon me than hunger and thirst. This unfortunate man has suffered long enough, since you have just told me that he has been your prisoner these ten years. Abridge his suffering. His good time has come; give him the benefit quickly. God will repay you in Paradise with years of felicity."

"You wish it?"—"I entreat you."—"What! in the very middle of

74

our repast?"—"I implore you; such an action is worth ten Bene-
dicites."—"It shall be as you desire; only, our supper will get cold."
—"Oh, never heed that!"

Baisemeaux leaned back to ring for François, and by a very natural motion turned round towards the door. The order had remained
on the table. Aramis seized the opportunity when Baisemeaux was
not looking to change the paper for another folded in the same manner, which he took from his pocket. "François," said the governor,
"let the major come up here with the turnkeys of the Bertaudière."
François bowed and quitted the room, leaving the two companions
alone.

CHAPTER XI

THE GENERAL OF THE ORDER

THERE was now a brief silence, during which Aramis never
removed his eyes from Baisemeaux for a moment. The latter seemed only half decided to disturb himself thus in the
middle of supper; and it was clear that he was seeking some pretext, whether good or bad, for delay, at any rate till after dessert.
And it appeared also that he had hit upon a pretext at last. "Eh!
but it is impossible," he cried.—"How impossible?" said Aramis.
"Give me a glimpse of this impossibility."—" 'Tis impossible to set
a prisoner at liberty at such an hour. Where can he go to,—he,
who is unacquainted with Paris?"—"He will go wherever he can."

"You see, now, one might as well set a blind man free!"—"I have
a carriage, and will take him wherever he wishes."—"You have an
answer for everything. François, tell Monsieur the Major to go
and open the cell of M. Seldon, No. 3 Bertaudière."

"Seldon!" exclaimed Aramis, very naturally. "You said Seldon,
I think?"—"I said Seldon, of course. 'Tis the name of the man to
be set free."—"Oh! you mean to say Marchiali?" said Aramis.

"Marchiali? oh, yes, indeed! No, no! Seldon."—"I think you are
making a mistake, M. Baisemeaux."—"I have read the order."—
"And I also."—"And I saw 'Seldon' in letters as large as that;" and
Baisemeaux held up his finger.—"And I read 'Marchiali,' in characters as large as this," said Aramis, holding up two fingers.

The Man in the Iron Mask

"To the proof; let us throw a light on the matter," said Baise-meaux, confident he was right. "There is the paper; you have only to read it."—"I read 'Marchiali,'" returned Aramis, spreading out the paper. "Look!" Baisemeaux looked, and his arms dropped suddenly. "Yes, yes," he said, quite overwhelmed; "yes, Marchiali. 'Tis plainly written 'Marchiali.' Quite true!"—"Ah!"

"How? The man of whom we have talked so much? The man whom they are every day telling me to take such care of?"—"There is 'Marchiali,'" repeated the inflexible Bishop of Vannes.—"I must own it, Monseigneur. But I understand absolutely nothing about it."—"You believe your eyes, at any rate."—"To tell me very plainly there is 'Marchiali.'"—"And in a good handwriting too."

"'Tis a wonder! I still see this order and the name of Seldon, Irishman. I see it. Ah! I even recollect that under this name there was a blot of ink."—"No, there is no ink; no, there is no blot." "Oh, but there was, though! I know it, because I rubbed the powder that was over the blot."—"In a word, be it how it may, dear M. Baisemeaux," said Aramis, "and whatever you may have seen, the order is signed to release Marchiali, blot or no blot."

"The order is signed to release Marchiali!" repeated Baisemeaux, mechanically endeavouring to regain his courage.—"And you are going to release this prisoner. If your heart dictates to you to deliver Seldon also, I declare to you I will not oppose it the least in the world." Aramis accompanied this remark with a smile, the irony of which effectually dispelled Baisemeaux's confusion of mind and restored his courage.

"Monseigneur," said the governor, "this Marchiali is the very same prisoner whom the other day a priest, confessor of *our order,* came to visit in so imperious and so secret a manner."—"I don't know that, Monsieur," replied the bishop.—"'Tis no very long time ago, dear M. d'Herblay."—"It is true. But *with us,* Monsieur, it is good that the man of to-day should no longer know what the man of yesterday did."—"In any case," said Baisemeaux, "the visit of the Jesuit confessor must have given happiness to this man."

Aramis made no reply, but recommended eating and drinking. As for Baisemeaux, no longer touching anything that was on the table, he again took up the order and examined it in every way. This investigation, under ordinary circumstances, would have made the ears of the impatient Aramis burn with anger; but the Bishop of Vannes

The General of the Order

did not become incensed for so little, especially when he had murmured to himself that to do so was dangerous. "Are you going to release Marchiali?" he said. "What mellow and fragrant sherry this is, my dear governor!"

"Monseigneur," replied Baisemeaux, "I shall release the prisoner Marchiali when I have summoned the courier who brought the order, and above all, when by interrogating him I have satisfied myself."—"The order is sealed, and the courier is ignorant of the contents. What do you want to satisfy yourself about?"—"Be it so, Monseigneur; but I shall send to the ministry, and M. de Lyonne will either confirm or withdraw the order."

"What is the good of all that?" asked Aramis, coldly.—"What good?"—"Yes; what is your object, I ask?"—"The object of never deceiving one's self, Monseigneur, of not failing in the respect which a subaltern owes to his superior officers, nor neglecting the duties of that service which one has voluntarily accepted."—"Very good; you have just spoken so eloquently that I cannot but admire you. It is true that a subaltern owes respect to his superiors; he is guilty when he deceives himself, and he should be punished if he disregard either the duties or laws of his office."

Baisemeaux looked at the bishop with astonishment. "It follows," pursued Aramis, "that you are going to ask advice in order to put your conscience at ease in the matter?"—"Yes, Monseigneur."—"And if a superior officer gives you orders, you will obey?"—"Never doubt it, Monseigneur."

"You know the king's signature very well, M. de Baisemeaux?" —"Yes, Monseigneur."—"Is it not on this order of release?"—"It is true, but it may—"—"Be forged, you mean?"—"That is possible, Monseigneur."—"You are right. And that of M. de Lyonne?"—"I see it plain enough on the order; but just as the king's signature may have been forged, so also, even more likely, may M. de Lyonne's."

"Your logic has the stride of a giant, M. de Baisemeaux," said Aramis; "and your reasoning is irresistible. But on what special grounds do you base your idea that these signatures are false?"— "On this: the absence of counter-signatures. Nothing checks his Majesty's signature; and M. de Lyonne is not there to tell me he has signed."

"Well, M. de Baisemeaux," said Aramis, bending an eagle glance on the governor, "I adopt so frankly your doubts, and your mode of clearing them up, that I will take a pen, if you will give me one." Baisemeaux gave him a pen. "And a sheet of white paper," added Aramis. Baisemeaux handed some paper. "Now, I—I, also—I, here present—incontestably, I—am going to write an order to which I am certain you will give credence, incredulous as you are!"

Baisemeaux turned pale at this icy assurance of manner. It seemed to him that that voice of Aramis, but just now so playful and so gay, had become funereal and sinister; that the wax-lights had changed into the tapers of a mortuary chapel, and the glasses of wine into chalices of blood. Aramis took a pen and wrote. Baisemeaux, in terror, read over his shoulder.

"A. M. D. G." wrote the bishop; and he drew a cross under these four letters, which signify *ad majorem Dei gloriam,* and thus continued:—"It is our pleasure that the order brought to M. de Baisemeaux de Montlezun, governor, for the king, of the castle of the Bastille, be held by him good and effectual, and be immediately carried into operation.

(Signed)   "D'Herblay,
"General of the Order, by the grace of God."

Baisemeaux was so profoundly astonished that his features remained contracted, his lips parted, and his eyes fixed. He did not move an inch, nor articulate a sound. Nothing could be heard in that large chamber but the buzzing of a little moth which was fluttering about the candles. Aramis, without even deigning to look at the man whom he had reduced to so miserable a condition, drew from his pocket a small case of black wax. He sealed the letter, and stamped it with a seal suspended at his breast, beneath his doublet; and when the operation was concluded, presented—still in silence—the missive to M. de Baisemeaux. The latter, whose hands trembled in a manner to excite pity, turned a dull and meaningless gaze upon the letter. A last gleam of feeling played over his features, and he fell, as if thunderstruck, on a chair.

"Come, come," said Aramis, after a long silence, during which the governor of the Bastille had slowly recovered his senses, "do not lead me to believe, dear Baisemeaux, that the presence of the general of the order is as terrible as that of the Almighty, and that men die merely from seeing him! Take courage, rouse yourself; give me your hand, and obey!"—Baisemeaux, reassured, if not satisfied,

The General of the Order

obeyed, kissed Aramis's hand, and rose from his chair. "Immediately?" he murmured.

"Oh, there is no pressing haste, my host; take your place again, and do the honours over this beautiful dessert."—"Monseigneur, I shall never recover such a shock as this,—I who have laughed, who have jested with you! I who have dared to treat you on a footing of equality!"—"Say nothing about it, old comrade," replied the bishop, who perceived how strained the cord was, and how dangerous it might be to break it; "say nothing about it. Let us each live in our own way: to you, my protection and my friendship; to me, your obedience. Exactly fulfilling these two requirements, let us live happily."

Baisemeaux reflected. He perceived, at a glance, the consequences of this withdrawal of a prisoner by means of a forged order; and putting in the scale the guarantee offered him by the official order of the general, did not consider it of any value.

Aramis divined this. "My dear Baisemeaux," said he, "you are a simpleton! Lose this habit of reflection when I give myself the trouble to think for you." At another gesture made by Aramis, Baisemeaux bowed again. "How shall I set about it?"—"What is the process for releasing a prisoner?"—"I have the regulations."—"Well, then, follow the regulations, my friend."

"I go with my major to the prisoner's room, and conduct him, if he is a personage of importance."—"But this Marchiali is not an important personage," said Aramis, carelessly.—"I don't know," answered the governor; as if he would have said, "It is for you to instruct me."—"Then, if you don't know it, I am right; so act towards Marchiali as you act towards one of obscure station."

"Good; the regulations so provide. They are to the effect that the turnkey, or one of the lower officials, shall bring the prisoner before the governor, in the office."—"Well, 'tis very wise, that; and then?"—"Then we return to the prisoner the valuables he wore at the time of his imprisonment, his clothes, and papers, if the minister's order has not otherwise directed."

"What was the minister's order as to this Marchiali?"—"Nothing; for the unhappy man arrived here without jewels, without papers, and almost without clothes."—"See how simple it all is! Indeed, Baisemeaux, you make a mountain of everything. Remain here, and make them bring the prisoner to the governor's house."

79

The Man in the Iron Mask

Baisemeaux obeyed. He summoned his lieutenant, and gave him an order, which the latter passed, on without disturbing himself about it, to the next whom it concerned. Half an hour afterwards they heard a gate shut in the court; it was the door to the dungeon which had just rendered up its prey to the free air. Aramis blew out all the candles which lighted the room but one, which he left burning behind the door. This flickering glare prevented the sight from resting steadily on any object. It multiplied tenfold the changing forms and shadows of the place by its wavering uncertainty. Steps drew near. "Go and meet your men," said Aramis to Baisemeaux.

The governor obeyed. The sergeant and turnkeys disappeared. Baisemeaux re-entered, followed by a prisoner. Aramis had placed himself in the shade; he saw without being seen. Baisemeaux, in an agitated tone of voice, made the young man acquainted with the order which set him at liberty. The prisoner listened, without making a single gesture or saying a word.

"You will swear,—the regulation requires it,"—added the governor, "never to reveal anything that you have seen or heard in the Bastille." The prisoner perceived a crucifix; he stretched out his hands, and swore with his lips. "And now, Monsieur, that you are free, whither do you intend going?" The prisoner turned his head, as if looking behind him for some protection which he had expected. Then was it that Aramis came out of the shadow. "I am here," he said, "to render the gentleman whatever service he may please to ask." The prisoner slightly reddened, and without hesitation passed his arm through that of Aramis. "God have you in his holy keeping!" he said, in a voice the firmness of which made the governor tremble as much as the form of the blessing astonished him.

Aramis, on shaking hands with Baisemeaux, said to him: "Does my order trouble you? Do you fear their finding it here, should they come to search?"—"I desire to keep it, Monseigneur," said Baisemeaux. "If they found it here, it would be a certain indication of my ruin, and in that case you would be a powerful and a last auxiliary for me."—"Being your accomplice, you mean?" answered Aramis, shrugging his shoulders. "Adieu, Baisemeaux!" said he.

The horses were in waiting, making the carriage shake with their impatience. Baisemeaux accompanied the bishop to the bottom of the steps. Aramis caused his companion to enter before him, then followed, and without giving the driver any further order, "Go on!" said he. The carriage rattled over the pavement of the courtyard. An officer with a torch went before the horses, and gave orders at every post to let them pass. During the time taken in opening all the barriers, Aramis barely breathed, and you might have heard his heart beat against his ribs. The prisoner, buried in a corner of the carriage, made no more sign of life than his companion. At length a jolt more severe than the others announced to them that they had cleared the last watercourse. Behind the carriage closed the last gate,—that in the Rue St. Antoine. No more walls either on the right or left; heaven everywhere, liberty everywhere, life everywhere! The horses, kept in check by a vigorous hand, went quietly as far as the middle of the faubourg. There they began to trot. Little by little, whether they warmed over it or whether they were urged, they gained in swiftness; and once past Bercy, the carriage seemed to fly, so great was the ardour of the coursers. These horses ran thus as far as Villeneuve-Saint-Georges, where relays were waiting. Then four instead of two whirled the carriage away in the direction of Melun, and pulled up for a moment in the middle of the forest of Sénart. No doubt the order had been given the postilion beforehand, for Aramis had no occasion even to make a sign.

"What is the matter?" asked the prisoner, as if waking from a long dream.—"The matter is, Monseigneur," said Aramis, "that before going further, it is necessary that your royal Highness and I should converse."—"I will wait an opportunity, Monsieur," answered the young prince.

"We could not have a better, Monseigneur; we are in the middle of a forest, and no one can hear us."—"The postilion?"—"The postilion of this relay is deaf and dumb, Monseigneur."—"I am at your service, M. d'Herblay."—"Is it your pleasure to remain in the carriage?"—"Yes; we are comfortably seated, and I like this carriage; it has restored me to liberty."

"Wait, Monseigneur; there is yet a precaution to be taken."—"What?"—"We are here on the highway; cavaliers or carriages travelling like ourselves might pass, and seeing us stopping deem us in some difficulty. Let us avoid offers of assistance, which would embarrass us."—"Give the postilion orders to conceal the carriage in one of the side avenues."—" 'Tis exactly what I wished to do, Monseigneur."

The Man in the Iron Mask

Aramis made a sign to the deaf and dumb driver of the carriage, whom he touched on the arm. The latter dismounted, took the leaders by the bridle, and led them over the velvet sward and the mossy grass of a winding alley, at the bottom of which, on this moonless night, the deep shades formed a curtain blacker than ink. This done, the man lay down on a slope near his horses, which on either side kept nibbling the young oak shoots.

"I am listening," said the young prince to Aramis; "but what are you doing there?"—"I am disarming myself of my pistols, of which we have no further need, Monseigneur."

CHAPTER XII

THE TEMPTER

"MY PRINCE," said Aramis, turning in the carriage towards his companion, "weak creature as I am, so unpretending in genius, so low in the scale of intelligent beings, it has never yet happened to me to converse with a man without penetrating his thoughts through that living mask which has been thrown over our mind in order to retain its expression. But to-night, in this darkness, in the reserve which you maintain, I can read nothing on your features, and something tells me that I shall have great difficulty in wresting from you a sincere declaration. I beseech you, then, not for love of me,—for subjects should never weigh as anything in the balance which princes hold,—but for love of yourself, to attend to every syllable I may utter, and to every tone of my voice,—which under our present grave circumstances will all have a sense and value as important as any words ever spoken in the world."—"I listen," repeated the young prince, decidedly, "without either eagerly seeking or fearing anything you are about to say to me;" and he sank still deeper in the thick cushions of the carriage, trying to deprive his companion not only of the sight of him, but even of the very idea of his presence.

Black was the darkness which fell wide and dense from the summits of the intertwining trees. The carriage, covered in by this vast roof, would not have received a particle of light, not even if a ray could have struggled through the wreaths of mist which were rising in the avenue of the wood.

"Monseigneur," resumed Aramis, "you know the history of the government which to-day controls France. The king issued from an infancy imprisoned like yours, obscure as yours, and confined as yours; only, instead of enduring, like yourself, this slavery in a prison, this obscurity in solitude, these straitened circumstances in concealment, he has borne all these miseries, humiliations, and distresses in full daylight, under the pitiless sun of royalty,—on an elevation so flooded with light, where every stain appears a miserable blemish, and every glory a stain. The king has suffered; it rankles in his mind, and he will avenge himself. He will be a bad king. I say not that he will pour out blood, like Louis XI. or Charles IX., for he has no mortal injuries to avenge; but he will devour the means and substance of his people, for he has himself suffered injuriously as to his own welfare and possessions. In the first place, then, I quite acquit my conscience, when I consider openly the merits and faults of this prince; and if I condemn him, my conscience absolves me."

Aramis paused, to leave the thoughts he had uttered sufficient time to eat deeply into the mind of his companion. "All that God does, he does well," continued the Bishop of Vannes; "and I am so persuaded of it that I have long been thankful to have been chosen depositary of the secret which I have aided you to discover. To a just Providence was necessary an instrument, at once penetrating, persevering, and convinced, to accomplish a great work. I am this instrument. I possess penetration, perseverance, conviction; I govern a mysterious people, who has taken for its motto the motto of God, *Patiens quia œternus.*" The prince moved. "I divine, Monseigneur, why you raise your head, and that my having rule over a people astonishes you. You did not know you were dealing with a king: oh, Monseigneur, king of a people very humble, very poor,—humble, because they have no force save when creeping; poor, because never, almost never in this world, do my people reap the harvest they sow, or eat the fruit they cultivate. They labour for an abstract idea; they heap together all the atoms of their power to form one man; and round this man, with the sweat of their labour, they create a misty halo which his genius shall, in turn, render a glory gilded with the rays of all the crowns in Christendom.

Such is the man you have beside you, Monseigneur. He has drawn you from the abyss for a great purpose, and he desires, in furtherance of this sublime purpose, to raise you above the powers of the earth,—above himself."

The prince lightly touched Aramis's arm. "You speak to me," he said, "of that religious order whose chief you are. For me the result of your words is, that the day you desire to hurl down the man you shall have raised, the event will be accomplished; and that you will keep under your hand your creature of to-day."—"Undeceive yourself, Monseigneur," replied the bishop. "I should not take the trouble to play this terrible game with your royal Highness, if I had not a double interest in winning. The day you are elevated, you are elevated for ever; you will overturn the footstool, as you rise, and will send it rolling so far that not even the sight of it will ever again recall to you its right to your remembrance."—"Oh, Monsieur!"

"Your movement, Monseigneur, arises from an excellent disposition. I thank you. Be well assured, I aspire to more than gratitude! I am convinced that when arrived at the summit you will judge me still more worthy to be your friend; and then, Monseigneur, we two will do such great deeds that ages hereafter shall speak of them."—"Tell me plainly, Monsieur,—tell me without disguise, —what I am to-day, and what you aim at my being to-morrow." "You are the son of King Louis XIII., brother of Louis XIV.; you are the natural and legitimate heir to the throne of France. In keeping you near him, as Monsieur has been kept,—Monsieur, your younger brother,—the king would reserve to himself the right of being legitimate sovereign. The doctors only and God could dispute his legitimacy. But the doctors always prefer the king who is to the king who is not. God has wrought against himself in wronging a prince who is an honest man. But God has willed that you should be persecuted; and this persecution to-day consecrates you king of France. You had then a right to reign, seeing that it is disputed; you had a right to be proclaimed, seeing that you have been concealed; you are of kingly blood, since no one has dared to shed your blood as your servants' has been shed. Now see what he has done for you,—this God whom you have so often accused of having in every way thwarted you! He has given you the features, figure, age, and voice of your brother; and the very causes of your persecu-

The Tempter

tion are about to become those of your triumphant restoration. To-morrow, after to-morrow,—from the very first, regal phantom, living shade of Louis XIV., you will sit upon his throne, whence the will of Heaven, confided in execution to the arm of man, will have hurled him without hope of return."

"I understand," said the prince; "my brother's blood will not be shed, then."—"You will be sole arbiter of his fate."—"The secret of which they made an evil use against me?"—"You will employ it against him. What did he do to conceal it? He concealed you. Living image of himself, you will defeat the conspiracy of Mazarin and Anne of Austria. You, my Prince, will have the same interest in concealing him, who will as a prisoner resemble you, as you will resemble him as king."

"I return to what I was saying to you. Who will guard him?"—"Who guarded you?"—"You know this secret,—you have made use of it with regard to myself. Who else knows it?"—"The queen-mother and Madame de Chevreuse."—"What will they do?"—"Nothing, if you choose."—"How is that?"—"How can they recognise you, if you act so that no one can recognise you?"

" 'Tis true; but there are grave difficulties."—"State them, Prince."—"My brother is married; I cannot take my brother's wife."—"I will cause Spain to consent to a divorce: it is in the interest of your new policy; it is human morality. All that is really noble and really useful in this world will find its account therein."

"The imprisoned king will speak."—"To whom do you think he should speak,—to the walls?"—"You mean, by walls, the men in whom you put confidence."

"If need be, yes. And besides, your royal Highness—"—"Besides?"—"I was going to say, that the designs of Providence do not stop on such a fair road. Every scheme of this calibre is completed by its results, like a geometrical calculation. The king in prison will not be for you the cause of embarrassment that you have been for the king enthroned. His soul is naturally proud and impatient; it is, morever, disarmed and enfeebled by being accustomed to honours, and by the licence of supreme power. God, who has willed that the concluding step in the geometrical calculation I have had the honour of describing to your royal Highness should be your accession to the throne and the destruction of him who is hurtful to you, has also determined that the conquered one shall soon end both his own and your sufferings. Therefore his soul and body have been adapted for but a brief agony. Put into prison as a private individual, left alone with your doubts, deprived of everything, you have met all with the force of uninterrupted custom. But your brother, a captive, forgotten, and in bonds, will not long endure the calamity; and Heaven will resume his soul at the appointed time,—that is to say, soon."

At this point in Aramis's gloomy analysis a bird of night uttered from the depths of the forest that prolonged and plaintive cry which makes every creature tremble. "I will exile the deposed king," said Philippe, shuddering; " 'twill be more humane."

"The king's good pleasure will decide the point," said Aramis. "But has the problem been well put? Have I brought out the solution according to the wishes or the foresight of your royal Highness?"—"Yes, Monsieur, yes; you have forgotten nothing,—except, indeed, two things."—"The first?"—"Let us speak of it at once, with the same frankness we have already used. Let us speak of the causes which may bring about the ruin of all the hopes we have conceived. Let us speak of the dangers we incur."

"They would be immense, infinite, terrific, insurmountable, if, as I have said, all things did not concur in rendering them absolutely of no account. There is no danger either for you or for me, if the constancy and intrepidity of your royal Highness are equal to that perfection of resemblance to your brother which Nature has bestowed upon you. I repeat it, there are no dangers,—only obstacles; a word, indeed, which I find in all languages, but have always ill understood, and, were I king, would have obliterated as useless and absurd."

"Yes, indeed, Monsieur; there is a very serious obstacle, an insurmountable danger, which you are forgetting."—"Ah!" said Aramis. —"There is conscience, which cries aloud; remorse, which lacerates."—"Oh! that is true," said the bishop; "there is a weakness of heart of which you remind me. Oh! you are right; that, indeed, is an immense obstacle. The horse afraid of the ditch leaps into the middle of it, and is killed! The man who tremblingly crosses his sword with that of another leaves loopholes by which death enters!"

"Have you a brother?" said the young man to Aramis.—"I am alone in the world," said the latter, with a hard, dry voice.—"But,

surely there is some one in the world whom you love?" added
Philippe.—"No one!—Yes, I love you."

The young man sank into so profound a silence that the sound
of his breathing seemed to Aramis like a roaring tumult. "Monseigneur," he resumed, "I have not said all I had to say to your
royal Highness; I have not offered you all the salutary counsels and
useful resources which I have at my disposal. It is useless to flash
bright visions before the eyes of one who loves darkness; useless,
too, is it to let the grand roar of the cannon sound in the ears of
one who loves repose and the quiet of the country. Monseigneur,
I have your happiness spread out before me in my thoughts. I will
let it fall from my lips; take it up carefully for yourself, who look
with such tender regard upon the bright heavens, the verdant
meadows, the pure air. I know a country full of delights, an unknown Paradise, a corner of the world where alone, unfettered, and
unknown, in the woods, amidst flowers, and streams of rippling
water, you will forget all the misery that human folly has so recently
allotted you. Oh, listen to me, my Prince! I do not jest. I have
a soul, and can read to the depths of your own. I will not take you,
unready for your task, in order to cast you into the crucible of my
own desires or my caprice or my ambition. Everything or nothing!
You are chilled, sick at heart, almost overcome by the excess of
emotion which but one hour's liberty has produced in you. For me,
that is a certain and unmistakable sign that you do not wish for
large and long respiration. Let us choose, then, a life more humble,
better suited to our strength. Heaven is my witness that I wish
your happiness to be the result of the trial to which I have exposed
you."

"Speak, speak!" said the prince, with a vivacity which did not
escape Aramis.—"I know," resumed the prelate, "in the Bas-Poitou,
a canton of which no one in France suspects the existence. Twenty
leagues of country,—it is immense, is it not? Twenty leagues, Monseigneur, all covered with water and herbage and reeds; the whole
studded with islands covered with woods. These large marshes,
covered with reeds as with a thick mantle, sleep silently and calmly
under the smiling sun. A few fishermen with their families indo-
lently pass their lives away there, with their large rafts of poplars
and alders, the flooring formed of reeds, and the roof woven out of
thick rushes. These barks, these floating houses, are wafted to and

fro by the changing winds. Whenever they touch a bank, it is but by chance; and so gently, too, that the sleeping fisherman is not awakened by the shock. Should he wish to land, it is because he has seen a large flight of landrails or plovers, of wild ducks, teal, widgeon, or woodcocks, which fall an easy prey to his nets or his gun. Silver shad, eels, greedy pike, red and grey mullet, fall in masses into his nets; he has but to choose the finest and largest, and return the others to the waters. Never yet has the foot of man, be he soldier or simple citizen,—never has any one, indeed, penetrated into that district. The sun's rays there are soft and tempered; in plots of solid earth, whose soil is rich and fertile, grows the vine, which nourishes with its generous juice its black and white grapes. Once a week a boat is sent to fetch the bread which has been baked at an oven,—the common property of all. There, like the seigneurs of early days,—powerful because of your dogs, your fishing-lines, your guns, and your beautiful reed-built house,—would you live, rich in the produce of the chase, in the plenitude of security. There would years of your life roll away, at the end of which, unrecognisable, transformed, you will have compelled Heaven to reshape your destiny. There are a thousand pistoles in this bag, Monseigneur,—more than sufficient to purchase the whole marsh of which I have spoken; more than enough to live there as many years as you have days to live; more than enough to constitute you the richest, the freest, and the happiest man in the country. Accept it, as I offer it to you,—sincerely, cheerfully. Forthwith, from the carriage here we will unharness two of the horses; the mute, my servant, shall conduct you—travelling by night, sleeping by day—to the locality I have mentioned; and I shall at least have the satisfaction of knowing that I have rendered to my prince the service that he himself preferred. I shall have made one man happy; and Heaven for that will hold me in better account than if I had made one man powerful,—for that is far more difficult. And now, Monseigneur, your answer to this proposition? Here is the money. Nay, do not hesitate! At Poitou you can risk nothing, except the chance of catching the fevers prevalent there; and even of them, the so-called wizards of the country may cure you for your pistoles. If you play the other game, you run the chance of being assassinated on a throne or of being strangled in a prison. Upon my soul, I assure you, now I compare them together, upon my life, I should hesitate."

"Monsieur," replied the young prince, "before I determine, let me alight from this carriage, walk on the ground, and consult that voice by which God speaks in unsullied Nature. Ten minutes, and I will answer."—"As you please, Monseigneur," said Aramis, bending before him with respect,—so solemn and august in its tone and address had been the voice which had just spoken.

CHAPTER XIII

CROWN AND TIARA

ARAMIS was the first to descend from the carriage; he held the door open for the young man. He saw him place his foot on the mossy ground with a trembling of the whole body, and walk round the carriage with an unsteady and almost tottering step. It seemed as if the poor prisoner were unaccustomed to walk on God's earth. It was the 15th of August, about eleven o'clock at night; thick clouds, portending a tempest, overspread the heavens, and shrouded all light and prospect beneath their heavy folds. The extremities of the avenues were imperceptibly detached from the copse by a lighter shadow of opaque grey, which upon closer examination became visible in the midst of the obscurity. But the fragrance which ascended from the grass, fresher and more penetrating than that which exhaled from the trees around him; the warm and balmy air which enveloped him for the first time in years; the ineffable enjoyment of liberty in an open country,— spoke to the prince in a language so intoxicating that notwithstanding the great reserve, we should almost say the dissimulation, of which we have tried to give an idea, he could not restrain his emotion, and breathed a sigh of joy. Then, by degrees, he raised his aching head and inhaled the perfumed air, as it was wafted in gentle gusts across his uplifted face. Crossing his arms on his chest as if to control this new sensation of delight, he drank in delicious draughts of that mysterious air which penetrates at night-time through lofty forests. The sky he was contemplating, the murmur-

The Man in the Iron Mask

ing waters, the moving creatures,—were not these real? Was not Aramis a madman to suppose that he had aught else to dream of in this world? Those exciting pictures of country life, so free from cares, from fears and troubles; that ocean of happy days which glitters incessantly before all youthful imaginations,—those were real allurements wherewith to fascinate an unhappy prisoner, worn out by prison life and emaciated by the close air of the Bastille. It was the picture, it will be remembered, drawn by Aramis when he offered to the prince the thousand pistoles which he had with him in the carriage, the enchanted Eden which the deserts of Bas-Poitou hid from the eyes of the world.

Similar to these were the reflections of Aramis as he watched, with an anxiety impossible to describe, the silent progress of the emotions of Philippe, whom he perceived gradually becoming more and more absorbed in his meditations. The young prince was offering up an inward prayer to Heaven for a ray of light upon that perplexity whence would issue his death or his life. It was an anxious time for the Bishop of Vannes, who had never before been so perplexed. Was his iron will, accustomed to overcome all obstacles, never finding itself inferior or vanquished, to be foiled in so vast a project from not having foreseen the influence which a few tree-leaves and a few cubic feet of air might have on the human mind? Aramis, overwhelmed by anxiety, contemplated the painful struggle which was taking place in Philippe's mind. This suspense lasted throughout the ten minutes which the young man had requested. During that eternity Philippe continued gazing with an imploring and sorrowful look towards the heavens. Aramis did not remove the piercing glance he had fixed on Philippe. Suddenly the young man bowed his head. His thoughts returned to the earth, his looks perceptibly hardened, his brow contracted, his mouth assumed an expression of fierce courage; and then again his look became fixed, but now it reflected the flame of mundane splendours,—now it was like the face of Satan on the mountain when he brought into view the kingdoms and the powers of earth as temptations to Jesus. Aramis's appearance then became as gentle as it had before been gloomy.

Philippe, seizing his hand in a quick, agitated manner, exclaimed: "Let us go where the crown of France is to be found!"—"Is this your decision, Monseigneur?" asked Aramis.—"It is."—"Irrevoc-

The brother of the king

ably so?" Philippe did not even deign to reply. He gazed earnestly at the bishop, as if to ask him if it were possible for a man to waver after having once made up his mind. "Those looks are flashes of fire which portray character," said Aramis, bowing over Philippe's hand. "You will be great, Monseigneur; I will answer for that."

"Let us resume our conversation. I wished to discuss two points with you: in the first place, the dangers or the obstacles we may meet with. That point is decided. The other is the conditions you intend to impose on me. It is your turn to speak, M. d'Herblay."— "The conditions, Monseigneur?"—"Doubtless. You will not check me in my course for a trifle, and you will not do me the injustice to suppose that I think you have no interest in this affair. Therefore, without subterfuge or hesitation, tell me the truth."

"I will do so, Monseigneur. Once a king—"—"When will that be?"—"To-morrow evening—I mean in the night."—"Explain to me how."—"When I shall have asked your Highness a question."— "Do so."

"I sent to your Highness a man in my confidence, with instructions to deliver some closely written notes, carefully drawn up, which will thoroughly acquaint your Highness with the different persons who compose and will compose your court."—"I perused all the notes."—"Attentively?"—"I know them by heart."

"And understood them? Pardon me, but I may venture to ask that question of a poor, abandoned captive of the Bastille. It will not be requisite in a week's time to question further a mind like yours, when you will then be in full possession of liberty and power."—"Interrogate me, then, and I will be a scholar repeating his lesson to his master."

"We will begin with your family, Monseigneur."—"My mother, Anne of Austria?—all her sorrows, her painful malady? Oh, I know her, I know her!"—"Your second brother?" asked Aramis, bowing.—"To these notes," replied the prince, "you have added portraits so faithfully painted that I am able to recognise the persons whose characters, manners, and history you have so carefully portrayed. Monsieur, my brother, is a fine, dark young man, with a pale face; he does not love his wife, Henrietta, whom I, Louis XIV., loved a little, and still flirt with, even although she made me weep on the day she wished to dismiss Mademoiselle de la Vallière from her service in disgrace."

The Man in the Iron Mask

"You will have to be careful with regard to watchfulness of the latter," said Aramis; "she is sincerely attached to the actual king. The eyes of a woman who loves are not easily deceived."—"She is fair; has blue eyes, whose affectionate gaze will reveal her identity. She halts slightly in her gait. She writes a letter every day, to which I shall have to send an answer by M. de Saint-Aignan."—"Do you know the latter?"—"As if I saw him; and I know the last verses he composed for me, as well as those I composed in answer to his."

"Very good. Do you know your ministers?"—"Colbert, an ugly, dark-browed man, but intelligent; his hair covering his forehead; a large, heavy, full head; the mortal enemy of M. Fouquet."—"We need not disturb ourselves about M. Colbert."—"No; because necessarily you will require me to exile him, will you not?" Aramis, struck with admiration at the remark, said, "You will become very great, Monseigneur."—"You see," added the prince, "that I know my lesson by heart; and with Heaven's assistance, and yours afterwards, I shall seldom go wrong."

"You have still a very awkward pair of eyes to deal with, Monseigneur."—"Yes; the captain of the musketeers, M. d'Artagnan, your friend."—"Yes; I can well say 'my friend.' "—"He who escorted La Vallière to Chaillot; he who delivered up Monk, in a box, to Charles II.; he who so faithfully served my mother; he to whom the crown of France owes so much that it owes everything. Do you intend to ask me to exile him also?"—"Never, Sire! D'Artagnan is a man to whom at a certain given time I will undertake to reveal everything. But be on your guard with him; for if he discovers our plot before it is revealed to him, you or I will certainly be killed or taken. He is a man of action."

"I will consider. Now tell me about M. Fouquet; what do you wish to be done with regard to him?"—"One moment more, I entreat you, Monseigneur; and forgive me if I seem to fail in respect in questioning you further."—"It is your duty to do so, and, more than that, your right also."

"Before we pass to M. Fouquet, I should very much regret forgetting another friend of mine."—"M. du Vallon, the Hercules of France, you mean. Oh! so far as he is concerned, his fortune is assured."—"No; it is not he of whom I intended to speak."—"The Comte de la Fère, then?"—"And his son,—the son of all four of us."

Crown and Tiara

"The lad who is dying of love for La Vallière, of whom my brother so disloyally deprived him? Be easy on that score! I shall know how to restore him. Tell me one thing, M. d'Herblay! Do men, when they love, forget the treachery that has been shown them? Can a man ever forgive the woman who has betrayed him? Is that a French custom; is it a law of the human heart?"—"A man who loves deeply, as deeply as Raoul loves Mademoiselle de la Vallière, finally forgets the fault of the woman he loves; but I do not know whether Raoul will forget."—"I will provide for that. Have you anything further to say about your friend?"—"No; that is all."

"Well, then, now for M. Fouquet. What do you wish me to do for him?"—"To continue him as superintendent, as he has hitherto acted, I entreat you."—"Be it so; but he is the first minister at present."—"Not quite so."—"A king ignorant and embarrassed as I shall be, will, as a matter of course, require a first minister of State."

"Your Majesty will require a friend."—"I have only one, and that is yourself."—"You will have many others by and by, but none so devoted, none so zealous for your glory."—"You will be my first minister of State."—"Not immediately, Monseigneur; for that would give rise to too much suspicion and astonishment."

"M. de Richelieu, the first minister of my grandmother, Marie de Médicis, was simply Bishop of Luçon, as you are Bishop of Vannes."—"I perceive that your royal Highness has studied my notes to great advantage; your amazing perspicacity overpowers me with delight."—"I know, indeed, that M. de Richelieu, by means of the queen's protection, soon became cardinal."—"It would be better," said Aramis, bowing, "that I should not be appointed first minister until after your royal Highness had procured my nomination as cardinal."

"You shall be nominated before two months are past, M. d'Herblay. But that is a matter of very trifling moment; you would not offend me if you were to ask more than that, and you would cause me serious regret if you were to limit yourself to that."—"In that case I have something still further to hope for, Monseigneur."—"Speak! speak!"

"M. Fouquet will not continue long at the head of affairs; he will soon get old. He is fond of pleasure, which at present is compatible

93

with his labours, thanks to the youthfulness which he still retains; but this youthfulness will disappear at the approach of the first serious annoyance, or upon the first illness he may experience. We will spare him the annoyance, because he is a brave and noble-hearted man; but we cannot save him from ill-health. So it is determined. When you shall have paid all M. Fouquet's debts, and restored the finances to a sound condition, M. Fouquet will be able to remain the sovereign ruler in his little court of poets and painters; we shall have made him rich. When that has been done, and I shall have become your royal Highness's prime minister, I shall be able to think of my own interests and yours."

The young man looked at his interlocutor. "M. de Richelieu, of whom we were speaking just now," said Aramis, "was very blamable in the fixed idea he had of governing France unaided. He allowed two kings—King Louis XIII. and himself—to be seated upon the same throne, when he might have installed them more conveniently upon two separate thrones."—"Upon two thrones?" said the prince, thoughtfully.—"In fact," pursued Aramis, quietly, "a cardinal, prime minister of France, assisted by the favour and by the countenance of his Most Christian Majesty the King of France; a cardinal to whom the king his master lends the treasures of the State, his army, his counsel,—such a man would be acting with twofold injustice in applying these mighty resources to France alone. Besides," added Aramis, with a searching look into the eyes of Philippe, "you will not be a king such as your father was,—delicate in health, slow in judgment, whom all things wearied; you will be a king governing by your brain and by your sword. You would have in the government of the State no more than you could manage unaided; I should only interfere with you. Besides, our friendship ought never to be, I do not say impaired, but even grazed by a secret thought. I shall have given you the throne of France; you will confer on me the throne of Saint Peter. Whenever your loyal, firm, and mailed hand shall have for its mate the hand of a pope such as I shall be, neither Charles V., who owned two-thirds of the habitable globe, nor Charlemagne, who possessed it entirely, will reach to the height of your waist. I have no alliances; I have no predilections. I will not throw you into persecutions of heretics, nor will I cast you into the troubled waters of family dissension; I will simply say to you: The whole universe is for us two,—for me

the minds of men, for you their bodies; and as I shall be the first to
die, you will have my inheritance. What do you say of my plan,
Monseigneur?"

"I say that you render me happy and proud, for no other reason
than that of having comprehended you thoroughly. M. d'Herblay,
you shall be cardinal, and when cardinal, my prime minister; and
then you will point out to me the necessary steps to be taken to
secure your election as pope, and I will take them. You can ask
what guarantees from me you please."—"It is useless. I shall never
act except in such a manner that you will be the gainer; I shall
never mount until I shall have first placed you upon the round of
the ladder immediately above me; I shall always hold myself sufficiently aloof from you to escape incurring your jealousy, sufficiently
near to sustain your personal advantage and to watch over your
friendship. All the contracts in the world are easily violated because the interest included in them inclines more to one side than
to another. With us, however, it will never be the case; I have no
need of guarantees."

"And so—my brother—will disappear?"—"Simply. We will remove him from his bed by means of a plank which yields to the
pressure of the finger. Having retired to rest as a crowned sovereign, he will awaken in captivity. Alone, you will rule from that
moment, and you will have no interest more urgent than that of
keeping me near you."—"I believe it. There is my hand, M.
d'Herblay."

"Allow me to kneel before you, Sire, most respectfully. We will
embrace each other on the day when we shall both have on our temples—you the crown, and I the tiara."—"Embrace me this very day;
and be more than great, more than skilful, more than sublime in
genius,—be good to me, be my father!"

Aramis was almost overcome as he listened to the voice of the
prince. He fancied he detected in his own heart an emotion hitherto
unknown to him; but this impression was speedily removed. "His
father!" he thought; "yes, his Holy Father." The two resumed their
places in the carriage, which sped rapidly along the road leading to
Vaux-le-Vicomte.

CHAPTER XIV

THE CHATEAU DE VAUX-LE-VICOMTE

THE Château de Vaux-le-Vicomte, situated about a league from Melun, had been built by Fouquet in 1653. There was then but little money in France; Mazarin had taken all that there was, and Fouquet had expended the remainder. However, as certain men have fertile faults and useful vices, Fouquet, in scattering broadcast millions of money in the construction of this palace, had found a means of bringing, as the result of his generous profusion, three illustrious men together,—Levau, the architect of the building; Lenôtre, the designer of the gardens; and Lebrun, the decorator of the apartments. If the Château de Vaux possessed a single fault with which it could be reproached, it was its grandiose, pretentious character. This mansion, built by a subject, bore a far greater resemblance to a royal residence than those that Wolsey fancied he must present to his master for fear of rendering him jealous. But if magnificence and splendour were displayed in any one particular part of this palace more than in another,—if anything could be preferred to the wonderful arrangement of the interior, to the sumptuousness of the gilding, and to the profusion of the painting and statues, it would be the park and gardens of Vaux. It was, as we have said, the 15th of August. The sun poured down its burning rays upon the heathen deities of marble and bronze. This magnificent palace had been got ready for the reception of the greatest reigning sovereign of the time. M. Fouquet's friends had transported thither, some their actors and their dresses, others their troops of sculptors and artists; others still their ready-mended pens, —floods of impromptus were contemplated. The cascades, somewhat rebellious nymphs though they were, poured forth their waters brighter than crystal; they scattered over the bronze tritons and nereids their waves of foam, which glistened in the rays of the sun. An army of servants were hurrying to and fro in squadrons in the courtyard and corridors; while Fouquet, who had only that morning arrived, moved about with a calm, observant glance, giving his last orders, after his intendants had inspected everything.

With a complete assurance that Aramis had made arrangements

96

The Château de Vaux-le-Vicomte

fairly to distribute the vast number of guests throughout the palace, and that he had not omitted to attend to any of the internal regulations for their comfort, Fouquet devoted his entire attention to the *ensemble*. In one direction Gourville showed him the preparations which had been made for the fireworks; in another, Molière led him over the theatre; at last, after he had visited the chapel, the salons, and the galleries, and was again going downstairs, exhausted with fatigue, Fouquet saw Aramis on the staircase. The prelate beckoned to him. The superintendent joined his friend, who paused before a large picture scarcely finished. Applying himself, heart and soul to his work, the painter, Lebrun, covered with perspiration, stained with paint, pale from fatigue and inspiration, was putting the last finishing touches with his rapid brush. It was the portrait of the king, whom they were expecting, dressed in the court suit which Percerin had condescended to show beforehand to the Bishop of Vannes. Fouquet placed himself before this portrait, which seemed to live, as one might say, in the cool freshness of its flesh and in its warmth of colour. He gazed upon it long and fixedly, estimated the prodigious labour that had been bestowed upon it, and not being able to find any recompense sufficiently great for this herculean effort, he passed his arm round the painter's neck, and embraced him. The superintendent, by this action, had ruined a suit of clothes worth a thousand pistoles, but he had invigorated Lebrun. It was a happy moment for the artist; it was an unhappy one for M. Percerin, who was walking behind Fouquet, and was engaged in admiring, in Lebrun's painting, the suit that he had made for his majesty,—a perfect work of art, as he called it, which was not to be matched except in the wardrobe of the superintendent. His distress and his exclamations were interrupted by a signal which had been given from the summit of the mansion. In the direction of Melun, in the still empty, open plain, the sentinels of Vaux had perceived the advancing procession of the king and the queens. His Majesty was entering into Melun with his long train of carriages and cavaliers.

"In an hour—" said Aramis to Fouquet.—"In an hour!" replied the latter, sighing.—"And the people who ask one another what is the good of these royal *fêtes!*" continued the Bishop of Vannes, laughing with his forced smile.—"Alas! I, too, who am not the people, ask the same thing."—"I will answer you in four-and-twenty hours, Monseigneur. Assume a cheerful countenance, for it is a day of joy."

"Well, believe me or not, as you like, D'Herblay," said the superintendent, with a swelling heart, pointing at the *cortége* of Louis, visible in the horizon, "the king certainly loves me but very little, nor do I care much for him; but I cannot tell you how it is that since he is approaching my house—"—"Well, what?"—"Well, then, since I know Louis is on his way hither, he is more sacred to me; he is my king, he is almost dear to me."

"*Dear!*—yes," said Aramis, playing upon the word, as the Abbé Terray did, at a later period, with Louis XV.—"Do not laugh, D'Herblay; I feel that if he were really to wish it, I could love that young man."—"You should not say that to me," returned Aramis, "but rather to M. Colbert."—"To M. Colbert!" exclaimed Fouquet. "Why so?"—"Because he would allow you a pension out of the king's privy purse, as soon as he becomes superintendent," said Aramis, preparing to leave as soon as he had dealt this last blow.

"Where are you going?" returned Fouquet, with a gloomy look.— "To my own apartment, to change my costume, Monseigneur."— "Where are you lodging, D'Herblay?"—"In the blue room on the second story."—"The room immediately over the king's room?" —"Precisely."—"You will be subject to very great restraint there. What an idea to condemn yourself to a room where you cannot stir or move about!"

"During the night, Monseigneur, I sleep or read in my bed."— "And your servants?"—"I have only one person with me. I find my reader quite sufficient. Adieu, Monseigneur! Do not over-fatigue yourself; keep yourself fresh for the arrival of the king."

"We shall see you by and by, I suppose, and your friend Du Vallon also?"—"He is lodging next to me, and is at this moment dressing." Then Fouquet, bowing, with a smile passed on, like a commander-in-chief who pays the different outposts a visit after the enemy has been signalled. Towards seven o'clock in the evening, without trumpets, without advanced guard, without outriders or musketeers, the king presented himself before the gate of Vaux, where Fouquet, who had been informed of his royal guest's approach, had been waiting for the last half-hour, with his head uncovered, surrounded by his household and his friends.

"What has this tailor done for you, my dear Porthos, that you are so pleased with him?"

The Château de Vaux-le-Vicomte

Fouquet held the stirrup of the king, who having dismounted bowed graciously, and more graciously still held out his hand to him, which Fouquet, in spite of a slight resistance on the king's part, carried respectfully to his lips. The king wished to wait in the first courtyard for the arrival of the carriages; nor had he long to wait. For the roads had been put into excellent order by the superintendent, and a stone would hardly have been found of the size of an egg the whole way from Melun to Vaux; so that the carriages, rolling along as though on a carpet, brought the ladies to Vaux, without jolting or fatigue, by eight o'clock. They were received by Madame Fouquet; and at the moment when they made their appearance, a light as bright as day burst forth from all the trees and vases and marble statues. This species of enchantment lasted until their Majesties had retired into the palace. All these wonders and magical effects,—which the chronicler has heaped up, or rather preserved, in his recital at the risk of rivalling the creations of a romancist,—these splendours whereby night seemed conquered and Nature corrected, together with every delight and luxury combined for the satisfaction of all the senses as well as of the mind, Fouquet really offered to his sovereign in that enchanting retreat, to which no monarch could at that time boast of possessing an equal.

We do not intend to describe the grand banquet, at which all the royal guests were present, nor the concerts, nor the fairylike and magical transformations and metamorphoses. It will be enough for our purpose to depict the countenance which the king assumed, and which, from being gay, soon wore a gloomy, constrained, and irritated expression. He remembered his own residence, and the mean style of luxury which prevailed there,—which comprised only that which was merely useful for the royal wants, without being his own personal property. The large vases of the Louvre, the old furniture and plate of Henry II., of Francis I., of Louis XI., were merely historical monuments,—they were nothing but specimens of art, relics left by his predecessors; while with Fouquet the value of the article was as much in the workmanship as in the article itself. Fouquet ate from a gold service, which artists in his own employ had modelled and cast for him. Fouquet drank wines of which the King of France did not even know the name, and drank them out of goblets each more precious than the whole royal cellar. What, too, could be said of the apartments, the hangings, the pictures, the servants and officers of every description, in Fouquet's household? What could be said of the mode of service in which etiquette was replaced by order, stiff formality by personal unrestrained comfort, and the happiness and contentment of the guest became the supreme law of all who obeyed the host? The swarm of busily engaged persons moving about noiselessly; the multitude of guests, who were, however, even less numerous than the servants who waited on them; the myriads of exquisitely prepared dishes, of gold and silver vases; the floods of dazzling light; the masses of unknown flowers, of which the hothouses had been despoiled, redundant with the luxuriance of unequalled beauty,—the harmony of all, which indeed was no more than the prelude of the promised *fête,* charmed all the guests, who testified their admiration over and over again, not by voice or gesture, but by deep silence and rapt attention,—those two languages of the courtier which acknowledge the hand of no master powerful enough to restrain them.

As for the king, his eyes filled with tears; he dared not look at the queen. Anne of Austria, whose pride, as it ever had been, was superior to that of any creature breathing, overwhelmed her host by the contempt with which she treated everything handed to her. The young queen, kind-hearted by nature and curious by disposition, praised Fouquet, ate with an exceedingly good appetite, and asked the names of the different fruits which were placed upon the table. Fouquet replied that he did not know their names. The fruits came from his own stores; he had often cultivated them himself, having an intimate acquaintance with the cultivation of exotic fruits and plants. The king felt and appreciated the delicacy of the reply, but was only the more humiliated at it; he thought that the queen was a little too familiar in her manners, and that Anne of Austria resembled Juno a little too much; his chief anxiety, however, was that he might remain cold and distant in his behaviour, bordering slightly on the limits of extreme disdain or of simple admiration.

Fouquet had foreseen all that; he was, in fact, one of those men who foresee everything. The king had expressly declared that so long as he remained under Fouquet's roof he did not wish his own different repasts to be served in accordance with the usual etiquette, and that he would consequently dine with the rest of the company; but by the thoughtful attention of the superintendent the king's dinner was served up separately, if one may so express it, in the middle of the general table. The dinner, wonderful in every respect, from the dishes of which it was composed, comprised everything the king liked, and which he generally preferred to anything else. Louis had no excuse—he, indeed, who had the keenest appetite in his kingdom —for saying that he was not hungry. Fouquet even did better still: he indeed, in obedience to the king's expressed desire, seated himself at the table; but as soon as the soups were served, he rose and personally waited on the king, while Madame Fouquet stood behind the queen-mother's arm-chair. The disdain of Juno and the sulky fits of temper of Jupiter could not resist this exhibition of kindly feeling and polite attention. The queen ate a biscuit dipped in a glass of San-Lucar wine; and the king ate of everything, saying to Fouquet, "It is impossible, Monsieur the Superintendent, to dine better any' where." Whereupon the whole court began, on all sides, to devour the dishes spread before them, with such enthusiasm that it looked like a cloud of Egyptian locusts settling down upon the uncut crops.

As soon, however, as his hunger was appeased, the king became dull and gloomy again; the more so in proportion to the satisfaction he fancied he had manifested, and particularly on account of the deferential manner which his courtiers had shown towards Fouquet. D'Artagnan, who ate a good deal and drank but little, without allowing it to be noticed, did not lose a single opportunity, but made a great number of observations which he turned to good profit. When the supper was finished, the king expressed a wish not to lose the promenade. The park was illuminated; the moon, too, as if she had placed herself at the orders of the Lord of Vaux, silvered the trees and lakes with her bright phosphoric light. The air was soft and balmy; the gravelled walks through the thickly set avenues yielded luxuriously to the feet. The *fête* was complete in every respect; for the king, having met La Vallière in one of the winding paths of the wood, was able to press her by the hand and say, "I love you," without any one overhearing him, except D'Artagnan who followed, and M. Fouquet who preceded him.

The night of enchantments stole on. The king having requested to be shown to his room, there was immediately a movement in every direction. The queens passed to their own apartments, accompanied by the music of theorbos and flutes. The king found his musketeers awaiting him on the grand flight of steps; for Fouquet had brought them on from Melun, and had invited them to supper. D'Artagnan's suspicions at once disappeared. He was weary; he had supped well and wished, for once in his life, thoroughly to enjoy a *fête* given by a man who was in every sense of the word a king. "M. Fouquet," he said, "is the man for me."

The king was conducted with the greatest ceremony to the chamber of Morpheus, of which we owe some slight description to our readers. It was the handsomest and the largest in the palace. Lebrun had painted on the vaulted ceiling the happy as well as disagreeable dreams with which Morpheus affects kings as well as other men: with everything lovely to which sleep gives birth,—its perfumes, its flowers and nectar, the wild voluptuousness or deep repose of the senses,—had the painter enriched his frescoes. It was a composition as soft and pleasing in one part as dark and terrible in another. The poisoned chalice; the glittering dagger suspended over the head of the sleeper; wizards and phantoms with hideous masks, those dim shadows more terrific than the brightness of flame or the blackness of night,—these he had made the companions of his more pleasing pictures.

No sooner had the king entered the room than a cold shiver seemed to pass through him; and when Fouquet asked him the cause of it, the king replied, turning pale, "I am sleepy."—"Does your Majesty wish for your attendants at once?"—"No; I have to talk with a few persons first," said the king. "Will you have the goodness to summon M. Colbert?" Fouquet bowed, and left the room.

CHAPTER XV

A GASCON, AND A GASCON AND A HALF

D'ARTAGNAN had lost no time; in fact, he was not in the habit of doing so. After having inquired for Aramis, he had looked for him in every direction until he had succeeded in finding him. Now, no sooner had the king entered Vaux than Aramis had retired to his own room, meditating doubtless some new piece of gallant attention for his Majesty's amusement. D'Artagnan desired the servants to announce him, and found on the second story, in a beautiful room called the blue room on account of the colour of

A Gascon, and a Gascon and a Half

its hangings, the Bishop of Vannes in company with Porthos and several of the modern Epicureans. Aramis came forward to embrace his friend, and offered him the best seat. As it was after a while generally remarked among those present that the musketeer was reserved, apparently wishing for an opportunity to converse privately with Aramis, the Epicureans took their leave. Porthos, however, did not stir; having dined exceedingly well, he was fast asleep in his armchair, and the freedom of conversation therefore was not interrupted by a third person. Porthos had a deep, harmonious snore; and people might talk in the midst of its loud bass without fear of disturbing him.

D'Artagnan felt that he was called upon to open the conversation. The encounter he had come to seek would be rough; so he delicately approached the subject. "Well, and so we have come to Vaux," he said.—"Why, yes, D'Artagnan. And how do you like the place?"—"Very much; and I like M. Fouquet also."—"Is he not a charming host?"—"No one could be more so."

"I am told that the king began by being very distant in his manner towards M. Fouquet, but that his Majesty became much more cordial afterwards."—"You did not notice it, then, since you say you have been told so?"—"No; I was engaged with those gentlemen who have just left the room about the theatrical performances and the tournament which are to take place to-morrow."

"Ah, indeed! you are the comptroller-general of the *fêtes* here, then?"—"You know I am a friend of all kinds of amusement where the exercise of the imagination is required; I have always been a poet in one way or another."—"Yes, I remember the verses you used to write; they were charming."—"I have forgotten them; but I am delighted to read the verses of others, when those others are known by the names of Molière, Pellisson, La Fontaine, etc."

"Do you know what idea occurred to me this evening, Aramis?" —"No; tell me what it was, for I should never be able to guess it, you have so many."—"Well, the idea occurred to me that the true king of France is not Louis XIV."—"What!" said Aramis, involuntarily, looking the musketeer full in the eyes.

"No; it is M. Fouquet." Aramis breathed again, and smiled. "Ah! you are like all the rest,—jealous," he said. "I would wager that it was M. Colbert who turned that pretty phrase. He comes of a mean race, does Colbert," said Aramis.—"Quite true."

The Man in the Iron Mask

"When I think, too," added the bishop, "that that fellow will be your minister within four months, and that you will serve him as blindly as you did Richelieu or Mazarin—"—"And as you serve M. Fouquet," said D'Artagnan.

"With this difference, though, that M. Fouquet is not M. Colbert."—"True, true," said D'Artagnan, as he pretended to become sad and full of reflection; and then, a moment after, he added, "Why do you tell me that M. Colbert will be minister in four months?"—"Because M. Fouquet will have ceased to be so," replied Aramis.—"He will be ruined, you mean?" said D'Artagnan.—"Completely so."

"Why does he give these *fêtes,* then?" said the musketeer, in a tone so full of thoughtful consideration, so natural, that the bishop was for the moment deceived by it. "Why did you not dissuade him from it?" The latter part of the sentence was just a little too much, and Aramis's former suspicions were again aroused. "It is done with the object of humouring the king."—"By ruining himself?"—"Yes, by ruining himself for the king."—"A singular calculation that!"—"Necessity."—"I don't see that, dear Aramis."

"Do you not? Have you not remarked M. Colbert's daily increasing antagonism, and that he is doing his utmost to drive the king to get rid of the superintendent?"—"One must be blind not to see it."—"And that a cabal is formed against M. Fouquet?"—"That is well known."—"What likelihood is there that the king would join a party formed against a man who will have spent everything he had to please him?"

"True, true," said D'Artagnan slowly, hardly convinced, yet curious to broach another phase of the conversation. "There are follies and follies," he resumed; "and I do not like those you are committing."—"To what do you allude?"—"As for the banquet, the ball, the concert, the theatricals, the tournaments, the cascades, the fireworks, the illuminations, and the presents,—these are all well and good, I grant; but why were not these expenses sufficient? Was it necessary to refurnish the entire house?"

"You are quite right. I told M. Fouquet that myself. He replied, that if he were rich enough he would offer the king a château new from the vanes at the top of the house to the very cellar, completely new inside and out; and that as soon as the king had left, he would burn the whole building and its contents, in order that it might not be made use of by any one else."—"How completely Spanish!"—"I told him so, and he then added this: 'Whoever advises me to spare expense, I shall look upon as my enemy.'"

"It is positive madness; and that portrait too!"—"What portrait?" said Aramis.—"That of the king; that surprise."—"That surprise?"—"Yes, for which you procured some samples at Percerin's." D'Artagnan paused. The shaft was discharged, and all he had to do was to wait and watch its effect. "That is merely an act of graceful attention," replied Aramis.

D'Artagnan went up to his friend, took hold of both his hands, and looking him full in the eyes said, "Aramis, do you still care for me a little?"—"What a question to ask!"—"Very good. One favour, then. Why did you take some samples of the king's costumes at Percerin's?"—"Come with me and ask poor Lebrun, who has been working upon them for the last two days and two nights."—"Aramis, that may be the truth for everybody else; but for me—"—"Upon my word, D'Artagnan, you astonish me."

"Be a little considerate for me. Tell me the exact truth; you would not like anything disagreeable to happen to me, would you?" —"My dear friend, you are becoming quite incomprehensible. What devil of a suspicion have you, then?"—"Do you believe in my instincts? Formerly you had faith in them. Well, then, an instinct tells me that you have some concealed project on foot."—"I—a project?"—"I am not sure of it."—"What nonsense!"—"I am not sure of it, but I would swear to it."

"Indeed, D'Artagnan, you cause me the greatest pain. Is it likely, if I have any project in hand that I ought to keep secret from you, I shall tell you about it? If I had one that I ought to reveal to you, I should have already told it to you."—"No, Aramis, no. There are certain projects which are never revealed until the favourable opportunity arrives."—"In that case, my dear fellow," returned the bishop, laughing, "the only thing now is, that the 'opportunity' has not yet arrived."

D'Artagnan shook his head with a sorrowful expression. "Oh, friendship, friendship!" he said, "what an idle word! Here is a man who, if I were but to ask it, would suffer himself to be cut in pieces for my sake."—"You are right," said Aramis, nobly.—"And this man, who would shed every drop of blood in his veins for me, will not open the smallest corner of his heart. Friendship, I repeat, is nothing but a shadow and a delusion, like everything else that shines in this world."—"It is not thus you should speak of our friendship," replied the bishop, in a firm, assured voice; "for ours is not of the same nature as those of which you have been speaking!"

"Look at us, Aramis! We are three out of the four. You are deceiving me, I suspect you, and Porthos sleeps; an admirable trio of friends, don't you think so?—a beautiful relic!"—"I can only tell you one thing, D'Artagnan, and I swear it on the Bible: I love you just as much as formerly. If ever I distrust you, it is on account of others, and not on account of either of us. In everything I may do and succeed in, you will find your share. Will you promise me the same favour?"

"If I am not mistaken, Aramis, these words of yours, at the moment you pronounce them, are full of generous intention."—"That is true."—"You are conspiring against M. Colbert. If that be all, *mordioux!* tell me so at once. I have the instrument, and will pull out the tooth."

Aramis could not restrain a smile of disdain which passed across his noble features. "And supposing that I were conspiring against Colbert, what harm would there be in that?"—"No, no; that would be too trifling a matter for you to take in hand, and it was not on that account you asked Percerin for those samples of the king's costumes. Oh, Aramis, we are not enemies, we are brothers! Tell me what you wish to undertake, and, upon the word of D'Artagnan, if I cannot help you, I will swear to remain neutral."—"I am undertaking nothing," said Aramis.

"Aramis, a voice speaks within me, and seems to enlighten my darkness; it is a voice which has never yet deceived me. It is the king you are conspiring against."—"The king!" exclaimed the bishop, pretending to be annoyed.—"Your face will not convince me. The king, I repeat."

"Will you help me?" said Aramis, smiling ironically.—"Aramis, I will do more than help you,—I will do more than remain neutral,—I will save you."—"You are mad, D'Artagnan."—"I am the wiser of the two, in this matter."—"You to suspect me of wishing to assassinate the king!"—"Who spoke of that at all?" said the musketeer.

"Well, let us understand each other. I do not see what any one can do to a legitimate king as ours is, if he does not assassinate him." D'Artagnan did not say a word. "Besides, you have your guards and your musketeers here," said the bishop.—"True."—"You are not in M. Fouquet's house, but in your own. You have at the present moment M. Colbert, who counsels the king against M. Fouquet all which perhaps you would wish to advise if I were not on his side."— "Aramis! Aramis! for mercy's sake, one word as a friend!"

"A friend's word is the truth itself. If I think of touching, even with my finger, the son of Anne of Austria, the true king of this realm of France; if I have not the firm intention of prostrating myself before his throne; if, according to my wishes, to-morrow here at Vaux will not be the most glorious day my king ever enjoyed,—may Heaven's lightning blast me where I stand!" Aramis had pronounced these words with his face turned towards the alcove of his bedroom, where D'Artagnan, seated with his back towards the alcove, could not suspect that any one was lying concealed. The earnestness of his words, the studied slowness with which he pronounced them, the solemnity of his oath, gave the musketeer the most complete satisfaction. He took hold of both Aramis's hands, and shook them cordially. Aramis had endured reproaches without turning pale; he blushed as he listened to words of praise. D'Artagnan, deceived, did him honour; but D'Artagnan, trustful and reliant, made him feel ashamed. 'Are you going away?" he said, as he embraced his friend in order to conceal the flush on his own face.— "Yes; my duty summons me. I have to get the watchword."

"Where are you lodged?"—"In the king's anteroom. And Porthos?"—"Take him away with you if you like, for he snores like a park of artillery."—"Ah! he does not stay with you, then?" said the captain.—"Not at all. He has his room to himself, but I don't know where."

"Very good!" said the musketeer, from whom this separation of the two associates removed his last suspicion; and he touched Porthos roughly on the shoulder. The latter replied by a yawn. "Come!" said D'Artagnan.—"What! D'Artagnan, my dear fellow, is that you? What a lucky chance! Oh, yes,—true; I am at the *fête* at Vaux."—"With your fine suit?"—"Yes; it was very attentive on the part of M. Coquelin de Volière, was it not?"

"Hush!" said Aramis. "You are walking so heavily that you will make the flooring give way."—"True," said the musketeer; "this room is above the dome."—"And I did not choose it for a fencing-room, I assure you," added the bishop. "The ceiling of the king's room has all the sweetness and calm delights of sleep. Do not forget, therefore, that my flooring is merely the covering of his ceiling. Good-night, my friends! In ten minutes I shall be fast asleep;" and Aramis accompanied them to the door, smiling pleasantly.

As soon as they were outside, Aramis bolted the door hurriedly, closed up the chinks of the windows, and then called out, "Monseigneur! Monseigneur!" Philippe made his appearance from the alcove, pushing aside a sliding panel placed behind the bed. "M. d'Artagnan entertains a great many suspicions, it seems," he said.—"Ah! you recognised M. d'Artagnan, then?"—"Before you called him by his name, even."—"He is your captain of musketeers."

"He is very devoted to *me*," replied Philippe, laying a stress upon the personal pronoun.—"As faithful as a dog; but he bites sometimes. If D'Artagnan does not recognise you before *the other* has disappeared, rely upon D'Artagnan to the end of the world; for in that case, if he has seen nothing, he will keep his fidelity. If he sees, when it is too late, he is a Gascon, and will never admit that he has been deceived."

"I thought so. What are we to do, now?"—"You will go and take up your post at our place of observation, and watch the moment of the king's retiring to rest, so as to learn how that ceremony is performed."—"Very good. Where shall I place myself?"

"Sit down on this folding-chair! I am going to push aside a portion of the flooring; you will look through the opening, which answers to one of the false windows made in the dome of the king's apartment. Can you see?"—"Yes," said Philippe, starting as at the sight of an enemy; "I see the king!"—"What is he doing?"—"He seems to wish some man to sit down close to him."

"M. Fouquet!"—"No, no; wait a moment—"—"The notes, my Prince, the portraits!"—"The man whom the king wishes to sit down in his presence is M. Colbert."

"Colbert sit down in the king's presence!" exclaimed Aramis; "it is impossible."—"Look!" Aramis looked through the opening in the flooring. "Yes," he said, "Colbert himself! Oh, Monseigneur! what are we about to hear, and what can result from this intimacy?" —"Nothing good for M. Fouquet, at all events." The prince was not mistaken.

We have seen that Louis XIV. had sent for Colbert, and that Colbert had arrived. The conversation began between them by the king's according to him one of the highest favours that he had ever

A Gascon, and a Gascon and a Half

given,—it is true that the king was alone with his subject,—"Colbert," said he, "sit down!"

The intendant, overcome with delight, for he had feared he should be dismissed, refused this unprecedented honour. "Does he accept?" said Aramis.—"No; he remains standing."—"Let us listen, then;" and the future king and the future pope listened eagerly to the simple mortals whom they beheld under their feet in a position to crush them if they had liked.

"Colbert," said the king, "you have annoyed me exceedingly to-day."—"I know it, Sire."—"Very good; I like that answer. Yes, you knew it, and there was courage in doing it."—"I ran the risk of displeasing your Majesty, but I risked also concealing what were your true interests from you."—"What! you were afraid of something on my account?"—"I was, Sire, even if it were of nothing more than an indigestion," said Colbert; "for one does not give his king such banquets as that of to-day, except it be to stifle him under the weight of good living."

Colbert awaited the effect of this coarse jest upon the king; and Louis XIV., who was the vainest and the most fastidiously delicate man in his kingdom, forgave Colbert his pleasantry. "The truth is," he said, "that M. Fouquet has given me too good a meal. Tell me, Colbert, where does he get all the money required for this enormous expenditure,—can you tell?"—"Yes, I know, Sire."—"You will show me?"—"Easily; to the very farthing."

"I know you are very exact."—"It is the principal qualification required in an intendant of finances."—"But all are not so."—"I thank your Majesty for a compliment so flattering from your lips."

"M. Fouquet, then, is rich, very rich; and I suppose every man knows he is so."—"Every one, Sire,—the living as well as the dead." —"What does that mean, M. Colbert?"—"The living are witnesses of M. Fouquet's wealth,—they admire and applaud the result produced; but the dead, wiser than we, know its sources, and they accuse him."—"So that M. Fouquet owes his wealth to certain sources?"—"The occupation of an intendant very often favours those who engage in it."

"You have something to say to me more confidentially, I perceive; do not be afraid, we are quite alone."—"I am never afraid of anything under the shelter of my own conscience and under the protection of your Majesty," said Colbert, bowing.—"If the dead, there-fore, were to speak—"—"They do speak sometimes, Sire. Read!"

"Ah!" murmured Aramis in the prince's ear, who close beside him listened without losing a syllable, "since you are placed here, Monseigneur, in order to learn the vocation of a king, listen to a piece of infamy truly royal. You are about to be a witness of one of those scenes which God alone, or rather which the devil alone, can conceive and execute. Listen attentively,—you will find your advantage in it."

The prince redoubled his attention, and saw Louis XIV. take from Colbert's hand a letter which the latter held out to him. "The late cardinal's handwriting," said the king.—"Your Majesty has an excellent memory," replied Colbert, bowing; "it is an immense advantage for a king who is destined for hard work to recognise handwritings at the first glance."

The king read Mazarin's letter; but as its contents are already known to the reader, in consequence of the misunderstanding between Madame de Chevreuse and Aramis, nothing further would be learned if we stated them here again. "I do not quite understand," said the king, greatly interested.

"Your Majesty has not yet acquired the habit of going through the public accounts."—"I see that it refers to money which had been given to M. Fouquet."—"Thirteen millions—a tolerably good sum." —"Yes. Well, and these thireen millions are wanting to balance the total of the accounts? That is what I do not very well understand. How was this deficit possible?"—"Possible, I do not say; but there is no doubt about its reality."

"You say that these thirteen millions are found to be wanting in the accounts?"—"I do not say so; but the registry does."—"And this letter of M. Mazarin indicates the employment of that sum, and the name of the person with whom it was deposited?"—"As your Majesty can judge for yourself."

"Yes; and the result is, then, that M. Fouquet has not yet restored the thirteen millions."—"That results from the accounts, certainly, Sire."—"Well, and consequently—"—"Well, Sire, consequently, inasmuch as M. Fouquet has not given back the thirteen millions, he must have appropriated them to his own purposes; and with those thirteen millions one could incur four times and a fraction as much expense and display as your Majesty was able to do at Fontainebleau, where we spent only three millions altogether, if you remember."

For a blunderer, the souvenir he had evoked was a very skilfully contrived piece of baseness; for in remembering his own *fête* the king, thanks to a word of Fouquet, had for the first time perceived its inferiority. Colbert received at Vaux what Fouquet had given him at Fontainebleau; and as a good financier, he returned it with the best possible interest. Having once disposed the king's mind in that way, Colbert had nothing further to accomplish. He perceived it; the king had become gloomy. Colbert awaited the first word from the king's lips with as much impatience as Philippe and Aramis did from their place of observation.

"Are you aware what is the natural consequence of all this, M. Colbert?" said the king, after a few moments' reflection.—"No, Sire, I do not know."—"Well, then, the fact of the appropriation of the thirteen millions, if it can be proved—"—"But it is so already."—"I mean if it were to be declared, M. Colbert."—"I think it will be to-morrow, if your Majesty—"—"Were we not under M. Fouquet's roof, you were going to say, perhaps," replied the king, with something of nobleness in his manner.—"The king is in his own palace wherever he may be, and especially in houses for which his own money has paid."

"I think," said Philippe, in a low tone to Aramis, "that the architect who constructed this dome ought, anticipating what use could be made of it, so to have contrived that it might easily be made to fall on the heads of scoundrels such as that M. Colbert."—"I thought so, too," replied Aramis; "but M. Colbert is so very near the king at this moment."—"That is true, and that would open the succession." —"Of which your younger brother would reap all the advantage, Monseigneur. But, stay! let us keep quiet and listen."

"We shall not have long to listen," said the young prince.—"Why not, Monseigneur?"—"Because, if I were the king, I should not say anything further."—"And what would you do?"—"I should wait until to-morrow morning to give myself time for reflection."

Louis XIV. at last raised his eyes, and finding Colbert attentively waiting for his next remark, said, hastily changing the conversation, "M. Colbert, I perceive it is getting very late, and I shall now retire to bed."—"Ah!" said Colbert, "I should have—"—"Till to-morrow. By to-morrow morning I shall have made up my mind."—"Very

good, Sire," returned Colbert, greatly incensed, although he restrained himself in the presence of the king. The king made a gesture of adieu, and Colbert withdrew with a respectful bow. "My
attendants!" cried the king; and they entered the apartment.

Philippe was about to quit his post of observation. "A moment
longer," said Aramis to him, with his accustomed gentleness of manner. "What has just now taken place is only a detail, and to-morrow
we shall have no occasion to think anything more about it; but the
ceremony of the king's retiring to rest, the etiquette observed in un-
dressing the king,—that, indeed, is important. Learn, Sire, and
study well how you ought to go to bed. Look, look!"

CHAPTER XVI

COLBERT

HISTORY will tell us, or rather history has told us, of the
various events of the following day,—of the splendid *fêtes*
given by the superintendent to his sovereign. There was
nothing but amusement and delight throughout the whole of the following day: there was a promenade, a banquet, a comedy, in which
to his great amazement Porthos recognized "M. Coquelin de Volière" as one of the actors, in the piece called "Les Fâcheux."

Full of preoccupation after the scene of the previous evening, and
hardly recovered from the effects of the poison which Colbert had
then administered to him, the king during the whole of the day, so
brilliant in its effects, so full of unexpected and startling novelties, in
which all the wonders of the *Arabian Nights' Entertainment* seemed
to be reproduced for his especial amusement,—the king, we say,
showed himself cold, reserved, and taciturn. Nothing could smooth
the frowns upon his face; every one who observed him noticed that
a deep feeling of resentment, of remote origin, increased by slow degrees, as the source becomes a river, thanks to the thousand threads
of water which increase its body, was keenly alive in the depths of
the king's heart. Towards the middle of the day only did he begin
to resume a little serenity of manner; by that time he had, in all
probability, made up his mind. Aramis, who followed him step by

step in his thoughts as in his walk, concluded that the event which he was expecting would soon occur. This time Colbert seemed to walk in concert with the Bishop of Vannes; and had he received for every annoyance which he inflicted on the king a word of direction from Aramis, he could not have done better. During the whole of the day the king, who in all probability wished to free himself from some of the thoughts which disturbed his mind, seemed to seek La Vallière's society as actively as he sought to avoid that of M. Colbert or M. Fouquet.

The evening came. The king had expressed a wish not to walk in the park until after cards in the evening. In the interval between supper and the promenade, cards and dice were introduced. The king won a thousand pistoles, and having won them put them in his pocket, and then rose, saying, "And now, gentlemen, to the park." He found the ladies of the court already there. The king, we have before observed, had won a thousand pistoles, and had put them in his pocket. But M. Fouquet had somehow contrived to lose ten thousand; so that among the courtiers there was still left a hundred and ninety thousand livres' profit to divide,—a circumstance which made the countenances of the courtiers and the officers of the king's household the most joyous in the world. It was not the same, how-ever, with the king's face; for notwithstanding his success at play, to which he was by no means insensible, there still remained a slight shade of dissatisfaction.

Colbert was waiting for him at the corner of one of the avenues; he was most probably waiting there by appointment, as Louis XIV., who had avoided him or who had seemed to avoid him, suddenly made him a sign, and they then struck into the depths of the park together. But La Vallière, too, had observed the king's gloomy aspect and kindling glances. She had remarked this; and as noth-ing which lay hidden or smouldering in his heart was impenetrable to her affection, she understood that this repressed wrath menaced some one. She put herself upon the road of vengeance, like an angel of mercy. Overcome by sadness, nervously agitated, deeply dis-tressed at having been so long separated from her lover, disturbed at the sight of that emotion which she had divined, she presented herself to the king with an embarrassed aspect, which in his evil mood the king interpreted unfavourably. Then, as they were alone, or nearly alone,—inasmuch as Colbert, as soon as he perceived the young girl approaching, had stopped and drawn back a dozen paces, —the king advanced towards La Vallière and took her by the hand. "Mademoiselle," he said to her, "should I be guilty of an indiscretion if I were to inquire if you are indisposed? You seem to breathe as if you were distressed, and your eyes are filled with tears."

"Oh, Sire, if I am distressed, and if my eyes are full of tears, it is for the sadness of your Majesty."—"My sadness? You are mistaken, Mademoiselle; no, it is not sadness I experience."—"What is it, then, Sire?"—"Humiliation."

"Humiliation? Oh, Sire, what a word for you to use!"—"I mean, Mademoiselle, that wherever I may happen to be, no one else ought to be the master. Well, then, look round you on every side, and judge whether I am not eclipsed—I, the King of France—before the king of these wide domains. Oh!" he continued, clinching his hands and teeth, "when I think that this king—"—"Well, Sire?" said Louise, terrified.—"That this king is a faithless, unworthy servant, who becomes proud with my stolen property— And therefore am I about to change this impudent minister's *fête* into a sorrow and mourning of which the nymph of Vaux, as the poets say, shall not soon lose the remembrance."

"Oh! your Majesty—"—"Well, Mademoiselle, are you about to take M. Fouquet's part?" said Louis, impatiently.—"No, Sire; I will only ask whether you are well informed. Your Majesty has more than once learned the value of accusations made at court." Louis XIV. made a sign for Colbert to approach. "Speak, M. Colbert," said the young king; "for I almost believe that Mademoiselle de la Vallière has need of your assurance before she can put any faith in the king's word. Tell Mademoiselle what M. Fouquet has done; and you, Mademoiselle, will perhaps have the kindness to listen. It will not be long."

Why did Louis XIV. insist upon it in such a manner? For a very simple reason,—his heart was not at rest; his mind was not thoroughly convinced; he imagined there was some dark, hidden, tortuous intrigue concealed beneath these thirteen million livres; and he wished that the pure heart of La Vallière, which had revolted at the idea of a theft or robbery, should approve even were it only by a single word, the resolution which he had taken, and which, nevertheless, he hesitated about carrying into execution. "Speak, Monsieur," said La Vallière to Colbert, who had advanced; "speak,

At that very moment a second sentinel stopped D'Artagnan

since the king wishes me to listen to you. Tell me, what is the crime with which M. Fouquet is charged?"—"Oh, not very heinous, Mademoiselle," he returned,—"a simple abuse of confidence."

"Speak, speak, Colbert; and when you shall have related it, leave us, and go and inform M. d'Artagnan that I have orders to give him."—"M. d'Artagnan, Sire!" exclaimed La Vallière; "but why send for M. d'Artagnan? I entreat you to tell me."—"*Pardieu!* in order to arrest this haughty Titan, who, true to his motto, threatens to scale my heaven."

"Arrest M. Fouquet, do you say?"—"Ah! does that surprise you?"—"In his own house?"—"Why not? If he be guilty, he is guilty in his own house as anywhere else."—"M. Fouquet, who at this moment is ruining himself for his sovereign!"—"I believe, Mademoiselle, you are defending this traitor!"

Colbert began to chuckle silently. The king turned round at the sound of this suppressed mirth. "Sire," said La Vallière, "it is not M. Fouquet I am defending; it is yourself."—"Me! you defend me?"—"Sire, you would be dishonouring yourself if you were to give such an order."—"Dishonour myself?" murmured the king, turning pale with anger. "In truth, Mademoiselle, you put a strange eagerness into what you say."—"I put eagerness not into what I say, but into serving your Majesty," replied the noble-hearted girl; "in that I would lay down my life, were it needed, and with the same eagerness, Sire."

Colbert seemed inclined to grumble. La Vallière, that gentle lamb, turned round upon him, and with a glance like lightning imposed silence upon him. "Monsieur," she said, "when the king acts well, if in doing so he does either myself or those who belong to me an injury, I have nothing to say; but were the king to confer a benefit either upon me or mine, and if he acted badly, I should tell him so."

"But it appears to me, Mademoiselle," Colbert ventured to say, "that I too love the king."—"Yes, Monsieur, we both love him, but each in a different manner," replied La Vallière, with such an accent that the heart of the young king was powerfully affected by it. "I love him so deeply that the whole world is aware of it, so purely that the king himself does not doubt my love. He is my king and my master; I am the humblest of his servants. But he who touches his honour touches my life. Now, I repeat that they dishonour the king who advise him to arrest M. Fouquet under his own roof."

Colbert hung down his head, for he felt that the king had abandoned him. However, as he bent his head, he murmured, "Mademoiselle, I have only one word to say."—"Do not say it, then, Monsieur; for I would not listen to it. Besides, what could you have to tell me? That M. Fouquet has been guilty of certain crimes? I know he has, because the king has said so; and from the moment the king said, 'I believe,' I have no occasion for other lips to say, 'I affirm.' But were M. Fouquet the vilest of men, I should say aloud, 'M. Fouquet's person is sacred to the king because he is the king's host. Were his house a den of thieves, were Vaux a cave of coiners or robbers, his home is sacred, his palace is inviolable, since his wife is living in it; and it is an asylum which even executioners would not dare to violate.' "

La Vallière paused, and was silent. In spite of himself, the king could not but admire her; he was overpowered by the passionate energy of her voice, by the nobleness of the cause she advocated. Colbert yielded, overcome by the inequality of the struggle. At last the king breathed again more freely, shook his head, and held out his hand to La Vallière. "Mademoiselle," he said gently, "why do you decide against me? Do you know what this wretched fellow will do, if I give him time to breathe again?"

"Is he not a prey which will always be within your grasp?"—"And if he escapes, and takes to flight?" exclaimed Colbert.—"Well, Monsieur, it will always remain on record, to the king's eternal honour, that he allowed M. Fouquet to flee; and the more guilty he may have been, the greater will the king's honour and glory appear, when compared with such misery and such shame."

Louis kissed La Vallière's hand, as he knelt before her. "I am lost!" thought Colbert; then suddenly his face brightened up again. "Oh, no, no, not yet!" he said to himself. And while the king, protected from observation by the thick covert of an enormous lime, pressed La Vallière to his breast with all the ardour of ineffable affection, Colbert tranquilly looked among the papers in his pocketbook, and drew out of it a paper folded in the form of a letter, slightly yellow, perhaps, but which must have been very precious, since the intendant smiled as he looked at it; he then bent a look full of hatred upon the charming group which the young girl and the king formed together,—a group which was revealed for a moment as the light of the approaching torches shone upon it.

Louis noticed the light reflected upon La Vallière's white dress. "Leave me, Louise," he said, "for some one is coming."—"Mademoiselle, Mademoiselle, some one is coming," cried Colbert, to expedite the young girl's departure.

Louise disappeared rapidly among the trees; and then, as the king, who had been on his knees before the young girl, was rising from his humble posture, Colbert exclaimed, "Ah! Mademoiselle de la Vallière has let something fall."—"What is it?" inquired the king.—"A paper,—a letter,—something white; look there, Sire!" The king stooped down immediately, and picked up the letter, crumpling it in his hand as he did so; and at the same moment the torches arrived, inundating the darkness of the scene with a flood of light as bright as day.

CHAPTER XVII

JEALOUSY

THE torches to which we have just referred, the eager attention which every one displayed, and the new ovation paid to the king by Fouquet arrived in time to suspend the effect of a resolution which La Vallière had already considerably shaken in Louis XIV.'s heart. He looked at Fouquet with a feeling almost of gratitude for having given La Vallière an opportunity of showing herself so generously disposed, so powerful in the influence she exercised over his heart. The moment of the last and greatest display had arrived. Hardly had Fouquet conducted the king towards the château, when a mass of fire burst from the dome of Vaux with a prodigious uproar, pouring a flood of dazzling light on every side, and illumining the remotest corner of the gardens. The fireworks began. Colbert, at twenty paces from the king, who was surrounded and *fêted* by the masters of Vaux, seemed, by the obstinate persistence of his gloomy thoughts, to do his utmost to recall Louis's attention, which the magnificence of the spectacle was already, in his opinion, too easily diverting.

The Man in the Iron Mask

Suddenly, just as Louis was on the point of holding his hand out to Fouquet, he perceived in it the paper which, as he believed, La Vallière had dropped at his feet as she hurried away. The still stronger magnet of love drew the young king's attention to the souvenir of his idol; and by the brilliant light, which increased momentarily in beauty, and drew forth from the neighbouring villages loud exclamations of admiration, the king read the letter, which he supposed was a loving and tender epistle that La Vallière had destined for him. But as he read it, a deathlike pallor stole over his face, and an expression of deep-seated wrath, illumined by the many-coloured fires, produced a terrible spectacle, which every one would have shuddered at, could they only have read his heart, which was torn by the most stormy passions. For him there was no more truce with jealousy and rage. From the moment when the dark truth was revealed to him, every gentler feeling disappeared,—piety, kindness, the religion of hospitality. In the bitter pang which wrung his heart, still too weak to hide his sufferings, he was almost on the point of uttering a cry of alarm, and calling his guards to gather round him. This letter which Colbert had thrown down at the king's feet had disappeared at Fontainebleau, after an attempt which Fouquet had made upon La Vallière's heart. Fouquet saw the king's pallor, and was far from guessing the evil. Colbert saw the king's anger, and rejoiced inwardly at the approach of the storm.

Fouquet's voice drew the young king from his wrathful reverie. "What is the matter, Sire?" inquired the superintendent, with an expression of graceful interest. Louis made a violent effort over himself, as he replied, "Nothing."—"I am afraid your Majesty is suffering?"

"I am suffering, and have already told you so, Monsieur; but it is nothing." The king, without waiting for the termination of the fireworks, turned towards the château. Fouquet accompanied him; and the whole court followed them, leaving the remains of the fireworks burning for their own amusement. The superintendent endeavoured again to question Louis XIV., but obtained no reply. He imagined that there had been some misunderstanding between Louis and La Vallière in the park, which had resulted in a slight quarrel; and that the king, who was not ordinarily sulky by disposition, but completely absorbed by his passion for La Vallière, had

118

taken a dislike to every one because his mistress had shown herself offended with him. This idea was sufficient to reassure him; he had even a friendly and kindly smile for the young king, when the latter wished him good-night. This, however, was not all the king had to submit to; he was obliged to undergo the usual ceremony, which on that evening was marked by the closest adherence to the strictest etiquette. The next day was the one fixed for the departure; it was but proper that the guests should thank their host, and should show him a little attention in return for the expenditure of his twelve millions. The only remark approaching to amiability which the king could find to say to Fouquet, as he took leave of him, was in these words: "M. Fouquet, you shall hear from me. Be good enough to desire M. d'Artagnan to come here!"

The blood of Louis XIV., who had so profoundly dissimulated his feelings, boiled in his veins; he was perfectly ready to get Fouquet's throat cut, as his predecessor had caused the assassination of the Maréchal d'Ancre. He concealed, beneath one of those royal smiles which are the lightning flashes to the thunderbolts of the State, the terrible resolution he had formed. Fouquet took the king's hand, and kissed it. Louis shuddered throughout his whole frame, but allowed Fouquet to touch his hand with his lips.

Five minutes afterwards, D'Artagnan, to whom the royal order had been communicated, entered Louis XIV.'s apartment. Aramis and Philippe were in theirs, still eagerly attentive and still listening. The king did not even give the captain of the musketeers time to approach his arm-chair, but ran forward to meet him. "Take care," he exclaimed, "that no one enters here!"—"Very good, Sire," replied the captain, whose glance had for a long time past analysed the ravages on the king's countenance. He gave the necessary order at the door; but returning to the king he said, "Is there some new trouble, your Majesty?"

"How many men have you here?" said the king, without making other reply to the question addressed to him.—"What for, Sire?"— "How many men have you, I say?" repeated the king, stamping upon the ground with his foot.—"I have the musketeers."

"Well; and what others?"—"Twenty guards and thirteen Swiss." —"How many men will be required to—"—"To do what, Sire?" replied the musketeer, opening his large, calm eyes.—"To arrest M. Fouquet."

The Man in the Iron Mask

D'Artagnan fell back a step. "To arrest M. Fouquet!" he burst forth.—"Are you going to tell me that it is impossible?" exclaimed the king, with cold and vindictive passion.—"I never said that anything is impossible," replied D'Artagnan, wounded to the quick.—"Very well; do it, then."

D'Artagnan turned on his heel, and made his way towards the door,—it was but a short distance, and he cleared it in half a dozen paces. When he reached it he suddenly paused, and said, "Your Majesty will forgive me; but in order to effect this arrest I should like written directions."—"For what purpose? and since when has the king's word been insufficient for you?"—"Because the word of a king when it springs from a feeling of anger may possibly change when the feeling changes."

"No more phrases, Monsieur; you have another thought besides that?"—"Oh, I always have thoughts; and thoughts which, unfortunately, others have not!" D'Artagnan replied impertinently. The king, in the tempest of his wrath, hesitated, and drew back in the face of that man, just as a horse crouches on his haunches under the strong hand of a rider. "What is your thought?" he exclaimed.— "This, Sire," replied D'Artagnan: "you cause a man to be arrested when you are still under his roof; and passion is alone the cause of that. When your anger shall have passed away you will regret what you have done; and then I wish to be in a position to show you your signature. If that mends nothing, it will at least show us that the king is wrong to lose his temper."

"Wrong to lose his temper!" shouted the king, with frenzy. "Did not my father, my grandfather too, before me, lose their temper, body of Christ!"—"The king your father and the king your grandfather never lost their temper except in the privacy of their own palace."—"The king is master wherever he may be."—"That is a flattering phrase which cannot proceed from any one but M. Colbert; but it happens not to be the truth. The king is at home in every man's house when he has driven its owner out of it."

The king bit his lips. "Can it be possible?" said D'Artagnan. "Here is a man who is ruining himself in order to please you, and you wish to have him arrested! *Mordioux!* Sire, if my name were Fouquet, and any one treated me in that manner, I would swallow at a single gulp ten pieces of fireworks, and I would set fire to them and blow myself and everybody else up to the sky. But it is all the same; it is your wish, and it shall be done."

"Go!" said the king; "but have you men enough?"—"Do you suppose I am going to take a whole host to help me? To arrest M. Fouquet is so easy that a child might do it! It is like drinking a glass of bitters: one makes an ugly face, and that is all."—"If he defends himself?"—"He! not at all likely. Defend himself when such extreme harshness as you are going to practise makes him king and martyr! Nay, I am sure that if he has a million livres left, which I very much doubt, he would be willing enough to give it in order to have such a termination as this. But what does that matter? It shall be done at once."

"Stay!" said the king; "do not make his arrest a public affair."—"That will be more difficult."—"Why so?"—"Because nothing is easier than to go up to M. Fouquet in the midst of a thousand enthusiastic guests who surround him, and say, 'In the king's name, I arrest you.' But to go up to him, to turn him first one way and then another, to drive him up into one of the corners of the chessboard in such a way that he cannot escape, to take him away from his guests and keep him a prisoner for you without one of them, alas! having heard anything about it,—that, indeed, is a real difficulty,—the greatest of all, in truth; and I hardly see how it is to be done."

"You had better say it is impossible, and you will have finished much sooner. *Mon Dieu!* I seem to be surrounded by people who prevent my doing what I wish."—"I do not prevent your doing anything. Are you decided?"—"Take care of M. Fouquet until I shall have made up my mind by to-morrow morning."—"That shall be done, Sire."—"And return, when I rise in the morning, for further orders; and now leave me to myself."

"You do not even want M. Colbert, then?" said the musketeer, firing this last shot as he was leaving the room. The king started. With his whole mind fixed on the thought of revenge, he had forgotten the cause and substance of the offence. "No, no one," he said; "no one here. Leave me!"

D'Artagnan quitted the room. The king closed the door with his own hands, and began to walk up and down his apartment at a furious pace, like a wounded bull in an arena who drags after him the coloured streamers and iron darts. At last he began to take comfort in the expression of his violent feelings. "Miserable wretch that he is! not only does he squander my finances, but with his ill-gotten plunder he corrupts secretaries, friends, generals, artists, and all; he even takes from me my mistress. Ah, that is the reason why that perfidious girl so boldly took his part! Gratitude! and who can tell whether it was not a stronger feeling,—love itself?" He gave himself up for a moment to his bitter reflections. "A satyr!" he thought, with that abhorrent hate with which young men regard those more advanced in life, who still think of love. "A faun who pursues a course of gallantry and has never met resistance; a man for silly women, who lavishes his gold and jewels in every direction, and who retains his staff of painters in order to take the portraits of his mistresses in the costume of goddesses!" The king trembled with passion as he continued: "He pollutes and profanes everything that belongs to me; he destroys everything that is mine; he will be my death at last! That man is too much for me; he is my mortal enemy, and he shall fall! I hate him,—I hate him,—I hate him!" and as he pronounced these words, he struck the arm of the chair in which he was sitting, violently over and over again, and then rose, like one in an epileptic fit. "To-morrow! to-morrow! oh, happy day!" he murmured; "when the sun rises, no other rival will that bright orb have but me. That man shall fall so low that when people look at the utter ruin which my anger shall have wrought, they will be forced to confess, at least, that I am indeed greater than he."

The king, who was incapable of mastering his emotions any longer, knocked over with a blow of his fist a small table placed close to his bedside, and in the bitterness of feeling from which he was suffering, almost weeping, and half suffocated by his passion, threw himself on his bed, dressed as he was, and bit the sheets in the extremity of his emotion, trying there to find at least repose of body. The bed creaked beneath his weight; and with the exception of a few broken sounds which escaped from his overburden chest, absolute silence soon reigned in the chamber of Morpheus.

Louis kissed La Vallière's hand, as he knelt before her

CHAPTER XVIII

HIGH TREASON

THE ungovernable fury which took possession of the king at the sight and at the perusal of Fouquet's letter to La Vallière by degrees subsided into a feeling of painful weariness. Youth, full of health and life, and requiring that what it loses should be immediately restored,—youth knows not those endless, sleepless nights which realise to the unhappy the fable of the liver of Prometheus, unceasingly renewed. In instances where the man of middle life in his acquired strength of will and purpose, and the old man in his state of exhaustion find an incessant renewal of their sorrow, a young man, surprised by the sudden appearance of a misfortune, weakens himself in sighs and groans and tears, in direct struggles with it, and is thereby far sooner overthrown by the inflexible enemy with whom he is engaged. Once overthrown, his sufferings cease. Louis was conquered in a quarter of an hour. Then he ceased to clinch his hands, and to burn with his looks the invisible objects of his hatred; he ceased to attack with violent imprecations M. Fouquet and La Vallière: from fury he subsided into despair, and from despair to prostration. After he had thrown himself for a few minutes to and fro convulsively on his bed, his nerveless arms fell quietly down; his head lay languidly on his pillow; his limbs, exhausted by his excessive emotions, still trembled occasionally, agitated by slight muscular contractions; and from his breast only faint and unfrequent sighs still issued.

Morpheus, the tutelary deity of the apartment which bore his name, towards whom Louis raised his eyes, wearied by his anger and reddened by his tears, showered down upon him copiously the sleep-inducing poppies, so that the king gently closed his eyes and fell asleep. Then it seemed to him, as it often happens in that first sleep, so light and gentle, which raises the body above the couch, the soul above the earth,—it seemed to him as if the god Morpheus, painted on the ceiling, looked at him with eyes quite human; that something shone brightly, and moved to and fro in the dome above the sleeper; that the crowd of terrible dreams, moving off for an instant, left uncovered a human face, with a hand resting against the mouth, and in

The Man in the Iron Mask

an attitude of deep and absorbed meditation. And strange enough, too, this man bore so wonderful a resemblance to the king himself, that Louis fancied he was looking at his own face reflected in a mirror; only, that face was saddened by a feeling of the profoundest pity. Then it seemed to him as if the dome gradually retired, escaping from his gaze, and that the figures and attributes painted by Lebrun became darker and darker as the distance became more and more remote. A gentle, easy movement, as regular as that by which a vessel plunges beneath the waves, had succeeded to the immovableness of the bed. Doubtless the king was dreaming; and in this dream the crown of gold which fastened the curtains together seemed to recede from his vision, just as the dome, to which it remained suspended, had done; so that the winged genius which with both its hands supported the crown seemed, though vainly so, to call upon the king, who was fast disappearing from it. The bed still sank. Louis, with his eyes open, could not resist the deception of this cruel hallucination. At last, as the light of the royal chamber faded away into darkness and gloom, something cold, gloomy, and inexplicable seemed to infect the air. No paintings, nor gold, nor velvet hangings were visible any longer,—nothing but walls of a dull grey colour, which the increasing gloom made darker every moment. And yet the bed still continued to descend; and after a minute, which seemed in its duration almost an age to the king, it reached a stratum of air black and still as death, and then it stopped. The king could no longer see the light in his room, except as from the bottom of a well we can see the light of day. "I am under the influence of a terrible dream," he thought. "It is time to arouse myself. Come, let us wake up!"

Every one has experienced what the above remark conveys; there is no one who in the midst of a suffocating nightmare has not said to himself, by the help of that light which still burns in the brain when every human light is extinguished, "It is nothing but a dream, after all." This was precisely what Louis XIV. said to himself. But when he said, "Let us wake up," he perceived that not only was he already awake, but still more that he had his eyes open also. He then looked around him. On his right hand and on his left two armed men stood silently, each wrapped in a huge cloak, and the face covered with a mask; one of them held a small lamp in his hand, whose glimmering light revealed the saddest picture a king could look upon.

Louis said to himself that his dream still lasted, and that all he had to do to cause it to disappear was to move his arms or to say something aloud. He darted from his bed, and found himself upon the damp ground. Then, addressing himself to the man who held the lamp in his hand, he said, "What is this, Monsieur, and what is the meaning of this jest?"—"It is no jest," replied, in a deep voice, the masked figure that held the lantern.

"Do you belong to M. Fouquet?" inquired the king, greatly astonished at his situation.—"It matters very little to whom we belong," said the phantom. "We are your masters; that is sufficient." The king, more impatient than intimidated, turned to the other masked figure. "If this is a comedy," he said, "you will tell M. Fouquet that I find it unseemly, and that I desire it should cease."

The second masked person to whom the king had addressed himself was a man of huge stature and vast circumference. He held himself erect and motionless as a block of marble. "Well," added the king, stamping his foot, "you do not answer!"—"We do not answer you, my good Monsieur," said the giant, in a stentorian voice, "because there is nothing to answer, except that you are the chief *fâcheux*, and that M. Coquelin de Volière forgot to include you in the number of his."

"At least, tell me what you want!" exclaimed Louis, folding his arms with a passionate gesture.—"You will know by and by," replied the man who held the lamp.—"In the meantime tell me where I am."—"Look!"

Louis looked all round him; but by the light of the lamp which the masked figure raised for the purpose, he could perceive nothing but the damp walls, which glistened here and there with the slimy traces of the snail. "Oh! oh! a dungeon," said the king.—"No, a subterranean passage."—"Which leads—"—"Will you be good enough to follow us?"—"I shall not stir from hence!" cried the king.

"If you are obstinate, my dear young friend," replied the taller and stouter of the two, "I will lift you up in my arms, will roll you up in a cloak, and if you are stifled there, why, so much the worse for you!" and as he said this he disengaged from beneath the cloak with which he had threatened the king a hand of which Milo of Crotona

The Man in the Iron Mask

would have envied him the possession on the day when he had that unhappy idea of rending his last oak.

The king dreaded violence; for he could well believe that the two men into whose power he had fallen had not gone so far with any idea of drawing back, and that they would consequently be ready to proceed to extremities if necessary. He shook his head, and said: "It seems I have fallen into the hands of a couple of assassins. Move on, then!"

Neither of the men answered a word to this remark. The one who carried the lantern walked first, the king followed him, while the second masked figure closed the procession. In this manner they passed along a winding gallery of some length, with as many staircases leading out of it as are to be found in the mysterious and gloomy palace of Ann Radcliffe. All these windings, throughout which the king heard the sound of falling water over his head, ended at last in a long corridor closed by an iron door. The figure with the lamp opened the door with one of the keys he wore suspended at his girdle, where during the whole of the time the king had heard them rattle. As soon as the door was opened and admitted the air, Louis recognised the balmy odours which the trees exhale after a hot summer's day. He paused hesitatingly for a moment or two; but his huge companion who followed him thrust him out of the subterranean passage.

"Another blow!" said the king, turning towards the one who had just had the audacity to touch his sovereign; "what do you intend to do with the King of France?"—"Try to forget that word," replied the man with the lamp, in a tone which as little admitted of reply as one of the famous decrees of Minos.—"You deserve to be broken on the wheel for the word you have just made use of," said the giant, as he extinguished the lamp his companion handed to him; "but the king is too kindhearted."

Louis, at that threat, made so sudden a movement that it seemed as if he meditated flight; but the giant's hand was placed on his shoulder, and fixed him motionless where he stood. "But tell me, at least, where we are going," said the king.—"Come!" replied the former of the two men, with a kind of respect in his manner, and leading his prisoner towards a carriage which seemed to be in waiting.

The carriage was completely concealed amid the trees. Two horses, with their feet fettered, were fastened by a halter to the

126

lower branches of a large oak. "Get in," said the same man, opening the carriage door and letting down the step. The king obeyed, seated himself at the back of the carriage, the padded door of which was shut and locked immediately upon him and his guide. As for the giant, he cut the fastenings by which the horses were bound, harnessed them himself, and mounted on the box of the carriage, which was unoccupied. The carriage set off immediately at a quick trot, turned into the road to Paris, and in the forest of Sénart found a relay of horses fastened to the trees in the same manner in which the first horses had been, and without a postilion. The man on the box changed the horses, and continued to follow the road towards Paris with the same rapidity, and entered the city about three o'clock in the morning. The carriage proceeded along the Faubourg St. Antoine, and after having called out to the sentinel, "By the king's order!" the driver conducted the horses into the circular enclosure of the Bastille, looking out upon the courtyard called La Cour du Gouvernement. There the horses drew up, reeking with sweat, at the flight of steps, and a sergeant of the guard ran forward.

"Go and wake the governor!" said the coachman, in a voice of thunder. With the exception of this voice, which might have been heard at the entrance of the Faubourg St. Antoine, everything remained as calm in the carriage as in the prison. Ten minutes afterwards, M. de Baisemeaux appeared in his dressing-gown on the threshold of the door. "What is the matter now?" he asked; "and whom have you brought me there?"

The man with the lantern opened the carriage door, and said two or three words to the one who acted as driver, who immediately got down from his seat, took up a short musket which he kept under his feet, and placed its muzzle on the prisoner's chest. "Fire at once if he speaks!" added, aloud, the man who alighted from the carriage. —"Very good!" replied his companion, without any other remark.

With this recommendation, the person who had accompanied the king in the carriage ascended the flight of steps, at the top of which the governor was awaiting him. "M. d'Herblay!" said the latter. "Hush!" said Aramis; "let us go into your room."—"Good heavens! what brings you here at this hour?"—"A mistake, my dear M. de Baisemeaux," Aramis replied quietly. "It appears that you were quite right the other day."—"What about?" inquired the governor.—"About the order of release, my dear friend."

The Man in the Iron Mask

"Tell me what you mean, Monsieur,—no, Monseigneur," said the governor, almost suffocated by surprise and terror.—"It is a very simple affair. You remember, dear M. de Baisemeaux, that an order of release was sent to you?"—"Yes, for Marchiali."—"Very good! we both thought that it was for Marchiali?"—"Certainly. You will recollect, however, that I did not believe it; that I was unwilling; that you compelled me."

"Oh, Baisemeaux, my good fellow, what a word to make use of!—advised, that was all."—"Advised,—yes, advised me to give him up to you; and that you carried him off with you in your carriage."— "Well, my dear M. de Baisemeaux, it was a mistake. It was discovered at the Ministry; so that I now bring you an order from the king to set at liberty Seldon,—that poor devil of a Scotchman, you know."

"Seldon! are you sure this time?"—"Well, read it yourself," added Aramis, handing him the order.—"Why," said Baisemeaux, "this order is the very same that has already passed through my hands." —"Indeed?"—"It is the very one I assured you I saw the other evening. *Parbleau!* I recognise it by the blot of ink."

"I do not know whether it is that; but, at any rate, it is the one I bring you."—"But, then, about the other?"—"What other?"— "Marchiali?"—"I have him here with me."

"But that is not enough for me. I require a new order to take him back again."—"Don't talk such nonsense, my dear Baisemeaux; you talk like a child! Where is the order you received respecting Marchiali?" Baisemeaux ran to his iron chest and took it out. Aramis seized hold of it, coolly tore it in four pieces, held them to the lamp, and burned them. "Good heavens! what are you doing?" exclaimed Baisemeaux, in an extremity of terror.

"Look at your position a little, my dear governor," said Aramis, with his imperturbable self-possession, "and you will see that it is very simple. You no longer possess any order justifying Marchiali's release."—"I am a lost man!"—"Far from it, my good fellow, since I have brought Marchiali back to you, and it is just the same as if he had never left."—"Ah!" said the governor, completely overcome by terror.

"Plain enough, you see; and you will go and shut him up immediately."—"I should think so, indeed."—"And you will hand over to me this Seldon, whose liberation is authorised by this order. In

128

this way you square your conduct; do you understand?"—"I—I—"
—"You do understand, I see," said Aramis. "Very good!"

Baisemeaux clasped his hands together. "But why, at all events,
after having taken Marchiali away from me, do you bring him back
again?" cried the unhappy governor, in a paroxysm of terror and
completely dumfounded.

"For a friend such as you are," said Aramis, "for so devoted a
servant, I have no secrets;" and he put his mouth close to Baisemeaux's ear, and he said in a low tone of voice, "you know the resemblance between that unfortunate fellow and—"—"And the king?
—yes."—"Very good; the very first use that Marchiali made of his
liberty was to pretend— Can you guess what?"—"How is it likely
I should guess?"—"To pretend that he was the King of France."—
"Oh, the wretch!" cried Baisemeaux.

"To dress himself up in clothes like those of the king, and attempt
to play the rôle of usurper."—"Gracious heavens!"—"That is the
reason why I have brought him back again, my dear friend. He is
mad, and lets every one see how mad he is."

"What is to be done, then?"—"That is very simple; let no one
hold any communication with him. You understand that when his
peculiar style of madness came to the king's ears, the king, who had
pitied his terrible affliction, and saw how his kindness of heart had
been repaid by such black ingratitude, became perfectly furious; so
that now,—and remember this very distinctly, dear M. de Baisemeaux, for it concerns you most closely,—so that there is now, I repeat, sentence of death pronounced against all those who may allow
him to communicate with any one else save me or the king himself.
You understand, Baisemeaux,—sentence of death!"—"Do I understand? *Morbleu!*"

"And now go down and conduct this poor devil back to his dungeon again, unless you prefer he should come up here."—"What
would be the good of that?"—"It would be better, perhaps, to enter
his name in the prison-book at once!"—"*Pardieu!*"—"Well, then,
have him up!"

Baisemeaux ordered the drums to be beaten and the bell to be
rung, as a warning to every one to retire in order to avoid meeting
a mysterious prisoner. Then, when the passages were free, he went
to take the prisoner from the carriage, at whose breast Porthos,
faithful to the directions which had been given him, still kept his

The Man in the Iron Mask

musket levelled. "Ah! is that you, miserable wretch?" cried the governor, as soon as he perceived the king. "Very good, very good!" and immediately, making the king get out of the carriage, he led him, still accompanied by Porthos, who had not taken off his mask, and Aramis, who again resumed his, up the stairs, to the second Bertaudière, and opened the door of the room in which Philippe for six long years had bemoaned his existence. The king entered the cell without pronouncing a single word; he was pale and haggard. Baisemeaux shut the door upon him, turned the key twice in the lock, and then returned to Aramis. "It is quite true," he said in a low tone, "that he has a rather strong resemblance to the king, but still less so than you said."—"So that," said Aramis, "you would not have been deceived by the substitution of the one for the other."—"What a question!"

"You are a most valuable fellow, Baisemeaux," said Aramis; "and now, set Seldon free!"—"Oh, yes; I was going to forget that. I will go and give orders at once."—"Bah! to-morrow will be time enough."—"To-morrow!—oh, no! This very minute!"

"Well, go off to your affairs! I shall go away to mine. But it is quite understood, is it not?"—"What is 'quite understood'?"—"That no one is to enter the prisoner's cell, except with an order from the king,—an order which I will myself bring."—"That is understood. Adieu, Monseigneur!"

Aramis returned to his companion. "Now, Porthos, my good fellow, back again to Vaux, and as fast as possible!"—"A man is light when he has faithfully served his king, and in serving him saved his country," said Porthos. "The horses will have nothing to draw. Let us be off!" and the carriage, lightened of a prisoner who in fact seemed to Aramis very heavy, passed across the drawbridge of the Bastille, which was raised again immediately behind it.

CHAPTER XIX

A NIGHT IN THE BASTILLE

SUFFERING in human life is proportioned to human strength. We will not pretend to say that God always apportions to a man's capability of endurance the anguish he permits him to suffer; such, indeed, would not be exact, since God permits the existence of death, which is sometimes the only refuge open to those who are too closely pressed,—too bitterly afflicted, so far as the body is concerned. Suffering is proportioned to strength in this sense,—that the weak suffer more, where the trial is the same, than the strong. And what are the elementary principles which compose human strength? Are they not—more than anything else—exercise, habit, experience? We shall not even take the trouble to demonstrate that; it is an axiom in morals as in physics.

When the young king, stupefied, crushed, found himself led to a cell in the Bastille, he fancied at first that death is like sleep, and has its dreams; that the bed had broken through the flooring of his room at Vaux; that death had resulted; and that, still carrying out his dream, Louis XIV., now dead, was dreaming of those horrors, impossible to realise in life, which are termed dethronement, imprisonment, and degradation of a king all-powerful but yesterday. To be a spectator, as palpable phantom, of his own wretched suffering; to float in an incomprehensible mystery between resemblance and reality; to hear everything, to see everything, without confusing the details of that agony,—"was it not," said the king to himself, "a torture the more terrible since it might be eternal?"

"Is this what is termed eternity,—hell?" Louis murmured at the moment the door closed upon him, shut by Baisemeaux himself. He did not even look around him; and in that chamber, leaning with his back against the wall, he allowed himself to be carried away by the terrible supposition that he was already dead, as he closed his eyes in order to avoid looking upon something even worse. "How can I have died?" he said to himself, almost insensible. "Could that bed have been let down by some artificial means? But, no! I do not remember to have received any contusion or any shock. Would they not rather have poisoned me at one my meals, or with the fumes of wax, as they did my ancestress Jeanne d'Albret?" Suddenly the chill of the dungeon seemed to fall like a cloak upon Louis's shoulders. "I have seen," he said, "my father lying dead upon his funereal couch, in his regal robes. That pale face, so calm and worn; those hands, once so skilful, lying nerveless by his side; those limbs stiffened by the icy grasp of death,—nothing there betokened a sleep disturbed by dreams. And yet what dreams God might have sent to him,—to him whom so many others had preceded, hurried away by him into eternal death! No, that king was still the king; he was enthroned still upon that funereal couch, as upon a velvet arm-chair; he had not abdicated aught of his majesty. God, who had not punished him, cannot punish me, who have done nothing."

A strange sound attracted the young man's attention. He looked round him, and saw on the mantel-shelf, just below an enormous crucifix coarsely painted in fresco on the wall, a rat of enormous size engaged in nibbling a piece of dry bread, but fixing all the time an intelligent and inquiring look upon the new occupant of the cell. The king could not resist a sudden impulse of fear and disgust. He moved back towards the door, uttering a loud cry; and as if he but needed this cry, which escaped from his breast almost unconsciously, to recognise himself, Louis knew that he was alive and in full possession of his natural senses. "A prisoner!" he cried. "I—I a prisoner!" He looked round him for a bell to summon some one to him. "There are no bells in the Bastille," he said, "and it is in the Bastille I am imprisoned. In what way can I have been made a prisoner? It is, of course, a conspiracy of M. Fouquet. I have been drawn into a snare at Vaux. M. Fouquet cannot be acting alone in this affair. His agent,—that voice I but just now heard was M. d'Herblay's; I recognised it. Colbert was right, then. But what is Fouquet's object? To reign in my place and stead? Impossible! Yet, who knows?" thought the king, relapsing into gloom. "Perhaps my brother the Duc d'Orléans is doing against me what my uncle, all through his life, wished to do against my father. But the queen? —My mother too? And La Vallière? Oh! La Vallière,—she will have been abandoned to Madame. Dear child!—yes, it is so; they have shut her up, as they have me. We are separated for ever!" and at this idea of separation the lover burst into tears, with sobs and groans.

"There is a governor in this place," the king continued, in a fury

A Night in the Bastille

of passion. "I will speak to him; I will summon him." He called; but no voice replied to his. He seized his chair, and hurled it against the massive oaken door. The wood resounded against the door, and awakened many a mournful echo in the profound depths of the staircase; but no one responded.

This was for the king a fresh proof of the slight regard in which he was held in the Bastille. Therefore, when his first fit of anger had passed away, having noticed a barred window, through which there passed a stream of light, lozenge-shaped, which must be the luminous dawn, Louis began to call out, at first gently, then louder and louder still; but no one replied to him. Twenty other attempts which he made, one after another, obtained no better success. His blood began to boil within him, and mount to his head. His nature was such that, accustomed to command, he trembled at the idea of disobedience. By degrees his anger increased. The prisoner broke the chair, which was too heavy for him to lift, and made use of it as a battering-ram to strike against the door. He struck with such force and rapidity that the perspiration soon began to pour down his face. The sound became tremendous and continuous; stifled cries replied in different directions.

This sound produced a strange effect upon the king; he paused to listen to it. It was the voices of the prisoners,—formerly his victims, now his companions. The voices ascended like vapours through the thick ceilings and the massive walls; they complained against the author of this noise, as doubtless their sighs and tears accused, in whispered tones, the author of their captivity. After having deprived so many persons of their liberty, the king had come among them to rob them of their sleep. This idea almost drove him mad; it redoubled his strength, or rather his will, bent upon obtaining some information or some result. With a portion of the broken chair he recommenced the noise. At the end of an hour Louis heard something in the corridor behind the door of his cell; and a violent blow which was returned upon the door itself made him cease his own.

"Ah, there! are you mad?" said a rude, brutal voice. "What is the matter with you this morning?"—"This morning!" thought the king, surprised; but he said aloud, politely, "Monsieur, are you the governor of the Bastille?"—"My good fellow, your head is out of sorts," replied the voice; "but that is no reason why you should make such a terrible disturbance. Be quiet, *mordieu!*"

"Are you the governor?" the king inquired again. He heard a door on the corridor close; the jailer had left without condescending to reply. When the king had assured himself of his departure, his fury knew no longer any bounds. As agile as a tiger, he leaped from the table to the window, and shook the iron bars. He broke a pane of glass, the pieces of which fell clanking into the courtyard below. He shouted with increasing hoarseness, "The governor, the governor!" This excess lasted fully an hour, during which time he was in a burning fever. With his hair in disorder and matted on his forehead, his dress torn and whitened, his linen in shreds, the king never rested until his strength was utterly exhausted; and it was not until then that he clearly understood the pitiless thickness of the walls, the impenetrable nature of the cement, invincible to all other influence save that of time, and that he possessed no other weapon but despair. He leaned his forehead against the door, and let the feverish throbbings of his heart calm by degrees; an additional pulsation would have made it burst.

"A moment will come when the food which is given to the prisoners will be brought to me. I shall then see some one; I shall speak to him, and get an answer." Then the king tried to remember at what hour the first repast of the prisoners was served in the Bastille; he was ignorant even of this detail. The feeling of remorse at this remembrance smote him like a keen thrust of a dagger,—that he should have lived for five-and-twenty years a king, and in the enjoyment of every happiness, without having bestowed a moment's thought on the misery of those who had been unjustly deprived of their liberty. The king blushed from shame. He felt that Heaven, in permitting this fearful humiliation, did no more than render to the man the same torture which was inflicted by that man upon so many others. Nothing could be more efficacious toward awakening religious feeling in that soul prostrated by the sense of suffering. But Louis dared not even kneel in prayer to God to entreat him to terminate his bitter trial.

"Heaven is right," he said; "Heaven acts wisely. It would be cowardly to pray to Heaven for that which I have so often refused to my own fellow-creatures." He had reached this stage of his reflections,—that is, of his agony of mind,—when the same noise was

A Night in the Bastille

again heard behind his door, followed this time by the sound of the key in the lock, and of the bolts withdrawn from their staples. The king bounded forward to be nearer to the person who was about to enter; but suddenly reflecting that it was a movement unworthy of a sovereign, he paused, assumed a noble and calm expression, which for him was easy enough, and waited with his back turned towards the window, in order to some extent to conceal his agitation from the eyes of the person who was about entering. It was only a jailer with a basket of provisions. The king looked at the man with anxiety, and waited for him to speak.

"Ah!" said the latter, "you have broken your chair, I should say! Why, you must have become quite mad."—"Monsieur," said the king, "be careful what you say; it will be a very serious affair for you."

The jailer placed the basket on the table, and looked at his prisoner steadily. "What do you say?" he said with surprise.—"Desire the governor to come to me," added the king, with dignity.—"Come, my boy," said the turnkey, "you have always been very quiet and reasonable; but you are getting vicious, it seems, and I wish to give you warning. You have broken your chair, and made a great disturbance; that is an offence punishable by imprisonment in one of the lower dungeons. Promise me not to begin over again, and I will not say a word about it to the governor."

"I wish to see the governor," replied the king, still controlling his passion.—"He will send you off to one of the dungeons, I tell you; so take care!"—"I insist upon it!—do you hear?"—"Ah! ah! your eyes are becoming wild again. Very good! I shall take away your knife."

The jailer did as he had said, closed the door and departed, leaving the king more astounded, more wretched and more alone than ever. In vain he began again to pound the door; in vain he threw the plates and dishes out of the window; not a sound was heard in answer. Two hours later he could not be recognised as a king, a gentleman, a man, a human being; he might rather be called a madman, tearing the door with his nails, trying to tear up the flooring of his cell, and uttering such wild and fearful cries that the old Bastille seemed to tremble to its very foundations for having revolted against its master. As for the governor, the jailer did not even think of disturbing him; the turnkeys and the sentinels had made their report, but what was the good of it? Were not these madmen common enough in the fortress, and were not the walls still stronger than they?

M. de Baisemeaux, thoroughly impressed with what Aramis had told him, and in perfect conformity with the king's order, hoped only that one thing might happen; namely, that the madman Marchiali might be mad enough to hang himself to the canopy of his bed or to one of the bars of the window. In fact, the prisoner was anything but a profitable investment for M. Baisemeaux, and became more annoying than agreeable to him. These complications of Seldon and Marchiali, these complications of deliverance and reincarceration, these complications of personal resemblance, would have found a very proper *dénouement*. Baisemeaux even thought he had remarked that D'Herblay himself would not be altogether dissatisfied with it. "And then, really," said Baisemeaux to his next in command, "an ordinary prisoner is already unhappy enough in being a prisoner; he suffers quite enough indeed to induce one to hope, in charity, that his death may not be far distant. With still greater reason, then, when the prisoner has gone mad, and may bite and make a disturbance in the Bastille,—why, in that case it is not simply an act of mere charity to wish him dead; it would be almost a commendable action quietly to put him out of his misery." And the good-natured governor thereupon sat down to his late breakfast.

CHAPTER XX

THE SHADOW OF FOUQUET

D'ARTAGNAN, still confused and oppressed by the conversation he had just had with the king, asked himself if he were really in possession of his senses; if the scene had occurred at Vaux; if he, D'Artagnan, were really the captain of the musketeers and Fouquet the owner of the château in which Louis XIV. was at that moment partaking of his hospitality. These reflections were not those of a drunken man, although everything was in prodigal profusion at Vaux, and the superintendent's wines had met with a distinguished reception at the *fête*.

The Shadow of Fouquet

The Gascon, however, was a man of calm self-possession; and when he touched his steel blade he was able to assume, figuratively, the coolness of that steel for his great occasions. "Well," he said, as he quitted the royal apartment, "I seem now to be mixed up historically with the destinies of the king and of the minister; it will be written that M. d'Artagnan, a younger son of a Gascon family, placed his hand on the shoulder of M. Nicholas Fouquet, the superintendent of the finances of France. My descendants, if I have any, will flatter themselves with the distinction which this arrest will confer, just as the members of the De Luynes family have done with regard to the estates of the poor Maréchal d'Ancre. But now the thing to be done is to execute the king's directions in a proper manner. It seems to me," added D'Artagnan to himself, "that if I am not a wretch, I shall let M. Fouquet know the purpose of the king in regard to him. Yet if I betray my master's secret, I shall be a false-hearted knave and a traitor,—a crime provided for and punishable by military laws, as proved by the fact that twenty times in the wars I have seen miserable fellows strung up for doing in little degree what my scruples counsel me to do on a larger scale. No, I think that a man of intelligence ought to get out of this difficulty with more skill than that."

D'Artagnan buried his head in his hands, tore his moustache in sheer vexation, and added: "For what reason is M. Fouquet disgraced? For three reasons: the first, because M. Colbert doesn't like him; the second, because he wished to fall in love with Mademoiselle de la Vallière; and, lastly, because the king likes M. Colbert and loves Mademoiselle de la Vallière. Oh, he is a lost man! Instead of going cold-bloodedly up to M. Fouquet and arresting him off-hand and shutting him up, I will try to conduct myself like a man who understands what good manners are. People will talk about it, of course; but they shall talk well of it, I am determined." And D'Artagnan, drawing by a gesture peculiar to himself his shoulder-belt over his shoulder, went straight off to Fouquet, who having taken leave of the ladies was preparing to sleep tranquilly after the triumphs of the day.

Fouquet had just retired to his room, still smiling, but more than half dead. He could listen to nothing more; he could hardly keep his eyes open; his bed seemed to possess a fascinating and irresistible attraction for him. Almost entirely alone, he was being as-

sisted by his *valet-de-chambre* to undress, when M. d'Artagnan
appeared at the entrance of the room.

"What! M. d'Artagnan?" said Fouquet, who had already taken
his right arm out of the sleeve of his doublet. "At your service,"
replied the musketeer.

"Come in, my dear M. d'Artagnan."—"Thank you."—"Have you
come to criticise the *fête?* You have an ingenious mind."—"By
no means."—"Are not your men looked after properly?"—"In every
way."—"You are not comfortably lodged, perhaps?"—"Nothing
could be better."

"In that case, I have to thank you for being so amiably disposed,
and I must not fail to express my obligations to you for all your
flattering kindness." These words were as much as to say, "My
dear D'Artagnan, pray go to bed, since you have a bed to lie down
on, and let me do the same."

D'Artagnan did not seem to understand. "Are you going to bed
already?" he said to the superintendent.—"Yes; have you anything
to say to me?"—"Nothing, Monsieur; nothing at all. You sleep in
this room, then?"—"Yes; as you see."

"Monsieur, you have given a most charming *fête* to the king."
—"Do you think so?"—"Oh, beautiful!"—"Is the king pleased?"
—"Enchanted!"—"Did he desire you to say as much to me?"—"He
would not choose so unworthy a messenger, Monseigneur."—"You
do not do yourself justice, M. d'Artagnan."

"Is that your bed there?"—"Yes! but why do you ask? Are
you not satisfied with your own?"—"May I speak frankly to you?"
—"Most assuredly."—"Well, then, I am not."

Fouquet started; and then replied, "Will you take my room, M.
d'Artagnan?"—"What! deprive you of it, Monseigneur? Never!"
—"What am I to do, then?"—"Allow me to share it with you."

Fouquet looked at the musketeer fixedly. "Ah! ah!" he said,
"you have just left the king?"—"I have, Monseigneur."—"And the
king wishes you to pass the night in my room?"—"Monseigneur—"
—"Very well, M. d'Artagnan, very well. You are master here."
—"I assure you, Monseigneur, that I do not wish to abuse—"

Fouquet turned to his valet, and said, "Leave us!" When the
man had left, he said to D'Artagnan, "You have something to say to
me?"—"I?"—"A man of your superior intelligence cannot have
come to talk with a man like myself, at such an hour as the present,

without grave motives."—"Do not interrogate me."—"On the con
trary, what do you want with me?"—"Nothing more than the pleasure of your society."

"Come into the garden, then," said the superintendent, suddenly,
"or into the park."—"No," replied the musketeer, hastily; "no."—
"Why?"—"The fresh air—"—"Come, admit at once that you arrest
me," said the superintendent to the captain.—"Never!" said the
latter.

"You intend to look after me, then?"—"Yes, Monseigneur, I do,
upon my honour."—"Upon your honour!—ah, that is quite another
thing! So I am to be arrested in my own house?"—"Do not say
such a thing."—"On the contrary, I will proclaim it aloud."—"If
you do so, I shall be compelled to persuade you to be silent."

"Very good! Violence towards me in my own house! Ah, that
is well done!"—"We do not seem to understand each other at all.
Stay a moment! There is a chess-board there; we will have a game,
if you have no objection."—"M. d'Artagnan, I am in disgrace,
then?"—"Not at all; but—"—"I am prohibited, I suppose, from
withdrawing from your sight."—"I do not understand a word you
are saying, Monseigneur; and if you wish me to withdraw, tell me
so."

"My dear M. d'Artagnan, your mode of action is enough to drive
me mad. I was almost sinking for want of sleep, but you have completely awakened me."—"I shall never forgive myself, I am sure;
and if you wish to reconcile me with myself, why, go to sleep in your
bed in my presence; I shall be delighted at it."—"I am under sur-
veillance, I see."—"I will leave the room, then."—"You are beyond
my comprehension."—"Good-night, Monseigneur," said D'Artagnan, as he pretended to withdraw.

Fouquet ran after him. "I will not lie down," he said. "Seriously,
and since you refuse to treat me as a man, and since you finesse with
me, I will try to set you at bay, as a hunter does a wild boar."—
"Bah!" cried D'Artagnan, pretending to smile.—"I shall order my
horses and set off for Paris," said Fouquet, sounding the heart of
the captain of the musketeers.—"If that be the case, Monseigneur,
it is very different."—"You will arrest me?"—"No; but I shall go
with you."

"That is quite sufficient, M. d'Artagnan," returned Fouquet, in a
cold tone of voice. "It is not idly that you have acquired your

reputation as a man of intelligence and full of resources; but with me that is quite superfluous. Let us two come to the point. Grant me a service. Why do you arrest me? What have I done?"—"Oh, I know nothing about what you may have done; but I do not arrest you—this evening."—"This evening!" said Fouquet, turning pale; "but to-morrow?"—"It is not to-morrow just yet, Monseigneur. Who can ever answer for the morrow?"

"Quick, quick, Captain! let me speak to M. d'Herblay."—"Alas! that is quite impossible, Monseigneur. I have strict orders to see that you hold no communication with any one."—"With M. d'Herblay, Captain,—with your friend!"—"Monseigneur, is M. d'Herblay the only person with whom you ought to be prevented from holding any communication?"

Fouquet coloured, and then assuming an air of resignation, said: "You are right, Monsieur; you have taught me a lesson that I ought not to have provoked. A fallen man cannot assert his right to anything, even to those whose fortunes he may have made; for a still greater reason he cannot claim anything from those to whom he may never have had the happiness of doing a service."—"Monseigneur!" —"It is true, M. d'Artagnan; you have always acted in the most admirable manner towards me,—in such a manner, indeed, as most becomes the man who is destined to arrest me. You, at least, have never asked me anything."

"Monseigneur," replied the Gascon, touched by his eloquent and noble tone of grief, "will you—I ask it as a favour—pledge me your word as a man of honour that you will not leave this room?"— "What is the use of it, dear M. d'Artagnan, since you keep watch and ward over me? Do you suppose that I should struggle against the most valiant sword in the kingdom?"—"It is not that at all, Monseigneur; but that I am going to look for M. d'Herblay, and consequently to leave you alone."

Fouquet uttered a cry of delight and surprise. "To look for M. d'Herblay, to leave me alone!" he exclaimed, clasping his hands together.—"Which is M. d'Herblay's room? The blue room, is it not?"—"Yes, my friend, yes."—"Your friend! thank you for that word, Monseigneur; you confer it upon me to-day, at least, even if you have never done so before."—"Ah, you have saved me!"

"It will take me a good ten minutes to go from hence to the blue room, and to return?" said D'Artagnan.—"Nearly so."—"And then to wake Aramis, who sleeps soundly when he sleeps at all, I put that down at another five minutes; making a total of fifteen minutes' absence. And now, Monseigneur, give me your word that you will not in any way attempt to make your escape, and that when I return I shall find you here again."—"I give it to you, Monsieur," replied Fouquet, with an expression of the warmest and deepest gratitude.

D'Artagnan disappeared. Fouquet looked at him as he quitted the room, waited with feverish impatience until the door was closed behind him, and as soon as it was shut, fled to his keys, opened two or three secret doors concealed in various articles of furniture in the room, looked vainly for certain papers, which doubtless he had left at St. Mandé, and which he seemed to regret not finding; then hurriedly seizing hold of letters, contracts, writings, he heaped them up into a pile, which he burned in the extremest haste upon the marble hearth of the fireplace, not even taking time to draw from the interior of it the vases and pots of flowers with which it was filled. As soon as he had finished, like a man who had just escaped an imminent danger, and whose strength abandons him as soon as the danger is past, he sank down, completely overcome, on a couch.

When D'Artagnan returned, he found Fouquet in the same position. The worthy musketeer had not the slightest doubt that Fouquet, having given his word, would not even think of failing to keep it; but he had thought it most likely that Fouquet would turn his (D'Artagnan's) absence to the best advantage in getting rid of all the papers, memorandums, and contracts which might possibly render his position, which was even now serious enough, still more dangerous. And so, lifting up his head like a dog who gains the scent, D'Artagnan perceived a certain odour resembling smoke, which he had fully expected to find in the atmosphere; and having found it, he made a movement of his head in token of satisfaction.

When D'Artagnan entered, Fouquet had, on his side, raised his head, and not one of D'Artagnan's movements had escaped him. The looks of the two men met, and they both saw that they had understood each other without exchanging a syllable. "Well!" asked Fouquet, the first to speak, "and M. d'Herblay?"—"Upon my word, Monseigneur," replied D'Artagnan, "M. d'Herblay must be desperately fond of walks by night, and composing verses by moonlight in the park of Vaux with some of your poets in all probability; for he is not in his room."

The Man in the Iron Mask

"What! not in his room?" cried Fouquet, whose last hope had thus escaped him; for without knowing in what way the Bishop of Vannes could assist him, he well knew that he could not expect assistance from any one else. "Or, indeed," continued D'Artagnan, "if he is in his own room, he has very good reasons for not answering."—"But surely you did not call him in such a manner that he could have heard you?"

"You can hardly suppose, Monseigneur, that having already exceeded my orders, which forbade my leaving you a single moment, —you can hardly suppose, I say, that I should have been mad enough to rouse the whole house and allow myself to be seen in the corridor of the Bishop of Vannes, in order that M. Colbert might state with positive certainty that I gave you time to burn your papers."—"My papers?"—"Of course; at least, that is what I should have done in your place. When any one opens a door for me, I always avail myself of it."—"Yes, yes, and I thank you; I have availed myself of it."

"And you have done right, *morbleu!* Every man has his own peculiar secrets, with which others have nothing to do. But let us return to Aramis, Monseigneur."—"Well, then, I tell you, you could not have called loudly enough, or he would have heard you."— "However softly any one may call Aramis, Monseigneur, he always hears when he has an interest in hearing. I repeat what I said before, —Aramis was not in his own room, or he had certain reasons for not recognising my voice, of which I am ignorant, and of which you even may be ignorant yourself, notwithstanding your liegeman is his greatness the Lord Bishop of Vannes."

Fouquet drew a deep sigh, rose from his seat, made three or four turns in his room, and finished by seating himself, with an expression of extreme dejection, upon his magnificent bed with velvet hangings and trimmed with the costliest lace.

D'Artagnan looked at Fouquet with feelings of the deepest and sincerest pity. Fouquet resumed his pensive attitude once more, and then, some moments after, said: "Where can M. d'Herblay be? I dare not ask you to send for him."—"You would not ask me, because I would not do it, M. Fouquet. People would learn it; and Aramis, who is not mixed up with the affair, might possibly be compromised and included in your disgrace."

"I will wait here till daylight," said Fouquet.—"Yes; that is

The Shadow of Fouquet

best."—"What shall we do when daylight comes?"—"I know nothing at all about it, Monseigneur."

"M. d'Artagnan, will you do me a favour?"—"Most willingly."— "You guard me, I remain; you are acting in the full discharge of your duty, I suppose?"—"Certainly."—"Very good, then; remain as close to me as my shadow, if you like. I prefer that shadow to any other."

D'Artagnan bowed. "But forget that you are M. d'Artagnan, captain of the musketeers; forget that I am M. Fouquet, superintendent of the finances, and let us talk about my affairs."—"*Peste!* a thorny subject that!"—"Truly?"—"Yes; but for your sake, M. Fouquet, I would do the impossible."

"Thank you. What did the king say to you?"—"Nothing."— "Ah! is that the way you talk?"—"The deuce!"—"What do you think of my situation?"—"Nothing."—"However, unless you have some ill-feeling against me—"—"Your position is a difficult one."— "In what respect?"—"Because you are under your own roof."

"However difficult it may be, yet I understand it very well."— "Do you suppose that with any one else but yourself I should have shown so much frankness?"—"What! so much frankness, do you say,—you who refuse to tell me the slightest thing?"—"At all events, then, so much ceremony and so much consideration."—"Ah! I admit that."

"One moment, Monseigneur! Let me tell you how I should have behaved towards any one but yourself. I should have arrived at your door just as your friends had left you, or if they had not yet gone I should have waited until they were leaving, and should then have caught them one after the other like rabbits; I should have locked them up quietly; I should have stolen softly along the carpet of your corridor, and with one hand upon you, before you suspected the slightest thing about it, I should have kept you safely until my master's breakfast in the morning. In this way I should have avoided all publicity, all disturbance, all opposition; but there would also have been no warning for M. Fouquet, no consideration for his feelings, none of those delicate concessions which are shown by persons who are essentially courteous in their natures whenever the decisive moment may arrive. Are you satisfied with that plan?"—"It makes me shudder."

"I thought you would not like it. It would have been very dis-

143

agreeable had I chosen to appear to-morrow without notice and to ask you for your sword."—"Oh, Monsieur, I should have died from shame and anger."

"Your gratitude is too eloquently expressed. I have not done enough to deserve it, I assure you."—"Most certainly, Monsieur, you will never get me to believe that."—"Well, then, Monseigneur, if you are satisfied with what I have done, and have somewhat recovered from the shock which I prepared you for as much as I could, let us allow the few hours that remain to pass away undisturbed. You are harassed, and require to arrange your thoughts; I beg you, therefore, to go to sleep, or pretend to go to sleep, either on your bed or in your bed. I shall sleep in this arm-chair; and when I fall asleep my rest is so sound that a cannon could not wake me."

Fouquet smiled.

"I except, however," continued the musketeer, "the case where one opens a door, whether secret or visible, whether to go out or to come in. Oh, for that my ear is sensitive to the last degree! Any creaking noise makes me start,—it is a matter of natural antipathy. Move about as much as you like; walk up and down in any part of the room; write, efface, destroy, burn: but do not touch either the key or the handle of the door; for I should start up in a moment, and that would shake my nerves terribly."

"M. d'Artagnan," said Fouquet, "you are certainly the most witty and the most courteous man I ever met; and you will leave me only one regret,—that of having made your acquaintance so late." D'Artagnan drew a deep sigh, which seemed to say, "Alas! you have perhaps made it too soon." He then settled himself in his arm-chair; while Fouquet, half lying on his bed and leaning on his arm, meditated upon his adventure. In this way both of them, leaving the candles burning, awaited the first dawn of the day; and when Fouquet happened to sigh too loudly, D'Artagnan only snored the louder. Not a single visit, not even from Aramis, disturbed their quietude; not a sound, even, was heard throughout the vast palace. Outside, the guards of honour and the patrols of the musketeers paced up and down; and the sound of their feet could be heard on the gravel walks. It was an additional soporific for the sleepers; while the murmuring of the wind through the trees and the unceasing music of the fountains still went on uninterruptedly, without being disturbed at the slight noises and trifling affairs of which the life and death of man consist.

CHAPTER XXI

THE MORNING

IN CONTRAST with the sad and terrible destiny of the king imprisoned in the Bastille, and tearing, in sheer despair, the bolts and bars of his dungeon, the rhetoric of the chroniclers of old would not fail to present the antithesis of Philippe lying asleep beneath the royal canopy.

The young prince descended from Aramis's room in the same way the king had descended from the apartment dedicated to Morpheus. The dome gradually and slowly sank down under Aramis's pressure, and Philippe stood beside the royal bed, which had ascended again, after having deposited its prisoner in the secret depths of the subterranean passage. Alone, in the presence of all the luxury which surrounded him; alone, in the presence of his power; alone, with the part he was about to be forced to act, Philippe's soul for the first time opened to the thousand varied emotions which are the vital throbs of a royal heart. But he could not help changing colour when he looked upon the empty bed, still tumbled by his brother's body. This mute accomplice had returned, after having served in the consummation of the enterprise; it returned with the traces of the crime; it spoke to the guilty author of that crime, with the frank and unreserved language which an accomplice never fears to use towards his companion in guilt,—it spoke the truth. Philippe bent over the bed, and perceived a pocket-handkerchief lying on it which was still damp with the cold sweat that had poured from Louis XIV.'s face. This sweat-bestained handkerchief terrified Philippe, as the blood of Abel terrified Cain.

"I am now face to face with my destiny," said Philippe, with his eyes on fire and his face livid. "Will it be more terrifying than my captivity has been sad and gloomy? Forced to pursue at every moment the usurpations of thought, shall I never cease to listen to the scruples of my heart? Yes; the king has lain on this bed. It is indeed his head that has left its impression on this pillow, his bitter tears that have stained this handkerchief; and yet I hesitate to throw myself on the bed, or to press in my hand the handkerchief which is embroidered with my brother's arms. Away with this weakness! Let me imitate M. d'Herblay, who asserts that a man's action should be always one degree above his thought; let me imitate M. d'Herblay, whose thoughts are of and for himself alone, who regards himself as a man of honour, so long as he injures or betrays his enemies only. I, I alone should have occupied this bed, if Louis XIV. had not, owing to my mother's criminal abandonment of me, stood in my way; and this handkerchief, embroidered with the arms of France, would, in right and justice, belong to me alone, if, as M. d'Herblay observes, I had been left in my place in the royal cradle! Philippe, son of France, take your place on that bed; Philippe, sole King of France, resume the blazonry which is yours! Philippe, sole heir presumptive to Louis XIII., your father, show yourself without pity or mercy for the usurper who at this moment has no remorse for all that you have suffered!" With these words, Philippe, notwithstanding an instinctive repugnance of feeling, and in spite of the shudder of terror which mastered his will, threw himself on the royal bed, and forced his muscles to press the still warm place where Louis XIV. had lain, while he buried his burning face in the handkerchief still moistened by his brother's tears. With his head thrown back and buried in the soft down of his pillow, Philippe perceived above him the crown of France, held, as we have stated, by the angel with golden wings.

Imagine, then, the royal intruder, his eyes gloomy, his body trembling. He is like a tiger led out of his way by a night of storm, who comes through the reeds by way of a ravine unknown to him, to lie down in the cave of an absent lion. The feline odour has attracted him,—that warm, moist atmosphere of his ordinary habitation. He has found a bed of dry herbs, and bones pulverised and pasty like marrow. He arrives; he turns about his flaming eyes, piercing the gloom; he shakes his streaming limbs and his body, covered with mire, and lies down heavily, his large nose resting on his enormous paws,—ready to sleep, but ready also to fight. From time to time the lightning blazing in the recesses of the cave, the noise of clashing branches, the sound of falling stones, the vague apprehension of danger, draw him from the lethargy occasioned by fatigue.

The Morning

Philippe listened attentively to every sound, his heart almost stifled by all his fears; but confident in his own strength, which was increased by the force of an overpowering resolute determination, he waited until some decisive circumstance should permit him to judge for himself. He hoped that some great danger would show him the way, like those phosphoric lights of the tempest which show the sailors the height of the waves against which they have to struggle. But nothing happened. Silence, the mortal enemy of restless hearts, the mortal enemy of ambitious minds, shrouded in the thickness of its gloom during the remainder of the night the future King of France, who lay there sheltered beneath his stolen crown. Towards the morning a shadow, rather than a body, glided into the royal chamber; Philippe expected his approach, and neither expressed nor exhibited any surprise.

"Well, M. d'Herblay?" he said.—"Well, Sire, all is done."—"How?"—"Exactly as we expected."—"Did he resist?"—"Terribly! tears and entreaties."—"And then?"—"Then stupor."—"But at last?"—"Oh, at last a complete victory, and absolute silence."

"Did the governor of the Bastille suspect anything?"—"Nothing."—"The resemblance, however—"—"That was the cause of the success."—"But the prisoner cannot fail to explain himself. Think well of that. I have myself been able to do that,—I, who had to contend with a power much better established than is mine."

"I have already provided for everything. In a few days, sooner perhaps, we will take the captive out of his prison, and will send him out of the country to a place of exile so remote—"—"People can return from exile, M. d'Herblay."—"To a place of exile so distant, I was going to say, that human strength and the duration of human life would not be enough for his return." And once more a cold look of intelligence passed between Aramis and the young king.

"And M. du Vallon?" asked Philippe, in order to change the conversation.—"He will be presented to you to-day, and confidentially will congratulate you on your escape from the danger to which that usurper has exposed you."—"What is to be done with him?"—"With M. du Vallon?"—"A dukedom, I suppose."—"Yes, a dukedom," replied Aramis, smiling in a significant manner.

"Why do you laugh, M. d'Herblay?"—"I laugh at the extreme caution of your Majesty."—"Cautious! why so?"—"Your Majesty is doubtless afraid that that poor Porthos may probably become a troublesome witness; and you wish to get rid of him."—"What! in making him a duke?"—"Certainly; you would assuredly kill him, for he would die from joy, and the secret would die with him."— "Good heavens!"—"Yes," said Aramis, phlegmatically; "I should lose a very good friend."

At this moment, and in the middle of this idle conversation, under the light tone of which the two conspirators concealed their joy and pride at their mutual success, Aramis heard something which made him prick up his ears.

"What is that?" said Philippe.—"The dawn, Sire."—"Well?"— "Well, before you retired to bed last night, you probably decided to do something this morning at the break of day."—"Yes; I told my captain of the musketeers," replied the young man, hurriedly, "that I should expect him."

"If you told him that, he will certainly be here, for he is a most punctual man."—"I hear a step in the vestibule."—"It must be he." —"Come, let us begin the attack," said the young king, resolutely.

"Be cautious, for heaven's sake; to begin the attack, and with D'Artagnan, would be madness. D'Artagnan knows nothing; he has seen nothing. He is a hundred leagues from suspecting our mystery; but if he comes into this room the first this morning, he will be sure to detect that something has taken place which he will think his business to occupy himself about. Before we allow D'Artagnan to penetrate into this room, we must air the room thoroughly, or introduce so many people into it that the keenest scent in the whole kingdom may be deceived by the traces of twenty different persons."

"But how can I send him away, since I have given him a rendezvous?" observed the prince, impatient to measure swords with so redoubtable an antagonist.—"I will take care of that," replied the bishop; "and in order to begin, I am going to strike a blow which will completely stupefy our man."—"He too is striking a blow, for I hear him at the door," added the prince, hurriedly. And, in fact, a knock at the door was heard at that moment. Aramis was not mistaken; for it was indeed D'Artagnan who adopted that mode of announcing himself.

The door opened. The captain thought that it was the king who had just opened it himself; and this supposition was not altogether inadmissible, considering the state of agitation in which he had left

The Morning

Louis XIV. on the previous evening. But instead of his royal master, whom he was on the point of saluting with the greatest respect, he perceived the long, calm features of Aramis. So extreme was his surprise that he could hardly refrain from uttering a loud exclamation. "Aramis!" he said.—"Good-morning, dear D'Artagnan," replied the prelate, coldly.—"You here?" stammered out the musketeer.

"His Majesty desires you to report that he is still sleeping, after having been greatly fatigued during the whole night."—"Ah!" said D'Artagnan, who could not understand how the Bishop of Vannes, who had been so indifferent a favourite the previous evening, had become in half-a-dozen hours the largest mushroom of fortune which had ever sprung up in a sovereign's bedroom. In fact, to transmit the orders of the king even to the mere threshold of that monarch's room, to serve as an intermediary of Louis XIV. so as to be able to give a single order in his name at a couple of paces from him, he must be greater than Richelieu had ever been to Louis XIII. D'Artagnan's expressive eye, his half-opened lips, his curling moustache, said as much, indeed, in the plainest language to the chief favourite, who remained calm and unmoved. "Moreover," continued the bishop, "you will be good enough, Monsieur the Captain of the Musketeers, to allow those only to pass into the king's room this morning who have special permission. His Majesty does not wish to be disturbed just yet."

"But," objected D'Artagnan, on the point of refusing to obey this order, and particularly of giving unrestrained passage to the suspicions which the king's silence had aroused,—"but, Monsieur the Bishop, his Majesty gave me a rendezvous for this morning."—"Later, later," said the king's voice from the bottom of the alcove,—a voice which made a cold shudder pass through the musketeer's veins. He bowed, amazed, confused, and stupefied by the smile with which Aramis seemed to overwhelm him as soon as those words had been pronounced.

"And then," continued the bishop, "as an answer to what you were coming to ask the king, my dear D'Artagnan, here is an order of his Majesty, which you will be good enough to attend to forthwith, for it concerns M. Fouquet." D'Artagnan took the order which was held out to him. "To be set at liberty!" he murmured. "Ah!"

149

"I am going with you," said the bishop.—"Where to?"—"To M. Fouquet; I wish to be a witness of his delight."—"Ah, Aramis, how you puzzled me just now!" said D'Artagnan, again.—"But you understand now, I suppose?"—"Of course I understand," he said aloud; but then he added in a low tone to himself, almost hissing the words through his teeth, "No, no! I do not understand yet. But it is all the same,—here is the order;" and then he added, "I will lead the way, Monseigneur," and he conducted Aramis to Fouquet's apartments.

CHAPTER XXII

THE KING'S FRIEND

FOUQUET was waiting with anxiety. When he saw D'Artagnan return, and when he perceived the Bishop of Vannes behind him, he could hardly restrain his delight; it was fully equal to his previous uneasiness. The mere sight of Aramis was a complete compensation to the superintendent for the unhappiness he had undergone in being arrested. The prelate was silent and grave, D'Artagnan completely bewildered by such an accumulation of events.

"Well, Captain, so you have brought M. d'Herblay to me?"—"And something better still, Monseigneur."—"What is that?"—"Liberty."—"I am free?"—"Yes,—by the king's order."

Fouquet interrogated Aramis with a look. "Oh, yes; you can thank M. the Bishop of Vannes," pursued D'Artagnan, "for it is indeed to him that you owe the change that has taken place in the king."—"Oh!" said Fouquet, more humiliated at the service than grateful at its success.—"But you," continued D'Artagnan, addressing Aramis,—"you who have become M. Fouquet's protector and patron,—can you not do something for me?"—"Anything you like, my friend," replied the bishop, in a calm voice.

"One thing only, then, and I shall be perfectly satisfied. How have you managed to become the favourite of the king, you who have never spoken to him more than twice in your life?"—"From a friend such as you are," said Aramis, "I cannot conceal anything."—"Ah, very good! tell me, then."

The King's Friend

"Very well. You think that I have seen the king only twice, while the fact is I have seen him more than a hundred times; only we have kept it very secret, that is all." And Aramis turned towards M. Fouquet, who was as much surprised as the musketeer. "Monseigneur," he resumed, "the king desires me to inform you that he is more than ever your friend, and that the beautiful *fête* so generously offered by you on his behalf has touched him to the heart."

And thereupon he saluted M. Fouquet with so much reverence of manner that the latter, unable to understand a man whose diplomacy was of so prodigious a character, remained incapable of uttering a single syllable, and equally incapable of thought or movement. D'Artagnan fancied that these two men had something to say to each other. Aramis turned towards him, and said in a quiet tone, "You will not forget, my friend, the king's order respecting those whom he intends to receive this morning on rising." These words were clear enough, and the musketeer understood them; he therefore bowed to Fouquet, and then to Aramis,—to the latter with a slight admixture of ironical respect,—and disappeared.

No sooner had he left than Fouquet, whose impatience had hardly been able to wait for that moment, darted towards the door to close it; and then returning to the bishop, he said, "My dear D'Herblay, I think it now high time you should explain to me what has passed, for, in plain and honest truth, I do not understand anything."

"We will explain all that to you," said Aramis, sitting down, and making Fouquet sit down also. "Where shall I begin?"—"With this, first of all. Why does the king set me at liberty? You and his Majesty have something particular, then, between you?"—"Yes."—"A secret, perhaps?"—"Yes, a secret."

"A secret of such a nature as to change his Majesty's interests?" —"You are indeed a man of superior intelligence, Monseigneur, and have made a very accurate guess. I have, in fact, discovered a secret of a nature to change the interests of the King of France."—"Ah!" said Fouquet, with the reserve of a man who does not wish to ask questions.

"Do you remember," said the bishop, casting down his eyes, "the birth of Louis XIV.?"—"As it were yesterday."—"Have you ever heard anything particular respecting his birth?"—"Nothing."— "That is where my secret begins. The queen, you must know, instead of being delivered of one son, was delivered of two children."

151

The Man in the Iron Mask

Fouquet looked up suddenly as he replied, "And the second is dead?"—"You will see. These twins seemed likely to be regarded as the pride of their mother and the hope of France; but the weak nature of the king, his superstitious feelings, made him apprehend a series of conflicts between two children whose rights were equal. He suppressed one of the twins. Both the children grew up,—the one on the throne, whose minister you are; the other, who is my friend, in gloom and isolation. He was brought up in the country, and then thrown into a fortress which goes by the name of the Bastille. The one was the most fortunate of men; the other the most unhappy of miserable beings."—"Does his mother not know this?" asked Fouquet.—"Anne of Austria knows it all."—"And the king?"—"Knows absolutely nothing."—"So much the better!" said Fouquet.

This remark seemed to make a great impression on Aramis; he looked at Fouquet with an anxious expression of countenance. "This poor prince," resumed Aramis, "was the unhappiest of men, when God undertook to come to his assistance."—"Oh! in what way?"

"You will see. The reigning king,—I say the reigning king: you can guess very well why?"—"No. Why?"—"Because being alike legitimately entitled from their birth, both ought to have been kings. Is not that your opinion?"—"It is, certainly."—"Unreservedly so?" —"Most unreservedly; twins are one person in two bodies."

"I am pleased that a legist of your learning and authority should have pronounced such an opinion. It is agreed, then, that both of them possessed the same rights, is it not?"—"Incontestably so! but, gracious heavens, what an extraordinary circumstance!"—"We are not at the end of it yet. Patience!"—"Oh, I shall find 'patience' enough." "Now we are coming to the point, Monseigneur! I think I shall not fail to excite a little interest in you. You are listening, I hope?"—"How can you ask me if I am listening? Go on."

Aramis walked softly all round the room, satisfied himself that they were alone and that all was silent, and then returned, and placed himself close to the arm-chair in which Fouquet awaited with the deepest anxiety the revelations he had to make. "I forgot to tell you," resumed Aramis, addressing himself to Fouquet, who listened to him with the most absorbed attention,—"I forgot to mention a most remarkable circumstance respecting these twins; namely, that God had formed them so like each other that He alone, if He should summon them to His tribunal, could distinguish the one from the

The King's Friend

other. Their own mother could not do it."—"Is it possible?" exclaimed Fouquet.

"The same noble character in their features, the same carriage, the same stature, the same voice."—"But their thoughts; degree of intelligence; their knowledge of human life?"—"There is inequality there, I admit, Monseigneur. Yes, for the prisoner of the Bastille is most incontestably superior in every way to his brother; and if from his prison this unhappy victim were to pass to the throne, France would not from the earliest period of its history, perhaps, have had a master more powerful by his genius and true nobleness of character." Fouquet buried his face in his hands, as if he were overwhelmed by the weight of this immense secret.

"My friend," said Aramis, emphasizing the word with a kind of disdainful familiarity, "what does God do in order to substitute one king for another?"—"God!" exclaimed Fouquet,—"God gives directions to His agent, who seizes upon the doomed victim, hurries him away, and seats the triumphant rival on the empty throne. But you forget that this agent is called death. Oh, M. d'Herblay! in Heaven's name, tell me if you have had the idea—"

"There is no question of that, Monseigneur,—you are going beyond the object in view. Who spoke of Louis XIV.'s death; who spoke of adopting the example of God in the strict method of his works? No; I wish you to understand that God effects His purposes without confusion, without scandal, without effort, and that men inspired by God succeed like him in all their undertakings, in all they attempt, in all they do."—"What do you mean?"—"I mean, my friend," returned Aramis, with the same intonation on the word "friend" that he had applied to it the first time,—"I mean that if there has been any confusion, scandal, and even effort in the substitution of the prisoner for the king, I defy you to prove it."

"What!" cried Fouquet, whiter than the handkerchief with which he wiped his temples; "what do you say?"—"Go to the king's apartment," continued Aramis, tranquilly; "and you who know the mystery, I defy even you to perceive that the prisoner of the Bastille is lying in his brother's bed."—"But the king?" stammered Fouquet, seized with horror at the intelligence.—"What king?" said Aramis, in his gentlest tone; "the one who hates you, or the one who likes you?"—"The king—of yesterday?"—"The king of yesterday! Be

153

quite easy on that score; he has gone to take the place in the Bastille which his victim has occupied for such a long time past."

"Great God! And who took him there?"—"I."—"You?"—"Yes, and in the simplest way. I carried him away last night; and while he was descending into gloom, the other was ascending into light. I do not think there has been any disturbance created in any way. A flash of lightning without thunder never awakens any one."

Fouquet uttered a thick, smothered cry, as if he had been struck by some invisible blow, and clasping his head between his clinched hands, he murmured, "You did that?"—"Cleverly enough, too; what do you think of it?"—"You have dethroned the king; you have imprisoned him?"—"It is done."—"And such an action was committed here at Vaux?"—"Yes; here at Vaux, in the Chamber of Morpheus. It would almost seem that it had been built in anticipation of such an act."—"And at what time did it occur?"—"Last night, between twelve and one o'clock."

Fouquet made a movement as if he were on the point of springing upon Aramis; he restrained himself. "At Vaux; under my roof!" he said in a half-strangled voice.—"I believe so; for it is still your house, and is likely to continue so, since M. Colbert cannot rob you of it now."—"It was under my roof, then, Monsieur, that you committed this crime!"

"This crime!" said Aramis, stupefied.—"This abominable crime!" pursued Fouquet, becoming more and more excited; "this crime more execrable than an assassination; this crime which dishonours my name for ever, and entails upon me the horror of posterity!"— "You are not in your senses, Monsieur," replied Aramis, in an irresolute tone of voice; "you are speaking too loudly. Take care!"—"I will call out so loudly that the whole world shall hear me."—"M. Fouquet, take care!"

Fouquet turned round towards the prelate, whom he looked full in the face. "You have dishonoured me," he said, "in committing so foul an act of treason, so heinous a crime upon my guest, upon one who was peacefully reposing beneath my roof. Oh, woe, woe is me!" —"Woe to the man, rather, who beneath your roof meditated the ruin of your fortune, your life. Do you forget that?"—"He was my guest; he was my king!"

Aramis rose, his eyes literally bloodshot, his mouth trembling convulsively. "Have I a man out of his senses to deal with?" he said.—

The king blushed with pleasure; he looked at Madame de Montespan with all the fire of love

The King's Friend

"You have an honourable man to deal with."—"You are mad!"—"A man who will prevent you from consummating your crime."—"You are mad!"—"A man who would sooner die, who would kill you even, rather than allow you to complete his dishonour." Aramis remained silent and motionless. "You do not reply?" said Fouquet.

Aramis raised his head gently, and a glimmer of hope might be seen once more to animate his eyes. "Reflect, Monseigneur," he said, "upon everything we have to expect. As the matter now stands, the king is still alive, and his imprisonment saves your life."

"Yes," replied Fouquet, "you may have been acting on my behalf; but I do not accept your service. At the same time, I do not wish your ruin. You will leave this house." Aramis stifled the exclamation which almost escaped his broken heart. "I am hospitable towards all who are dwellers beneath my roof," continued Fouquet, with an air of inexpressible majesty; "you will not be more fatally lost than he whose ruin you have consummated."

"You will be so," said Aramis, in a hoarse, prophetic voice,—"you will be so, believe me."—"I accept the augury, M. d'Herblay; but nothing shall stop me. You will leave Vaux; you must leave France. I give you four hours to place yourself out of the king's reach." —"Four hours?" said the Bishop of Vannes, scornfully and incredulously.

"Upon the word of Fouquet, no one shall follow you before the expiration of that time. You will therefore have four hours' advance of those whom the king may wish to despatch after you."—"Four hours!" repeated Aramis, in a thick, smothered voice.

"It is more than you will need to get on board a vessel, and flee to Belle-Isle, which I give you as a place of refuge."—"Ah!" murmured Aramis.—"Belle-Isle is as much mine for you as Vaux is mine for the king. Go, D'Herblay, go! as long as I live, not a hair of your head shall be injured."—"Thank you," said Aramis, with a cold irony of manner.

"Go at once, then, and give me your hand, before we both hasten away,—you to save your life, I to save my honour."

Both of them darted out of the room by a secret staircase which led down to the inner courtyard. Fouquet ordered his best horses, while Aramis paused at the foot of the staircase which led to Porthos's apartment. He reflected for some time, while Fouquet's carriage left the stone-paved courtyard at full gallop.

155

The Man in the Iron Mask

"Shall I go alone," said Aramis to himself, "or warn the prince? Oh, fury! Warn the prince, and then—do what? Take him with me? Carry this accusing witness about with me everywhere? War, too, would follow,—civil war, implacable in its nature! And without any resource—alas, it is impossible! What will he do without me? Without me he will be utterly destroyed! Yet who knows? let destiny be fulfilled! Condemned he was, let him remain so, then! God! Demon! Lost! I am lost! What can be done? Flee to Belle-Isle? Yes, and leave Porthos behind me, to talk and relate the whole affair to every one,—Porthos, who will suffer, perhaps! I will not let poor Porthos suffer. Porthos shall leave with me, and shall follow my destiny. It must be so." And Aramis, apprehensive of meeting any one to whom his hurried movements might appear suspicious, ascended the staircase without being perceived. Porthos, but just returned from Paris, slept already the sleep of the just; his huge body forgot its fatigue as his mind forgot its thoughts. Aramis entered, light as a shadow, and placed his nervous grasp on the giant's shoulder. "Come, Porthos," he cried, "come!"

Porthos obeyed, rose from his bed, and opened his eyes, even before opening his mind. "We are going off," said Aramis.—"Ah!" returned Porthos.—"We shall go mounted, and faster than we have ever gone in our lives."—"Ah!" repeated Porthos.—"Dress yourself, my friend."

And he helped the giant to dress himself, and thrust his gold and diamonds into his pocket. While he was thus engaged, a slight noise attracted his attention, and he saw D'Artagnan looking at them from the open doorway. Aramis started.

"What the devil are you doing there in such an agitated manner?" said the musketeer.—"Hush!" said Porthos.—"We are going off on a mission," added the bishop.—"You are very fortunate," said the musketeer.—"Oh, dear me!" said Porthos, "I feel so wearied; I would much prefer to sleep. But the service of the king—"

"Have you seen M. Fouquet?" inquired Aramis of D'Artagnan. —"Yes; this very minute, in a carriage."—"What did he say to you?"—"He bade me adieu."—"Was that all?"—"What else do you think he could say? Am I worth anything now, since you have all got into such high favour?"

"Listen," said Aramis, embracing the musketeer; "your good

156

times are returning again. You will have no more occasion to be jealous of any one."—"Ah, bah!"—"I predict that something will happen to you to-day which will increase your importance."—"Really?"—"You know that I know all the news?"—"Oh, yes!"

"Come, Porthos, are you ready? Let us go."—"I am quite ready, Aramis."—"Let us embrace D'Artagnan first."—"*Pardieu!*"—"But the horses?"—"Oh! there is no want of them here. Will you have mine?"—"No; Porthos has his own stud. So adieu; adieu!"

The two fugitives mounted their horses beneath the eyes of the captain of the musketeers, who held Porthos's stirrup for him, and gazed after them until they were out of sight. "On any other occasion," thought the Gascon, "I should say that those gentlemen were making their escape; but in these days politics seem so changed that this is called going on a mission. I have no objection. Let me attend to my own affairs;" and he philosophically entered his apartments.

CHAPTER XXIII

HOW THE COUNTERSIGN WAS RESPECTED AT THE BASTILLE

FOUQUET tore along as fast as his horses could drag him. On the way he trembled with horror at the idea of what had just been revealed to him. "What must have been," he thought, "the youth of those extraordinary men, who, even as age is stealing fast upon them, still are able to conceive such plans, and to carry them out without flinching!"

At one moment he asked himself whether all that Aramis had just been recounting to him was not a dream only, and whether the fable itself was not the snare; so that when he should arrive at the Bastille he might find an order of arrest, which would send him to join the dethroned king. Strongly impressed with this idea, he gave certain sealed orders on his route, while fresh horses were harnessed to his carriage. These orders were addressed to M. d'Artagnan and to certain others whose fidelity to the king was far above suspicion. "In this way," said Fouquet to himself, "prisoner or not, I shall have performed the duty which I owe to my honour. The orders will not reach them until after my return, if I should return free, and consequently they will not have been unsealed. I shall then take them back again. If I am delayed, it will be because some misfortune will have befallen me; and in that case assistance will be sent for me as well as for the king."

Prepared in this manner, the superintendent arrived at the Bastille; he had travelled at the rate of five leagues and a half an hour. Every circumstance of delay which Aramis had escaped in his visit to the Bastille befell Fouquet. It was in vain that he gave his name, in vain that he endeavoured to be recognized; he could not succeed in obtaining an entrance. By dint of entreaties, threats, and commands, he succeeded in inducing a sentinel to speak to one of the subalterns, who went and told the major. As for the governor, they did not even dare to disturb him. Fouquet sat in his carriage, at the outer gate of the fortress, chafing with rage and impatience, awaiting the return of the officer, who at last reappeared with a somewhat sulky air. "Well," said Fouquet impatiently, "what did the major say?"—"Well, Monsieur," replied the soldier, "the major laughed in my face. He told me that M. Fouquet was at Vaux, and that even were he at Paris, M. Fouquet would not rise at so early an hour as the present."

"*Mordieu!* you are a set of fools," cried the minister, darting out of the carriage; and before the subaltern had had time to shut the gate, Fouquet sprang through it, and ran forward in spite of the soldier, who cried out for assistance. Fouquet gained ground, regardless of the cries of the man, who however, having at last come up with Fouquet, called out to the sentinel of the second gate, "Look out, look out, sentinel!" The man crossed his pike before the minister; but the latter, robust and active, and carried away too by his passion, wrested the pike from the soldier, and struck him a violent blow on the shoulder with it. The subaltern, who approached too closely, received his part of the blows as well. Both of them uttered loud and furious cries, at the sound of which the whole of the first body of the advanced guard poured out of the guard-house. Among them there was one, however, who recognised the superintendent, and who called out, "Monseigneur! ah, Monseigneur! Stop, stop, you fellows!" and he effectually checked the soldiers, who were on the point of avenging their companions. Fouquet desired them to open the gate; but they refused to do so without the countersign. He desired them to inform the governor of his presence; but the latter had already heard the disturbance at the gate. He ran forward, followed by his major, and accompanied by a picket of twenty men, persuaded that an attack was being made on the Bastille. Baisemeaux also recognised Fouquet immediately, and dropped his sword, which he had held brandishing about in his hand.

"Ah, Monseigneur!" he stammered, "how can I excuse—"—"Monsieur," said the superintendent, flushed with anger, and heated by his exertions, "I congratulate you. Your watch and ward are admirably kept." Baisemeaux turned pale, thinking that this remark was said ironically, and portended a furious burst of anger. But Fouquet had recovered his breath, and beckoning towards him the sentinel and the subaltern, who were rubbing their shoulders, he said, "There are twenty pistoles for the sentinel, and fifty for the officer. Pray receive my compliments, gentlemen. I will not fail to speak to his Majesty about you. And now, M. Baisemeaux, a word with you."

And he followed the governor to his official residence, accompanied by a murmur of general satisfaction. Baisemeaux was already trembling with shame and uneasiness. Aramis's early visit from that moment seemed to involve consequences which a functionary was justified in apprehending. It was quite another thing, however, when Fouquet, in a sharp tone of voice, and with an imperious look, said, "You have seen M. d'Herblay this morning?"

"Yes, Monseigneur."—"And are you not horrified at the crime of which you have made yourself an accomplice?"—"Well," thought Baisemeaux, "good so far;" and then he added aloud, "But what crime, Monseigneur, do you allude to?"—"That for which you can be quartered alive, Monsieur,—do not forget that! But this is not a time to show anger. Conduct me immediately to the prisoner."—"To what prisoner?" said Baisemeaux, tremblingly.

"You pretend to be ignorant! Very good; it is the best thing for you to do,—for if, in fact, you were to admit your participation in it, it would be all over with you. I wish, therefore, to seem to believe in your assumption of ignorance."—"I entreat you, Monseigneur—"—"That will do. Lead me to the prisoner."—"To Marchiali?"—"Who is Marchiali?"—"The prisoner who was brought back this morning by M. d'Herblay."—"He is called Marchiali?" said the superintendent, his conviction somewhat shaken by Baisemeaux's cool manner.—"Yes, Monseigneur; that is the name under which he was inscribed here."

Fouquet looked steadily at Baisemeaux, as if to read his very heart, and perceived that the man was speaking with absolute sincerity. Besides, on observing his face for a moment, he could not believe that Aramis would have chosen such a confidant.

"It is the prisoner," said the superintendent to Baisemeaux, "whom M. d'Herblay carried away the day before yesterday?"—"Yes, Monseigneur."—"And whom he brought back this morning?" added Fouquet, quickly, for he understood immediately the mechanism of Aramis's plan.—"Precisely, Monseigneur."

"And his name is Marchiali, you say?"—"Yes; Marchiali. If Monseigneur has come here to remove him, so much the better, for I was going to write about him."—"What has he done, then?"—"Ever since this morning, he has annoyed me extremely. He has had such terrible fits of passion as almost to make me believe that he would bring the Bastille itself down about our ears."—"I will soon relieve you of his presence," said Fouquet.—"Ah! so much the better."

"Conduct me to his prison."—"Will Monseigneur give me the order?"—"What order?"—"An order from the king."—"Wait until I sign you one."—"That will not be sufficient, Monseigneur; I must have an order from the king."

Fouquet assumed an irritated expression. "As you are so scrupulous," he said, "with regard to allowing prisoners to leave, show me the order by which this one was set at liberty." Baisemeaux showed him the order to release Seldon. "Very good," said Fouquet; "but Seldon is not Marchiali."—"But Marchiali is not at liberty; he is here."—"But you said that M. d'Herblay carried him away and brought him back again."—"I did not say so."—"So surely did you say it that I almost seem to hear it now."—"It was a slip of my tongue, then, Monseigneur."—"Take care, M. Baisemeaux, take care!"—"What influences me, Monseigneur, is the king's service. I am doing my duty. Give me an order from him, and you shall enter."

"Stay, Monsieur the Governor! I give you my word that if you allow me to see the prisoner I will give you an order from the king at once."—"Give it to me now, Monseigneur."—"And that if you refuse me I will have you and all your officers arrested on the spot."

"Stop, Monseigneur!" cried Baisemeaux. "I understand absolutely nothing of the whole matter; but so many misfortunes, even were it madness itself that had set them at work, might happen here in a couple of hours that the king, by whom I shall be judged, will see whether I have been wrong in withdrawing the countersign before so many imminent catastrophes. Come with me to the keep, Monseigneur; you shall see Marchiali." Fouquet darted out of the room, followed by Baisemeaux wiping the perspiration from his face. "What a terrible morning!" he said; "what a disgrace!"—"Walk faster!" replied Fouquet.

Baisemeaux made a sign to the jailer to precede them. He was afraid of his companion,—which the latter could not fail to perceive. "A truce to this child's-play!" said Fouquet, roughly. "Let the man remain here; take the keys yourself, and show me the way. Not a single person, do you understand, must hear what is going to take place here."—"Ah!" said Baisemeaux, undecided.—"Again," cried Fouquet. "Ah! say 'No' at once, and I will leave the Bastille, and will myself carry my own despatches."

Baisemeaux bowed his head, took the keys, and unaccompanied except by the minister, ascended the staircase. As they advanced up the spiral staircase, certain smothered murmurs became distinct cries and fearful imprecations. "What is that?" asked Fouquet.— "That is your Marchiali," said the governor; "that is the way madmen howl." And he accompanied that reply with a glance more indicative of injurious allusions, as far as Fouquet was concerned, than of politeness.

The latter trembled; he had just recognized, in one cry more terrible than any that had preceded it, the king's voice. He paused on the staircase, trying to snatch the bunch of keys from Baisemeaux, who thought this new madman was going to dash out his brains with one of them. "Give me the keys at once!" cried Fouquet, tearing them from his hand. "Which is the key of the door I am to open?"—"That one."

A fearful cry, followed by a violent blow against the door, made the whole staircase resound with the echo. "Leave this place!" said Fouquet to Baisemeaux, in a threatening voice.—"I ask nothing better," murmured the latter. "There will be a couple of madmen face to face; and the one will kill the other, I am sure."—"Go!" repeated Fouquet. "If you place your foot on this staircase before I call you, remember that you shall take the place of the meanest prisoner in the Bastille."—"This job will kill me, I am sure!" muttered Baisemeaux, as he withdrew with tottering steps.

The prisoner's cries became more and more terrible. When Fouquet had satisfied himself that Baisemeaux had reached the bottom of the staircase, he inserted the key in the first lock. It was then that he heard the hoarse, choking voice of the king crying out in a frenzy of rage, "Help, help! I am the king!" The key of the second door was not the same as the first, and Fouquet was obliged to look for it on the bunch. The king, meanwhile, furious and almost mad with rage and passion, shouted at the top of his voice, "It was M. Fouquet who brought me here! help me against M. Fouquet! I am the king! help the king against M. Fouquet!" These cries tore the minister's heart with mingled emotions. They were followed by frightful blows levelled against the door with a part of the broken chair with which the king had armed himself. Fouquet at last succeeded in finding the key. The king was almost exhausted; he no longer articulated, he roared: "Death to Fouquet! Death to the traitor Fouquet!" The door flew open.

CHAPTER XXIV

THE KING'S GRATITUDE

THE two men were on the point of darting towards each other, when they suddenly stopped, as a mutual recognition took place, and each uttered a cry of horror. "Have you come to assassinate me, Monsieur?" said the king, when he recognized Fouquet.—"The king in this state!" murmured the minister.

Nothing could be more terrible, indeed, than the appearance of Louis at the moment Fouquet had surprised him; his clothes were in tatters; his shirt, open and torn to rags, was stained with sweat, and with the blood which streamed from his lacerated breast and arms. Haggard, pale, foaming, his hair dishevelled, Louis XIV. presented a vivid picture of despair, hunger, and fear, combined in

Fouquet

The King's Gratitude

one figure. Fouquet was so touched, so affected and disturbed, that he ran to the king with his arms stretched out and his eyes filled with tears. Louis held up the massive piece of wood of which he had made such a furious use.

"Sire," said Fouquet, in a voice trembling with emotion, "do you not recognize the most faithful of your friends?"—"A friend,— you!" repeated Louis, gnashing his teeth in a manner which betrayed his hate and desire for speedy vengeance.—"The most respectful of your servants," added Fouquet, throwing himself on his knees. The king let the rude weapon fall from his grasp. Fouquet approached him, kissed his knees, and took him tenderly in his arms. "My king, my child," he said, "how you must have suffered!"

Louis, recalled to himself by the change of situation, looked at himself, and ashamed of his disordered state, ashamed of his conduct, ashamed of the protection he was receiving, drew back. Fouquet did not understand this movement; he did not perceive that the king's pride would never forgive him for having been a witness of so much weakness. "Come, Sire," he said, "you are free."

"Free?" repeated the king. "Oh! you set me at liberty, then, after having dared to lift up your hand against me?"—"You do not believe that!" exclaimed Fouquet, indignantly; "you cannot believe me to be guilty of such an act."

And rapidly, warmly even, he related the whole particulars of the intrigue, the details of which are already known to the reader. While the recital continued, Louis suffered the most horrible anguish of mind; and when it was finished, the magnitude of the danger he had run struck him far more than the importance of the secret relating to his twin brother. "Monsieur," he said suddenly to Fouquet, "this double birth is a falsehood; you cannot have been deceived by it."—"Sire!"—"It is impossible, I tell you, that the honour, the virtue of my mother can be suspected. And my first minister, has he not already done justice on the criminals?"

"Reflect, Sire, before you are carried away by your anger," replied Fouquet. "The birth of your brother—"—"I have only one brother; and that is *Monsieur*. You know it as well as myself. There is a plot, I tell you, beginning with the governor of the Bastille."

"Be careful, Sire, for this man has been deceived as every one else

has by the prince's likeness to yourself."—"Likeness? absurd!"—
"This Marchiali must, however, be very like your Majesty to be able
to deceive every one," Fouquet persisted.—"Ridiculous!"—"Do not
say so, Sire; those who had prepared everything in order to face and
deceive your ministers, your mother, your officers of state, the members of your family, must be quite confident of the resemblance
between you."

"There is truth in that," murmured the king; "but where are
these persons, then?"—"At Vaux."—"At Vaux! and you suffer
them to remain there?"—"My most pressing duty seemed to be
your Majesty's release. I have accomplished that duty; and now
whatever your Majesty may command, shall be done. I await your
orders."

Louis reflected for a few minutes. "Muster all the troops in
Paris," he said.—"All the necessary orders are given for that purpose," replied Fouquet.—"You have given orders?" exclaimed the
king.—"For that purpose,—yes, Sire! your Majesty will be at the
head of ten thousand men in an hour."

The only reply the king made was to take hold of Fouquet's hand
with such an expression of feeling that it was very easy to perceive
how strongly he had until that remark maintained his suspicions of
the minister, notwithstanding the latter's intervention. "And with
these troops," he said, "we shall go at once and besiege in your
house the rebels who by this time will have established and in-
trenched themselves there."—"I should be surprised if that were
the case," replied Fouquet.—"Why?"—"Because their chief,—the
very soul of the enterprise,—having been unmasked by me, the
whole plan seems to me to have miscarried."

"You have unmasked this false prince also?"—"No, I have not
seen him."—"Whom have you seen, then?"—"The leader of the
enterprise is not that unhappy young man; the latter is merely an
instrument, destined through his whole life to wretchedness, I
plainly perceive."—"Most certainly."—"It is M. l'Abbé d'Herblay,
Bishop of Vannes."

"Your friend?"—"He was my friend, Sire," replied Fouquet,
nobly.—"An unfortunate circumstance for you," said the king, in a
less generous tone of voice.—"Such friendship, Sire, had nothing
dishonourable in it so long as I was ignorant of the crime."

"You should have foreseen it."—"If I am guilty, I place myself in your Majesty's hands."—"Ah, M. Fouquet, it was not that I meant," returned the king, sorry to have shown the bitterness of his thought in such a manner. "Well; I assure you that notwithstanding the mask with which the villain covered his face, I had something like a vague suspicion that it might be he. But with this chief of the enterprise there was a man of prodigious strength; the one who menaced me with a force almost herculean, what is he?"

"It must be his friend the Baron du Vallon, formerly one of the musketeers."—"The friend of D'Artagnan; the friend of the Comte de la Fère? Ah!" exclaimed the king, as he paused at the name of the latter, "we must not forget that connection between the conspirators and M. de Bragelonne."

"Sire, Sire, do not go too far! M. de la Fère is the most honourable man in France. Be satisfied with those whom I deliver up to you."—"With those whom you deliver up to me, you say? Very good, for you will deliver up those who are guilty to me."—"What does your Majesty understand by that?" inquired Fouquet.—"I understand," replied the king, "that we shall soon arrive at Vaux with a large body of troops, that we will lay violent hands upon that nest of vipers, and that not a soul shall escape."

"Your Majesty will put these men to death?" cried Fouquet.— "To the very meanest of them."—"Oh, Sire!"—"Let us understand each other, M. Fouquet," said the king, haughtily. "We no longer live in times when assassination was the only, the last resource of kings. No, Heaven be praised! I have parliaments who judge in my name, and I have scaffolds on which my supreme will is executed."

Fouquet turned pale. "I will take the liberty of observing to your Majesty that any proceedings instituted respecting these matters would bring down the greatest scandal upon the dignity of the throne. The august name of Anne of Austria must never be allowed to pass the lips of the people accompanied by a smile."—"Justice must be done, however, Monsieur."—"Good, Sire; but the royal blood cannot be shed on a scaffold."

"The royal blood! you believe that?" cried the king, with fury in his voice, stamping on the ground. "This double birth is an invention; and in that invention particularly do I see M. d'Herblay's crime. That is the crime I wish to punish, rather than their violence or their insult."—"And punish it with death, Sire?"—"With death! yes, Monsieur."

"Sire," said the superintendent, with firmness, as he raised his head proudly, "your Majesty will take the life, if you please, of your brother Philippe of France; that concerns you alone, and you will doubtless consult the queen-mother upon the subject. Whatever she may order will be ordered well. I do not wish to mix myself up in it, not even for the honour of your crown; but I have a favour to ask of you, and I beg to submit it to you."—"Speak," said the king, in no little degree agitated by his minister's last words. "What do you require?"—"The pardon of M. d'Herblay and of M. du Vallon."—"My assassins?"—"Two rebels, Sire; that is all."

"Oh! I understand, then, you ask me to forgive your friends."— "My friends!" said Fouquet, deeply wounded.—"Your friends, certainly; but the safety of the State requires that an exemplary punishment should be inflicted on the guilty."

"I will not permit myself to remind your Majesty that I have just restored you to liberty, and have saved your life."—"Monsieur!"—"I will only remind your Majesty that had M. d'Herblay wished to play the part of an assassin, he could very easily have assassinated your Majesty this morning in the forest of Sénart, and all would have been over."

The king started. "A pistol-bullet through the head," pursued Fouquet, "and the disfigured features of Louis XIV., which no one could have recognised, would have been M. d'Herblay's complete absolution." The king turned pale with fear at the idea of the danger he had escaped. "If M. d'Herblay," continued Fouquet, "had been an assassin, he had no occasion to inform me of his plan in order to succeed. Freed from the real king, it would have been impossible to guess the false one. And if the usurper had been recognised by Anne of Austria, he would still have been a son for her. The usurper, so far as M. d'Herblay's conscience was concerned, was still a king of the blood of Louis XIII. Moreover, the conspirator in that course would have had security, secrecy, and impunity. A pistol-bullet would have procured him all that. For the sake of Heaven, Sire, grant me his forgiveness!"

The king, instead of being touched by that picture, so faithful in all its details, of Aramis's generosity, felt himself painfully humiliated. His unconquerable pride revolted at the idea that a man had

The King's Gratitude

held suspended at the end of his finger the thread of his royal life. Every word which Fouquet thought would be efficacious in procuring his friend's pardon, carried another drop of poison to the already rankling heart of Louis XIV. Nothing could bend him. Addressing himself to Fouquet, he said, "I really don't know, Monsieur, why you should solicit the pardon of these men. What good is there in asking that which can be obtained without solicitation?"

"I do not understand you, Sire."—"It is not difficult either. Where am I now?"—"In the Bastille, Sire."—"Yes; in a dungeon. I am looked upon as a madman, am I not?"—"Yes, Sire."—"And no one is known here but Marchiali?"—"Certainly."—"Well; change nothing in the position of affairs. Let the madman rot in the dungeon of the Bastille, and M. d'Herblay and M. du Vallon will stand in no need of my forgiveness. Their new king will absolve them."

"Your Majesty does me a great injustice, Sire; and you are wrong," replied Fouquet, dryly. "I am not child enough, nor is M. d'Herblay silly enough, to have omitted to make all these reflections; and if I had wished to make a new king, as you say, I had no occasion to have come here to force open all the gates and doors of the Bastille, to free you from this place. That would show a want of common-sense even. Your Majesty's mind is disturbed by anger; otherwise you would be far from offending groundlessly the very one of your servants who has rendered you the most important service of all."

Louis perceived that he had gone too far, that the gates of the Bastille were still closed upon him; while, by degrees, the floodgates were gradually being opened behind which the generous-hearted Fouquet had restrained his anger. "I did not say that to humiliate you, Heaven knows, Monsieur," he replied. "Only you are addressing yourself to me in order to obtain a pardon, and I answer you according as my conscience dictates. And so, judging by my conscience, the criminals we speak of are not worthy of consideration of forgiveness." Fouquet was silent. "What I do is as generous," added the king, "as what you have done, for I am in your power. I will even say, it is more generous, inasmuch as you place before me certain conditions upon which my liberty, my life, may depend, and to reject which is to make a sacrifice of them both."

"I was wrong, certainly," replied Fouquet. "Yes; I had the appearance of extorting a favour. I regret it, and entreat your Majesty's forgiveness."—"And you are forgiven, my dear M. Fouquet," said the king, with a smile which restored the serene expression of his features, which so many circumstances had altered since the preceding evening.

"I have my own forgiveness," replied the minister, with some degree of persistence; "but M. d'Herblay and M. du Vallon?"—"They will never obtain theirs as long as I live," replied the inflexible king. "Do me the kindness not to speak of it again."—"Your Majesty shall be obeyed."

"And you will bear me no ill-will for it?"—"Oh, no, Sire,—for I anticipated it."—"You had 'anticipated' that I should refuse to forgive those gentlemen?"—"Certainly; and all my measures were taken in consequence."—"What do you mean to say?" cried the king, surprised.

"M. d'Herblay came, so to speak, to deliver himself into my hands. M. d'Herblay left to me the happiness of saving my king and my country. I could not condemn M. d'Herblay to death; nor could I, on the other hand, expose him to your Majesty's most justifiable wrath,—it would have been just the same as if I had killed him myself."—"Well; and what have you done?"—"Sire, I gave M. d'Herblay the best horses in my stables, and four hours' start over those your Majesty will despatch after him."

"Be it so!" murmured the king. "But still, the world is large enough for those whom I may send to overtake your horses, notwithstanding the 'four hours' start' which you have given to M. d'Herblay."—"In giving him those four hours, Sire, I knew I was giving him his life; and he will save his life."—"In what way?"—"After having galloped as hard as possible, with the four hours' start over your musketeers, he will reach my château of Belle-Isle, where I have given him a safe asylum."

"That may be! but you forget that you have made me a present of Belle-Isle."—"But not for you to arrest my friends."—"You take it back again, then?"—"As far as that goes,—yes, Sire."—"My musketeers will capture it, and the affair will be at an end."—"Neither your musketeers nor your whole army could take Belle-Isle," said Fouquet, coldly. "Belle-Isle is impregnable."

The king became livid; a lightning flash darted from his eyes. Fouquet felt that he was lost, but he was not one to shrink when the voice of honour spoke loudly within him. He bore the king's wrathful gaze; the latter swallowed his rage, and after a few moments' silence, said, "Are we going to return to Vaux?"—"I am at your Majesty's orders," replied Fouquet, with a low bow; "but I think that your Majesty can hardly dispense with changing your clothes previous to appearing before your court."

"We shall pass by the Louvre," said the king. "Come." And they left the prison, passing before Baisemeaux, who looked completely bewildered, as he saw Marchiali once more leave, and in his helplessness tore out the few remaining hairs he had left. It is true that Fouquet wrote and gave him an authority for the prisoner's release, and that the king wrote beneath it, "Seen and approved, Louis,"—a piece of madness that Baisemeaux, incapable of putting two ideas together, acknowledged by giving himself a terrible blow with his fist on his jaws.

CHAPTER XXV

THE FALSE KING

IN THE meantime, usurped royalty was playing out its part bravely at Vaux. Philippe gave orders that for his *petit lever,* the *grandes entrées,* already prepared to appear before the king, should be introduced. He determined to give this order notwithstanding the absence of M. d'Herblay, who did not return,—and our readers know for what reason. But the prince, not believing that that absence could be prolonged, wished, as all rash spirits do, to try his valour and his fortune independently of all protection and all counsel. Another reason urged him to this,—Anne of Austria was about to appear; the guilty mother was about to stand in the presence of her sacrificed son. Philippe was not willing, if he should betray any weakness, to render the man a witness of it before whom he was bound henceforth to display so much strength.

Philippe opened his folding-doors, and several persons entered silently. Philippe did not stir while his *valets de chambre* dressed him. He had watched, the evening before, all the habits of his brother, and played the king in such a manner as to awaken no suspicion. He was then completely dressed in his hunting costume when he received his visitors. His own memory and the notes of Aramis announced everybody to him, first of all Anne of Austria, to whom Monsieur gave his hand, and then Madame with M. de Saint-Aignan. He smiled at seeing these countenances, but trembled on recognizing his mother. That figure so noble, so imposing, ravaged by pain, pleaded in his heart the cause of that famous queen who had immolated a child to reasons of state. He found his mother still handsome. He knew that Louis XIV. loved her; and he promised himself to love her likewise, and not to prove a cruel chastisement for her old age. He contemplated his brother with a tenderness easily to be understood. The latter had usurped nothing over him, had cast no shade over his life; a separate branch, he allowed the stem to rise without heeding its elevation or the majesty of its life. Philippe promised himself to be a kind brother to this prince, who required nothing but gold to minister to his pleasures. He bowed with a friendly air to De Saint-Aignan, who was all reverences and smiles, and tremblingly held out his hand to Henrietta, his sister-in-law, whose beauty struck him; but he saw in her eyes an expression of coldness which would facilitate, as he thought, their future relations. "How much more easy," thought he, "it will be to be the brother of that woman than her gallant, if she evinces towards me a coldness that my brother could not have for her, and which is imposed upon me as a duty." The only visit he dreaded at this moment was that of the queen; his heart, his mind, had just been shaken by so violent a trial that in spite of their firm temperament they would not, perhaps, support another shock. Happily the queen did not come.

Then began, on the part of Anne of Austria, a political dissertation upon the welcome M. Fouquet had given to the house of France. She mixed up hostilities with compliments addressed to the king, and questions as to his health with little maternal flatteries and diplomatic artifices. "Well, my son," said she, "are you convinced with regard to M. Fouquet?"

"Saint-Aignan," said Philippe, "have the goodness to go and inquire after the queen." At these words, the first which Philippe had pronounced aloud, the slight difference that there was between his voice and that of the king was sensible to maternal ears, and Anne of Austria looked earnestly at her son. De Saint-Aignan left the room, and Philippe continued, "Madame, I do not like to hear M. Fouquet ill-spoken of,—you know I do not; and you have even spoken well of him yourself."—"That is true; therefore I only question you on the state of your sentiments with respect to him."

"Sire," said Henrietta, "I, on my part, have always liked M. Fouquet. He is a man of good taste; he is a superior man."—"A superintendent who is never sordid or niggardly," added Monsieur, "and who pays in gold all the orders I have on him."—"Every one in this thinks too much of himself, and nobody for the State," said the old queen. "M. Fouquet—it is a fact—M. Fouquet is ruining the State."

"Well, mother," replied Philippe, in rather a lower key, "do you likewise constitute yourself the buckler of M. Colbert?"—"How is that?" replied the old queen, rather surprised.—"Why, in truth," replied Philippe, "you speak that just as your old friend Madame de Chevreuse would speak."

At that name Anne of Austria turned pale and bit her lips. Philippe had irritated the lioness. "Why do you mention Madame de Chevreuse to me?" said she; "and what sort of humour are you in to-day towards me?" Philippe continued: "Is not Madame de Chevreuse always in league against somebody? Has not Madame de Chevreuse been to pay you a visit, mother?"—"Monsieur, you speak to me now in such a manner that I can almost fancy I am listening to your father."

"My father did not like Madame de Chevreuse, and with good reason," said the prince. "For my part, I like her no better than he did; and if she thinks proper to come here as she formerly did, to sow divisions and hatreds under the pretext of begging money, why —"—"Well, what?" said Anne of Austria, proudly, herself provoking the storm.—"Well," replied the young man, firmly, "I will drive Madame de Chevreuse out of my kingdom,—and with her all who meddle with secrets and mysteries."

He had not calculated the effect of this terrible speech, or perhaps he wished to judge of the effect of it,—like those who suffering from a chronic pain, and seeking to break the monotony of that suffering, touch their wound to procure a sharper pang. Anne of Austria was near fainting. Her eyes, open but meaningless, ceased to see for several seconds; she stretched out her arms towards her other son, who supported and embraced her without fear of irritating the king. "Sire," murmured she, "you treat your mother cruelly."

"In what, Madame?" replied he. "I am only speaking of Madame de Chevreuse; does my mother prefer Madame de Chevreuse to the security of the State and to the security of my person? Well, then, Madame, I tell you Madame de Chevreuse is returned to France to borrow money, and that she addressed herself to M. Fouquet to sell him a certain secret."—"'A certain secret'!" cried Anne of Austria.—"Concerning pretended robberies that monsieur the superintendent had committed; which is false," added Philippe. "M. Fouquet rejected her offers with indignation, preferring the esteem of the king to all complicity with intriguers. Then Madame de Chevreuse sold the secret to M. Colbert; and as she is insatiable, and was not satisfied with having extorted a hundred thousand crowns from that clerk, she has sought still higher, and has endeavoured to find still deeper springs. Is that true, Madame?"— "You know all, Sire," said the queen, more uneasy than irritated.

"Now," continued Philippe, "I have good reason to dislike this fury, who comes to my court to plan the dishonour of some and the ruin of others. If God has suffered certain crimes to be committed, and has concealed them in the shade of his clemency, I will not permit Madame de Chevreuse to have the power to counteract the designs of God."

The latter part of this speech had so agitated the queen-mother that her son had pity on her. He took her hand and kissed it tenderly; she did not perceive that in that kiss, given in spite of repulsions and bitternesses of the heart, there was a pardon for eight years of horrible suffering. Philippe allowed the silence of a moment to swallow the emotions that had just developed themselves. Then, with a cheerful smile, "We will not go to-day," said he; "I have a plan." And turning towards the door, he hoped to see Aramis, whose absence began to alarm him. The queen-mother wished to leave the room. "Remain, mother," said he; "I wish you to make your peace with M. Fouquet."—"I bear no ill-will towards M. Fouquet; I only dreaded his prodigalities."—"We will put that to rights, and will take nothing of the superintendent but his good qualities."

"What is your Majesty looking for?" said Henrietta, seeing the prince's eyes constantly turned towards the door, and wishing to let fly a little poisoned arrow at his heart,—for she supposed he was ex-

The False King

pecting La Vallière or a letter from her.—"My sister," said the young man, who had divined her thought, thanks to that marvellous perspicuity of which fortune was from that time about to allow him the exercise,—"my sister, I am expecting a most distinguished man, a most able counsellor, whom I wish to present to you all, recommending him to your good graces— Ah! come in, then, D'Artagnan."

"What does your Majesty wish?" said D'Artagnan, appearing.— "Where is M. l'Evêque de Vannes, your friend?"—"Why, Sire—"— "I am waiting for him, and he does not come. Let him be sought for."

D'Artagnan remained for an instant stupefied; but soon, reflecting that Aramis had left Vaux secretly with a mission from the king, he concluded that the king wished to preserve the secret of it, "Sire," replied he, "does your Majesty absolutely require M. d'Herblay to be brought to you?"—"Absolutely is not the word," said Philippe,— "I do not want him so particularly as that; but if he can be found—" —"I thought so," said D'Artagnan to himself.

"Is this M. d'Herblay, Bishop of Vannes?" said Anne of Austria. —"Yes, Madame."—"A friend of M. Fouquet?"—"Yes, Madame, an old musketeer." Anne of Austria blushed. "One of the four braves who formerly performed such wonders." The old queen repented of having wished to bite; she broke off the conversation, in order to preserve the rest of her teeth. "Whatever may be your choice, Sire," said she, "I have no doubt it will be excellent." All bowed in support of that sentiment.

"You will find in him," continued Philippe, "the depth and penetration of M. de Richelieu, without the avarice of M. de Mazarin!" —"A prime minister, Sire?" said Monsieur, in a fright.—"I will tell you all about that, brother; but it is strange that M. d'Herblay is not here!" He called out, "Let M. Fouquet be informed that I wish to speak to him— Oh, before you, before you; do not retire!"

M. de Saint-Aignan returned, bringing satisfactory news of the queen, who only kept her bed from precaution, and to have strength to carry out all the king's wishes. While some were seeking M. Fouquet and Aramis, Philippe quietly continued his experiments, and no one of the family, officers, or servants had the least suspicion; his air, voice, and manners were so like the king's. On his side, Philippe, applying to all countenances the faithful description furnished by his

The Man in the Iron Mask

accomplice Aramis, conducted himself so as not to give birth to a doubt in the minds of those who surrounded him.

Nothing from that time could disturb the usurper. With what strange facility had Providence just reversed the most elevated fortune of the world to substitute the most humble in its stead! Philippe admired the goodness of God with regard to himself, and seconded it with all the resources of his admirable nature. But he felt at times something like a shadow gliding between him and the rays of his new glory. Aramis did not appear. The conversation had languished in the royal family; Philippe, preoccupied, forgot to dismiss his brother and Madame Henrietta. The latter were astonished, and began by degrees to lose all patience. Anne of Austria stooped towards her son's ear, and addressed some words to him in Spanish. Philippe was completely ignorant of that language, and grew pale at this unexpected obstacle. But as if the spirit of the imperturbable Aramis had covered him with his infallibility, instead of appearing disconcerted, Philippe rose. "Well! what?" said Anne of Austria.

"What is all that noise?" said Philippe, turning round towards the door of the second staircase. And a voice was heard saying, "This way! this way! A few steps more, Sire!"—"The voice of M. Fouquet," said D'Artagnan, who was standing close to the queen-mother. "Then M. d'Herblay cannot be far off," added Philippe.

But he then saw what he little thought to see so near to him. All eyes were turned towards the door at which M. Fouquet was expected to enter; but it was not M. Fouquet who entered. A terrible cry resounded from all corners of the chamber. It is not given to men, even to those whose destiny contains the strangest elements and accidents the most wonderful, to contemplate a spectacle similar to that which presented itself in the royal chamber at that moment. The half-closed shutters admitted the entrance of only an uncertain light, passing through large velvet curtains lined with silk. In this soft shade the eyes were by degrees dilated, and every one present saw others rather with faith than with positive sight. In these circumstances, however, not one of the surrounding details could escape; and any new object which presented itself appeared as luminous as if it had been enlightened by the sun. So it was with Louis XIV., when he showed himself pale and frowning in the doorway of the secret stairs. The face of Fouquet appeared behind him, impressed with sorrow and sternness. The queen-mother, who perceived Louis XIV., and who held the hand of Philippe, uttered the cry of which we have spoken, as if she had beheld a phantom. Monsieur was bewildered, and kept turning his head in astonishment from one to the other. Madame made a step forward, thinking she saw the form of her brother-in-law reflected in a glass; and, in fact, the illusion was possible.

The two princes, both pale as death,—for we renounce the hope of being able to describe the fearful state of Philippe,—both trembling, and clinching their hands convulsively, measured each other with their looks and darted their eyes, like poniards, into each other. Mute, panting, bending forward, they appeared as if about to spring upon an enemy. The unheard-of resemblance of countenance, gesture, shape, height, even of costume,—produced by chance, for Louis XIV. had been to the Louvre and put on a violet-coloured suit,—the perfect likeness of the two princes completed the consternation of Anne of Austria. And yet she did not at once guess the truth. There are misfortunes in life that no one will accept; people would rather believe in the supernatural and the impossible. Louis had not reckoned upon these obstacles. He expected that he had only to appear and be acknowledged. A living sun, he could not endure the suspicion of parity with any one. He did not admit that every torch should not become darkness at the instant he shone out with his conquering ray. At the aspect of Philippe, then, he was perhaps more terrified than any one round him, and his silence, his immobility, were this time a concentration and a calm which precede violent explosions of passion.

But Fouquet! who could paint his emotion and stupor in presence of this living portrait of his master! Fouquet thought Aramis was right,—that this new-comer was a king as pure in his race as the other, and that for having repudiated all participation in this *coup d'état*, so skilfully got up by the general of the Jesuits, he must be a mad enthusiast unworthy of ever again dipping his hands in a political work. And then it was the blood of Louis XIII. which Fouquet was sacrificing to the blood of Louis XIII.; it was to a selfish ambition he was sacrificing a noble ambition; it was to the right of keeping he sacrificed the right of having! The whole extent of his fault was revealed to him by the simple sight of the pretender. All that passed in the mind of Fouquet was lost upon the persons present. He had five minutes to concentrate his meditations upon this point of the case of conscience; five minutes,—that is to say, five ages,—during which the two kings and their family scarely found time to breathe after so terrible a shock.

D'Artagnan, leaning against the wall in front of Fouquet, with his hand to his brow, asked himself the cause of such a wonderful prodigy. He could not have said at once why he doubted, but he knew assuredly that he had reason to doubt, and that in this meeting of the two Louis XIV.'s lay all the mystery which during late days had rendered the conduct of Aramis so suspicious to the musketeer. These ideas were, however, enveloped in thick veils. The actors in this assembly seemed to swim in the vapours of a confused waking.

Suddenly Louis XIV., more impatient and more accustomed to command, ran to one of the shutters, which he opened, tearing the curtains in his eagerness. A flood of living light entered the chamber, and made Philippe draw back to the alcove. Louis seized upon this movement with eagerness, and addressing himself to the queen, "My mother," said he, "do you not acknowledge your son, since every one here has forgotten his king?" Anne of Austria started, and raised her arms towards heaven, without being able to articulate a single word. "My mother," said Philippe, with a calm voice, "do you not acknowledge your son?" And this time, in his turn, Louis drew back.

As to Anne of Austria, struck in both head and heart with remorse, she was no longer able to stand. No one aiding her, for all were petrified, she sank back in her *fauteuil,* breathing a weak, trembling sigh. Louis could not endure this spectacle and this affront. He bounded towards D'Artagnan, upon whom the vertigo was beginning to gain, and who staggered as he caught at the door for support. *"A moi, mousquetaire!"* said he. "Look us in the face and say which is the paler, he or I!" This cry roused D'Artagnan, and stirred in his heart the fibre of obedience. He shook his head, and without more hesitation, he walked straight up to Philippe, upon whose shoulder he laid his hand, saying, "Monsieur, you are my prisoner!"

Philippe did not raise his eyes towards heaven, nor stir from the spot, where he seemed nailed to the floor, his eye intently fixed upon the king, his brother. He reproached him by a sublime silence with all his misfortunes past, with all his tortures to come. Against this

The False King

language of the soul Louis XIV. felt he had no power; he cast down his eyes, and led away precipitately his brother and sister, forgetting his mother, sitting motionless within three paces of the son whom she left a second time to be condemned to death. Philippe approached Anne of Austria, and said to her in a soft and nobly agitated voice, "If I were not your son, I should curse you, my mother, for having rendered me so unhappy."

D'Artagnan felt a shudder pass through the marrow of his bones. He bowed respectfully to the young prince, and said as he bent, "Excuse me, Monseigneur; I am but a soldier, and my oaths are his who has just left the chamber."—"Thank you, M. d'Artagnan; but what is become of M. d'Herblay?"—"M. d'Herblay is in safety, Monseigneur," said a voice behind them; "and no one, while I live and am free, shall cause a hair to fall from his head."

"M. Fouquet!" said the prince, smiling sadly.—"Pardon me, Monseigneur," said Fouquet, kneeling; "but he who is just gone out from hence was my guest."—"Here are," murmured Philippe, with a sigh, "brave friends and good hearts. They make me regret the world. On, M. d'Artagnan, I follow you!"

At the moment the captain of the musketeers was about to leave the room with his prisoner, Colbert appeared, and after delivering to D'Artagnan an order from the king, retired. D'Artagnan read the paper, and then crushed it in his hand with rage. "What is it?" asked the prince.—"Read, Monseigneur," relied the musketeer. Philippe read the following words, hastily traced by the hand of the king:—

"M. d'Artagnan will conduct the prisoner to the Ile Ste. Marguerite. He will cover his face with an iron visor, which the prisoner cannot raise without peril of his life."

"It is just," said Philippe, with resignation; "I am ready."—"Aramis was right," said Fouquet, in a low voice to the musketeer, "this one is quite as much of a king as the other."—"More," replied D'Artagnan. "He needs only you and me."

The Man in the Iron Mask

CHAPTER XXVI

IN WHICH PORTHOS THINKS HE IS PURSUING A DUCHY AND RAOUL PREPARES FOR AN EXPEDITION

ARAMIS and Porthos, having profited by the time granted them by Fouquet, did honour to the French cavalry by their speed. Porthos did not clearly understand for what kind of mission he was forced to display so much velocity; but as he saw Aramis spurring on furiously, he, Porthos, spurred on in the same manner. They had soon, in this manner, placed twelve leagues between them and Vaux; they were then obliged to change horses, and organise a sort of post arrangement. It was during a relay that Porthos ventured to interrogate Aramis discreetly. "Hush!" replied the latter; "know only that our fortune depends upon our speed."

"I shall be made a duke!" said Porthos, aloud. He was speaking to himself. "That is possible," replied Aramis, smiling after his own fashion, as the horse of Porthos passed him. Thus they travelled on for eight long hours, and then arrived at Orléans. It was four o'clock in the afternoon. Aramis, searching his recollections, judged that nothing demonstrated pursuit to be possible. It would be without example that a troop capable of taking him and Porthos should be furnished with relays sufficient to perform forty leagues in eight hours. Thus, admitting pursuit, which was not at all manifest, the fugitives were five hours in advance of their pursuers.

A noise of horses and voices was heard from the extremity of the road to Blois, the spacious country house to which Athos and his son Raoul had retired. Mounted torch-bearers shook their torches merrily among the trees of their route, and turned round from time to time to avoid distancing the horsemen who followed them. These flames, this noise, this dust of a dozen richly caparisoned horses, formed a strange impression in the middle of the night. The entrance gate appeared in a blaze as the flambeaux stopped and appeared to inflame the road. A cry was heard of "M. le Duc de Beaufort!" and Athos sprang towards the door of his house. But the duke had already alighted from his horse, and was looking around him.

Anne of Austria

Porthos Thinks He is Pursuing a Duchy

"I am here, Monseigneur," said Athos.—"Ah, good-evening, dear Count," said the prince, with that frank cordiality which won him so many hearts. "Is it too late for a friend?"—"Ah, my dear Prince, come in!" said the count. And M. de Beaufort leaning on the arm of Athos, they entered the house, followed by Raoul, who walked respectfully and modestly among the officers of the prince, with several of whom he was acquainted.

The prince turned round at the moment when Raoul, in order to leave him alone with Athos, was shutting the door, and preparing to go with the other officers into an adjoining apartment. "Is that the young man I have heard Monsieur the Prince speak so highly of?" asked M. de Beaufort.—"It is, Monseigneur."—"He is quite the soldier; let him stay, Count, we cannot spare him."

"Remain, Raoul, since Monseigneur permits it," said Athos.— "*Ma foi!* he is tall and handsome!" continued the duke. "Will you give him to me, Monseigneur, if I ask him of you?"—"How am I to understand you, Monseigneur?" said Athos.

"Why, I call upon you to bid you farewell."—"Farewell?"— "Yes, in good truth. Have you no idea of what I am about to be?"— "Why, what you have always been, Monseigneur,—a valiant prince and an excellent gentleman."—"I am going to be an African prince, —a Bedouin gentleman. The king is sending me to make conquests among the Arabs."—"What do you tell me, Monseigneur?"— "Strange, is it not? I, the Parisian *par essence*,—I, who have reigned in the faubourgs, and have been called King of the Halles— I am going to pass from the Place Maubert to the minarets of Djid-gelli; I become from a Frondeur and adventurer!"

"Oh, Monseigneur, if you did not yourself tell me that—"—"It would not be credible, would it? Believe me, nevertheless, and let us bid each other farewell. This is what comes of getting into favour again."—"Into favour?"—"Yes. You smile? Ah, my dear Count, do you know why I have accepted this enterprise; can you guess?"

"Because your Highness loves glory above everything."—"Oh, no; there is no glory in firing muskets at savages. I see no glory in that, for my part, and it is more probable that I shall there meet with something else. But I have wished, and still wish earnestly, my dear Count, that my life should have this last facet, after all the whimsical exhibitions I have made in fifty years. For, in short, you

179

must admit that it is sufficiently strange to be born the grandson of a king, to have made war against kings, to have been reckoned among the powers of the age, to have maintained my rank, to feel Henry IV. within me, to be great Admiral of France, and then to go and get killed at Djidgelli among all those Turks, Saracens, and Moors!"

"Monseigneur, you dwell strangely upon that subject," said Athos, in an agitated voice. "How can you suppose that so brilliant a destiny will be extinguished in that remote and miserable scene?"— "And can you believe, just and simple man as you are, that if I go into Africa for this ridiculous motive, I will not endeavour to come out of it without ridicule? Will I not give the world cause to speak of me? and to be spoken of nowadays, when there are Monsieur the Prince, M. de Turenne, and many others, my contemporaries, I, Admiral of France, grandson of Henry IV., King of Paris,—have I anything left but to get myself killed? *Cordieu!* I will be talked of, I tell you; I will be killed, whether or not,—if not there, somewhere else."

"Why, Monseigneur, this is only exaggeration; and hitherto you have demonstrated nothing of that kind but in bravery."—*"Peste!* my dear friend, there is bravery in facing scurvy, dysentery, locusts, and poisoned arrows, as my ancestor Saint Louis did. Do you know those fellows still use poisoned arrows? And then, you know me of old, I fancy; and you know that when I once make up my mind to a thing, I do it in earnest."

The duke began to laugh; then, addressing Raoul, who from the beginning of this conversation had sunk into a profound reverie, "Young man," said he, "I know there is to be found here a certain De Vouvray wine, and I believe—" Raoul left the room precipitately to order the wine. In the meantime, M. de Beaufort took the hand of Athos.

"What do you mean to do with him?" asked he.—"Nothing, at present, Monseigneur."—"Ah, yes, I know,—since the passion of the king for La Vallière."—"Yes, Monseigneur."—"That is all true then, is it? I think I know her, that little Vallière. She is not particularly handsome, if I remember rightly."—"No, Monseigneur," said Athos.

"Now, here is poor Raoul, who is your son, I believe."—"Yes, he is my son, Monseigneur."—"And the poor lad has been cut out by the king, and he frets."—"Better than that, Monseigneur, he abstains."

"You are going to let the boy rust in idleness; you are wrong. Come, give him to me!"—"My wish is to keep him at home, Monseigneur. I have no longer anything in the world but him, and as long as he is willing to remain—"—"Well, well," replied the duke. "I could, nevertheless, have soon put matters to rights again. I assure you, I think he has in him the stuff of which marshals of France are made; I have seen more than one produced from such material." —"That is very possible, Monseigneur; but it is the king who makes marshals of France, and Raoul will never accept anything of the king."

Raoul interrupted this conversation by his return. He preceded Grimaud, whose still steady hands carried the salver with one glass and a bottle of the duke's favourite wine.

"You are a charming friend," replied the Duc de Beaufort, who drank and passed the goblet to his companion. "But that is not all," continued he; "I am still thirsty, and I wish to do honour to this handsome young man who stands here. I carry good luck with me, Viscount," said he to Raoul; "wish for something while drinking out of my glass, and the plague stifle me if what you wish does not come to pass!" He held the goblet to Raoul, who hastily moistened his lips, and replied with the same promptitude, "I have wished for something, Monseigneur." His eyes sparkled with a gloomy fire, and the blood mounted to his cheeks; he terrified Athos, if only with his smile.

"And what have you wished for?" replied the duke, sinking back into his arm-chair, while with one hand he returned the bottle to Grimaud and with the other gave him a purse.—"Will you promise me, Monseigneur, to grant me what I wish for?"—"*Pardieu!* That is agreed upon."—"I wished, Monsieur the Duke, to go with you to Djidgelli."

Athos became pale, and was unable to conceal his agitation. The duke looked at his friend, as if desirous to assist him to parry this unexpected blow. "That is difficult, my dear Viscount, very difficult," added he, in a lower tone of voice.

"Pardon me, Monseigneur, I have been indiscreet," replied Raoul, in a firm voice; "but as you yourself invited me to wish—"—"To wish to leave me?" said Athos.—"Oh, Monsieur—can you imagine—" —"Well, *mordieu!*" cried the duke, "the young viscount is right!

The Man in the Iron Mask

What can he do here? He will rot with grief." Raoul blushed; and the prince, excited, continued, "War is a distraction. We gain everything by it; we can lose only one thing by it,—life; then so much the worse!"—"That is to say, memory," said Raoul, eagerly; "and that is to say, so much the better!"

He repented of having spoken so warmly when he saw Athos rise and open the window—which was doubtless to conceal his emotion. Raoul sprang towards the count, but the latter had already overcome his emotion, and turned to the lights with a serene and impassive countenance.

"Well, come," said the duke, "let us see! Shall he go, or shall he not? If he goes, Count, he shall be my aide-de-camp, my son."—"Monseigneur!" cried Raoul, bending his knee.—"Monseigneur!" cried Athos, taking the hand of the duke; "Raoul shall do just as he likes."—"Oh, no, Monsieur, just as you like," interrupted the young man.

"Par la corbleu!" said the prince, in his turn, "it is neither the count nor the viscount that shall have his way,—it is I. I will take him away. The navy offers a superb future, my friend." Raoul smiled again so sadly that this time Athos was wounded to the heart, and replied to him by a severe look. Raoul comprehended it all; he recovered his calmness, and was so guarded that not another word escaped him. The duke at length rose, on observing the advanced hour, and said with much animation, "I am in great haste, but if I am told I have lost time in talking with a friend, I will reply that I have gained a good recruit."

"Pardon me, Monsieur the Duke," interrupted Raoul, "do not tell the king so, for it is not the king I will serve."—"Eh, my friend, whom then will you serve? The times are past when you might have said, 'I belong to M. de Beaufort.' No, nowadays, we all belong to the king, great or small. Therefore, if you serve on board my vessels, there can be nothing equivocal in it, my dear Viscount; it will be the king you will serve."

Athos waited with a kind of impatient joy for the reply about to be made to this embarrassing question by Raoul, the intractable enemy of the king, his rival. The father hoped that the obstacle would overcome the desire. He was thankful to M. de Beaufort, whose lightness or generous reflection had thrown an impediment in the way of the departure of a son now his only joy.

Porthos Thinks He is Pursuing a Duchy

Raoul, still firm and tranquil, replied, "Monsieur the Duke, the objection you make I have already considered in my mind. I will serve on board your vessels, because you do me the honour to take me with you; but I shall there serve a more powerful master than the king,—I shall serve God!"—"God! how so?" said the duke and Athos together.—"My intention is to make profession, and become a Knight of Malta," added Bragelonne, letting fall one by one words more icy than the drops which fall from the bare trees after the tempests of winter.

"Here is your commission," said the prince to Raoul a few days later. "I had prepared it, reckoning upon you. You will go on before me as far as Antibes."—"Yes, Monseigneur."—"Here is the order;" and De Beaufort gave Raoul the order. "Do you know anything of the sea?"—"Yes, Monseigneur; I have travelled with Monsieur the Prince."

"That is well. All these barges and lighters must be in attendance to form an escort, and carry my provisions. The army must be prepared to embark in a fortnight at latest."—"That shall be done, Monseigneur."—"The present order gives you the right to visit and search all the isles along the coast; you will there make the enrolments and levies you may want for me."—"Yes, Monsieur the Duke."

"And as you are an active man, and will work freely, you will spend much money."—"I hope not, Monseigneur."—"But I reckon you will. My intendant has prepared orders of a thousand livres, drawn upon the cities of the south; he will give you a hundred of them. Now, dear Viscount, begone!"

Athos interrupted the prince. "Keep your money, Monseigneur; war is to be made among the Arabs with gold as well as lead."—"I wish to try the contrary," replied the duke; "and then, you are acquainted with my ideas upon the expedition,—plenty of noise, plenty of fire, and, if so it must be, I shall disappear in the smoke." Having spoken thus, M. de Beaufort began to laugh; but his mirth was not reciprocated by Athos and Raoul. He perceived this at once. "Ah," said he, with the courteous egotism of his rank and his age, "you are such people as a man should not see after dinner; you are cold, stiff, and dry, when I am all fire, all suppleness, and all wine.

183

No, devil take me! I shall always see you fasting, Viscount; and you, Count, if you wear such a face as that, I will see no more."

He said this, pressing the hand of Athos, who replied with a smile, "Monseigneur, do not talk so grandly because you happen to have plenty of money. I predict that within a month you will be dry, stiff, and cold in presence of your strong-box, and that then, having Raoul at your elbow, fasting, you will be surprised to see him gay, animated, and generous, because he will have some new crowns to offer you."—"God grant it may be so!" cried the delighted duke. "Count, stay with me."

"No, I shall go with Raoul; the mission with which you charge him is a troublesome and a difficult one. Alone, it would be too much for him to execute. You do not observe, Monseigneur, that you have given him a command of the first order."—"Bah!"—"And in the navy!"—"That may be true. But when people resemble him, do they not do all that is required of them?"

"Monseigneur, I believe you will find nowhere so much zeal and intelligence, so much real bravery, as in Raoul; but if he failed in your embarkation, you would only meet with what you deserve."—"Humph! you are scolding me, then?"—"Prince, to provision a fleet, to assemble a flotilla, to enrol your maritime force, would take an admiral a year. Raoul is a cavalry officer, and you allow him a fortnight!"—"I tell you he will get through."—"He may; but I will help him."—"To be sure you will,—I reckoned upon you; and still further, I believe that when we are once at Toulon you will not let him depart alone."—"Oh!" said Athos, shaking his head.

"Patience! patience!"—"Monseigneur, permit us to take our leave."—"Go, then, and may my good fortune attend you!"— "Adieu, Monseigneur; and may your good fortune attend you likewise!"

"Here is an expedition admirably begun!" said Athos to his son. "No provisions, no reserves, no store flotilla! What can be done thus?"—"Humph!" murmured Raoul; "if all are going to do as I am, provisions will not be wanted."—"Monsieur," replied Athos, sternly, "do not be unjust and senseless in your egotism, or your grief, whichever you please to call it. If you set out for this war solely with the intention of getting killed in it, you stand in need of nobody, and it was scarcely worth while to recommend you to M. de Beaufort. But when you have been introduced to the prince commandant; when you have accepted the responsibility of a post in his army,—the question is no longer about you, but about all those poor soldiers who as well as you have hearts and bodies, who will weep for their country and endure all the necessities of their human condition. Remember, Raoul, that an officer is a minister as useful as a priest, and that he ought to have more charity than a priest."

"Monsieur, I know it, and have practised it; I would have continued to do so still, but—"—"You forget also that you are of a country which is proud of its military glory; go and die if you like, but do not die without honour and without advantage to France. Cheer up, Raoul! do not let my words grieve you; I love you, and wish to see you perfect."—"I love your reproaches, Monsieur," said the young man mildly; "they alone may cure me, because they prove to me that some one loves me still."

"And now, Raoul, let us be off, the weather is so fine, the heavens are so pure,—those heavens which we shall always find above our heads, which you will see more pure still at Djidgelli, and which will speak to you of me there, as they speak to me here of God."

The two gentlemen, after having agreed on this point, talked over the wild freaks of the duke, convinced that France would be served in a very incomplete manner, as regarded both spirit and practice, in the ensuing expedition; and having summed up his policy under the word "vanity," they set forward, in obedience to their will even more than to their destiny. The sacrifice was accomplished.

CHAPTER XXVII

THE SILVER PLATE

THE journey passed off pretty well. Athos and his son traversed France at the rate of fifteen leagues per day; sometimes more, sometimes less, according to the intensity of Raoul's grief. It took them a fortnight to reach Toulon.

When Raoul began his labour of classing the flotilla, and got together the *chalands* and lighters to send them to Toulon, one of the fishermen told the count that his boat had been laid up to refit since a trip he had made on account of a gentleman who was in great haste

185

to embark. Athos, believing that this man was telling a falsehood in order to be left at liberty to fish, and so gain more money when all his companions were gone, insisted upon having the details.

The fisherman informed him that six days previously a man had come in the night to hire his boat, for the purpose of visiting the Island of St. Honorat. The price was agreed upon; but the gentleman had arrived with an immense carriage-case, which he insisted upon embarking in spite of all the difficulties which opposed themselves to that operation. The fisherman had wished to retract; he had even threatened, but his threats had procured him nothing but a shower of blows from the gentleman's cane, which fell upon his shoulders, sharp and long. Swearing and grumbling, he had recourse to the syndic of his brotherhood at Antibes, who administer justice among themselves and protect one another; but the gentleman had exhibited a certain paper, at the sight of which the syndic, bowing to the very ground, had enjoined obedience upon the fisherman, and abused him for having been refractory. They then departed with the freight.

"But all this does not tell us," said Athos, "how you have injured your boat."—"This is the way. I was steering towards St. Honorat as the gentleman had desired me; but he changed his mind, and pretended that I could not pass to the south of the abbey."—"And why not?"—"Because, Monsieur, there is in front of the square tower of the Benedictines, towards the southern point, the bank of the *Moines*."—"A rock?" asked Athos.—"Level with the water, and below it; a dangerous passage, but one I have cleared a thousand times. The gentleman required me to land him at Ste. Marguerite."

"Well?"—"Well, Monsieur!" cried the fisherman, with his provençal accent, "a man is a sailor, or he is not; he knows his course, or he is nothing but a fresh-water lubber. I was obstinate, and wished to try the channel. The gentleman took me by the collar, and told me quietly he would strangle me. My mate armed himself with a hatchet, and so did I: we had the affront of the night before to pay him off for. But the gentleman drew his sword, and used it in such an astonishingly rapid manner that we neither of us could get near him. I was about to hurl my hatchet at his head, and I had a right to do so, hadn't I, Monsieur? for a sailor aboard is master, as a citizen is in his chamber,—I was going, then, in self-defence, to cut the gentleman in two, when all at once (believe me or not, Monsieur) the great carriage-case opened of itself, I don't know how, and there

Raoul ran to pick up a silver plate

came out of it a sort of a phantom, his head covered with a black helmet and a black mask, something terrible to look upon, which came towards me threatening with its fist."—"And that was?" said Athos. —"That was the Devil, Monsieur,—for the gentleman, with great glee, cried out on seeing him, 'Ah, thank you, Monseigneur!'"

"A strange story!" murmured the count, looking at Raoul.—"And what did you do?" asked the latter of the fisherman.—"You must know, Monsieur, that two poor men like us were already too few to fight against two gentlemen; but against the Devil, ah! Well, we didn't stop to consult each other,—we made but one jump into the sea, for we were within seven or eight hundred feet of the shore."— "Well, and then?"—"Why, and then, Monseigneur, as there was a little wind from the southwest, the boat drifted into the sands of Ste. Marguerite."

"Oh! but the two travellers?"—"Bah! you need not be uneasy about them! It was pretty plain that one was the Devil, and protected the other,—for when we recovered the boat, after she got afloat again, instead of finding these two creatures injured by the shock, we found nothing, not even the carriage-case."

"Very strange! very strange!" repeated the count. "But since that what have you done, my friend?"—"I made my complaint to the governor of Ste. Marguerite, who brought my finger under my nose while telling me if I plagued him with such silly stories he would have me flogged."—"What! did the governor say so?"—"Yes, Monsieur; and yet my boat was injured, seriously injured, for the prow is left upon the point of Ste. Marguerite, and the carpenter asks a hundred and twenty livres to repair it."—"Very well," replied Raoul; "you will be exempted from the service. Go."

"We will go to Ste. Marguerite, shall we?" said the count to Bragelonne, as the man walked away.—"Yes, Monsieur, for there is something to be cleared up; that man does not seem to me to have told the truth."—"Nor to me, Raoul. The story of the masked man and the carriage-case having disappeared may be told to conceal some violence these fellows have committed upon their passenger in the open sea, to punish him for his persistence in embarking."

"I formed the same suspicion; the carriage-case was more likely to contain property than a man."—"We shall see to that, Raoul. This gentleman very much resembles D'Artagnan; I recognise his mode of proceeding. Alas! we are no longer the young invincibles of former days. Who knows whether the hatchet or the iron bar of this miserable coaster has not succeeded in doing that which the best blades of Europe, balls, and bullets have not been able to do in forty years?"

That same day they set out for Ste. Marguerite's, on board a *chasse-marée* come from Toulon under orders. The impression they felt on landing was a singularly pleasing one. The isle was full of flowers and fruits. In its cultivated part it served as a garden for the governor. Orange, pomegranate and fig trees bent beneath the weight of their golden or purple fruits. All around this garden, in the uncultivated parts, the red partridges ran about in coveys among the brambles and tufts of junipers, and at every step of the count and Raoul a terrified rabbit quitted his thyme and heath to scuttle away to his burrow. In fact, this fortunate isle was uninhabited. Flat, offering nothing but a tiny bay for the convenience of embarkation, under the protection of the governor, who went shares with them, smugglers made use of it as a provisional *entrepôt*, under condition of not killing the game or devastating the garden. With this compromise, the governor was in a situation to be satisfied with a garrison of eight men to guard his fortress, in which twelve cannon accumulated their coats of mouldy green. The governor was a sort of happy farmer, harvesting wines, figs, oil, and oranges, preserving his citrons and *cédrats* in the sun of his casemates. The fortress, encircled by a deep ditch, its only guardian, raised like three heads its three turrets connected with one another by terraces covered with moss.

Athos and Raoul wandered for some time round the fences of the garden without finding any one to introduce them to the governor. They ended by making their own way into the garden. It was at the hottest time of the day. Everything sought shelter beneath grass or stone. The heavens spread their fiery veils as if to stifle all noises, to envelop all existences; the rabbit under the broom, the fly under the leaf, slept as the wave did beneath the heavens. Athos saw nothing living but a soldier upon the terrace beneath the second and third courts, who was carrying a basket of provisions on his head. This man returned almost immediately without his basket, and disappeared in the shade of his sentry-box. Athos supposed this man must have been carrying dinner to some one, and after having done so, returned to dine himself. All at once they heard some one call out, and raising their heads, perceived in the frame of the bars

The Silver Plate

of the window something of a white colour, like a hand that was waved backwards and forwards,—something shining, like a polished weapon struck by the rays of the sun. And before they were able to ascertain what it was they saw, a luminous train accompanied by a hissing sound in the air called their attention from the donjon to the ground. A second dull noise was heard from the ditch, and Raoul ran to pick up a silver plate which was rolling along the dry sand. The hand which had thrown this plate made a sign to the two gentlemen and then disappeared. Athos and Raoul, approaching each other, began an attentive examination of the dusty plate; and they discovered, in characters traced upon the bottom of it with the point of a knife, this inscription:—

"I AM THE BROTHER OF THE KING OF FRANCE: A PRISONER TO-DAY, A MADMAN TO-MORROW. FRENCH GENTLEMEN AND CHRISTIANS, PRAY TO GOD FOR THE SOUL AND THE REASON OF THE SON OF YOUR MASTERS."

The plate fell from the hands of Athos while Raoul was endeavouring to make out the meaning of these dismal words. At the same instant they heard a cry from the top of the donjon. As quick as lightning Raoul bent down his head, and forced down that of his father likewise. A musket-barrel glittered from the crest of the wall. A white smoke floated like a plume from the mouth of the musket, and a ball was flattened against a stone within six inches of the two gentlemen. Another musket appeared, which was aimed at them.

"*Cordieu!*" cried Athos. "What! are people assassinated here? Come down, cowards as you are!"—"Yes, come down!" cried Raoul, furiously shaking his fist at the citadel.

One of the assailants—he who was about to fire—replied to these cries by an exclamation of surprise; and as his companion, who wished to continue the attack, had reseized his loaded musket, he who had cried out threw up the weapon, and the ball flew into the air. Athos and Raoul, seeing them disappear from the platform, expected that they would come to them, and waited with a firm demeanour. Five minutes had not elapsed when a stroke upon a drum called the eight soldiers of the garrison to arms, and they showed themselves on the other side of the ditch with their muskets in hand. At the head of these men was an officer, whom Athos and Raoul recognised as the one who had fired the first musket. The man ordered the soldiers to "make ready." "We are going to be shot!" cried Raoul; "but, sword in hand, at least let us leap the ditch. We shal certainly kill two of these scoundrels when their muskets are empty.'

And suiting the action to the word, Raoul was springing forward followed by Athos, when a well-known voice resounded behind them "Athos! Raoul!"—"D'Artagnan!" replied the two gentlemen.

"Recover arms! *Mordioux!*" cried the captain to the soldiers. "I was sure I could not be mistaken!"—"What is the meaning of this?" asked Athos. "What! were we to be shot without warning?"—"It was I who was going to shoot you; and if the governor missed you, I should not have missed you, my dear friends. How fortunate it is that I am accustomed to take a long aim, instead of firing at the instant I raise my weapon! I thought I recognized you. Ah, my dear friends, how fortunate!" and D'Artagnan wiped his brow,— for he had run fast, and emotion with him was not feigned.

"How!" said Athos; "and is the gentleman who fired at us the governor of the fortress?"—"In person."—"And why did he fire at us? What have we done to him?"—"*Pardieu!* You received what the prisoner threw to you?"—"That is true."—"That plate,—the prisoner has written something on the bottom of it, has he not?"— "Yes."—"Good heavens! I was afraid he had."

And D'Artagnan, with all the marks of mortal alarm, seized the plate to read the inscription. When he had read it, a fearful pallor spread over his countenance. "Oh, good heavens!" repeated he. "Silence! here is the governor."—"And what will he do to us? Is it our fault?" asked Raoul.—"It is true, then?" said Athos, in a sub-dued voice; "it is true?"

"Silence, I tell you, silence! If he only believes you can read, if he only suspects you have understood— I love you, my dear friends, I will be killed for you; but—"—" 'But—' " said Athos to Raoul.— "But I could not save you from perpetual imprisonment, if I saved you from death. Silence, then! silence again!"

The governor came up, having crossed the ditch upon a plank bridge. "Well," said he to D'Artagnan, "what stops us?"—"You are Spaniards; you do not understand a word of French," said the captain, eagerly to his friends in a low voice. "Well!" replied he, addressing the governor, "I was right; these gentlemen are two Spanish captains with whom I was acquainted at Ypres, last year. They don't know a word of French."—"Ah!" said the governor, sharply. "And yet they were trying to read the inscription on the plate."

D'Artagnan took it out of his hands, effacing the characters with the point of his sword. "How!" cried the governor; "what are you doing? I cannot read them now!"—"It is a state secret," replied D'Artagnan, bluntly; "and as you know that according to the king's orders it is under the penalty of death that any one should penetrate it, I will, if you like, allow you to read it and have you shot immediately afterwards."

During this apostrophe—half serious, half ironical—Athos and Raoul preserved the coolest, most unconcerned silence. "But, is it possible," said the governor, "that these gentlemen do not comprehend at least some words?"—"Suppose they do! If they do understand a few spoken words it does not follow that they should understand what is written. They cannot even read Spanish. A noble Spaniard, remember, ought never to know how to read."

The governor was obliged to be satisfied with these explanations; but he was still tenacious. "Invite these gentlemen to come to the fortress," said he.—"That I will willingly do. I was about to propose it to you." The fact is, the captain had quite another idea, and would have wished his friends a hundred leagues off. But he was obliged to make the best of it. He addressed the two gentlemen in Spanish, giving them a polite invitation, which they accepted. They all turned towards the entrance of the fort, and the incident being exhausted, the eight soldiers returned to their delightful leisure, for a moment disturbed by this unexpected adventure.

CHAPTER XXVIII

CAPTIVE AND JAILERS

WHEN they had entered the fort, and while the governor was making some preparations for the reception of his guests, "Come," said Athos, "let us have a word of explanation while we are alone."—"It is simply this," replied the musketeer. "I have conducted hither a prisoner, who the king commands shall not be seen. You came here; he has thrown something to you through the lattice of his window. I was at dinner with the governor; I saw the object thrown, and I saw Raoul pick it up. It does not take long to understand this. I understood it; and I thought you in intelligence with my prisoner. And then—"

"And then—you commanded us to be shot."—"*Ma foi!* I admit it; but if I was the first to seize a musket, fortunately I was the last to take aim at you."—"If you had killed me, D'Artagnan, I should have had the good fortune to die for the royal house of France; and it would be an honour to die by your hand,—you, its noblest and most loyal defender."

"What the devil, Athos, do you mean by the royal house?" stammered D'Artagnan. "You don't mean that you, a well-informed and sensible man, can place any faith in the nonsense written by an idiot?"—"I do believe in it."—"With the more reason, my dear Chevalier, for your having orders to kill all those who do believe in it," said Raoul.

"That is because," replied the captain of the musketeers,—"because every calumny, however absurd it may be, has the almost certain chance of becoming popular."—"No, D'Artagnan," replied Athos, in a low tone; "but because the king is not willing that the secret of his family should transpire among the people, and cover with shame the executioners of the son of Louis XIII."

"Do not talk in such a childish manner, Athos, or I shall begin to think you have lost your senses. Besides, explain to me how it is possible Louis XIII. should have a son in the Isle of Ste. Marguerite?"—"A son whom you have brought hither masked, in a fishing-boat," said Athos. "Why not?" D'Artagnan was brought to a pause. "Ah, ah!" said he; "whence do you know that a fishing-boat—"—"Brought you to Ste. Marguerite with the carriage-case containing the prisoner,—with a prisoner whom you styled Monseigneur. Oh, I am acquainted with all that," resumed the count. D'Artagnan bit his moustache.

"If it were true," said he, "that I had brought hither in a boat and with a carriage a masked prisoner, nothing proves that this prisoner must be a prince,—a prince of the house of France."—"Oh! ask that of Aramis," replied Athos, coolly.—"Of Aramis!" cried the musketeer, quite at a stand. "Have you seen Aramis?"—"After his discomfiture at Vaux, yes. I have seen Aramis, a fugitive, pursued, ruined; and Aramis has told me enough to make me believe in the complaints that this unfortunate young man inscribed upon the silver plate."

D'Artagnan's head sunk upon his breast with confusion. "This is the way," said he, "in which God turns to nothing that which men call their wisdom! A fine secret must that be of which twelve or fifteen persons hold the tattered fragments! Athos, cursed be the chance which has brought you face to face with me in this affair! for now—"

"Well," said Athos, with his customary mild severity, "is your secret lost because I know it? Consult your memory, my friend. Have I not borne secrets as heavy as this?"—"You have never borne one so dangerous," replied D'Artagnan, in a tone of sadness. "I have something like a sinister idea that all who are concerned with this secret will die, and die unfortunately."—"The will of God be done!" said Athos; "but here is your governor."

D'Artagnan and his friends immediately resumed their parts. The governor, suspicious and hard, behaved towards D'Artagnan with a politeness almost amounting to obsequiousness. With respect to the travellers, he contented himself with offering them good cheer, and never taking his eye from them. Athos and Raoul observed that he often tried to embarrass them by sudden attacks, or to catch them off their guard; but neither the one nor the other gave him the least advantage. What D'Artagnan had said was probable, if the governor did not believe it to be quite true. They rose from the table to repose awhile.

"What is this man's name? I don't like the looks of him," said Athos to D'Artagnan, in Spanish.—"De Saint-Mars," replied the captain.—"He will be, then, the prince's jailer?"—"Eh! how can I tell? I may be kept at Ste. Marguerite for ever."

"Oh, no, not you!"—"My friend, I am in the situation of a man who finds a treasure in the midst of a desert. He would like to carry it away, but he cannot; he would like to leave it, but he dare not. The king will not dare to recall me, for fear no one else would serve him as faithfully as I; he regrets not having me near him, from being aware that no one will be of so much service near his person as myself. But it will happen as it may please God."—"But," observed Raoul, "your not being certain proves that your situation here is provisional, and you will return to Paris."

"Ask these gentlemen," interrupted the governor, "what was their purpose in coming to Ste. Marguerite."—"They came because they had heard that there was a convent of Benedictines at St. Honorat which is considered curious; and from being told there was excellent shooting in the island."—"That is quite at their service, as well as yours," replied De Saint-Mars. D'Artagnan politely thanked him. "When will they depart?" added the governor.—"To-morrow," replied D'Artagnan.

M. de Saint-Mars went to make his rounds, and left D'Artagnan alone with the pretended Spaniards. "Oh!" exclaimed the musketeer, "here is a life with a society that suits me but little. I command this man; and he bores me, *mordioux!* Come, let us have a shot or two at the rabbits; the walk will be beautiful, and not fatiguing. The isle is but a league and a half in length, upon a breadth of a league, —a real park. Let us try to amuse ourselves."—"As you please, D'Artagnan; not for the sake of amusing ourselves, but to gain an opportunity for talking freely."

D'Artagnan made a sign to a soldier, who brought the gentlemen some guns, and then returned to the fort. "And now," said the musketeer, "answer me the question put to you by that black-looking Saint-Mars. What did you come to do at the Lérins Isles?"—"To bid you farewell."—"Bid me farewell! What do you mean by that? Is Raoul going anywhere?"—"Yes."—"Then I will lay a wager it is with M. de Beaufort."—"With M. de Beaufort it is, my dear friend; you always guess rightly."—"From habit."

After the shooting, as they were passing over the ramparts to a gallery of which D'Artagnan had the key, they saw M. de Saint-Mars directing his steps towards the chamber inhabited by the prisoner. Upon a sign from D'Artagnan, they concealed themselves in an angle of the staircase. "What is it?" said Athos.—"You will see. Look! the prisoner is returning from chapel."

And by the red flashes of the lightning against the violet fog which the wind spread upon the background of the sky, they saw pass gravely, at six paces behind the governor, a man clothed in black and masked by a visor of polished steel soldered to a helmet of the same nature, which altogether enveloped the whole of his head. The fire of the heavens cast red reflections upon the polished surface, and these reflections, flying off capriciously, seemed to be angry looks launched by this unfortunate, instead of imprecations. In the middle of the gallery, the prisoner stopped for a moment to contemplate the infinite horizon, to inhale the sulphurous perfumes of the tempest, to drink in thirstily the hot rain, and to breathe a sigh resembling a smothered roar. "Come on, Monsieur," said De Saint-Mars, sharply to the prisoner, for he already became uneasy at seeing him look so long beyond the walls. "Monsieur, come on!"

"Say Monseigneur!" cried Athos, from his corner, with a voice so solemn and terrible that the governor trembled from head to foot. Athos always wished respect to be paid to fallen majesty. The prisoner turned round. "Who spoke?" asked De Saint-Mars.—"It was I," replied D'Artagnan, showing himself promptly. "You know that is the order."—"Call me neither Monsieur nor Monseigneur," said the prisoner in his turn, in a voice that penetrated to the very soul of Raoul; "call me ACCURSED!" He passed on, and the iron door creaked after him.

"That is truly an unfortunate man!" murmured the musketeer, in a hollow whisper, pointing out to Raoul the chamber inhabited by the prince.

Scarcely had D'Artagnan re-entered his apartment with his two friends, when one of the soldiers of the fort came to inform him that the governor was seeking for him. A bark which Raoul had perceived at sea, and which appeared so eager to gain the port, came to Ste. Marguerite with an important despatch for the captain of the musketeers. On opening it, D'Artagnan recognised the writing of the king: "I should think," said Louis XIV., "that you must have completed the execution of my orders, M. d'Artagnan; return then immediately to Paris, and join me at the Louvre."—"There is the end of my exile!" cried the musketeer, with joy; "God be praised, I am no longer a jailer!" and he showed the letter to Athos.

"So then you must leave us?" replied the latter, in a melancholy tone.—"Yes; but to meet again, dear friend, seeing that Raoul is old enough now to go alone with M. de Beaufort, and will prefer that his father should go back in company with M. d'Artagnan, rather than that he should travel two hundred leagues solitarily to reach home at La Fère; would you not, Raoul?"—"Certainly," stammered the latter, with an expression of tender regret.

"No, no, my friend," interrupted Athos, "I will never quit Raoul till the day his vessel shall have disappeared on the horizon. As long as he remains in France, he shall not be separated from me."—"As you please, dear friend; but we will, at least, leave Ste. Marguerite together. Take advantage of the bark which will convey me back to Antibes."—"With all my heart; we cannot too soon be at a distance from this fort, and from the spectacle which saddened us so just now."

The three friends quitted the little isle, after paying their respects to the governor, and by the last flashes of the departing tempest they took their farewell of the white walls of the fort. D'Artagnan parted from his friends that same night, after having seen fire set to the carriage-case upon the shore by the orders of De Saint-Mars, according to the advice the captain had given him.

CHAPTER XXIX

BELLE-ISLE-EN-MER

IT WAS two o'clock in the afternoon. The king, full of impatience, went to his cabinet on the terrace, and kept opening the door of the corridor to see what his secretaries were doing.

D'Artagnan was summoned. "Monsieur," said the king, "you will go immediately and take possession of the isle and fief of Belle-Isle-en-Mer."—"Yes, Sire. Alone?"—"You will take a sufficient number of troops to prevent delay, in case the place should be contumacious." A murmur of adulatory incredulity arose from the group of courtiers. "That is to be done," said D'Artagnan.

"I saw the place in my infancy," resumed the king, "and I do not wish to see it again. You have heard me? Go, Monsieur, and do not return without the keys of the place. A commission which, if you carry it out well, will be worth a marshal's bâton to you."

"Why do you employ the words, 'if you carry it out well'?"—"Because it is difficult."—"Ah! in what respect?"—"You have friends in Belle-Isle, M. d'Artagnan; and it is not an easy thing for men like you to march over the bodies of their friends to obtain success."

A quarter of an hour after, the captain received the written order from the king to blow up the fortress of Belle-Isle in case of resistance, with the power of life and death over all the inhabitants or refugees, and an injunction not to allow one to escape. "He was right," thought D'Artagnan,—"my bâton of a marshal of France will cost the lives of my two friends. Only they seem to forget that my friends are not more stupid than the birds, and that they will not wait for the hand of the fowler to extend their wings. I will show them that hand so plainly that they will have quite time enough to see it. Poor Porthos! poor Aramis! No; my fortune shall not cost your wings a feather."

Having thus determined, D'Artagnan assembled the royal army, embarked it at Paimbœuf, and set sail without losing a moment.

At the extremity of the pier, upon the promenade which the furious sea beats at evening tide, two men, holding each other by the arm, were conversing in an animated and expansive tone, without the possibility of any other human being hearing their words, borne away, as they were, one by one, by the gusts of wind with the white foam swept from the crests of the waves. The sun had just gone down in the vast sheet of ocean, red like a gigantic crucible. From time to time, one of these men, turning towards the east, cast an anxious, inquiring look over the sea. The other, interrogating the features of his companion, seemed to seek for information in his looks. Then, both silent, both busied with dismal thoughts, they resumed their walk. Every one has already perceived that those two men were our proscribed heroes, Porthos and Aramis, who had taken refuge in Belle-Isle since the ruin of their hopes, since the discomfiture of the vast plan of M. d'Herblay.

"It is of no use your saying anything to the contrary, my dear Aramis," repeated Porthos, inhaling vigorously the saline air with which he filled his powerful chest. "It is of no use, Aramis. The disappearance of all the fishing-boats that went out two days ago is not an ordinary circumstance. There has been no storm at sea; the weather has been constantly calm, not even the slightest gale; and even if we had had a tempest, all our boats would not have foundered. I repeat, it is strange. This complete disappearance astonishes me, I tell you."

"True," murmured Aramis. "You are right, friend Porthos; it is true, there is something strange in it."—"And further," added Porthos, whose ideas the assent of the Bishop of Vannes seemed to enlarge,—"and further, have you remarked that if the boats have perished, not a single plank has been washed ashore?"—"I have remarked that as well as you."—"Have you remarked, besides, that the only two boats we had left in the whole island, and which I sent in search of the others—"

Aramis here interrupted his companion by a cry, and by so sudden a movement that Porthos stopped as if he were stupefied. "What do you say, Porthos? What! You have sent the two boats—"—"In search of the others. Yes; to be sure I have," replied Porthos, quite simply.—"Unhappy man! What have you done? Then we are indeed lost," cried the bishop.

"Lost! What did you say?" exclaimed the terrified Porthos. "How lost, Aramis? How are we lost?" Aramis bit his lips. "Nothing! nothing! Your pardon, I meant to say—"—"What?"—"That if we were inclined—if we took a fancy to make an excursion by sea, we could not."

"Very good! and why should that vex you? A fine pleasure, *ma foi!* For my part, I don't regret it at all. What I regret is certainly not the more or less amusement we can find at Belle-Isle; what I regret, Aramis, is Pierrefonds, is Bracieux, is Le Vallon, is my beautiful France! Here we are not in France, my dear friend; we are —I know not where. Oh! I tell you in the full sincerity of my soul,— and your affection will excuse my frankness,—but I declare to you I am not happy at Belle-Isle. No; in good truth, I am not happy!" Aramis breathed a stifled sigh. "Dear friend," replied he, "that is why it is so sad a thing you have sent the two boats we had left in search of those which disappeared two days ago. If you had not sent them away, we would have departed."

" 'Departed!' And the orders, Aramis?"—"What orders?"— *"Parbleu!* Why, the orders you have been constantly and on all occasions repeating to me,—that we were to hold Belle-Isle against the usurper. You know very well!"—"That is true!" murmured Aramis again.—"You see, then, plainly, my friend, that we could not depart; and that the sending away of the boats in search of the others is not prejudicial to us in any way."

Aramis was silent; and his vague glance, luminous as that of a gull, hovered for a long time over the sea, interrogating space, and seeking to pierce the very horizon.

"With all that, Aramis," continued Porthos, who adhered to his idea, and that the more closely since the bishop had found it correct, —"with all that, you give me no explanation about what can have happened to these unfortunate boats. I am assailed by cries and

complaints whichever way I go. The children cry at seeing the deso-
lation of the women, as if I could restore the absent husbands and
fathers. What do you suppose, my friend, and what ought I
to answer them?"—"Suppose everything, my good Porthos, and say
nothing."

This reply did not satisfy Porthos at all. He turned away, grumbling some words in a very ill humour. Aramis stopped the valiant
soldier. "Do you remember," said he, in a melancholy tone, pressing
the two hands of the giant between his own with an affectionate cordiality, "do you remember, my friend, that in the glorious days of
our youth—do you remember, Porthos, when we were all strong and
valiant—we and the other two—if we had then had an inclination to
return to France, do you think this sheet of salt water would have
stopped us?"—"Oh!" said Porthos; "six leagues!"

"If you had seen me get astride of a plank, would you have remained on land, Porthos?"—"No, *pardieu!* No, Aramis. But nowadays what sort of a plank should we want, my friend,—I, in
particular?" And the Seigneur de Bracieux cast a proud glance over
his colossal rotundity, with a loud laugh. "And do you mean seriously to say that you are not a little tired of Belle-Isle also, and that
you would not prefer the comforts of your dwelling,—of your episco-
pal palace at Vannes? Come, confess!"—"No," replied Aramis,
without daring to look at Porthos.

"Let us stay where we are, then," said his friend, with a sigh which
in spite of the efforts he made to restrain it escaped from his breast.
"Let us remain! let us remain! And yet," added he,—"and yet, if
we seriously wished, but that decidedly, if we had a fixed idea, one
firmly taken, to return to France, and there were no boats—"

"Have you remarked another thing, my friend?—that is, since the
disappearance of our boats, during the two days' absence of the fishermen, not a single small boat has landed on the shores of the isle?"
—"Yes, certainly; you are right. I have remarked it also; and the
observation was the more naturally made, for before the last two
fatal days we saw boats and shallops arrive by dozens."

"I must inquire," said Aramis, suddenly, and with emphasis.
"And then, if I had a raft constructed—"—"But there are some ca-
noes, my friend; shall I go on board one?"—"A canoe! a canoe!
Can you think of such a thing, Porthos? A canoe to be upset in!

No, no," said the Bishop of Vannes; "it is not our trade to ride upon the waves. We will wait; we will wait."

And Aramis continued walking about with increased agitation. Porthos, who grew tired of following all the feverish movements of his friend; Porthos, who in his calmness and trust understood nothing of the sort of exasperation which was betrayed by the bishop's continual convulsive starts,—Porthos stopped him. "Let us sit down upon this rock," said he. "Place yourself there, close to me, Aramis, and I conjure you for the last time to explain to me in a manner I can comprehend,—explain to me what we are doing here."—"Porthos!" said Aramis, much embarrassed.

"I know that the false king wished to dethrone the true king. That is a fact that I understand. Well—"—"Yes," said Aramis.—"I know that the false king formed the project of selling Belle-Isle to the English. I understand that too."—"Yes."—"I know that we engineers and captains came and threw ourselves into Belle-Isle to take the direction of the works and the command of the ten companies levied and paid by M. Fouquet, or rather the ten companies of his son-in-law. All that is plain."

Aramis arose in a state of great impatience. He might be said to be a lion importuned by a gnat. Porthos held him by the arm. "But what I cannot understand, what in spite of all the efforts of my mind and all my reflections I cannot comprehend and never shall comprehend, is, that instead of sending us troops, instead of sending us reinforcements of men, munitions, and provisions, they leave us without boats, they leave Belle-Isle without arrivals, without help; it is that instead of establishing with us a correspondence, whether by signals or written or verbal communications, they intercept all relations with us. Tell me, Aramis; answer me, or rather, before answering me, will you allow me to tell you what I have thought? Will you hear what my idea is, what imagination I have conceived?" The bishop raised his head. "Well, Aramis," continued Porthos, "I have thought, I have had an idea; I have imagined that an event has taken place in France. I dreamed of M. Fouquet all the night; I dreamed of dead fish, broken eggs, chambers badly furnished, meanly kept. Bad dreams, my dear D'Herblay; very unlucky, such dreams!"

"Porthos, what is that yonder?" interrupted Aramis, rising suddenly, and pointing out to his friend a black spot upon the empurpled line of the water.—"A boat!" said Porthos; "yes, it is a boat! Ah!

we shall have some news at last."—"There are two!" cried the bishop, on discovering another mast; "two! three! four!"—"Five!" said Porthos, in his turn. "Six! seven! Ah! *mon Dieu! mon Dieu!* it is a whole fleet!"

"Our boats returning, probably," said Aramis, very uneasily, in spite of the assurance he affected.—"They are very large for fishing-boats," observed Porthos; "and do you not remark, my friend, that they come from the Loire?"—"They come from the Loire—yes—" —"And look! everybody here sees them as well as ourselves; look, the women and children are beginning to get upon the jetty!"

An old fisherman passed. "Are those our boats yonder?" asked Aramis. The old man looked steadily into the horizon. "No, Monseigneur," replied he; "they are lighter-boats in the king's service." —"Boats in the royal service?" replied Aramis, starting. "How do you know that?" said he.—"By the flag."

"But," said Porthos, "the boat is scarcely visible; how the devil, my friend, can you distinguish the flag?"—"I see there is one," replied the old man; "our boats, or trade-lighters, do not carry any. That sort of craft is generally used for the transport of troops."— "Ah!" said Aramis.

"Vivat!" cried Porthos, "they are sending us reinforcements; don't you think they are, Aramis?"—"Probably."—"Unless it is the English coming."—"By the Loire? That would have an ill look, Porthos, for they must have come through Paris!"—"You are right; they are reinforcements, decidedly, or provisions."

Aramis leaned his head upon his hands and made no reply. Then, all at once, "Porthos," said he, "have the alarm sounded."—"The alarm! do you think of such a thing?"—"Yes, and let the cannoneers mount to their batteries; let the artillery-men be at their pieces, and be particularly watchful of the coast batteries." Porthos opened his eyes to their widest extent. He looked attentively at his friend, to convince himself that he was in his proper senses.

"I will do it, my dear Porthos," continued Aramis, in his most bland tone; "I will go and have these orders executed myself if you do not go, my friend."—"Well, I will go instantly!" said Porthos, going to execute the order, casting all the while looks behind him to see if the Bishop of Vannes were not making a mistake, and if, on returning to more rational ideas, he would not recall him. The alarm was sounded, the trumpets brayed, and drums rolled; the great bell of the belfry was put in motion. The dikes and piers were quickly filled with the curious and soldiers; the matches sparkled in the hands of the artillery-men, placed behind the large cannon bedded in their stone carriages. When every man was at his post, when all the preparations for the defence were made, "Permit me, Aramis, to try to comprehend," whispered Porthos, timidly, in Aramis's ear.—"My dear friend, you will comprehend but too soon," murmured M. d'Herblay, in reply to this question of his lieutenant.

"The fleet which is coming yonder with sails unfurled straight towards the port of Belle-Isle, is a royal fleet, is it not?"—"But as there are two kings in France, Porthos, to which of these two kings does this fleet belong?"

"Oh, you open my eyes!" replied the giant, stunned by this argument. And Porthos, whose eyes his friend's reply had just opened, or rather, had thickened the bandage which covered his sight, went with his best speed to the batteries to overlook his people and exhort every one to do his duty. In the meantime Aramis, with his eyes fixed on the horizon, saw the ships continue to draw nearer. The people and the soldiers, mounted upon all the summits or irregularities of the rocks, could distinguish the masts, then the lower sails, and at last the hulls of the lighters, bearing at the masthead the royal flag of France. It was quite night when one of these vessels which had created such a sensation among the inhabitants of Belle-Isle was moored within cannon-shot of the place. It was soon seen, notwithstanding the darkness, that a sort of agitation reigned on board this vessel, from the side of which a skiff was lowered, of which the three rowers, bending to their oars, took the direction of the port, and in a few instants struck land at the foot of the fort. The commander of this yawl jumped on shore. He had a letter in his hand, which he waved in the air, and seemed to wish to communicate with somebody. This man was soon recognised by several soldiers as one of the pilots of the island. He was the skipper of one of the two boats kept back by Aramis, which Porthos, in his anxiety with regard to the fate of the fishermen who had disappeared for two days, had sent in search of the missing boats. He asked to be conducted to M. d'Herblay. Two soldiers, at a signal from the sergeant, placed him between them and escorted him. Aramis was upon the quay. The envoy presented himself before the Bishop of Vannes. The darkness was almost complete, notwithstanding the torches borne at a small distance by the soldiers who were following Aramis in his rounds.

"Well, Jonathas, from whom do you come?"—"Monseigneur, from those who captured me."—"Who captured you?"—"You know, Monseigneur, we set out in search of our comrades?"—"Yes,—and afterwards?"—"Well, Monseigneur, within a short league we were captured by a *chasse-marée* belonging to the king."—"Ah!" said Aramis.—"Of which king?" cried Porthos. Jonathas started.

"Speak!" continued the bishop.—"We were captured, Monseigneur, and joined to those who had been taken yesterday morning." —"What was the cause of the mania for capturing you all?" said Porthos.—"Monsieur, to prevent us from telling you."

Porthos was again at a loss to comprehend. "And they have released you to-day?" asked he.—"That I might tell you they have captured us, Monsieur."—"Trouble upon trouble!" thought honest Porthos.

During this time Aramis was reflecting. "Humph!" said he; "then I suppose it is a royal fleet blockading the coasts?"—"Yes, Monseigneur."—"Who commands it?"—"The captain of the king's musketeers."—"D'Artagnan?"—"D'Artagnan!" exclaimed Porthos. —"I believe that is the name."—"And did he give you this letter?" —"Yes, Monseigneur."—"Bring the torch nearer."—"It is his writing," said Porthos.

Aramis eagerly read the following lines:—

"Order of the king to take Belle-Isle; order to put the garrison to the sword if they resist; order to make prisoners all the men of the garrison.   (Signed)   "D'ARTAGNAN."

Aramis turned pale, and crushed the paper in his hands. "What is it?" asked Porthos.—"Nothing, my friend, nothing. Tell me, Jonathas."—"Monseigneur!"—"Did you speak to M. d'Artagnan?" —"Yes, Monseigneur."—"What did he say to you?"—"That for more ample information he would speak with Monseigneur."— "Where?"—"On board his own vessel."

" 'On board his vessel'!" and Porthos repeated, " 'On board his vessel'!"—"Monsieur the musketeer," continued Jonathas, "told me to take you both on board my canoe and bring you to him."—"Let us go at once!" exclaimed Porthos; "dear D'Artagnan!"

But Aramis stopped him. "Are you mad?" cried he. "Who knows that it is not a snare?"—"Of the other king?" said Porthos, mysteriously.

"A snare, in fact,—that's what it is, my friend!"—"Very possibly. What is to be done, then? If D'Artagnan sends for us—"—"Who assures you that D'Artagnan sends for us?"—"Yes, but—but his writing—"—"Writing is easily counterfeited. This looks counterfeited—trembling—"—"You are always right; but in the meantime we know nothing." Aramis was silent. "It is true," said the good Porthos; "we do not want to know anything."

"What shall I do?" asked Jonathas.—"You will return on board this captain's vessel."—"Yes, Monseigneur."—"And will tell him that we beg he will himself come to the island."—"Ah, I comprehend!" said Porthos.

"Yes, Monseigneur," replied Jonathas; "but if the captain should refuse to come to Belle-Isle?"—"If he refuses, as we have cannon, we will make use of them."—"What! against D'Artagnan?"—"If it is D'Artagnan, Porthos, he will come. Go, Jonathas, go!"

Ma foi! I no longer comprehend anything," murmured Porthos. —"I will make you comprehend all, my dear friend; the time for it is come. Sit down upon this gun-carriage, open your ears, and listen well to me."—"Oh, *pardieu!* I shall listen,—no fear of that."

"May I depart, Monseigneur?" cried Jonathas.—"Yes; go and bring back an answer. Allow the canoe to pass, you men there!" and the canoe pushed off to regain the fleet. Aramis took Porthos by the hand, and began the explanations.

CHAPTER XXX

THE EXPLANATIONS OF ARAMIS

"WHAT I have to say to you, friend Porthos, will probably surprise you, but it will instruct you."—"I like to be surprised," said Porthos, in a kindly tone; "do not spare me, therefore, I beg. I am hardened against emotions; don't fear, speak out."

"It is difficult, Porthos, it is—difficult; for in truth—I warn you

—again—I have very strange things, very extraordinary things, to tell you."—"Oh, you speak so well, my friend, that I could listen to you for days together. Speak, then, I beg; and—stop, I have an idea: I will, to make your task more easy, to assist you in telling me such things, question you."—"I shall be pleased at your doing so."

"What are we going to fight for, Aramis?"—"If you put to me many such questions as that, if that is your way of assisting my task of revelation,—by such questions as that,—Porthos, you will not help me at all. On the contrary, that is precisely the Gordian knot. But, my friend, with a man like you, good, generous, and devoted, the confession must be made bravely. I have deceived you, my worthy friend."

"You have deceived me!"—"Good heavens! yes."—"Was it for my good, Aramis?"—"I thought so, Porthos; I thought so sincerely, my friend."—"Then," said the honest Seigneur de Bracieux, "you have rendered me a service, and I thank you for it,—for if you had not deceived me, I might have deceived myself. In what, then, have you deceived me?"—"In that I was serving the usurper against whom Louis XIV. at this moment is directing his efforts."

"The usurper!" said Porthos, scratching his head. "That is— well, I do not too clearly comprehend that!"—"He is one of the two kings who are contending for the crown of France."—"Very well! Then you were serving him who is not Louis XIV.?"—"You have hit upon the matter in a word."

"It results that—"—"It results that we are rebels, my poor friend."—"The devil! the devil!" cried Porthos, much disappointed.—"Oh, but, dear Porthos, be calm! we shall still find means of getting out of the affair, trust me."—"It is not that which makes me uneasy," replied Porthos; "that which alone touches me is that ugly word 'rebels.'"

"Ah! but—"—"And so the duchy that was promised me—"—"It was the usurper who was to give it to you."—"And that is not the same thing, Aramis," said Porthos, majestically.

"My friend, if it had only depended upon me, you should have become a prince." Porthos began to bite his nails after a melancholy fashion. "That is where you have been wrong," continued he, "in deceiving me; for that promised duchy I reckoned upon. Oh,

The Man in the Iron Mask

I reckoned upon it seriously, knowing you to be a man of your word, Aramis."—"Poor Porthos! pardon me, I implore you!"

"So then," continued Porthos, without replying to the bishop's prayer,—"so then, it seems, I have quite fallen out with Louis XIV.?"—"Oh, I will settle all that, my good friend; I will settle all that. I will take it upon myself alone!"

"Aramis!"—"No, no, Porthos, I conjure you, let me act. No false generosity; no inopportune devotedness! You knew nothing of my projects; you have done nothing of yourself. With me it is different. I alone am the author of the plot. I stood in need of my inseparable companion; I called upon you, and you came to me in remembrance of our ancient device, 'All for one, one for all.' My crime was that of being an egotist."—"Now, that is the word I like," said Porthos; "and seeing that you have acted entirely for yourself, it is impossible for me to blame you. It is so natural." And upon this sublime reflection, Porthos pressed the hand of his friend cordially.

In presence of this ingenuous greatness of soul, Aramis felt himself little. It was the second time he had been compelled to bend before real superiority of heart, much more powerful than splendour of mind. He replied by a mute and energetic pressure to the kind endearment of his friend. "Now," said Porthos, "that we have come to an explanation, now that I am perfectly aware of our situation with respect to Louis XIV., I think, my friend, it is time to make me comprehend the political intrigue of which we are the victims,—for I plainly see there is a political intrigue at the bottom of all this."

"D'Artagnan, my good Porthos, D'Artagnan is coming, and will detail it to you in all its circumstances; but excuse me, I am overcome with grief, bowed down by pain, and I have need of all my presence of mind, of all my reflection, to extricate you from the false position in which I have so imprudently involved you; but nothing can be more clear, nothing more plain, than your position henceforth. The king, Louis XIV., has now but one enemy; that enemy is myself, myself alone. I have made you a prisoner, you have followed me; to-day I liberate you, you fly back to your prince. You can perceive, Porthos, there is not a single difficulty in all this."—"Do you think so?" said Porthos.—"I am quite sure of it."—"Then why," said the admirable good sense of Porthos,—"then why, if we are in such an easy position, why, my friend, do we prepare cannon,

The Explanations of Aramis

muskets, and engines of all sorts? It seems to me it would be much more simple to say to Captain D'Artagnan, 'My dear friend, we have been mistaken; that error is to be repaired. Open the door to us; let us pass through, and good-day!' "

"Ah! that!" said Aramis, shaking his head.—"Why do you say 'that'? Do you not approve of my plan, my friend?"—"I see a difficulty in it."—"What is it?"—"The possibility that D'Artagnan may come with orders which will oblige us to defend ourselves."

"What! defend ourselves against D'Artagnan? Folly! Against the good D'Artagnan?" Aramis once more replied by shaking his head. "Porthos," at length he said, "if I have had the matches lighted and the guns pointed; if I have had the signal of alarm sounded; if I have called every man to his post upon the ramparts, —those good ramparts of Belle-Isle which you have so well fortified,—it is for something. Wait to judge; or rather, no, do not wait—"—"What can I do?"

"If I knew, my friend, I would have told you."—"But there is one thing much more simple than defending ourselves,—a boat, and away for France where—"—"My dear friend," said Aramis, smiling with a sort of melancholy, "do not let us reason like children; let us be men in counsel and execution. But, hark! I hear a hail for landing at the port. Attention, Porthos, serious attention!"

"It is D'Artagnan, do doubt," said Porthos, in a voice of thunder, approaching the parapet.—"Yes, it is I," replied the captain of the musketeers, running lightly up the steps of the pier, and gaining rapidly the little esplanade upon which his two friends waited for him. As soon as he came towards them Porthos and Aramis observed an officer who followed D'Artagnan, treading apparently in his very steps. The captain stopped upon the stairs of the pier when half-way up. His companion imitated him.

"Make your men draw back," cried D'Artagnan to Porthos and Aramis; "let them retire out of hearing." The order being given by Porthos was executed immediately. Then D'Artagnan, turning towards him who followed him, said, "Monsieur, we are no longer here on board the king's fleet, where, in virtue of your order, you spoke so arrogantly to me just now."—"Monsieur," replied the officer, "I did not speak arrogantly to you; I simply but rigorously obeyed what I had been commanded. I have been directed to follow you; I follow you. I am directed not to allow you to communicate with any one without taking cognizance of what you do; I am present therefore at your interview."

D'Artagnan trembled with rage, and Porthos and Aramis, who heard this dialogue, trembled likewise, but with uneasiness and fear. D'Artagnan, biting his moustache with that vivacity which denoted in him the state of exasperation closely to be followed by a terrible explosion, approached the officer. "Monsieur," said he, in a low voice, the more impressive, because affecting a calm, and filled with storm,—"Monsieur, when I sent a canoe hither, you wished to know what I wrote to the defenders of Belle-Isle. You produced an order to that effect; and in my turn I instantly showed you the note I had written. When the skipper of the boat sent by me returned; when I received the reply of these two gentlemen [pointing to Aramis and Porthos],—you heard every word the messenger said. All that was plainly in your orders, all that was well followed, well executed, punctiliously enough, was it not?"

"Yes, Monsieur," stammered the officer; "yes, without doubt, but—"—"Monsieur," continued D'Artagnan, growing warm,— "Monsieur," when I manifested the intention of quitting my vessel to cross to Belle-Isle, you insisted on coming with me. I did not hesitate; I brought you with me. You are now at Belle-Isle, are you not?"

"Yes, Monsieur; but—"—"But—the question no longer is of M. Colbert, who has given you that order, or of any one in the world whose instructions you are following; the question now is of a man who is a clog upon M. d'Artagnan, and who is alone with M. d'Artagnan upon steps whose base is bathed by thirty feet of salt water, —a bad position for that man, a bad position, Monsieur, I warn you."

"But, Monsieur, if I am a restraint upon you," said the officer timidly and almost faintly, "it is my duty which—"—"Monsieur, you have had the misfortune, you, or those who sent you, to insult me. It is done. I cannot seek redress from those who employ you, —they are unknown to me, or are at too great a distance. But you are under my hand, and I swear that if you make one step behind me when I lift a foot to go up to those gentlemen,—I swear to you by my name, I will cleave your head with my sword, and pitch you into the water. Oh, that must come which will come! I have only

The Explanations of Aramis

been six times angry in my life, Monsieur, and in the five times which have preceded this, I have killed my man."

The officer did not stir; he became pale under this terrible threat, and replied with simplicity, "Monsieur, you are wrong in acting against the orders given me." Porthos and Aramis, mute and trembling at the top of the parapet, cried to the musketeer, "Dear D'Artagnan, take care!"

D'Artagnan made them a sign to keep silence, raised his foot with a terrifying calmness to mount the stair, and turned round, sword in hand, to see if the officer followed him. The officer made a sign of the cross and followed. Porthos and Aramis, who knew their D'Artagnan, uttered a cry, and rushed down to prevent the blow which they thought they already heard. But D'Artagnan, passing his sword into his left hand, said to the officer, in an agitated voice, "Monsieur, you are a brave man. You will better comprehend what I am going to say to you now than what I have just said to you." —"Speak, M. d'Artagnan, speak!" replied the brave officer.

"These gentlemen we have just seen, and against whom you have orders, are my friends."—"I know they are, Monsieur."—"You can understand if I ought to act towards them as your instructions prescribe."—"I understand your reserves."—"Very well; permit me, then, to converse with them without a witness."

"M. d'Artagnan, if I yielded to your request, if I did that which you beg me to do, I should break my word; but if I do not do it, I shall disoblige you. I prefer the one to the other. Converse with your friends, and do not despise me, Monsieur, for doing for the sake of you, whom I esteem and honour,—do not despise me for committing for you, and you alone, an unworthy act." D'Artagnan, much agitated, passed his arms rapidly round the neck of the young man, and went up to his friends. The officer, enveloped in his cloak, sat down on the damp weed-covered steps.

"Well!" said D'Artagnan to his friends, "such is my position, as you see." They all three embraced. All three pressed one another in their arms as in the glorious days of their youth.

"What is the meaning of all these rigours?" said Porthos.—"You ought to have some suspicions of what it is," said D'Artagnan.— "Not much, I assure you, my dear Captain,—for, in fact, I have done nothing; no more has Aramis," the worthy baron hastened to say.

The Man in the Iron Mask

D'Artagnan darted a reproachful look at the prelate which penetrated that hardened heart. "Dear Porthos!" cried the Bishop of Vannes.

"You see what has been done against you," said D'Artagnan,— "interception of all that is coming to or going from Belle-Isle. Your boats are all seized. If you had endeavoured to fly, you would have fallen into the hands of the cruisers which plough the sea in all directions on the watch for you. The king wants you to be taken, and he will take you." And D'Artagnan tore several hairs from his grey moustache. Aramis became sombre, Porthos angry. "My idea was this," continued D'Artagnan: "to make you both come on board, to keep you near me, and restore you your liberty. But now, who can say that when I return to my ship I may not find a superior; that I may not find secret orders which will take from me my command, and give it to another, who will dispose of you and me and deprive us of all resources?"

"We must remain at Belle-Isle," said Aramis, resolutely; "and I assure you, for my part, I will not surrender easily." Porthos said nothing.

D'Artagnan remarked the silence of his friend. "I have another trial to make of this officer, of this brave fellow who accompanies me, whose courageous resistance makes me very happy,—for it denotes an honest man, who, although an enemy, is a thousand times better than a complaisant coward. Let us try to learn from him what he has the right of doing, and what his orders permit or forbid."—"Let us try," said Aramis.

D'Artagnan came to the parapet, leaned over towards the steps of the pier, and called the officer, who immediately came up. "Monsieur," said D'Artagnan, after having exchanged the most cordial courtesies, natural between gentlemen who know and appreciate each other worthily,—"Monsieur, if I wished to take away these gentlemen from this place, what would you do?"—"I should not oppose it, Monsieur; but having direct orders, formal orders, to take them under my guard, I should detain them."

"Ah!" said D'Artagnan.—"It is all over," said Aramis, gloomily. Porthos did not stir. "But still take Porthos," said the Bishop of Vannes; "he can prove to the king, I will help him in doing so, and you also can, M. d'Artagnan, that he has had nothing to do in this affair."

The Explanations of Aramis

"Hum!" said D'Artagnan. "Will you come? Will you follow me, Porthos? The king is merciful."—"I beg to reflect," said Porthos, nobly.—"You will remain here, then?"—"Until fresh orders," said Aramis, with vivacity.—"Until we have had an idea," resumed D'Artagnan; "and I now believe that will not be a long time, for I have one already."

"Let us say adieu, then," said Aramis; "but in truth, my good Porthos, you ought to go."—"No!" said the latter, laconically.— "As you please," replied Aramis, a little wounded in his nervous susceptibility at the morose tone of his companion. "Only I am reassured by the promise of an idea from D'Artagnan,—an idea I fancy I have divined."

"Let us see," said the musketeer, placing his ear near Aramis's mouth. The latter spoke several words rapidly, to which D'Artagnan replied, "That is it precisely."—"Infallible, then!" cried Aramis. —"During the first emotion that this resolution will cause, take care of yourself, Aramis."—"Oh, don't be afraid!"

"Now, Monsieur," said D'Artagnan to the officer, "thanks, a thousand thanks! You have made yourself three friends for life."— "Yes," added Aramis. Porthos alone said nothing, but merely bowed.

D'Artagnan, having tenderly embraced his two old friends, left Belle-Isle with the inseparable companion M. Colbert had given him. Thus, with the exception of the explanation with which the worthy Porthos had been willing to be satisfied, nothing apparently was changed in the condition of the one or of the other. 'Only," said Aramis, "there is D'Artagnan's idea."

D'Artagnan did not return on board without examining to the bottom the idea he had discovered. Now, we know that when D'Artagnan did examine, he was accustomed to see through. As to the officer, become mute again, he left him full leisure to meditate. Therefore, on putting his foot on board his vessel, moored within cannon-shot of the island, the captain of the musketeers had already got together all his means, offensive and defensive.

He immediately assembled his council, which consisted of the officers serving under his orders. These were eight in number,—a chief of the maritime forces; a major directing the artillery; an engineer; the officer we are acquainted with; and four lieutenants. Having assembled them in the chamber of the poop, D'Artagnan arose, took off his hat, and addressed them thus: "Gentlemen, I have been to reconnoitre Belle-Isle-en-Mer, and I have found in it a good and solid garrison; moreover, preparations are made for a defence that may prove troublesome. I therefore intend to send for two of the principal officers of the place that we may converse with them. Having separated them from their troops and their cannon, we shall be better able to deal with them,—particularly with good reasoning. Is this your opinion, gentlemen?"

The major of artillery rose. "Monsieur," said he, with respect, but with firmness, "I have heard you say that the place is preparing to make a troublesome defence. The place is, then, as you know, determined upon rebellion?" D'Artagnan was visibly put out by this reply; but he was not a man to allow himself to be subdued by so little, and resumed. "Monsieur," said he, "your reply is just. But you are ignorant that Belle-Isle is a fief of M. Fouquet, and the ancient kings gave the right to the seigneurs of Belle-Isle to arm their people."

The major made a movement. "Oh, do not interrupt me," continued D'Artagnan. "You are going to tell me that that right to arm themselves against the English was not a right to arm themselves against their king. But it is not M. Fouquet, I suppose, who holds Belle-Isle at this moment, since I arrested M. Fouquet the day before yesterday. Now, the inhabitants and defenders of Belle-Isle know nothing of that arrest. You would announce it to them in vain. It is a thing so unheard of and extraordinary, so unexpected, that they would not believe you. A Breton serves his master, and not his masters; he serves his master till he has seen him dead. Now, the Bretons, as I know, have not seen the body of M. Fouquet. It is not then surprising that they hold out against everything which is not M. Fouquet or his signature."

The major bowed in sign of assent. "That is why," continued D'Artagnan, "I propose to cause two of the principal officers of the garrison to come on board my vessel. They will see you, gentlemen; they will see the forces we have at our disposal; they will consequently know what they have to expect, and the fate that attends them in case of rebellion. We will assure them, upon our honour, that M. Fouquet is a prisoner, and that all resistance can be only prejudicial to them. We will tell them that when the first cannon is fired there will be no mercy to be expected from the king.

The Explanations of Aramis

Then, I hope it at least, they will no longer resist. They will yield without fighting, and we shall have a place given up to us in a friendly way which it might cost us much trouble to subdue."

The officer who had followed D'Artagnan to Belle-Isle was preparing to speak, but D'Artagnan interrupted him. "Yes, I know what you are going to tell me, Monsieur; I know that there is an order by the king to prevent all secret communications with the defenders of Belle-Isle, and that is exactly why I do not offer to communicate but in the presence of my staff." And D'Artagnan made an inclination of the head to his officers, which was intended to give a value to that condescension.

The officers looked at one another as if to read their opinions in their eyes, with the evident intention of acting, after they should have agreed, according to the desire of D'Artagnan. And already the latter saw with joy that the result of their consent would be the sending a boat to Porthos and Aramis, when the king's officer drew from his pocket a folded paper, which he placed in the hands of D'Artagnan. This paper bore upon its superscription the number "1." "What, still another!" murmured the surprised captain.— "Read, Monsieur," said the officer, with a courtesy that was not free from sadness.

D'Artagnan, full of mistrust, unfolded the paper, and read these words:—

"Prohibition to M. d'Artagnan to assemble any council whatever, or to deliberate in any way before Belle-Isle be surrendered and the prisoners shot.

(Signed)   "Louis."

D'Artagnan repressed the movement of impatience that ran through his whole body, and with a gracious smile, "That is well, Monsieur," said he; "the king's orders shall be obeyed."

The Man in the Iron Mask

CHAPTER XXXI

RESULT OF THE IDEAS OF THE KING AND THE IDEAS OF D'ARTAGNAN

THE blow was direct; it was severe, mortal. D'Artagnan, furious at having been anticipated by an idea of the king, did not however yet despair; and reflecting upon the idea he had brought back from Belle-Isle, he derived from it a new means of safety for his friends. "Gentlemen," said he, suddenly, "since the king has charged some other than myself with his secret orders, it must be because I no longer possess his confidence, and I should be really unworthy of it if I had the courage to hold a command subject to so many injurious suspicions. I will go then immediately and carry my resignation to the king. I give it before you all, enjoining you all to fall back with me upon the coast of France in such a way as not to compromise the safety of the forces his Majesty has confided to me. For this purpose, return all to your posts and command the return; within an hour we shall have the flood-tide. To your posts, gentlemen! I suppose," added he, on seeing that all were prepared to obey him except the surveillant officer, "you have no orders to object, this time?"

And D'Artagnan almost triumphed while speaking these words. This plan was the safety of his friends. The blockade once raised, they might embark immediately, and set sail for England or Spain without fear of being molested. While they were making their escape, D'Artagnan would return to the king, would justify his return by the indignation which the mistrust of Colbert had raised in him; he would be sent back with full powers, and he would take Belle-Isle,—that is to say, the cage, after the birds had flown. But to this plan the officer opposed a second order of the king. It was thus conceived:—

"From the moment M. d'Artagnan shall have manifested the desire of giving in his resignation, he shall no longer be reckoned leader of the expedition, and every officer placed under his orders shall be held no longer to obey him. Moreover, the said M. d'Artagnan, having lost that quality of leader of the army sent against Belle-Isle, shall set out immediately for France, in company with the officer

214

who will have remitted the message to him, who will consider him as a prisoner for whom he is answerable."

Brave and careless as he was, D'Artagnan turned pale. Everything had been calculated with a depth which for the first time in thirty years recalled to him the solid foresight and the inflexible logic of the great cardinal. He leaned his head on his hand, thoughtful, scarcely breathing. "If I were to put this order in my pocket," thought he, "who would know it, or who would prevent my doing it? Before the king had had time to be informed, I should have saved those poor fellows yonder. Let us exercise a little audacity! My head is not one of those which the executioner strikes off for disobedience. We will disobey!" But at the moment he was about to adopt this plan, he saw the officers around him reading similar orders which the infernal agent of the thoughts of Colbert had just distributed to them. The case of disobedience had been foreseen as the others had been.

"Monsieur," said the officer, coming up to him, "I await your good pleasure to depart."—"I am ready, Monsieur," replied D'Artagnan, grinding his teeth.

The officer immediately commanded a canoe to receive M. d'Artagnan and himself. At sight of this D'Artagnan became almost mad with rage. "How," stammered he, "will you carry on the direction of the different corps?"—"When you are gone, Monsieur," replied the commander of the fleet, "it is to me the direction of the whole is committed."

"Then, Monsieur," rejoined Colbert's man, addressing the new leader, "it is for you that this last order that has been remitted to me is intended. Let us see your powers."—"Here they are," said the marine officer, exhibiting a royal signature.

"Here are your instructions," replied the officer, placing the folded paper in his hands; and turning towards D'Artagnan, "Come, Monsieur," said he, in an agitated voice (such despair did he behold in that man of iron), "do me the favour to depart at once."—"Immediately!" articulated D'Artagnan, feebly, subdued, crushed by implacable impossibility. And he let himself slide down into the little boat, which started, favoured by wind and tide, for the coast of France. The king's guards embarked with him. The musketeer still preserved the hope of reaching Nantes quickly, and of pleading the cause of his friends eloquently enough to incline the king to mercy. The boat flew like a swallow. D'Artagnan distinctly saw the land of France profiled in black against the white clouds of night.

"Ah, Monsieur," said he, in a low voice, to the officer, to whom for an hour he had ceased speaking, "what would I give to know the instructions for the new commander! They are all pacific, are they not? and—"

He did not finish; the sound of a distant cannon rolled over the waters, then another, and two or three still louder. D'Artagnan shuddered. "The fire is opened upon Belle-Isle," replied the officer. The canoe had just touched the soil of France.

CHAPTER XXXII

THE ANCESTORS OF PORTHOS

WHEN D'Artagnan had quitted Aramis and Porthos, the latter returned to the principal fort to converse with the greater liberty. Porthos, still thoughtful, was a constraint upon Aramis, whose mind had never felt itself more free.

"Dear Porthos," said he, suddenly, "I will explain D'Artagnan's idea to you."—"What idea, Aramis?"—"An idea to which we shall owe our liberty within twelve hours."—"Ah, indeed!" said Porthos, much astonished; "let us hear it."

"Did you remark in the scene our friend had with the officer that certain orders restrained him with regard to us?"—"Yes, I did remark that."—"Well, D'Artagnan is going to give in his resignation to the king; and during the confusion which will result from his absence, we will get away,—or rather, you will get away, Porthos, if there is a possibility of flight only for one." Here Porthos shook his head, and replied, "We will escape together, Aramis, or we will remain here together."

"You are a generous heart," said Aramis; "but your melancholy uneasiness afflicts me."—"I am not uneasy," said Porthos.—"Then you are angry with me?"—"I am not angry with you."—"Then why, my friend, do you put on such a dismal countenance?"—"I will tell

216

you; I am making my will;" and while saying these words, the good Porthos looked sadly in the face of Aramis.

"Your will!" cried the bishop. "What then! do you think yourself lost?"—"I feel fatigued; it is the first time, and there is a custom in our family."—"What is it, my friend?"

"My grandfather was a man twice as strong as I am."—"Indeed!" said Aramis; "then your grandfather must have been Samson himself."—"No,—his name was Antoine. Well, he was of about my age when, setting out one day for the chase, he felt his legs weak,—he who had never before known that infirmity."—"What was the meaning of that fatigue, my friend?"—"Nothing good, as you will see,—for having set out, complaining still of the weakness of his legs, he met a wild boar, which made head against him. He missed him with his arquebuse, and was ripped up by the beast, and died directly."

"There is no reason in that why you should alarm yourself, dear Porthos."—"Oh, you will see. My father was as strong again as I am. He was a rough soldier under Henry III. and Henry IV.; his name was not Antoine, but Gaspard,—the same as M. de Coligny's. Always on horseback, he had never known what lassitude was. One evening, as he rose from table, his legs failed him."—"He had supped heartily, perhaps," said Aramis; "and that was why he staggered."—"Bah! A friend of M. de Bassompierre? nonsense! No, no; he was astonished at feeling this lassitude, and said to my mother, who laughed at him, 'Would not one believe I was going to meet with a wild boar, as the late M. du Vallon, my father, did?' "

"Well?" said Aramis.—"Well, braving this weakness, my father insisted upon going down into the garden, instead of going to bed. His foot slipped on the first stair; the staircase was steep; my father fell against a stone angle, in which an iron hinge was fixed. The hinge opened his temple, and he lay dead upon the spot."

Aramis raised his eyes to his friend. "These are two extraordinary circumstances," said he; "let us not infer that there may succeed a third. It is not becoming in a man of your strength to be superstitious, my brave Porthos. Besides, when were your legs seen to fail? Never have you been so firm, so superb; why, you could carry a house on your shoulders!"—"At this moment," said Porthos, "I feel myself pretty active; but at times I vacillate, I sink; and lately this phenomenon, as you call it, has occurred four times. I will not say that this frightens me, but it annoys me. Life is an agreeable thing. I have money, I have fine estates, I have horses that I love; I have also friends I love,—D'Artagnan, Athos, Raoul, and you."

The admirable Porthos did not even take the trouble to conceal from Aramis the rank he gave him in his friendship. Aramis pressed his hand. "We will still live many years," said he, "to preserve in the world specimens of rare men. Trust yourself to me, my friend; we have no reply from D'Artagnan—that is a good sign. He must have given orders to get the vessels together and clear the seas. On my part, I have just issued directions that a boat should be rolled upon rollers to the mouth of the great cavern of Locmaria, which you know, where we have so often lain in wait for foxes."—"Yes, and which terminates at the little creek by a trench which we discovered the day that splendid fox escaped that way."—"Precisely. In case of misfortunes, a boat is to be concealed for us in that cavern; indeed, it must be there by this time. We will wait a favourable moment; and during the night, to sea!"

"That is a good idea; what shall we gain by it?"—"We shall gain by it that nobody knows that grotto or rather its issue, except ourselves and two or three hunters of the island, we shall gain by it that if the island is occupied, the scouts, seeing no boat upon the shore, will never imagine we can escape, and will cease to watch."—"I understand."—"Well,—the legs?"—"Oh, excellent, just now."

"You see, then, plainly that everything conspires to give us quietude and hope. D'Artagnan will clear the sea and give us liberty of action. No more royal fleet or descent to be dreaded. *Vive Dieu!* Porthos, we have still half a century of good adventures before us; and if I once touch Spanish ground, I swear to you," added the bishop, with a terrible energy, "that your brevet of duke is not remote as it now appears."—"We will live in hope," said Porthos, a little enlivened by the reviving warmth of his companion.

All at once a cry resounded in their ears: "To arms! to arms!" This cry, repeated by a hundred voices, brought to the chamber where the two friends were conversing surprise to the one and uneasiness to the other. Aramis opened the window; he saw a crowd of people running with torches. Women were seeking places of safety; the armed men were hastening to their posts.

"The fleet! the fleet!" cried a soldier, who recognised Aramis.— "The fleet?" repeated the latter.—"Within half-cannon-shot," con-

The enormous rock sank down, pressed by the two others
which pushed in from the sides

tinued the soldier.—"To arms!" cried Aramis.—"To arms!" repeated Porthos, formidably. And both rushed forth towards the
pier, to place themselves within the shelter of the batteries. Boats
laden with soldiers were seen approaching; they took three directions for the purpose of landing at three points at once.

"What must be done?" said an officer of the guard.—"Stop them;
and if they persist, fire!" said Aramis. Five minutes after, the
cannonade began. These were the shots that D'Artagnan had heard
as he landed in France. But the boats were too near the pier to
allow the cannon to aim correctly. They landed, and the combat
began hand to hand.

"What's the matter, Porthos?" said Aramis to his friend.—"Nothing! nothing!—only my legs. It is really incomprehensible; they
will be better when we charge." In fact, Porthos and Aramis did
charge with such vigour, they so thoroughly animated their men,
that the Royalists re-embarked precipitately without gaining anything but the wounds they carried away.

The retreat proved, however, to be only a ruse. A short time after-
ward, as they were resting in the fortress, "Hark!" cried Aramis, "I
hear a voice which liberates mine by dominating over it."—"Cannon?" said Porthos.—"Cannon and musketry too!" cried the bishop.

On hearing at a distance among the rocks these sinister reports
of a combat which they thought had ceased, "What can that be?"
asked Porthos.—"Eh, *pardieu!*" cried Aramis; "this is just what I
expected."—"What is that?"—"The attack was nothing but a feint,
—And while their companions allowed themselves to be repulsed, a
second expedition effected a landing on the other side of the island.
We are lost, then," said the Bishop of Vannes, quietly.

"Lost! that is possible," replied the Seigneur de Pierrefonds; "but
we are not taken or hung." And so saying, he rose from the table,
went straight to the wall, and coolly took down his sword and pistols, which he examined with the care of an old soldier who was preparing for battle, and who feels that his life in a great measure
depends upon the excellence and the good condition of his arms.

At the report of the cannon, at the news of the surprise which
might deliver up the isle to the royal troops, the terrified crowd
rushed precipitately to the fort to demand assistance and advice
from their leaders. Aramis, pale and downcast, between two torches,
showed himself at the window which looked into the principal court

full of soldiers waiting for orders and bewildered inhabitants imploring succour. The crowd collected under the window uttered a prolonged growl of anger and terror. "The soldiers of Louis XIV. have entered the island," continued Aramis. "From this time it would no longer be a combat between them and you,—it would be a massacre. Go, then; go and forget. This time I command you in the name of the Lord." The mutineers retired slowly, submissive and silent.

Aramis turned to Porthos. "And now, my friend, since we have saved these poor people from being helplessly slaughtered by superior forces, let us try to make our own escape."—"But how, dear Aramis?" questioned Porthos.—"We are going to escape by the cavern. If you please," replied Aramis, joyously. "Forward, my friend Porthos; our boat awaits us, and the king has not caught us yet."

CHAPTER XXXIII

THE GROTTO OF LOCMARIA

THE cavern of Locmaria was sufficiently distant from the pier to render it necessary for our friends to husband their strength to arrive there. Besides, the night was advancing; midnight had struck at the fort. Porthos and Aramis were loaded with money and arms. They walked, then, across the heath which is between the pier and the cavern, listening to every noise, and endeavouring to avoid ambushes. From time to time, on the road, which they had carefully left on their left hand, passed fugitives coming from the interior at the news of the landing of the royal troops. Aramis and Porthos, concealed behind some projecting mass of rock, collected the words which escape from the poor people, who fled trembling, carrying with them their most valuable effects, and tried, while listening to their complaints, to draw something from them for their own interest. At length, after a rapid course, frequently interrupted by cautious delays, they reached the deep grotto into which the foreseeing Bishop of Vannes had taken care to have rolled upon cylinders a good boat capable of keeping the sea at this fine season.

The Grotto of Locmaria

"My good friend," said Porthos, after having respired vigorously, "we are arrived, it seems. But I thought you spoke of three men,— three servants who were to accompany us. I don't see them; where are they?"—"Why should you see them, dear Porthos?" replied Aramis. "They are certainly waiting for us in the cavern, and, no doubt, are resting for a moment after having accomplished their rough and difficult task." He stopped Porthos, who was preparing to enter the cavern. "Will you allow me, my friend," said he to the giant, "to pass in first? I know the signal I have given to these men, who, not hearing it, would be very likely to fire upon you or slash away with their knives in the dark."

"Go on, then, Aramis; go on,—go first. You are all wisdom and prudence; go on. Ah! there is that fatigue of which I spoke to you. It has just seized me again." Aramis left Porthos sitting at the entrance of the grotto, and bowing his head, he penetrated into the interior of the cavern, imitating the cry of the owl. A little plaintive cooing, a scarcely distinct cry, replied from the depths of the cave. Aramis pursued his way cautiously, and soon was stopped by the same kind of cry as he had first uttered, and this cry sounded within ten paces of him.

"Are you there, Yves?" said the bishop.—"Yes, Monseigneur; Goennec is here likewise. His son accompanies us."—"That is well. Are all things ready?"—"Yes, Monseigneur."—"Go to the entrance of the grotto, my good Yves, and you will there find the Seigneur de Pierrefonds, who is resting after the fatigues of our journey; and if he should happen not to be able to walk, lift him up, and bring him hither to me."

The three men obeyed; but the recommendation Aramis had given to his servants was useless. Porthos, refreshed, had already himself begun the descent, and his heavy step resounded among the cavities formed and supported by columns of silex and granite. As soon as the Seigneur de Bracieux had rejoined the bishop, the Bretons lighted a lantern with which they were furnished, and Porthos assured his friend that he felt as strong as ever.

"Let us visit the canoe," said Aramis, "and see in the first place what it will hold."—"Do not go too near with the light," said the skipper Yves; "for, as you desired me, Monseigneur, I have placed under the bench of the poop, in the coffer you know of, the barrel of powder, and the musket-charges that you sent me from the fort."

The Man in the Iron Mask

"Very well," said Aramis; and taking the lantern himself, he examined minutely all parts of the canoe with the precautions of a man who is neither timid nor ignorant in the face of danger. The canoe was long, light, drawing little water, thin of keel,—in short, one of those which have always been so well constructed at Belle-Isle,—a little high in its sides, solid upon the water, very manageable, furnished with planks which in uncertain weather form a sort of bridge over which the waves glide, and which protect the rowers. In two well-closed coffers placed beneath the benches of the prow and the poop, Aramis found bread, biscuit, dried fruits, a quarter of bacon, a good provision of water in leathern bottles,—the whole forming rations sufficient for people who did not mean to quit the coast, and would be able to revictual, if necessity demanded. The arms, eight muskets and as many horse-pistols, were in good condition, and all loaded. There were additional oars, in case of accident, and that little sail called *trinquette,* which assists the speed of the canoe at the same time the boatmen row, and is so useful when the breeze is slack. When Aramis had seen all these things, and appeared satisfied with the result of his inspection, "Let us consider, Porthos," said he, "whether to endeavour to get the boat out by the unknown extremity of the grotto, following the descent and the shade of the cavern, or whether it be better to make it slide upon the rollers through the bushes in the open air, levelling the road of the little beach, which is but twenty feet high, and gives at its foot, in the tide, three or four fathoms of good water upon a sound bottom."

"It must be as you please, Monseigneur," replied the skipper, Yves, respectfully; "but I don't believe that by the slope of the cavern, and in the dark in which we shall be obliged to manœuvre our boat, the road will be so convenient as in the open air. I know the beach well, and can certify that it is as smooth as a grass-plot in a garden; the interior of the grotto, on the contrary, is rough,—without again reckoning, Monseigneur, that at the extremity we shall come to the trench which leads into the sea and which perhaps the canoe will not pass."—"I have made my calculations," said the bishop, "and I am certain it would pass."

"So be it; I wish it may, Monseigneur," the skipper insisted. "But your Greatness knows very well that to make it reach the extremity of the trench, there is an enormous stone to be lifted,—that under which the fox always passes, and which closes the trench

The Grotto of Locmaria

like a door."—"That can be raised," said Porthos; "that is nothing."—"Oh! I know that Monseigneur has the strength of ten men," replied Yves; "but that is giving Monseigneur a great deal of trouble."

"I think the skipper may be right," said Aramis; "let us try the open passage."—"The more so, Monseigneur," continued the fisherman, "that we should not be able to embark before day, it would require so much labour; and that as soon as daylight appears, a good *vedette* placed outside the grotto would be necessary, indispensable even, to watch the manœuvres of the lighters or the cruisers that are upon the look-out for us."—"Yes, yes, Yves, your reasons are good; we will go by the beach."

And the three robust Bretons went to the boat, and were beginning to place their rollers underneath it to put in motion, when the distant barking of dogs was heard, proceeding from the interior of the island. Aramis darted out of the grotto, followed by Porthos. Dawn just tinted with purple and white the waves and the plain; through the dim light the young melancholy firs waved their tender branches over the pebbles, and long flights of crows were skimming with their black wings over the thin fields of buckwheat. In a quarter of an hour it would be clear daylight; the awakened birds joyously announced it to all nature. The barkings which had been heard, which had stopped the three fishermen engaged in moving the boat, and had brought Aramis and Porthos out of the cavern, were prolonged in a deep gorge within about a league of the grotto.

"It is a pack of hounds," said Porthos; "the dogs are upon a scent."—"Who can be hunting at such a moment as this?" said Aramis.—"And this way, particularly," continued Porthos, "this way, where they may expect the army of the Royalists."—"The noise comes nearer. Yes, you are right, Porthos, the dogs are on a scent. But, Yves!" cried Aramis, "come here! come here!"

Yves ran towards him, letting fall the cylinder which he was about to place under the boat when the bishop's call interrupted him. "What is the meaning of this hunt, Skipper?" said Porthos.—"Eh, Monseigneur, I cannot understand it," replied the Breton. "It is not at such a moment that the Seigneur de Locmaria would hunt. No; and yet the dogs—"—"Unless they have escaped from the kennel."—"No," said Goennec, "they are not the Seigneur de Locmaria's hounds."

The Man in the Iron Mask

"In common prudence," said Aramis, "let us go back into the grotto; the voices evidently draw nearer, we shall soon know what we have to expect." They re-entered, but had scarcely proceeded a hundred steps in the darkness when a noise like the hoarse sigh of a creature in distress resounded through the cavern, and breathless, running, terrified, a fox passed like a flash of lightning before the fugitives, leaped over the boat and disappeared, leaving behind it its sour scent, which was perceptible for several seconds under the low vaults of the cave.

"The fox!" cried the Bretons, with the joyous surprise of hunters. —"Accursed chance!" cried the bishop; "our retreat is discovered." —"How so?" said Porthos; "are we afraid of a fox?"—"Eh, my friend, what do you mean by that, and why do you name the fox? It is not the fox alone, *pardieu!* But don't you know, Porthos, that after the fox come hounds, and after the hounds men?"

Porthos hung his head. As if to confirm the words of Aramis, they heard the yelping pack coming with frightful swiftness upon the trail of the animal. Six foxhounds burst out at once upon the little heath, with a cry resembling the noise of a triumph.—"There are the dogs plain enough!" said Aramis, posted on the look-out behind a chink between two rocks; "now, who are the huntsmen?" —"If it is the Seigneur de Locmaria's," replied the skipper, "he will leave the dogs to hunt the grotto, for he knows them, and will not enter in himself, being quite sure that the fox will come out at the other side; it is there he will go and wait for him."

"It is not the Seigneur de Locmaria who is hunting," replied Aramis, turning pale, in spite of his efforts to maintain a good countenance.—"Who is it, then?" said Porthos.—"Look!"

Porthos applied his eye to the slit, and saw at the summit of a hillock a dozen horsemen urging on their horses in the track of the dogs, shouting, "Tally-ho! tally-ho!"—"The guards," said he.— "Yes, my friend, the king's guards."—"The king's guards, do you say, Monseigneur?" cried the Bretons, becoming pale in their turn.

The hounds at the same moment rushed into the grotto like an avalanche, and the depths of the cavern were filled with their deafening cries. "Ah, the devil!" said Aramis, resuming all his coolness at the sight of this certain, inevitable danger. "I know well we are lost, but we have at least one chance left. If the guards who follow their hounds happen to discover there is an issue to the grotto,

The Grotto of Locmaria

there is no more help for us, for on entering they must see both us and our boat. The dogs must not go out of the cavern. The masters must not enter."—"That is clear," said Porthos.

"You understand," added Aramis, with the rapid precision of command; "there are six dogs which will be forced to stop at the great stone under which the fox has glided, but at the too narrow opening of which they shall be themselves stopped and killed."

The Bretons sprang forward, knife in hand. In a few minutes there was a lamentable concert of growls and mortal howlings, and then—nothing.—"That's well!" said Aramis, coolly; "now for the masters!"—"What is to be done with them?" said Porthos.—"Wait their arrival, conceal ourselves, and kill them."

"Kill them!" replied Porthos.—"There are sixteen," said Aramis, —"at least for the time being."—"And well armed," added Porthos, with a smile of consolation.—"It will last about ten minutes," said Aramis. "To work!" And with a resolute air he took up a musket, and placed his hunting-knife between his teeth. "Yves, Goennec, and his son," continued he, "will pass the muskets to us. You, Porthos, will fire when they are close. We shall have brought down eight before the others are aware of anything, that is certain; then we all—there are five of us—will despatch the other eight, knife in hand."

In spite of the sort of divination which was the remarkable side of the character of Aramis, the event, subject to the chances of things over which uncertainty presides, did not fall out exactly as the Bishop of Vannes had foreseen. One, named Biscarrat, better mounted than his companions, arrived first at the opening of the grotto, and comprehended that the fox and the dogs were all engulfed in it. But, struck by that superstitious terror which every dark and subterraneous way naturally impresses upon the mind of man, he stopped at the outside of the grotto, and waited till his companions should have assembled round him. "Well?" asked the young men, coming up out of breath, and unable to understand the meaning of his inaction.

"Well, I cannot hear the dogs; they and the fox must be all engulfed in this cavern."—"They were too close up," said one of the guards, "to have lost scent all at once; besides, we should hear them from one side or another. They must, as Biscarrat says, be in this grotto."—"But then," said one of the young men, "why don't they give tongue?"—"It is strange!" said another.

"Well, but," said a fourth, "let us go into this grotto. Is it forbidden that we should enter it?"—"No," replied Biscarrat "only, as it looks as dark as a wolf's mouth, we might break our necks in it." —"Witness the dogs," said a guard, "who seem to have broken theirs."

"What the devil can have become of them?" asked the young men, in chorus; and every master called his dog by his name, whistled to him in his favourite note, without a single reply to either the call or the whistle. "It is perhaps an enchanted grotto," said Biscarrat. "Let us see;" and jumping from his horse, he made a step into the grotto.

"Stop! stop! I will accompany you," said one of the guards, on seeing Biscarrat preparing to disappear in the shade of the cavern's mouth. "No," replied Biscarrat,—"there must be something extraordinary in the place; don't let us risk ourselves all at once. If in ten minutes you do not hear of me, you can come in,—but then all at once."—"Be it so," said the young men, who besides did not see that Biscarrat ran much risk in the enterprise, "we will wait for you;" and without dismounting from their horses, they formed a circle round the grotto.

Biscarrat entered then alone, and advanced through the darkness till he came in contact with the muzzle of Porthos's musket. The resistance against his breast astonished him; he raised his hand and laid hold of the icy barrel. At the same instant Yves lifted a knife against the young man, and let it fall upon him with all the force of a Breton's arm.

"Biscarrat! Biscarrat!" cried several voices from the outside, coming like a whirlwind into the cave.

"Biscarrat! Biscarrat!" cried the voices, still nearer; and the shadows of several human forms projected into the interior of the grotto. Aramis and Porthos listened with the intense attention of men whose lives depend upon a breath of air.

"Messieurs," said one of the young men, "there is something mysterious in the grotto. Well, for my part, I am very curious to see what it is, even if it were the Devil. To the grotto, Messieurs! to the grotto!"—"To the grotto!" repeated all the voices. And the echo of the cavern carried like a menace to Porthos and Aramis, "To the grotto! to the grotto!"

The guards penetrated farther and farther, with cries that grew weaker as they advanced. All at once, a discharge of musketry, growling like thunder, exploded beneath the vault. At the same instant cries, howlings, and imprecations burst forth, and the little troop of gentlemen reappeared—some pale, some bleeding—all enveloped in a cloud of smoke, which the outward air seemed to draw from the depths of the cavern. A second discharge laid five upon the icy sand; and as it was impossible to see whence this murderous thunder issued, the others fell back with a terror that can be better imagined than described. There were only six gentlemen left.

"Seriously," said one of the survivors, "is it the Devil?"—"*Ma foi!* it is much worse," said another.

"Good!" said the officer who had shown so much coolness in the affair. "Here are reinforcements coming." In fact, a company of the guards, left in the rear by their officers, whom the ardour of the chase had carried away,—from seventy-five to eighty men,—arrived in good order, led by their captain and the first lieutenant. The five officers hastened to meet their soldiers; and in a language the eloquence of which may be easily imagined, they related the adventure and asked for aid. The captain interrupted them. "Where are your companions?" demanded he.—"Dead!"

"But there were sixteen of you!"—"Ten are dead. Biscarrat is in the cavern, and we are five."—"Biscarrat is then a prisoner?"— "Probably."—"Come on! Come on!" cried all the troop; and they advanced into the cavern.

CHAPTER XXXIV

AN HOMERIC SONG

I T IS time to pass into the other camp, and to describe at once the combatants and the field of battle. Aramis and Porthos had gone to the grotto of Locmaria with the expectation of finding in that place their canoe, ready moored, as well as the three Bretons, their assistants; and they at first hoped to make the boat pass through the little issue of the cavern, concealing in that fashion both their labours and their flight. The arrival of the fox and the dogs had obliged them to remain concealed. The grotto extended the space of about a hundred *toises* to a little slope dominating a creek. Formerly a temple of the Celtic divinities when Belle-Isle was still called Calonèse, this grotto had seen more than one human sacrifice accomplished in its mysterious depths. The first entrance to the cavern was by a moderate descent, above which heaped up rocks formed a low arcade; the interior, very unequal as to the ground, dangerous from the rocky inequalities of the vault, was subdivided into several compartments which commanded one another and were joined by means of several rough broken steps, fixed right and left in enormous natural pillars. At the third compartment the vault was so low, the passage so narrow, that the boat would scarcely have passed without touching the two sides; nevertheless, in a moment of despair, wood softens and stone becomes compliant under the breath of human will. Such was the thought of Aramis, when, after having fought the fight, he decided upon flight,—a flight certainly dangerous, since all the assailants were not dead, and since admitting the possibility of putting the boat to sea, they would have to fly in open day, before the eyes of the conquered, who, on discovering how few they were, would be eager in pursuit.

When the two discharges had killed ten men, Aramis, habituated to the windings of the cavern, went to reconnoitre them one by one, and counted them, for the smoke prevented seeing on beyond; and he immediately commanded that the canoe should be rolled as far as the great stone, the closure of the liberating issue. Porthos collected all his strength, and took the canoe in his arms and lifted it, while the Bretons made it run rapidly along the rollers. They had descended into the third compartment; they had arrived at the stone which walled up the outlet. Porthos seized this gigantic stone at its base, applied his robust shoulder to it, and gave a heave which made this wall crack. A cloud of dust fell from the vault with the ashes of ten thousand generations of sea-birds, whose nests stuck like cement to the rock. At the third shock the stone gave way; it oscillated for a minute. Porthos, placing his back against the neighbouring rock, made an arch with his foot which drove the block out of the calcareous masses which served for hinges and cramps. The stone fell; and daylight was visible, brilliant, radiant, which rushed into the cavern by the opening, and the blue sea appeared to the delighted Bretons. They then began to lift the boat over the barricade. Twenty more *toises*, and it might glide into the ocean. It was during this time that the company arrived, was drawn up by the captain, and disposed for either an escalade or an assault.

Aramis watched over everything, to favour the labours of his friends. He saw the reinforcements; he counted the men; he convinced himself at a single glance of the insurmountable peril to which a fresh combat would expose them. To escape by sea at the moment the cavern was about to be invaded, was impossible. In fact, the daylight which had just been admitted to the last two compartments had exposed to the soldiers the boat rolling towards the sea, and the two rebels within musket-shot; and one of their discharges would riddle the boat if it did not kill the five navigators. Besides, supposing everything,—suppose the boat should escape with the men on board of it how could the alarm be suppressed, how could notice to the royal lighters be prevented? What could hinder the poor canoe, followed by sea and watched from the shore, from succumbing before the end of the day? Aramis, digging his hands into his gray hair with rage, invoked the assistance of God and the assistance of the Devil. Calling to Porthos, who was working alone more than all the rollers,—whether of flesh or of wood,—"My friend," said he, "our adversaries have just received a reinforcement."

"Ah, ah!" said Porthos, quietly, "what is to be done, then?"—"To recommence the combat," said Aramis, "is hazardous."—"Yes," said Porthos, "for it is difficult to suppose that out of two one should not be killed; and certainly, if one of us were killed, the other would get himself killed also." Porthos spoke these words with that natural heroism which, with him, was greater than all material forces.

Aramis felt it like a spur to his heart. "We shall neither of us be killed if you do what I tell you, friend Porthos."—"Tell me what?" —"These people are coming down into the grotto."—"Yes."—"We could kill about fifteen of them, but not more."—"How many are there in all?" asked Porthos.—"They have received a reinforcement of seventy-five men."—"Seventy-five and five, eighty. Ah, ah!" said Porthos.

"If they fire all at once they will riddle us with balls."—"Certainly they will."—"Without reckoning," added Aramis, "that the detonations might occasion fallings in of the cavern."—"Ay," said

Porthos; "a piece of falling rock just now grazed my shoulder a little."—"You see, then?"—"Oh! it is nothing."

"We must determine upon something quickly. Our Bretons are going to continue to roll the canoe towards the sea."—"Very well." —"We two will keep the powder, the balls, and muskets here."— "But only two, my dear Aramis,—we shall never fire three shots together," said Porthos, innocently; "the defence by musketry is a bad one."—"Find a better, then."

"I have found one," said the giant, suddenly; "I will place myself in ambuscade behind the pillar with this iron bar; and invisible, unattackable, if they come in floods, I can let my bar fall on their skulls thirty times in a minute. Eh! what do you think of the project? You smile!"—"Excellent, dear friend, perfect! I approve it greatly; only you will frighten them, and half of them will remain outside to take us by famine. What we want, my good friend, is the entire destruction of the troop; a single man left standing ruins us."

"You are right, my friend, but how can we attract them, pray?" —"By not stirring, my good Porthos."—"Well, we won't stir, then; but when they shall be all together—"—"Then leave it to me; I have an idea."—"If so, and your idea be a good one,—and your idea is most likely to be good,—I am satisfied."

"To your ambuscade, Porthos, and count how many enter!"— "But you, what will you do?"—"Don't trouble yourself about me; I have my work."—"I think I can hear voices."—"It is they! To your post! Keep within reach of my voice and hand."

Porthos took refuge in the second compartment, which was absolutely black with darkness. Aramis glided into the third; the giant held in his hand an iron bar of about fifty pounds weight. Porthos handled this lever, which had been used in rolling the boat, with marvellous facility. During this time, the Bretons had pushed the boat to the beach. In the enlightened compartment, Aramis, stooping and concealed, was busied in some mysterious manœuvre. A command was given in a loud voice. It was the last order of the captain. Twenty-five men jumped from the upper rocks into the first compartment of the grotto, and having taken their ground, began to fire. The echoes growled; the hissing of the balls cut the air; an opaque smoke filled the vault.

"To the left! to the left!" cried the captain, who had discovered the passage to the second chamber, and who animated by the smell of powder wished to guide his soldiers in that direction. The troop accordingly precipitated themselves to the left,—the passage gradually growing narrower. The captain, with his hands stretched forward, devoted to death, marched in advance of the muskets. "Come on! come on!" exclaimed he, "I see daylight!"—"Strike! Porthos!" cried the sepulchral voice of Aramis.

Porthos breathed a sigh; but he obeyed. The iron bar fell full and direct upon the captain's head, who was dead before he had ended his cry. Then the formidable lever rose ten times in ten seconds, made ten corpses. The soldiers could see nothing; they heard sighs and groans; they stumbled over dead bodies, but as they had no conception of the cause of all this, they came forward jostling one another. The implacable bar, still falling, annihilated the first platoon without a single sound having warned the second, which was quietly advancing. But this second platoon, commanded by the lieutenant, had broken a thin fir growing on the shore, and with its resinous branches twisted together, the captain had made a torch.

On arriving at the compartment where Porthos, like the exterminating angel, had destroyed all he touched, the first rank drew back in terror. No firing had replied to that of the guards, and yet their way was stopped by a heap of dead bodies,—they literally walked in blood. Porthos was still behind his pillar. The lieutenant, on lighting up with the trembling flame of the fir this frightful carnage, of which he in vain sought the cause, drew back towards the pillar behind which Porthos was concealed. Then a gigantic hand issued from the shade and fastened on the throat of the lieutenant, who uttered a stifled rattle; his outstretched arms beating the air, the torch fell and was extinguished in blood. A second after, the corpse of the lieutenant fell close to the extinguished torch and added another body to the heap of dead which blocked up the passage.

All this was effected as mysteriously as if by magic. On hearing the rattling in the throat of their leader, the soldiers who accompanied him had turned round; they had caught a glimpse of his extended arms, his eyes starting from their sockets, and then the torch fell and they were left in darkness. By an unreflective, instinctive, mechanical impulse the lieutenant cried, "Fire!" Immediately a volley of musketry flamed, thundered, roared in the cavern, bringing down enormous fragments from the vaults. The cavern was lighted for an instant by this discharge, and then immediately returned to a darkness rendered still thicker by the smoke. To this succeeded a profound silence, broken only by the steps of the third brigade, now entering the cavern.

CHAPTER XXXV

THE DEATH OF A TITAN

AT THE moment when Porthos, more accustomed to the darkness than all these men coming from open daylight, was looking round him to see if in this night Aramis were not making him some signal, he felt his arm gently touched, and a voice low as a breath murmured in his ear, "Come,"—"Oh!" said Porthos.—"Hush!" said Aramis, still more softly.

And amid the noise of the third brigade, which continued to advance, amid the imprecations of the guards left alive, of the dying breathing their last sigh, Aramis and Porthos glided imperceptibly along the granite walls of the cavern. Aramis led Porthos into the last compartment but one, and showed him in a hollow of the rocky wall a barrel of powder weighing from seventy to eighty pounds, to which he had just attached a match. "My friend," said he to Porthos, "you will take this barrel, the match of which I am going to set fire to, and throw it amid our enemies; can you do so?"— "*Parbleu!*" replied Porthos; and he lifted the barrel with one hand. "Light it!"—"Stop," said Aramis, "till they are all massed together, and then, my Jupiter, hurl your thunderbolt among them."—"Light it," repeated Porthos.

"On my part," continued Aramis, "I will join our Bretons, help them to get the canoe to the sea, and will wait for you on the shore. Throw your barrel strongly, and hasten to us."—"Light it," said Porthos, a third time. "But do you understand me?"—"*Parbleu!*" said Porthos, with laughter that he did not even attempt to restrain; "when a thing is explained to me, I understand it. Go, and give me the light."

Aramis gave the burning match to Porthos, who held out his arm to him to press, his hands being engaged. Aramis pressed the arm of Porthos with both his hands, and fell back to the outlet of the

The Death of a Titan

cavern, where the three rowers awaited him. Porthos, left alone, applied the spark bravely to the match. The spark—a feeble spark, first principle of a conflagration—shone in the darkness like a fire-fly, then was deadened against the match which it inflamed. Porthos enlivened the flame with his breath. The smoke was a little dispersed, and by the light of the sparkling match objects might for two seconds be distinguished. It was a short but a splendid spec-tacle,—that of this giant, pale, bloody, his countenance lighted by the fire of the match burning in surrounding darkness! The sol-diers saw him; they saw the barrel he held in his hand; they at once understood what was going to happen. Then these men, already filled with fright at the sight of what had been accomplished, filled with terror at thinking of what was going to be accomplished, uttered together one shriek of agony. Some endeavoured to fly, but they encountered the third brigade, which barred their passage; others mechanically took aim and attempted to fire their discharged mus-kets; others fell upon their knees. Two or three officers cried out to Porthos to promise him his liberty if he would spare their lives. The lieutenant of the third brigade commanded his men to fire; but the guards had before them their terrified companions, who served as a living rampart for Porthos.

We have said that the light produced by the spark and the match did not last more than two seconds; but during these two seconds this is what it illumined: in the first place, the giant, enlarged in the darkness; then, at ten paces from him, a heap of bleeding bodies, crushed, mutilated, in the midst of which was still visible some last struggle of agony which lifted the mass as a last breath raises the sides of a shapeless monster expiring in the night. Every breath of Porthos, while enlivening the match, sent towards this heap of bodies a sulphurous hue mingled with streaks of purple. In addi-tion to this principal group, scattered about the grotto as the chance of death or the surprise of the blow had stretched them, some iso-lated bodies seemed to threaten by their gaping wounds. Above the ground, soaked by pools of blood, rose, heavy and sparkling, the short, thick pillars of the cavern, of which the strongly marked shades threw out the luminous particles. And all this was seen by the tremulous light of a match attached to a barrel of powder,—that is to say, a torch which, while throwing a light upon the dead past, showed the death to come.

The Man in the Iron Mask

As I have said, this spectacle did not last above two seconds. During this short space of time, an officer of the third brigade got together eight men armed with muskets, and, through an opening, ordered them to fire upon Porthos. But they who received the order to fire trembled so that three guards fell by the discharge, and the five other balls went hissing to splinter the vault, plough the ground, or indent the sides of the cavern.

A burst of laughter replied to this volley; then the arm of the giant swung round; then was seen to pass through the air, like a falling star, the train of fire. The barrel, hurled a distance of thirty feet, cleared the barricade of the dead bodies and fell amid a group of shrieking soldiers, who threw themselves on their faces. The officer had followed the brilliant train in the air; he endeavoured to precipitate himself upon the barrel and tear out the match before it reached the powder it contained. Useless devotion! The air had made the flame attached to the conductor more active; the match, which at rest might have burned five minutes, was consumed in thirty seconds, and the infernal work exploded.

Furious vortices, hissings of sulphur and nitre, devouring ravages of the fire, the terrible thunder of the explosion,—this is what the second which followed the two seconds we have described disclosed in that cavern, equal in horrors to a cavern of demons. The rocks split like planks of deal under the axe. A jet of fire, smoke, and *debris* sprang up from the middle of the grotto, enlarging as it mounted. The great walls of silex tottered and fell upon the sand; and the sand itself—an instrument of pain when launched from its hardened bed—riddled the face with its myriads of cutting atoms. Cries, howlings, imprecations, and lives,—all were extinguished in one great crash.

The first three compartments became a gulf into which fell back again, according to its weight, every vegetable, mineral, or human fragment. Then the lighter sand and ashes fell in their turns, stretching like a grey winding-sheet and smoking over these dismal remains.

As to Porthos, after having hurled the barrel of powder amid his enemies, he had fled as Aramis had directed him and had gained the last compartment, into which air, light, and sunshine penetrated through the opening. And scarcely had he turned the angle which separated the third compartment from the fourth, when he perceived

The Death of a Titan

at a hundred paces from him the boat dancing on the waves. There were his friends; there was liberty; there was life after victory. Six more of his formidable strides and he would be out of the vault; out of the vault, two or three vigorous springs and he would reach the canoe. Suddenly he felt his knees give way; his knees appeared powerless, his legs yielded under him. "Oh, oh!" murmured he, "there is my fatigue seizing me again! I can walk no farther! What is this?"

Aramis perceived him through the opening; unable to conceive what could induce him to stop thus, he cried, "Come on, Porthos! come on! come quickly!"—"Oh!" replied the giant, making an effort which acted upon every muscle of his body, "oh! but I cannot!" While saying these words he fell upon his knees, but with his robust hands he clung to the rocks, and raised himself up again.

"Quick! quick!" repeated Aramis, bending forward towards the shore, as if to draw Porthos to him with his arms.—"Here I am," stammered Porthos, collecting all his strength to make one step more.—"In the name of Heaven, Porthos, make haste! the barrel will blow up!"—"Make haste, Monseigneur!" shouted the Bretons to Porthos, who was floundering as in a dream.

But there was no longer time; the explosion resounded, the earth gaped, the smoke which rushed through the large fissures obscured the sky; the sea flowed back as if driven by the blast of fire which darted from the grotto as if from the jaws of a gigantic chimera; the reflux carried the boat out twenty *toises;* the rocks cracked to their base, and separated like blocks under the operation of wedges; a portion of the vault was carried up towards heaven, as if by rapid currents; the rose-coloured and green fire of the sulphur, the black lava of the argillaceous liquefactions clashed and combated for an instant beneath a majestic dome of smoke; then at first oscillated, then declined, then fell successively the long angles of rock, which the violence of the explosion had not been able to uproot from their bed of ages; they bowed to one another like grave and slow old men, then prostrated themselves, and were embedded for ever in their dusty tomb.

This frightful shock seemed to restore to Porthos the strength he had lost; he arose, himself a giant among these giants. But at the moment he was flying between the double hedge of granite phantoms, these latter, which were no longer supported by the corresponding links, began to roll with a crash around this Titan, who looked as if precipitated from heaven amid the rocks which he had just been launching at it. Porthos felt the earth beneath his feet shaken by this long rending. He extended his vast hands to the right and left to repulse the falling rocks. A gigantic block was held back by each of his extended hands; he bent his head, and a third granite mass sank between his two shoulders. For an instant the arms of Porthos had given way, but the Hercules united all his forces, and the two walls of the prison in which he was buried fell back slowly and gave him place. For an instant he appeared in this frame of granite like the ancient angel of chaos; but in pushing back the lateral rocks, he lost his point of support for the monolith which weighed upon his strong shoulders, and the monolith lying upon him with all its weight, brought the giant down upon his knees. The lateral rocks, for an instant pushed back, drew together again and added their weight to that of the other, which would have been sufficient to crush ten men. The giant fell without crying for help; he fell while answering Aramis with words of encouragement and hope, for, thanks to the powerful arch of his hands, for an instant he might believe that, like Enceladus, he should shake off the triple load. But by degrees Aramis saw the block sink; the hands contracted for an instant, the arms stiffened for a last effort, gave way, the extended shoulders sank wounded and torn, and the rock continued to lower gradually.

"Porthos! Porthos!" cried Aramis, tearing his hair, "Porthos! where are you? Speak!"—"There, there!" murmured Porthos, with a voice growing evidently weaker; "patience! patience!" Scarcely had he pronounced these words, when the impulse of the fall augmented the weight! the enormous rock sank down, pressed by the two others which sank in from the sides, and, as it were, swallowed up Porthos in a sepulchre of broken stones. On hearing the dying voice of his friend, Aramis had sprung to land. Two of the Bretons followed him, each with a lever in his hand,—one being sufficient to take care of the boat. The last sighs of the valiant struggler guided them amid the ruins. Aramis, animated, active, and young as at twenty, sprang towards the triple mass, and with his hands, delicate as those of a woman, raised by a miracle of vigour a corner of the immense sepulchre of granite. Then he caught a glimpse, in the darkness of that grave, of the still brilliant eye of his friend, to whom the momentary lifting of the mass restored a moment of respiration. The two men came rushing up, grasped their iron levers, united their triple strength, not merely to raise it, but to sustain it. All was useless. The three men slowly gave way with cries of grief, and the rough voice of Porthos, seeing them exhaust themselves in a useless struggle, murmured in a bantering tone those last words which came to his lips with the last breath, "Too heavy!"

After which the eye darkened and closed, the face became pale, the hand whitened, and the Titan sank quite down, breathing his last sigh. With him sank the rock, which even in his agony he had still held up. The three men dropped the levers, which rolled upon the tumulary stone. Then, breathless, pale, his brow covered with sweat, Aramis listened, his breast oppressed, his heart ready to break. Nothing more! The giant slept the eternal sleep, in the sepulchre which God had made to his measure.

CHAPTER XXXVI

THE EPITAPH OF PORTHOS

ARAMIS, silent, icy, trembling like a timid child, arose shivering from the stone. A Christian does not walk upon tombs. But though capable of standing, he was not capable of walking. It might be said that something of Porthos, dead, had just died within him. His Bretons surrounded him; Aramis yielded to their kind exertions, and the three sailors, lifting him up, carried him into the canoe. Then, having laid him down upon the bench near the tiller, they took to their oars, preferring to get off by rowing rather than to hoist a sail, which might betray them. Of all that levelled surface of the ancient grotto of Locmaria, of all that flattened shore, one single little hillock attracted their eyes. Aramis never removed his from it; and at a distance out in the sea, in proportion as the shore receded, the menacing and proud mass of rock seemed to draw itself up, as formerly Porthos used to do, and raise a smiling and invincible head towards heaven,—like that of the honest and valiant friend, the strongest of the four, and yet the first dead.

The Man in the Iron Mask

Strange destiny of these men of brass! The most simple of heart allied to the most crafty; strength of body guided by subtlety of mind; and in the decisive moment, when strength alone could save mind and body, a stone, a rock, a vile and material weight, triumphed over strength, and falling upon the body, drove out the mind.

But scarcely half an hour after the sail had been hoisted, the rowers became inactive, reclined upon their benches, and making an eye-shade with their hands, pointed out to one another a white spot which appeared on the horizon, as motionless in appearance as is a gull rocked by the insensible respiration of the waves. But that which might have appeared motionless to the ordinary eyes was moving at a quick rate to the experienced eye of the sailor; that which appeared stationary on the ocean was cutting a rapid way through it. For some time, seeing the profound torpor in which their master was plunged, the sailors did not dare to rouse him, and satisfied themselves with exchanging their conjectures in low and anxious tones. Aramis, in fact, so vigilant, so active,—Aramis, whose eye, like that of a lynx, watched without ceasing, and saw better by night than by day,—Aramis seemed to sleep in the despair of his soul. An hour passed thus, during which daylight gradually disappeared, but during which also the sail in view gained so swiftly on the boat that Goennec, one of the three sailors, ventured to say aloud, "Monseigneur, we are chased!"

Aramis made no reply; the ship still gained upon them. Then, of their own accord, two of the sailors, by the direction of the skipper Yves, lowered the sail, in order that that single point which appeared above the surface of the waters should cease to be a guide to the eye of the enemy who was pursuing them. On the part of the ship in sight, on the contrary, two more small sails were run up at the extremities of the masts. Unfortunately, it was the time of the finest and longest days of the year, and the moon, in all her brilliancy, succeeded to that inauspicious day. The vessel which was pursuing the little boat before the wind had then still half an hour of twilight, and a whole night almost as light as day. "Monseigneur! Monseigneur! we are lost!" said the skipper. "Look! they see us although we have lowered our sail."—"That is not to be wondered at," murmured one of the sailors, "since they say that, by the aid of the Devil, the people of the cities have made instruments with which

The Epitaph of Porthos

they see as well at a distance as near, by night as well as by day."

Aramis took a telescope from the bottom of the boat, arranged it silently, and passing it to the sailor, "Here," said he, "look!" The sailor hesitated. "Don't be alarmed," said the bishop, "there is no sin in it; and if there is any sin, I will take it upon myself." The sailor lifted the glass to his eye, and uttered a cry. He believed that the vessel, which appeared to be distant about cannon-shot, had suddenly and at a single bound cleared the distance. But on withdrawing the instrument from his eye, he saw that, except the way which the vessel had been able to make during that short instant, it was still at the same distance.

"So," murmured the sailor, "they can see us as we see them?"—"They see us," said Aramis, and sank again into his impassiveness. —"How,—they see us?" said the skipper Yves. "Impossible!"—"Well, Skipper, look for yourself," said the sailor. And he passed to him the glass.

"Monseigneur assures me that the Devil has nothing to do with this?" asked the skipper. Aramis shrugged his shoulders. The skipper lifted the glass to his eye. "Oh, Monseigneur," said he, "it is a miracle. They are there; it seems as if I were going to touch them. Twenty-five men at least! Ah! I see the captain forward. He holds a glass like this, and is looking at us. Ah! he turns round and gives an order; they are rolling a piece of cannon forward—they are charging it—they are pointing it. *Miséricorde!* they are firing at us!"

And by a mechanical movement the skipper took the glass off, and the objects, sent back to the horizon, appeared again in their true aspect. The vessel was still at the distance of nearly a league, but the manœuvre announced by the skipper was not less real. A light cloud of smoke appeared under the sails, more blue than they, and spreading like a flower opening; then, at about a mile from the little canoe, they saw the ball take the crown off two or three waves, dig a white furrow in the sea and disappear at the end of that furrow, as inoffensive as the stone with which, at play, a boy "makes ducks and drakes." That was at once a menace and a warning.

"What is to be done?" asked the skipper.—"They will sink us!" said Goennec, "give us absolution, Monseigneur!" And the sailors fell on their knees before him. "You forget that they can see you," said he.—"That is true!" said the sailors, ashamed of their weakness. "Give us your orders, Monseigneur; we are ready to die for you."

"Let us wait," said Aramis.—"How,—let us wait?"—"Yes; do you not see, as you just now said, that if we endeavour to fly, they will sink us?"—"But perhaps," the skipper ventured to say—"perhaps by the favour of the night we could escape them."—"Oh!" said Aramis, "they probably have some Greek fire to light their own course and ours likewise."

At the same moment, as if the little vessel wished to reply to the words of Aramis, a second cloud of smoke mounted slowly to the heavens, and from the bosom of that cloud sparkled an arrow of flame, which described its parabola like a rainbow, and fell into the sea, where it continued to burn, illuminating a space of a quarter of a league in diameter. The Bretons looked at one another in terror. "You see plainly," said Aramis, "it will be better to wait for them."

The oars dropped from the hands of the sailors, and the boat ceasing to make way, rocked motionless on the summits of the waves. Night came on, but the vessel still approached nearer. It might be said it redoubled its speed with the darkness. From time to time, as a bloody-necked vulture rears its head out of its nest, the formidable Greek fire darted from its sides, and cast its flame into the ocean like an incandescent snow. At last it came within musket-shot. All the men were on deck, arms in hand; the cannoneers were at their guns, the matches were burning. It might be thought that they were about to board a frigate and to combat a crew superior in number to their own, and not to take the canoe manned by four persons. "Surrender!" cried the commander of the vessel through his speaking-trumpet.

The sailors looked at Aramis. Aramis made a sign with his head. The skipper Yves waved a white cloth at the end of a gaff. This was a way of striking their flag. The vessel came on like a racehorse. It launched a fresh Greek fire which fell within twenty paces of the little canoe, and threw a stronger light upon them than the most ardent ray of the sun could have done. "At the first sign of resistance," cried the commander of the vessel, "fire!" And the soldiers brought their muskets to the shoulder.

"Did not we say we surrendered?" said the skipper Yves.—"Living! living, Captain!" cried some excited soldiers, "they must be taken living!"—"Well, yes,—living," said the captain. Then turning towards the Bretons, "Your lives are all safe, my friends, cried he, "except the Chevalier d'Herblay."

Aramis started imperceptibly. For an instant his eye was fixed upon the depths of the ocean enlightened by the last flashes of the Greek fire,—flashes which ran along the sides of the waves, played upon their crests like plumes, and rendered still more dark, more mysterious, and more terrible the abysses they covered. "Do you hear, Monseigneur?" said the sailors.—"Yes."—"What are your orders?"—"Accept!"

"But you, Monseigneur?" Aramis leaned still more forward, and played with the ends of his long white fingers with the green water of the sea, to which he turned smiling as to a friend. "Accept!" repeated he.

"We accept," repeated the sailors; "but what security have we?" —"The word of a gentleman," said the officer. "By my rank and by my name I swear that all but M. le Chevalier d'Herblay shall have their lives spared. I am lieutenant of the king's frigate the *Pomona*, and my name is Louis Constant de Pressigny."

With a rapid gesture Aramis,—already bent over the side of the boat towards the sea,—with a rapid gesture Aramis raised his head, drew himself up, and with a flashing eye and a smile upon his lips, "Throw out the ladder, Messieurs," said he, as if the command had belonged to him. He was obeyed. Then Aramis, seizing the rope-ladder, ascended first; but instead of the terror which was expected to be displayed upon his countenance, the surprise of the sailors of the vessel was great when they saw him walk straight up to the commander with a firm step, look at him earnestly, make a sign to him with his hand,—a mysterious and unknown sign, at the sight of which the officer turned pale, trembled, and bowed his head. Without saying a word, Aramis then raised his hand close to the eyes of the commander, and showed him the collet of a ring which he wore on the ring-finger of his left hand; and while making this sign, Aramis, draped in cold, silent and haughty majesty, had the air of an emperor giving his hand to be kissed. The commandant, who for a moment had raised his head, bowed a second time with marks of the most profound respect. Then stretching his hand out in his turn towards the poop,—that is to say, towards his own cabin,—he drew back to allow Aramis to go first. The three Bretons, who had come on board after their bishop, looked at one another, stupefied. The crew were struck with silence. Five minutes after, the commander called the second lieutenant, who returned immediately, ordering the head to be put towards Corunna. While the given order was executed, Aramis reappeared upon the deck, and took a seat near the railing. The night had fallen, the moon had not yet risen; and yet Aramis looked incessantly towards Belle-Isle. Yves then approached the captain, who had returned to take his post in the stern, and said in a low and humble voice, "What course are we to follow, Captain?" —"We take what course Monseigneur pleases," replied the officer.

Aramis passed the night leaning upon the railing. Yves, on approaching him the next morning, remarked that, "the night must have been very humid, for the wood upon which the bishop's head had rested was soaked with dew." Who knows?—that dew was, perhaps, the first tears which had ever fallen from the eyes of Aramis! What epitaph would have been equal to that, good Porthos?

CHAPTER XXXVII

KING LOUIS XIV

THE king was seated in his cabinet, with his back turned towards the door of entrance. In front of him was a mirror in which while turning over his papers he could see with a glance those who came in. He did not take any notice of the entrance of D'Artagnan, but laid over his letters and plans the large silk cloth which he made use of to conceal his secrets from the importunate. D'Artagnan understood his play, and kept in the background; so that at the end of a minute, the king, who heard nothing and could see only with the corner of his eye, was obliged to cry, "Is not M. d'Artagnan there?"

"I am here, Sire," replied the musketeer, advancing.—"Well, Monsieur," said the king, fixing his clear eye upon D'Artagnan, "what have you to say to me?"—"I, Sire!" replied the latter, who watched the first blow of his adversary to make a good retort; "I have nothing to say to your Majesty, unless it be that you have caused me to be arrested, and here I am."

The king was going to reply that he had not had D'Artagnan arrested, but the sentence appeared too much like an excuse, and he was silent. D'Artagnan likewise reserved an obstinate silence. "Monsieur," at length resumed the king, "what did I charge you to go and do at Belle-Isle? Tell me, if you please."

The king, while speaking these words, looked fixedly at his captain. Here D'Artagnan was too fortunate,—the king made for him so fine an opening. "I believe," replied he, "that your Majesty does me the honour to ask what I went to Belle-Isle to do?"—"Yes, Monsieur."—"Well, Sire, I know nothing about it; it is not of me that that question should be asked, but of that infinite number of officers of all kinds to whom have been given an infinite number of orders of all kinds, while to me, head of the expedition, nothing precise was ordered."

The king was wounded; he showed it by his reply. "Monsieur," said he, "orders have only been given to such as were judged faithful."—"And therefore I have been astonished, Sire," retorted the musketeer, "that a captain like myself, who rank with a marshal of France, should have found himself under the orders of five or six lieutenants or majors, good to make spies of, possibly, but not at all fit to conduct warlike expeditions. It was upon this subject I came to demand an explanation of your Majesty."

"It was wrong to send me in pursuit of two men whose lives M. Fouquet, your Majesty's preserver, had implored you to save. Still further, these men were my friends. They did not attack your Majesty; they succumbed to a blind anger. Besides, why were they not allowed to escape? What crime had they committed? I admit that you may contest with me the right of judging of their conduct. But why suspect me before the action? Why surround me with spies? Why disgrace me before the army? Why me, in whom you have to this time showed the most entire confidence,—me, who for thirty years have been attached to your person, and have given you a thousand proofs of devotedness,—for it must be said, now that I am accused; why compel me to see three thousand of the king's soldiers march in battle against two men?"—"One would say you have forgotten what these men have done to me!" said the king, in a hollow voice, "and that it was no merit of theirs that I was not lost."—"Sire, one would say that you forget I was there."

"Enough, M. d'Artagnan, enough of these dominating concerns which arise to keep the sun from my interests. I am founding a state in which there shall be but one master, as I promised you formerly; the moment is come for keeping my promise. You wish to be, according to your tastes or your friendships, free to destroy my plans and save my enemies; I will break you, or I will abandon you. Seek a more compliant master. I know full well that another king would not conduct himself as I do, and would allow himself to be dominated over by you at the risk of sending you some day to keep company with M. Fouquet and the others; but I have a good memory, and for me services are sacred titles to gratitude, to impunity. You shall only have this lesson, M. d'Artagnan, as the punishment of your want of discipline; and I will not imitate my predecessors in their anger, not having imitated them in their favour. And then, other reasons make me act mildly towards you: in the first place, because you are a man of sense, a man of great sense, a man of heart, and you will be a good servant to him who shall have mastered you; secondly, because you will cease to have any motives for insubordination. Your friends are destroyed or ruined by me. These supports upon which your capricious mind instinctively relied I have made to disappear. At this moment, my soldiers have taken or killed the rebels of Belle-Isle."

D'Artagnan became pale. "Taken or killed!" cried he. "Oh, Sire, if you thought what you tell me, if you were sure you were telling me the truth, I should forget all that is just, all that is magnanimous in your words, to call you a barbarous king and an unnatural man. But I pardon you these words," said he, smiling with pride; "I pardon them to a young prince who does not know, who cannot comprehend, what such men as M. d'Herblay, M. du Vallon, and myself are. Taken or killed! Ah, ah, Sire! tell me, if the news is true, how much it has cost you in men and money. We will then reckon if the game has been worth the stakes."

As he spoke thus, the king went up to him in great anger and said, "M. d'Artagnan, your replies are those of a rebel! Tell me, if you please, who is King of France? Do you know any other?"—"Sire," replied the captain of the musketeers, coldly, "I remember that one morning at Vaux you addressed that question to people who did not know how to answer it, while I, on my part, did answer it. If I recognised my king on that day, when the thing was not easy, I think it would be useless to ask it of me now, when your Majesty is alone with me."

King Louis XIV

At these words, Louis cast down his eyes. It appeared to him that the shade of the unfortunate Philippe passed between D'Artagnan and himself, to evoke the remembrance of that terrible adventure. Almost at the same moment an officer entered and placed a despatch in the hands of the king, who, in his turn, changed colour while reading it. "Monsieur," said he, "what I learn here you would know later; it is better I should tell you, and that you should learn it from the mouth of your king. A battle has taken place at Belle-Isle."—"Oh! ah!" said D'Artagnan, with a calm air, though his heart beat enough to break through his chest. "Well, Sire?"—"Well, Monsieur; and I have lost a hundred and six men." A beam of joy and pride shone in the eyes of D'Artagnan. "And the rebels?" said he. —"The rebels have fled," said the king.

D'Artagnan could not restrain a cry of triumph. "Only," added the king, "I have a fleet which closely blockades Belle-Isle, and I am certain no boat can escape."—"So that," said the musketeer, brought back to his dismal ideas, "if these two gentlemen are taken—"— "They will be hanged," said the king, quietly.—"And do they know it?" replied D'Artagnan, repressing a shudder.—"They know it, because you must have told them yourself; and all the country knows it."

"Then, Sire, they will never be taken alive, I will answer for that." —"Ah!" said the king, negligently, taking up his letter again. "Very well, they will be dead then, M. d'Artagnan, and that will come to the same thing, since I should only take them to have them hanged." D'Artagnan wiped the sweat which flowed from his brow.

"I have told you," pursued Louis XIV., "that I would one day be to you an affectionate, generous, and constant master. You are now the only man of former times worthy of my anger or my friendship. I will not be sparing of either to you, according to your conduct. Could you serve a king, M. d'Artagnan, who should have a hundred other kings, his equals, in the kingdom? Could I, tell me, do with such weakness the great things I meditate? Have you ever seen an artist effect solid work with a rebellious instrument? Far from us, Monsieur, those old leavens of feudal abuses! The Fronde, which threatened to ruin the monarchy, has emancipated it. I am master at home, Captain D'Artagnan, and I shall have servants who, wanting perhaps your genius, will carry devotedness and obedience up to heroism. Of what consequence, I ask you, of what consequence is it that God has given no genius to arms and legs? It is to the head he has given it; and the head, you know, all the rest obey. I myself am the head." D'Artagnan started. Louis XIV. continued as if he had seen nothing, although this emotion had not at all escaped him. "Now, let us conclude between us two that bargain which I promised to make with you one day when you found me very small, at Blois. Do me justice, Monsieur, when you think that I do not make any one pay for the tears of shame I then shed. Look around you: lofty heads have bowed. Bow yours, or choose the exile that will best suit you. Perhaps, when reflecting upon it, you will find that this king has a generous heart, who reckons sufficiently upon your loyalty to allow you to leave him, knowing you to be dissatisfied, and the possessor of a great state secret. You are a brave man, I know. Why have you judged me before trial? Judge me from this day forward, D'Artagnan, and be as severe as you please."

D'Artagnan remained bewildered, mute, undecided for the first time in his life. He had just found an adversary worthy of him. This was no longer trick, it was calculation; it was no longer violence, it was strength; it was no longer passion, it was will; it was no longer boasting, it was wisdom. This young man who had brought down Fouquet and could do without D'Artagnan, deranged all the somewhat headstrong calculations of the musketeer.

"Come, let us see what stops you?" said the king, kindly. "You have given in your resignation; shall I refuse to accept it? I admit that it may be hard for an old captain to recover his good-humour." —"Oh!" replied D'Artagnan, in a melancholy tone, "that is not my most serious care. I hesitate to take back my resignation because I am old in comparison with you, and I have habits difficult to abandon. Henceforward, you must have courtiers who know how to amuse you,—madmen who will get themselves killed to carry out what you call your great works. Great they will be, I feel; but if by chance I should not think them so? I have seen war, Sire; I have seen peace; I have served Richelieu and Mazarin; I have been scorched with your father at the fire of Rochelle, riddled with thrusts like a sieve, having made a new skin ten times, as serpents do. After affronts and injustices, I have a command which was formerly something, because it gave the bearer the right of speaking as he liked to his king. But your captain of the musketeers will henceforward be an officer guarding the lower doors. Truly, Sire, if that is to be the employment from this time, seize the opportunity of our being on good terms to take it from me. Do not imagine that I bear malice. No, you have tamed me, as you say; but it must be confessed that in taming me you have lessened me,—by bowing me, you have convicted me of weakness. If you knew how well it suits me to carry my head high, and what a pitiful mien I shall have while scenting the dust of your carpets! Oh, Sire, I regret sincerely, and you will regret as I do, those times when the King of France saw in his vestibules all those insolent gentlemen, lean, always swearing,—cross-grained mastiffs, who could bite mortally in days of battle. Those men were the best of courtiers for the hand which fed them,—they would lick it; but for the hand that struck them, oh, the bite that followed! A little gold on the lace of their cloaks, a little more portliness of figure, a little sprinkling of grey in their dry hair, and you will behold the handsome dukes and peers, the haughty marshals of France. But why should I tell you all this? The king is my master; he wills that I should make verses; he wills that I should polish the mosaics of his antechambers with satin shoes. *Mordioux!* that is difficult, but I have got over greater difficulties than that. I will do it. Why will I do it? Because I love money? I have enough. Because I am ambitious? My career is bounded. Because I love the court? No; I will remain because I have been accustomed for thirty years to go and take the order of the king, and to have said to me, 'Good-evening, D'Artagnan,' with a smile I did not beg for. That smile I will beg for! Are you content, Sire?" And D'Artagnan bowed his silvered head, upon which the smiling king placed his white hand with pride.

"Thanks, my old servant, my faithful friend," said he. "As, reckoning from this day, I have no longer any enemies in France, it remains with me to send you to a foreign field to gather your marshal's bâton. Depend upon me for finding you an opportunity. In the meantime, eat of my best bread and sleep tranquilly."—"That is all kind and well!" said D'Artagnan, much agitated. "But those poor men at Belle-Isle,—one of them, in particular, so good and so brave?"—"Do you ask their pardon of me?"—"Upon my knees, Sire!"—"Well, then, go and take it to them, if it be still time. But do you answer for them?"—"With my life, Sire!"

"Go, then. To-morrow I set out for Paris. Return by that time, for I do not wish you to leave me in future."—"Be assured of that,

The Man in the Iron Mask

Sire," said D'Artagnan, kissing the royal hand. And with a heart swelling with joy, he rushed out of the castle on his way to Belle-Isle.

The king had returned to Paris, and with him D'Artagnan, who in twenty-four hours, having made with the greatest care all possible inquiries at Belle-Isle, had learned nothing of the secret so well kept by the heavy rock of Locmaria, which had fallen on the heroic Porthos. The captain of the musketeers only knew what those two valiant men,—what these two friends, whose defence he had so nobly taken up, whose lives he had so earnestly endeavoured to save,—aided by three faithful Bretons, had accomplished against a whole army. He had been able to see, launched on the neighbouring heath, the human remains which had stained with blood the stones scattered among the flowering broom. He learned also that a boat had been seen far out at sea, and that, like a bird of prey, a royal vessel had pursued, overtaken, and devoured this poor little bird which was flying with rapid wings. But there D'Artagnan's certainties ended. The field of conjectures was thrown open at this boundary. Now, what could he conjecture? The vessel had not returned. It is true that a brisk wind had prevailed for three days; but the corvette was known to be a good sailor and solid in its timbers; it could not fear gales of wind, and it ought, according to the calculation of D'Artagnan, to have either returned to Brest, or come back to the mouth of the Loire. Such was the news, ambiguous, it is true, but in some degree reassuring to him personally, which D'Artagnan brought to Louis XIV. when the king, followed by all the court, returned to Paris.

Louis, satisfied with his success—Louis, more mild and more affable since he felt himself more powerful—had not ceased for an instant to ride close to the carriage door of Mademoiselle de la Vallière. Everybody had been anxious to amuse the two queens, so as to make them forget this abandonment of the son and the husband. Everything breathed of the future; the past was nothing to anybody: only that past came like a painful and bleeding wound to the hearts of some tender and devoted spirits. Scarcely was the king reinstalled in Paris when he received a touching proof of this. Louis XIV. had just risen and taken his first repast, when his captain of the musketeers presented himself before him. D'Artagnan was pale and looked unhappy. The king, at the first glance, perceived the change in a countenance generally so unconcerned. "What is the matter, D'Artagnan?" said he.

"Sire, a great misfortune has happened to me."—"Good heavens! what is it?"—"Sire, I have lost one of my friends, M. du Vallon, in the affair of Belle-Isle." And while speaking these words, D'Artagnan fixed his falcon eye upon Louis XIV., to catch the first feeling that would show itself.

"I knew it," replied the king, quietly.—"You knew it, and did not tell me?" cried the musketeer.—"To what good? Your grief, my friend, is so worthy of respect! It is my duty to treat it kindly. To have informed you of this misfortune, which I knew would pain you so greatly, D'Artagnan, would have been, in your eyes, to have triumphed over you. Yes, I knew that M. du Vallon had buried himself beneath the rocks of Locmaria; I knew that M. d'Herblay had taken one of my vessels with its crew, and had compelled it to convey him to Bayonne. But I was willing that you should learn these matters in a direct manner, in order that you might be convinced that my friends are with me respected and sacred; that always the man in me will immolate himself to men, while the king is so often found to sacrifice men to his majesty and power."

"But, Sire, how could you know?"—"How do you yourself know, D'Artagnan?"—"By this letter, Sire, which M. d'Herblay, free and out of danger, writes me from Bayonne."—"Look here," said the king, drawing from a casket placed upon the table close to the seat upon which D'Artagnan was leaning a letter copied exactly from that of M. d'Herblay; "here is the very letter which Colbert placed in my hands a week before you received yours. I am well served, you may perceive."

"Yes, Sire," murmured the musketeer; "you were the only man whose fortune was capable of dominating the fortunes and strength of my two friends. You have used it, Sire; but you will not abuse it, will you?"—"D'Artagnan," said the king, with a smile beaming with kindness, "I could have M. d'Herblay carried off from the territories of the King of Spain, and brought here alive to inflict justice upon him. But, D'Artagnan, be assured I will not yield to this first and natural impulse. He is free; let him continue free."

"Oh, Sire! you will not always remain so clement, so noble, so generous as you have shown yourself with respect to me and M.

d'Herblay; you will have about you councillors who will cure you of that weakness."—"No, D'Artagnan, you are mistaken when you accuse my council of urging me to pursue rigorous measures. The advice to spare M. d'Herblay comes from Colbert himself."—"Oh, Sire!" said D'Artagnan, extremely surprised.

"As for you," continued the king, with a kindness very uncommon with him, "I have several pieces of good news to announce to you; but you shall know them, my dear Captain, the moment I have finished my accounts. I have said that I wish to make, and would make, your fortune; that promise will soon be a reality."

CHAPTER XXXVIII

THE OLD AGE OF ATHOS

WHILE all these affairs appeared to be separating for ever the four musketeers, formerly bound together in a manner that seemed indissoluble, Athos, left alone after the departure of Raoul, began to pay his tribute to that death by anticipation which is called the absence of those we love. Returned to his house at Blois, he daily felt the decline of the vigour of a nature which for so long a time had appeared infallible. Age, which had been kept back by the presence of the beloved object, arrived with that *cortége* of pains and inconveniences which increases in proportion as its coming is delayed. Athos had no longer his son's presence to incite him to walk firmly, with his head erect, as a good example; he had no longer in those brilliant eyes of the young man an ever-ardent focus at which to rekindle the fire of his looks. And then, it must be said, this nature, exquisite in its tenderness and its reserve, no longer finding anything that comprehended its feelings, gave itself up to grief with all the warmth with which vulgar natures give themselves up to joy. The Comte de la Fère, who had remained a young man up to his sixty-second year; the warrior who had preserved his strength in spite of fatigues, his freshness of mind in spite of misfortunes, his mild serenity of soul and body in spite of Milady, in spite of Mazarin, in spite of La Vallière,—Athos had become an old man in a week from the moment at which he had lost the support of his latter

The Old Age of Athos

youth. Still handsome though bent, noble but sad,—gently, and tottering under his grey hairs, he sought since his solitude the glades where the rays of the sun penetrated through the foliage of the walks. He discontinued all the vigorous exercises he had enjoyed through life, since Raoul was no longer with him. The servants, accustomed to see him stirring with the dawn at all seasons, were astonished to hear seven o'clock strike before their master had quitted his bed. Athos remained in bed with a book under his pillow; but he did not sleep, neither did he read. Remaining in bed that he might no longer have to carry his body, he allowed his soul and spirit to wander from their envelope, and return to his son or to God.

His people were sometimes terrified to see him for hours together absorbed in a silent reverie, mute and insensible; he no longer heard the timid step of the servant who came to the door of his chamber to watch the sleeping or waking of his master. It sometimes happened that he forgot that the day had half passed away, that the hours for the first two meals were gone by. Then he was awakened. He rose, descended to his shady walk, then came out a little into the sun, as if to partake its warmth for a minute with his absent child; and then the dismal, monotonous walk was resumed, until, quite exhausted, he regained the chamber and the bed,—his domicile by choice. For several days the count did not speak a word; he refused to receive the visits that were paid him, and during the night he was seen to relight his lamp and pass long hours in writing letters or examining parchments.

Athos's *valet de chambre* observed that he shortened his walk every day by several turns. The great alley of limes soon became too long for feet that used to traverse it a hundred times in a day. The count walked feebly as far as the middle trees, seated himself upon a mossy bank which sloped towards a side path, and there waited the return of his strength, or rather the return of night. Very shortly a hundred steps exhausted him. At length Athos refused to rise at all; he declined all nourishment, and his terrified people,—although he did not complain, although he had a smile on his lips, although he continued to speak with his sweet voice,—his people went to Blois in search of the old physician of the late Monsieur, and brought him to the Comte de la Fère in such a fashion that he could see the count without being himself seen. For this purpose they placed him in a closet adjoining the chamber of the patient, and

251

implored him not to show himself, in the fear of displeasing their master, who had not asked for a physician. The doctor obeyed: Athos was a sort of model for the gentlemen of the country; the Blaisois boasted of possessing this sacred relic of the old French glories. Athos was a great seigneur, compared with such nobles as the king improvised by touching with his yellow and prolific sceptre the dry trunks of the heraldic trees of the province.

People respected Athos, we say, and they loved him. The physician could not bear to see his people weep, and to see flock round him the poor of the canton, to whom Athos gave life and consolation by his kind words and his charities. He examined, therefore, from the depths of his hiding-place, the nature of that mysterious malady which bent down and devoured more mortally every day a man but lately so full of life and of a desire to live. He remarked upon the cheeks of Athos the purple of fever, which fires itself and feeds itself,—slow fever, pitiless, born in a fold of the heart, sheltering itself behind that rampart, growing from the suffering it engenders, at once cause and effect of a perilous situation. The count spoke to nobody, we say; he did not even talk to himself. His thought feared noise; it approached to that degree of over-excitement which borders upon ecstasy. Man thus absorbed, though he does not yet belong to God, already belongs no longer to earth. The doctor remained for several hours studying this painful struggle of the will against a superior power; he was terrified at seeing those eyes always fixed, always directed towards an invisible object, at seeing beat with the same movement that heart from which never a sigh arose to vary the melancholy state. Sometimes the acuteness of pain awakens hope in the mind of a physician. Half a day passed away thus. The doctor formed his resolution like a brave man, like a man of firm mind; he issued suddenly from his place of retreat, and went straight up to Athos, who saw him without evincing more surprise than if he had not perceived the apparition. "Monsieur the Count, I crave your pardon," said the doctor, coming up to the patient with open arms; "but I have a reproach to make you. You shall hear me." And he seated himself by the pillow of Athos, who with difficulty roused himself from his preoccupation. "What is the matter, Doctor?" asked the count, after a silence.

"Why, the matter is, you are ill, Monsieur, and have had no advice."—"I! ill!" said Athos, smiling.—"Fever, consumption, weak-

The Old Age of Athos

ness, decay, Monsieur the Count."—"Weakness!" replied Athos; "is that possible? I do not get up."

"Come, come, Monsieur the Count, no subterfuges; you are a good Christian?" —"I hope so," said Athos.—"Would you kill yourself?"—"Never, Doctor."—"Well, Monsieur, you are in a fair way of doing so; to remain thus is suicide. Get well, Monsieur the Count! get well!"

"Of what? Find the disease first. For my part, I never knew myself better. Never did the sky appear more blue to me; never did I value more my flowers."—"You have a concealed grief."— "Concealed! not at all. I have the absence of my son, Doctor,— that is my malady, and I do not conceal it."—"Monsieur the Count, your son lives, he is strong, he has all the future before him of men of his merit and of his race; live for him—"—"But I do live, Doctor; oh! be satisfied of that," added he, with a melancholy smile. "As long as Raoul lives, it will be plainly known,—for as long as he lives, I shall live."

"What do you say?"—"A very simple thing. At this moment, Doctor, I allow my life to be in a state of suspense. A forgetful, dissipated, indifferent life would be above my strength now that I have Raoul no longer with me. You do not ask the lamp to burn when the spark has not lighted the flame; do not ask me to live noisily and brilliantly. I vegetate, I prepare myself, I wait. Look, Doctor; you remember those soldiers we have so often seen together at the ports, where they were waiting to embark,—lying down, indifferent, half upon one element, half upon the other. They were neither at the place where the sea was going to carry them nor at the place where the earth was going to lose them; baggage prepared, minds upon the stretch, looks fixed,—they waited. I repeat that word; it is the one which describes my present life. Lying down, like the soldiers, my ear on the alert for the reports that may reach me, I wish to be ready to set out at the first summons. Who will make me that summons,—life or death, God or Raoul? My baggage is packed; my soul is prepared; I await the signal. I wait, Doctor, I wait!"

The doctor knew the temper of that mind; he appreciated the strength of that body. He reflected for a moment, told himself that words were useless, remedies absurd; and he left the château, exhorting Athos's servants not to leave him for a moment.

253

The Man in the Iron Mask

The doctor being gone, Athos evinced neither anger nor vexation at having been disturbed. He did not even desire that all letters that came should be brought to him directly. He knew very well that every distraction which should arrive would be a joy, a hope, which his servants would have paid with their blood to procure him. Sleep had become rare. By force of thought, Athos forgot himself, for a few hours at most, in a reverie more profound, more obscure than other people would have called a reverie. The momentary repose which this forgetfulness afforded the body, fatigued the soul,—for Athos lived a double life during these wanderings of his understanding. One night, he dreamed that Raoul was dressing himself in a tent to go upon an expedition commanded by M. de Beaufort in person. The young man was sad; he clasped his cuirass slowly, and slowly he girded on his sword. "What is the matter?" asked his father, tenderly.—"What afflicts me is the death of Porthos, our so dear friend," replied Raoul. "I suffer here for the grief you will feel at home."

And the vision disappeared with the slumber of Athos. At daybreak one of his servants entered his master's apartments, and gave him a letter which came from Spain. "The writing of Aramis," thought the count; and he read. "Porthos is dead!" cried he, after the first lines. "Oh, Raoul, Raoul, thanks! thou keepest thy promise, thou warnest me!" Athos, seized with a mortal sweat, fainted, without any other cause than his weakness. Everything was soon prepared in his chamber, and they put him to bed.

The count fell asleep, but his disturbed slumber resembled suffering more than repose. The servant who watched him saw several times the expression of interior torture imprinted upon his features. Perhaps Athos was dreaming.

The fever rose; it invaded the chest, where the fire soon caught, according to the expression of the physician, who had been brought back from Blois. It soon reached the head. The physician made two successive bleedings, which unlodged it, but left the patient very weak, and without power of action except in his brain; and yet this redoubtable fever had ceased. It attacked with its last strokes the stiffened extremities; and as midnight struck it yielded.

The physician, seeing the incontestable improvement, returned to Blois, after having ordered some prescriptions, declaring that the count was saved. Then began for Athos a strange, indefinable

The Old Age of Athos

state. Free to think, his mind turned towards Raoul, that beloved son. His imagination painted the fields of Africa in the environs of Djidgelli, where M. de Beaufort was to land his army. There were grey rocks, rendered green in certain parts by the waters of the sea when it lashed the shore in storms and tempests. Beyond the shore, strewed over with these rocks like tombs, ascended, in form of an amphitheatre among mastic-trees and cactus, a sort of village, full of smoke, confused noises, and terrified movements. Suddenly, from the bosom of this smoke arose a flame, which, gaining headway, presently covered the whole surface of this village, and increased by degress, including in its red vortices tears, cries, arms extended towards heaven. There was, for a moment, a frightful *pêle-mêle* of timbers falling, of swords broken, of stones calcined, of trees burned and disappearing. It was a strange thing that in this chaos, in which Athos distinguished raised arms, in which he heard cries, sobs, and groans, he did not see one human figure. The cannon thundered at a distance, musketry cracked, the sea moaned, flocks made their escape, bounding over the verdant slope; but not a soldier to apply the match to the batteries of cannon, not a sailor to assist in manœuvring the fleet, not a shepherd for the flocks. After the ruin of the village and the destruction of the forts which commanded it,—a ruin and a destruction operated magically without the co-operation of a single human being,—the flame was extinguished, the smoke began to descend, then diminished in intensity, paled, and disappeared entirely. Night then came over the scene,—a night dark upon the earth, brilliant in the firmament. The large, blazing stars which sparkled in the African sky shone without lighting anything even around them.

A long silence ensued, which gave, for a moment, repose to the troubled imagination of Athos; and as he felt that that which he saw was not terminated, he applied his observation more attentively to the strange spectacle which his imagination had presented. This spectacle was soon continued for him. A mild and pale moon arose behind the declivities of the coast, and streaking at first the undulating ripples of the sea, which appeared to have calmed after the roarings it had sent forth during the vision of Athos,—the moon, we say, shed its diamonds and opals upon the briers and bushes of the hill. The grey rocks, like so many silent and attentive phantoms, appeared to raise their verdant heads to examine likewise the field of battle by the light of the moon; and Athos perceived that that field, entirely empty during the combat, was now strewn with fallen bodies.

An inexpressible shudder of fear and horror seized the soul of Athos when he recognized the white and blue uniform of the soldiers of Picardy, with their long pikes and blue handles, and their muskets marked with the *fleur-de-lis* on the butts; when he saw all the gaping, cold wounds looking up to the azure heavens as if to demand back of them the souls to which they had opened a passage; when he saw the slaughtered horses, stiff, with their tongues hanging out at one side of their mouths, sleeping in the icy blood pooled around them, staining their furniture and their manes; when he saw the white horse of M. de Beaufort, with his head beaten to pieces, in the first ranks of the dead. Athos passed a cold hand over his brow, which he was astonished not to find burning. He was convinced by this touch that he was present as a spectator, without fever, on the day after a battle fought upon the shores of Djidgelli by the army of the expedition which he had seen leave the coasts of France and disappear in the horizon, and of which he had saluted with thought and gesture the last cannon-shot fired by the duke as a signal of farewell to his country.

Who can paint the mortal agony with which his soul followed, like a vigilant eye, the trace of those dead bodies, and examined them, one after the other, to see if Raoul slept among them? Who can express the intoxication of joy with which Athos bowed before God, and gave thanks for not having seen him he sought with so much fear among the dead? In fact, fallen dead in their ranks, stiff, icy, all these dead, easy to be recognized, seemed to turn with kindness and respect towards the Comte de la Fère, to be the better seen by him during his funereal inspection. But yet he was astonished while viewing all these bodies, not to perceive the survivors. To such a point did the illusion extend, that this vision was for the father a real voyage made by him into Africa, to obtain more exact information respecting his son.

Fatigued, therefore, with having traversed seas and continents, he sought repose under one of the tents sheltered behind a rock, on the top of which floated the white *fleurdelisé* pennon. He looked for a soldier to conduct him to the tent of M. de Beaufort. Then, while his eye was wandering over the plain, turning in all directions, he saw a white form appear behind the resinous myrtles. This figure was clothed in the costume of an officer; it held in its hand a broken sword; it advanced slowly towards Athos, who, stopping short and fixing his eyes upon it, neither spoke nor moved, but wished to open his arms, because in this silent and pale officer he had just recognized Raoul. The count attempted to utter a cry; but it remained stifled in his throat. Raoul with a gesture directed him to be silent, placing his finger on his lips and drawing back by degrees, without Athos being able to see any motion of his legs. The count, more pale than Raoul, more trembling, followed his son, traversing painfully briers and bushes, stones and ditches, Raoul appearing not to touch the earth, and no obstacle impeding the lightness of his march. The count, whom the inequalities of the path fatigued, soon stopped exhausted. Raoul still continued to beckon him to follow him. The tender father, to whom love restored strength, made a last effort and climbed the mountain after the young man, who drew him onward by his gesture and his smile.

At length Athos gained the crest of the hill, and saw, thrown out in black upon the horizon whitened by the moon, the airy, visionary form of Raoul. Athos stretched out his hand to get closer to his beloved son upon the plateau, and the latter also stretched out his; but suddenly, as if the young man had been drawn away in spite of himself, still retreating, he left the earth; and Athos saw the clear blue sky shine between the feet of his child and the ground of the hill. Raoul rose insensibly into the void, still smiling, still inviting with a gesture; he departed towards heaven. Athos uttered a cry of terrified tenderness. He looked below again. He saw a camp destroyed, and all those white bodies of the royal army, like so many motionless atoms. And then, when raising his head, he saw still, still, his son beckoning him to ascend with him.

Athos was at this part of his marvellous vision when the charm was suddenly broken by a great noise rising from the outward gates of the house. A horse was heard galloping over the hard gravel of the great alley; and the sound of noisy and animated conversations ascended to the chamber in which the count was dreaming. Athos did not stir from the place he occupied; he scarcely turned his head towards the door to ascertain the sooner what these noises could be. A heavy step ascended the stairs; the horse which had recently galloped with such rapidity departed slowly towards the stables.

The Man in the Iron Mask

Great hesitation appeared in the steps which by degrees approached the chamber of Athos. A door then was opened, and Athos, turning a little towards the part of the room the noise came from, cried in a weak voice, "It is a courier from Africa, is it not?"—"No, Monsieur the Count," replied a voice which made the father of Raoul start upright in his bed.

"Grimaud!" murmured he; and the sweat began to pour down his cheeks. The old servant and companion appeared in the doorway. It was no longer a Grimaud still young with courage and devotion. He was a stern and pale old man, his clothes covered with dust, his few scattered hairs whitened by old age. He trembled while leaning against the door-frame, and was near falling on seeing by the light of the lamps the countenance of his master. These two men, who had lived so long together in a community of intelligence, and whose eyes, accustomed to economise expressions, knew how to say so many things silently,—these two old friends, one as noble as the other in heart, if they were unequal in fortune and birth, remained silent while looking at each other. By the exchange of a single glance they had just read to the bottom of each other's heart. Grimaud bore upon his countenance the impression of a grief already old, of a familiarity with sorrow. He appeared now to have at his command but one interpreter of his thought. As formerly he was accustomed not to speak, he now had accustomed himself not to smile. Athos read at a glance all these shades upon the visage of his faithful servant, and in the same tone he would have employed to speak to Raoul in his dream, "Grimaud," said he, "Raoul is dead, is he not?"

Behind Grimaud the other servants listened breathlessly, with their eyes fixed upon the bed of their sick master. They heard the terrible question, and an awful silence ensued. "Yes," replied the old man, heaving up the monosyllable from his chest with a hoarse broken sigh.

Then arose voices of lamentation, which groaned without measure, and filled with regrets and prayers the chamber where the agonised father searched with his eyes the portrait of his son. This was for Athos a transition which led him to his dream. Without uttering a cry, without shedding a tear, patient, mild, resigned as a martyr, he raised his eyes towards heaven, in order to there see again, rising above the mountain of Djidgelli, the beloved shade

Aramis, bishop of Vannes

which was leaving him at the moment of Grimaud's arrival. Without doubt, while looking towards the heavens, when resuming his marvellous dream, he returned to the same road by which the vision, at once so terrible and so sweet, had led him before; for after having gently closed his eyes, he re-opened them and began to smile,— he had just seen Raoul, who had smiled upon him. With his hands clasped upon his breast, his face turned towards the window, bathed by the fresh air of night, which brought to his pillow the aroma of the flowers and the woods, Athos entered, never again to come out of it, into the contemplation of that paradise which the living never see. God willed, no doubt, to open to this elect the treasures of eternal beatitude at the hour when other men tremble with the idea of being severely received by the Lord, and cling to this life they know, in the dread of the other life of which they get a glimpse by the dismal murky torches of death. Athos was guided by the pure and serene soul of his son, which aspired to be like the paternal soul. Everything for this just man was melody and perfume in the rough road which souls take to return to the celestial country. After an hour of this ecstasy, Athos softly raised his hands as white as wax; the smile did not quit his lips, and he murmured low, so low as scarcely to be audible, these three words addressed to God or to Raoul, "HERE I AM!" And his hands fell down slowly, as if he himself had laid them on the bed.

Death had been kind and mild to this noble creature. It had spared him the tortures of the agony, the convulsions of the last departure; it had opened with an indulgent finger the gates of eternity to that noble soul worthy of all its respect. God had no doubt ordered it thus, that the pious remembrance of this death should remain in the hearts of those present and in the memory of other men,—a death which made the passage from this life to the other seem desirable to those whose existence upon this earth leads them not to dread the last judgment. Athos preserved, even in the eternal sleep, his placid and sincere smile,—an ornament which was to accompany him to the tomb. The quietude of his features, the peacefulness of his departure, made his servants for a long time doubt whether he had really quitted life.

EPILOGUE

FOUR years after the scene we have just described, two horsemen, well mounted, traversed Blois early in the morning, for the purpose of arranging a birding-party which the king intended to make in that uneven plain which the Loire divides in two, and which borders on the one side on Meung, on the other on Amboise. These were the captain of the king's harriers and the governor of the falcons,—personages greatly respected in the time of Louis XIII., but rather neglected by his successor. These two horsemen, having reconnoitred the ground, were returning, their observations made, when they perceived some little groups of soldiers here and there whom the sergeants were placing at distances at the opening of the enclosures. These were the king's musketeers. Behind them came, upon a good horse, the captain, known by his richly embroidered uniform. His hair was grey, his beard was becoming so. He appeared a little bent, although sitting and handling his horse gracefully. He was looking about him watchfully.

"M. d'Artagnan does not get any older," said the captain of the harriers to his colleague the falconer; "with ten years more than either of us, he has the seat of a young man on horseback."—"That is true," replied the falconer. "I haven't seen any change in him for the last twenty years." But this officer was mistaken; D'Artagnan in the last four years had lived twelve years. Age imprinted its pitiless claws at each corner of his eyes; his brow was bald; his hands, formerly brown and nervous, were getting white, as if the blood began to chill there.

D'Artagnan accosted the officers with the shade of affability which distinguishes superior men, and received in return for his courtesy two most respectful bows. "Ah! what a lucky chance to see you here, M. d'Artagnan!" cried the falconer.

"It is rather I who should say that, Messieurs," replied the captain, "for nowadays the king makes more frequent use of his musketeers than of his falcons."—"Ah! it is not as it was in the good old times," sighed the falconer. "Do you remember, M. d'Artagnan, when the late king flew the pie in the vineyards beyond Beaugency? Ah, *dame!* you were not captain of the musketeers at that time, M. d'Artagnan."

Epilogue

"And you were nothing but under-corporal of the tiercels," replied D'Artagnan, laughing. "Never mind that; it was a good time, seeing that it is always a good time when we are young. Good-day, Monsieur the Captain of the harriers."—"You do me honour, Monsieur the Count," said the latter. D'Artagnan made no reply. The title of count had not struck him; D'Artagnan had been a count four years.

"Are you not very much fatigued with the long journey you have had, Monsieur the Captain?" continued the falconer. "It must be full two hundred leagues from hence to Pignerol."—"Two hundred and sixty to go, and as many to come back," said D'Artagnan, quietly.—"And," said the falconer, "is *he* well?"—"Who?" asked D'Artagnan.—"Why, poor M. Fouquet," continued the falconer, still in a low voice. The captain of the harriers had prudently withdrawn.

"No," replied D'Artagnan, "the poor man frets terribly; he cannot comprehend how imprisonment can be a favour. He says that the parliament had absolved him by banishing him, and that banishment is liberty. He does not imagine that they have sworn his death, and that to save his life from the claws of the parliament would be to incur too much obligation to God."—"Ah, yes; the poor man had a near chance of the scaffold," replied the falconer; "it is said that M. Colbert had given orders to the governor of the Bastille, and that the execution was ordered."

"Enough!" said D'Artagnan, pensively, and with a view to cutting short the conversation.—"Yes," said the captain of the harriers, approaching, "M. Fouquet is now at Pignerol; he has richly deserved it. He has had the good fortune to be conducted there by you; he had robbed the king enough." D'Artagnan cast at the master of the dogs one of his evil looks, and said to him, "Monsieur, if any one told me that you had eaten your dogs' meat, not only would I refuse to believe it, but, still more, if you were condemned to the whip or the jail for it, I should pity you, and would not allow people to speak ill of you. And yet, Monsieur, honest man as you may be, I assure you that you are not more so than poor M. Fouquet was."

After having undergone this sharp rebuke, the captain of the harriers hung his head, and allowed the falconer to get two steps in advance of him nearer to D'Artagnan. "He is content," said the

The Man in the Iron Mask

falconer, in a low voice, to the musketeer; "we all know that harriers are in fashion nowadays. If he were a falconer he would not talk in that way."

D'Artagnan smiled in a melancholy manner at seeing this great political question resolved by the discontent of such humble interests. He for a moment ran over in his mind the glorious existence of the superintendent, the crumbling away of his fortunes, and the melancholy death that awaited him; and, to conclude, "Did M. Fouquet love falconry?" said he.—"Oh, passionately, Monsieur!" replied the falconer, with an accent of bitter regret and a sigh that was the funeral oration of Fouquet.

D'Artagnan allowed the ill-humour of the one and the regrets of the other to pass, and continued to advance into the plain. They could already catch glimpses of the huntsmen at the issues of the wood, the feathers of the outriders passing like shooting stars across the clearings, and the white horses cutting with their luminous apparitions the dark thickets of the copses.

"But," resumed D'Artagnan, "will the sport be long? Pray, give us a good swift bird, for I am very tired. Is it a heron or a swan?" —"Both, M. d'Artagnan," said the falconer; "but you need not be alarmed, the king is not much of a sportsman. He does not sport on his own account; he only wishes to give amusement to the ladies."

The words "to the ladies" were so strongly accented that it set D'Artagnan listening. "Ah!" said he, looking at the falconer with surprise. The captain of the harriers smiled, no doubt with a view of making it up with the musketeer. "Oh, you may safely laugh," said D'Artagnan; "I know nothing of current news. I arrived only yesterday, after a month's absence. I left the court mourning the death of the queen-mother. The king was not willing to take any amusement after receiving the last sigh of Anne of Austria; but everything has an end in this world. Well! then he is no longer sad? So much the better."

"And everything begins as well as ends," said the captain of the dogs, with a coarse laugh.—"Ah!" said D'Artagnan a second time, —he burned to know; but dignity would not allow him to interrogate persons below him,—"there is something new, then, it appears?"

The captain gave him a significant wink; but D'Artagnan was

Epilogue

unwilling to learn anything from this man. "Shall we see the king early?" asked he of the falconer.—"At seven o'clock, Monsieur, I shall fly the birds."—"Who comes with the king? How is Madame? How is the queen?"—"Better, Monsieur."—"Has she been ill, then?"—"Monsieur, since the last chagrin she had, her Majesty has been unwell."

"What chagrin? You need not fancy your news is old. I am but just returned."—"It appears that the queen, a little neglected since the death of her mother-in-law, complained to the king, who replied to her, 'Do I not sleep with you every night, Madame? What more do you want?' " —"Ah!" said D'Artagnan,—"poor woman! She must heartily hate Mademoiselle de la Vallière."

"Oh, no! not Mademoiselle de la Vallière," replied the falconer. —"Who, then—" The horn interrupted this conversation. It summoned the dogs and the hawks. The falconer and his companion set off immediately, leaving D'Artagnan alone in the midst of the suspended sentence. The king appeared at a distance, surrounded by ladies and horsemen. All the troop advanced in beautiful order, at a foot's pace, the horns of various sorts animating the dogs and the horses. It was a movement, a noise, a mirage of light, of which nothing now can give an idea, unless it be the fictitious splendour or false majesty of a theatrical spectacle. D'Artagnan, with an eye little weakened, distinguished behind the group three carriages. The first was intended for the queen; it was empty. D'Artagnan, who did not see Mademoiselle de la Vallière by the king's side, on looking about for her, saw her in the second carriage. She was alone with two of her women, who seemed as dull as their mistress. On the left hand of the king, upon a high-spirited horse, restrained by a bold and skilful hand, shone a lady of the most dazzling beauty. The king smiled upon her, and she smiled upon the king. Loud laughter followed every word she spoke.

"I must know that woman," thought the musketeer; "who can she be?" And he stooped towards his friend the falconer, to whom he addressed the question he had put to himself. The falconer was about to reply, when the king, perceiving D'Artagnan, said, "Ah, Count! you are returned then! Why have I not seen you?" —"Sire," replied the captain, "because your Majesty was asleep when I arrived, and not awake when I resumed my duties this morning."—"Still the same!" said Louis, in a loud voice, denoting

The Man in the Iron Mask

satisfaction. "Take some rest, Count; I command you to do so. You will dine with me to-day."

A murmur of admiration surrounded D'Artagnan like an immense caress. Every one was eager to salute him. Dining with the king was an honour his Majesty was not so prodigal of as Henry IV. had been. The king passed a few steps in advance, and D'Artagnan found himself in the midst of a fresh group, among whom shone M. Colbert. "Good-day, M. d'Artagnan," said the minister, with affable politeness; "have you had a pleasant journey?"—"Yes, Monsieur," said D'Artagnan, bowing to the neck of his horse.—"I heard the king invite you to his table for this evening," continued the minister; "you will meet an old friend there."

"An old friend of mine?" asked D'Artagnan, plunging painfully into the dark waves of the past which had swallowed up for him so many friendships and so many hatreds.—"M. le Duc d'Alaméda, who is arrived this morning from Spain."

"The Duc d'Alaméda?" said D'Artagnan, reflecting in vain.—"I!" said an old man, white as snow, sitting bent in his carriage, which he caused to be thrown open to make room for the musketeer.—"Aramis!" cried D'Artagnan, struck with stupor. And, inert as he was, he suffered the thin arm of the old nobleman to rest trembling on his neck.

Colbert, after having observed them in silence for a minute, put his horse forward, and left the two old friends together. "And so," said the musketeer, taking the arm of Aramis, "you, the exile, the rebel, are again in France?"—"And I shall dine with you at the king's table," said Aramis, smiling. "Yes; will you not ask yourself what is the use of fidelity in this world? Stop! let us allow poor La Vallière's carriage to pass. See how uneasy she is! How her eye, dimmed with tears, follows the king, who is riding on horseback yonder!"—"With whom?"—"With Mademoiselle de Tonnay-Charente, now become Madame de Montespan," replied Aramis.

"She is jealous; is she then deserted?"—"Not quite yet, but soon will be." They chatted together while following the sport, and Aramis's coachman drove them so cleverly that they got up at the moment when the falcon, attacking the bird, beat him down and fell upon him. The king alighted; Madame de Montespan followed his example. They were in front of an isolated chapel, concealed by

Epilogue

large trees, already despoiled of their leaves by the first winds of autumn. Behind this chapel was an enclosure entered only by a latticed gate. The falcon had beat down his prey in the enclosure belonging to this little chapel, and the king was desirous of going in to take the first feather, according to custom. The *cortége* formed a circle round the building and the hedges, too small to receive so many.

D'Artagnan held back Aramis by the arm as he was about, like the rest, to alight from his carriage, and in a broken voice, "Do you know, Aramis," said he, "whither chance has conducted us?"— "No," replied the duke.—"Here repose people I have known," said D'Artagnan, much agitated.

Aramis, without divining anything, and with a trembling step, penetrated into the chapel by a little door which D'Artagnan opened for him. "Where are they buried?" said he.—"There, in the enclosure. There is a cross, you see, under that little cypress. The little cypress is planted over their tomb. Don't go to it; the king is going that way,—the heron has fallen just there."

Aramis stopped, and concealed himself in the shade. They then saw, without being seen, the pale face of La Vallière, who, neglected in her carriage, had at first looked on with a melancholy heart from the door, and then, carried away by jealousy, had advanced into the chapel, whence, leaning against a pillar, she contemplated in the enclosure the king smiling and making signs to Madame de Montespan to approach, as there was nothing to be afraid of. Madame de Montespan complied; she took the hand the king held out to her, and he, plucking out the first feather from the heron, which the falconer had strangled, placed it in the hat of his beautiful companion. She, smiling in her turn, kissed the hand tenderly which made her this present. The king blushed with pleasure; he looked at Madame de Montespan with all the fire of love. "What will you give me in exchange?" said he.

She broke off a little branch of cypress and offered it to the king, intoxicated with hope. "Humph!" said Aramis to D'Artagnan; "the present is but a sad one, for that cypress shades a tomb."—"Yes, and the tomb is that of Raoul de Bragelonne," said D'Artagnan, aloud; "of Raoul, who sleeps under that cross with Athos his father."

A groan was heard behind them. They saw a woman fall fainting to the ground. Mademoiselle de la Vallière had seen and heard all.

The Man in the Iron Mask

"Poor woman!" muttered D'Artagnan, as he helped the attendants to carry back to her carriage her who from that time was to suffer.

That evening D'Artagnan was seated at the king's table, near M. Colbert and M. le Duc d'Alaméda. The king was very gay. He paid a thousand little attentions to the queen, a thousand kindnesses to Madame, seated at his left hand, and very sad. It might have been supposed to be that calm time when the king used to watch the eyes of his mother for assent or dissent to what he had just spoken. Of mistresses there was no question at this dinner. The king addressed Aramis two or three times, calling him Monsieur the Ambassador, which increased the surprise already felt by D'Artagnan at seeing his friend the rebel so marvellously well received at court.

The king, on rising from table, gave his hand to the queen and made a sign to Colbert, whose eye watched that of his master. Colbert took D'Artagnan and Aramis on one side. The king began to chat with his sister, while Monsieur, very uneasy, entertatined the queen with a preoccupied air, without ceasing to watch his wife and brother from the corner of his eye. The conversation between Aramis, D'Artagnan, and Colbert turned upon indifferent subjects. They spoke of preceding ministers; Colbert related the feats of Mazarin, and had those of Richelieu related to him. D'Artagnan could not overcome his surprise at finding this man, with heavy eyebrows and a low forehead, contain so much sound knowledge and cheerful humour. Aramis was astonished at that lightness of character which permitted a serious man to retard with advantage the moment for a more important conversation, to which nobody made any allusion, although all three interlocutors felt the imminence of it.

It was very plain from the embarrassed appearance of Monsieur how much the conversation of the king and Madame annoyed him. The eyes of Madame were almost red; was she going to complain? Was she going to commit a little scandal in open court? The king took her on one side, and in a tone so tender that it must have reminded the princess of the time when she was loved for herself, "Sister," said he, "why do I see tears in those beautiful eyes?"—"Why—Sire—" said she.—"Monsieur is jealous, is he not, sister?" She looked towards Monsieur,—an infallible sign that they were talking about him. "Yes," said she.

"Listen to me," said the king; "if your friends compromise you, it is not Monsieur's fault." He spoke these words with so much kind-

Epilogue

ness that Madame, encouraged,—she who had had so many griefs for so long a time,—was near bursting into tears, so full was her heart. "Come, come, dear sister," said the king, "tell me your griefs. By the word of a brother, I pity them; by the word of a king, I will end them."

She raised her fine eyes, and in a melancholy tone, "It is not my friends who compromise me," said she. "They are either absent or concealed; they have been brought into disgrace with your Majesty, —they, so devoted, so good, so loyal!"—"You say this on account of De Guiche, whom I have exiled at the desire of Monsieur?"— "And who, since that unjust exile, has endeavoured once every day to get himself killed!"

"Unjust, do you say, sister?"—"So unjust, that if I had not had the respect mingled with friendship that I have always entertained for your Majesty—"—"Well?"—"Well! I would have asked my brother Charles, upon whom I can always—" The king started. "What then?"—"I would have asked him to have it represented to you that Monsieur and his favourite, M. le Chevalier de Lorraine, ought not with impunity to constitute themselves the executioners of my honour and my happiness."

"The Chevalier de Lorraine," said the king,—"that dismal fellow?"—"He is my mortal enemy. While that man lives in my household, where Monsieur retains him and delegates his powers to him, I shall be the most miserable woman in this kingdom."

"So," said the king, slowly, "you call your brother of England a better friend than I am?"—"Actions speak for themselves, Sire."— "And you would prefer going to ask assistance there—"—"To my own country!" said she, with pride; "yes, Sire."—"You are the grandchild of Henry IV. as well as myself, my friend. Cousin and brother-in-law, does not that amount pretty nearly to the title of brother-german?"—"Then," said Henrietta, "act!"

"Let us form an alliance."—"Begin."—"I have, you say, unjustly exiled De Guiche."—"Oh, yes," said she, blushing.—"De Guiche shall return."—"So far, well."—"And now you say that I am wrong in having in your household the Chevalier de Lorraine, who gives Monsieur ill advice respecting you?"—"Remember well what I tell you, Sire: the Chevalier de Lorraine some day— Observe, if ever I come to an ill end, I accuse beforehand the Chevalier de Lorraine; he has a soul capable of any crime!"—"The

The Man in the Iron Mask

Chevalier de Lorraine shall no longer annoy you; I promise you that."

"Then that will be a true preliminary of alliance, Sire,—I sign; but since you have done your part, tell me what shall be mine."—"Instead of embroiling me with your brother Charles, you must make him my more intimate friend than ever."—"That is very easy."—"Oh! not quite so much so as you may think, for in ordinary friendship persons embrace or exercise hospitality, and that only costs a kiss or a return,—easy expenses; but in political friendship—"

"Ah! it's a political friendship, is it?"—"Yes, my sister; and then, instead of embraces and feasts, it is soldiers—it is soldiers all living and well equipped—that we must serve up to our friend; vessels we must offer, all armed with cannons and stored with provisions. It hence results that we have not always our coffers in a fit state to form such friendships."—"Ah! you are quite right," said Madame; "the coffers of the king of England have been very sonorous for some time."—"But you, my sister, who have so much influence over your brother,—you can obtain more than an ambassador ever could obtain."

"To effect that I must go to London, my dear brother."—"I have thought so," replied the king, eagerly; "and I have said to myself that such a voyage would do your spirits good."—"Only," interrupted Madame, "it is possible I should fail. The king of England has dangerous counsellors."

"Counsellors, do you say?"—"Precisely. If, by chance, your Majesty had any intention—I am only supposing so—of asking Charles II. his alliance for a war—"—"For a war?"—"Yes; well, then the counsellors of the king, who are to the number of seven,—Mademoiselle Stewart, Mademoiselle Wells, Mademoiselle Gwyn, Miss Orchay, Mademoiselle Zunga, Miss Daws, and the Countess of Castlemaine,—will represent to the king that war costs a great deal of money; that it is far better to give balls and suppers at Hampton Court than to equip vessels of the line at Portsmouth and Greenwich."—"And then your negotiations will fail?"—"Oh! those ladies cause all negotiations to fail that they don't make themselves."

"Do you know the idea that has struck me, sister?"—"No; tell me what it is."—"It is that by searching well around you, you

Epilogue

might perhaps find a female counsellor to take with you to your brother whose eloquence might paralyse the ill-will of the seven others."—"That is really an idea, Sire; and I will search."—"You will find what you want."—"I hope so."

"A pretty person is necessary; an agreeable face is better than an ugly one, is it not?"—"Most assuredly."—"An animated, lively, audacious character?"—"Certainly."—"Nobility,—that is, enough to enable her to approach the king without awkwardness; little enough, so that she may not trouble herself about the dignity of her race."—"Quite just."—"And who knows a little English."— "*Mon Dieu!* why, some one," cried Madame, "like Mademoiselle de Kéroualle, for instance!"

"Oh! why, yes!" said Louis XIV.; "you have found—it is you who have found, my sister."—"I will take her; she will have no cause to complain, I suppose."—"Oh, no; I will name her *séductrice plénipotentiaire* at once, and will add the dowry to the title."— "That is well."—"I fancy you already on your road, my dear little sister, and consoled for all your griefs."

"I will go on two conditions. The first is, that I shall know what I am negotiating about."—"This is it. The Dutch, you know, insult me daily in their gazettes, and by their republican attitude. I don't like republics."—"That may easily be conceived, Sire."— "I see with pain that these kings of the sea—they call themselves so —keep trade from France in the Indies, and that their vessels will soon occupy all the ports of Europe. Such a power is too near me, sister."

"They are your allies, nevertheless."—"That is why they were wrong in having the medal you have heard of struck,—a medal which represents Holland stopping the sun, as Joshua did, with this legend: *The sun has stopped before me.* There is not much fraternity in that, is there?"—"I thought you had forgotten that miserable affair."—"I forget nothing, my sister. And if my true friends, such as your brother Charles, are willing to second me—" The princess remained pensively silent. "Listen to me; there is the empire of the seas to be shared. In this partition, which England submits to, could I not represent the second party as well as the Dutch?"—"We have Mademoiselle de Kéroualle to treat that question," replied Madame.

"Your second condition for going, if you please, sister?"—"The consent of Monsieur, my husband."—"You shall have it."—"Then consider me gone, my brother."

On hearing these words, Louis XIV., turned round towards the corner of the room in which D'Artagnan, Colbert, and Aramis stood, and made an affirmative sign to his minister. Colbert then broke the conversation at the point where it happened to be, and said to Aramis, "Monsieur the Ambassador, shall we talk about business?" D'Artagnan immediately withdrew, from politeness. He directed his steps towards the chimney, within hearing of what the king was going to say to Monsieur, who, evidently uneasy, had gone to him. The face of the king was animated. Upon his brow was stamped a will, the redoubtable expression of which already met with no more contradiction in France, and soon would meet with no more in Europe.

"Monsieur," said the king to his brother, "I am not pleased with M. le Chevalier de Lorraine. You, who do him the honour to protect him, must advise him to travel for a few months." These words fell with a crush of an avalanche upon Monsieur, who adored this favourite, and concentrated all his affections in him. "In what has the chevalier been able to displease your Majesty?" cried he, darting a furious look at Madame.—"I will tell you that when he is gone," replied the impassive king. "And also when Madame, here, shall have crossed over into England."—"Madame! into England!" murmured Monsieur, seized with stupor.—"In a week, my brother," continued the king, "while we two will go whither I will tell you." And the king turned upon his heel after having smiled in his brother's face, to sweeten a little the bitter draught he had given him.

During this time, Colbert was talking with the Duc d'Alaméda. "Monsieur," said he to Aramis, "this is the moment for us to come to an understanding. I have made your peace with the king, and I owed that clearly to a man of your merit; but as you have often expressed friendship for me, an opportunity presents itself for giving me a proof of it. You are, besides, more a Frenchman than a Spaniard. Shall we have, answer me frankly, the neutrality of Spain, if we undertake anything against the United Provinces?"—"Monsieur," replied Aramis, "the interest of Spain is very clear. To embroil Europe with the United Provinces, against which subsists the ancient rancour arising from their acquisition of liberty, is our

Epilogue

policy; but the King of France is allied with the United Provinces. You are not ignorant, besides, that it would be a maritime war, and that France is not in a state to make such a one with advantage."

Colbert, turning round at this moment, saw D'Artagnan, who was seeking an interlocutor, during the "aside" of the king and Monsieur. He called him, at the same time saying in a low voice to Aramis, "We may talk with M. d'Artagnan, I suppose?"—"Oh, certainly," replied the ambassador.

"We were saying, M. d'Alaméda and I," said Colbert, "that war with the United Provinces would be a maritime war."—"That's evident enough," replied the musketeer.—"And what do you think of it, M. d'Artagnan?"—"I think that to carry on that maritime war you must have a very large land army."

"What did you say?" said Colbert, thinking he had misunderstood him.—"Why a land army?" said Aramis.—"Because the king will be beaten by sea if he has not the English with him; and when beaten by sea, he will be soon invaded, either by the Dutch in his ports, or by the Spaniards by land."—"And Spain neutral?" asked Aramis.—"Neutral as long as the king shall be the stronger," rejoined D'Artagnan.

Colbert admired that sagacity which never touched a question without illumining it thoroughly. Aramis smiled; he had long known that in diplomacy D'Artagnan acknowledged no master. Colbert, who like all proud men dwelt upon his fantasy with a certainty of success, resumed the subject, "Who told you, M. d'Artagnan, that the king had no navy?"—"Oh! I have taken no heed of these details," replied the captain. "I am but a middling sailor. Like all nervous people I hate the sea; and yet I have an idea that with ships, France being a seaport with two hundred heads, we should have sailors."

Colbert drew from his pocket a little oblong book divided into two columns. On the first were the names of vessels, on the other the figures recapitulating the number of cannon and men requisite to equip these ships. "I have had the same idea as you," said he to D'Artagnan; "and I have had an account drawn up of the vessels we have altogether,—thirty-five vessels."—"Thirty-five vessels! that is impossible!" cried D'Artagnan.—"Something like two thousand pieces of cannon," said Colbert. "That is what the king possesses at this moment. With thirty-five vessels we can make three squadrons, but I must have five."

"Five!" cried Aramis.—"They will be afloat before the end of the year, gentlemen; the king will have fifty ships of the line. With those we may venture on a contest, may we not?"—"To build vessels," said D'Artagnan, "is difficult, but possible. As to arming them, how is that to be done? In France there are neither foundries nor military docks."

"Bah!" replied Colbert, with a gay tone, "I have instituted all that this year and a half past, did you not know it? Don't you know M. d'Infreville?"—"D'Infreville?" replied D'Artagnan; "no." —"He is a man I have discovered; he has a speciality,—he knows how to set men to work. It is he who at Toulon has had the cannon made, and has cut the woods of Bourgogne. And then, Monsieur the Ambassador, you may not believe what I am going to tell you, but I have a further idea."—"Oh, Monsieur!" said Aramis, civilly, "I always believe you."

"Figure to yourself that, calculating upon the character of the Dutch, our allies, I said to myself, 'They are merchants, they are friends with the king; they will be happy to sell to the king what they fabricate for themselves. Then the more we buy—' Ah! I must add this: I have Forant,—do you know Forant, D'Artagnan?" Colbert, in his warmth, forgot himself; he called the captain simply "D'Artagnan," as the king did. But the captain only smiled at it. "No," replied he, "I don't know him."—"That is another man I have discovered with a genius for buying. This Forant has purchased for me three hundred and fifty thousand pounds of iron in balls, two hundred thousand pounds of powder, twelve cargoes of Northern timber, matches, grenades, pitch, tar,—I know not what! —with a saving of seven per cent. upon what all those articles would cost me made in France."

"That is a good idea," replied D'Artagnan,—"to have Dutch balls cast which will return to the Dutch."—"Is it not,—with loss too?" And Colbert laughed aloud. He was delighted with his own joke. "Still further," added he, "these same Dutch are building for the king at this moment six vessels after the model of the best of their marine. Destouches—ah! perhaps you don't know Destouches?"—"No, Monsieur."—"He is a man who has a glance singularly sure to discern, when a ship is launched, what are the

Epilogue

defects and qualities of that ship,—that is valuable, please to observe! Nature is truly whimsical. Well, this Destouches appeared to me to be a man likely to be useful in port, and he is superintending the construction of six vessels of seventy-eight guns, which the Provinces are building for his Majesty. It results from all this, my dear M. d'Artagnan, that the king, if he wished to quarrel with the Provinces, would have a very pretty fleet. Now, you know better than anybody else if the land army is good."

D'Artagnan and Aramis looked at each other, wondering at the mysterious labours this man had effected in a few years. Colbert understood them, and was touched by this best of flatteries. "If we in France were ignorant of what was going on," said D'Artagnan, "out of France still less must be known."

"That is why I told Monsieur the Ambassador," said Colbert, "that Spain, promising its neutrality, England helping us—"—"If England assists you," said Aramis, "I engage for the neutrality of Spain."—"I take you at your word," hastened Colbert to reply with his blunt *bonhomie*. "And, *à propos* of Spain, you have not the 'Golden Fleece,' M. d'Alaméda. I heard the king say the other day that he should like to see you wear the *grand cordon* of Saint Michael." Aramis bowed. "Oh!" thought D'Artagnan, "and Porthos is no longer here! What ells of ribbon would there be for him in these largesses! Good Porthos!"

"M. d'Artagnan," resumed Colbert, "between us two, you will have, I would wager, an inclination to lead your musketeers into Holland. Can you swim?" and he laughed like a man in a very good humour.—"Like an eel," replied D'Artagnan.—"Ah! but there are some rough passages of canals and marshes yonder, M. d'Artagnan, and the best swimmers are sometimes drowned there."—"It is my profession to die for his Majesty," said the musketeer. "Only as it is seldom that in war much water is met with without a little fire, I declare to you beforehand that I will do my best to choose fire. I am getting old; water freezes me, fire warms, M. Colbert."

And D'Artagnan looked so handsome in juvenile vigour and pride as he pronounced these words that Colbert, in his turn, could not help admiring him. D'Artagnan perceived the effect he had produced. He remembered that the best tradesman is he who fixes a high price upon his goods when they are valuable. He prepared, then, his price in advance. "So then," said Colbert, "we go into

Holland?"—"Yes," replied D'Artagnan; "only—"—"Only?" said M. Colbert.—"Only," repeated D'Artagnan, "there is in everything the question of interest, and the question of self-love. It is a very fine title,—that of captain of the musketeers; but observe this; we have now the king's guards and the military household of the king. A captain of musketeers ought either to command all that, and then he would absorb a hundred thousand livres a year for expenses of representation and table—"

"Well; but do you suppose, by chance, that the king would haggle with you?" said Colbert.—"Eh, Monsieur, you have not understood me," replied D'Artagnan, sure of having carried the question of interest; "I was telling you that I,—an old captain, formerly chief of the king's guard, having precedence of the marshals of France,—I saw myself one day in the trenches with two equals, the captain of the guards and the colonel commanding the Swiss. Now, at no price will I suffer that. I have old habits; I will stand to them."

Colbert felt this blow, but he was prepared for it. "I have been thinking of what you said just now," said he.—"About what, Monsieur?"—"We were speaking of canals and marshes in which people are drowned."—"Well!"—"Well; if they are drowned, it is for want of a boat, a plank, or a stick."—"Of a stick [bâton], however short it may be," said D'Artagnan.—"Exactly," said Colbert; "and therefore I never heard of an instance of a marshal of France being drowned."

D'Artagnan became pale with joy, and in not a very firm voice, he said, "People would be very proud of me in my country, if I were a marshal of France; but a man must have commanded an expedition as chief to obtain the bâton."—"Monsieur," said Colbert, "here is in this pocket-book, which you will study, a plan of a campaign; you are to carry it into execution next spring with a body of troops which the king puts under your orders."

D'Artagnan took the book tremblingly, and his fingers meeting with those of Colbert, the minister pressed the hand of the musketeer loyally. "Monsieur," said he, "we had both a revenge to take, one over the other. I have begun; it is now your turn!"—"I will do you justice, Monsieur," replied D'Artagnan, "and implore you to tell the king that the first opportunity that shall offer, he may depend upon a victory or seeing me dead."—"Then I will have

Death of D'Artagnan

the *fleurs-de-lis* for your marshal's bâton prepared immediately," said Colbert.

On the morrow of this day, Aramis, who was setting out for Madrid to negotiate the neutrality of Spain, came to embrace D'Artagnan at his hotel. "Let us love each other for four," said D'Artagnan; "we are now but two."—"And you will perhaps never see me again, dear D'Artagnan," said Aramis; "if you knew how I have loved you! I am old, I am extinguished, I am dead."

"My friend," said D'Artagnan, "you will live longer than I shall. Diplomacy commands you to live; but, for my part, honour condemns me to die."—"Bah! such men as we are, Monsieur the Marshal," said Aramis, "only die satiated with joy or glory."—"Ah!" replied D'Artagnan, with a melancholy smile, "I assure you, Monsieur the Duke, I feel very little appetite for either." They once more embraced, and two hours later they were separated.

THE DEATH OF D'ARTAGNAN

CONTRARY to what generally happens, whether in politics or morals, each kept his promise and did honour to his engagements.

The king recalled M. de Guiche and banished M. le Chevalier de Lorraine, so that Monsieur became ill in consequence. Madame set out for London, where she applied herself so earnestly to make her brother, Charles II., have a taste for the political counsels of Mademoiselle de Kéroualle, that the alliance between England and France was signed, and the English vessels, ballasted by a few millions of French gold, made a terrible campaign against the fleets of the United Provinces. Charles II. had promised Mademoiselle de Kéroualle a little gratitude for her good counsels; he made her Duchess of Portsmouth. Colbert had promised the king vessels, munitions, and victories. He kept his word, as is well known. In fine, Aramis, upon whose promises there was least dependence to be placed, wrote Colbert the following letter on the subject of the negotiations which he had undertaken at Madrid:—

The Man in the Iron Mask

"M. COLBERT,—I have the honour to send to you the R. P. d'Oliva, General *ad interim* of the Society of Jesus, my provisional successor. The reverend father will explain to you, M. Colbert, that I reserve to myself the direction of all the affairs of the Order which concern France and Spain; but that I am not willing to retain the title of general, which would throw too much light upon the course of the negotiations with which his Catholic Majesty wishes to entrust me. I shall resume that title by the command of his Majesty when the labours I have undertaken in concert with you, for the great glory of God and his Church, shall be brought to a good end. The R. P. d'Oliva will inform you likewise, Monsieur, of the consent which his Catholic Majesty gives to the signature of a treaty which assures the neutrality of Spain in the event of a war between France and the United Provinces. This consent will be valid, even if England, instead of being active, should satisfy herself with remaining neutral. As to Portugal, of which you and I have spoken, Monsieur, I can assure you it will contribute with all its resources to assist the most Christian king in his war. I beg you, M. Colbert, to preserve to me your friendship, as also to believe in my profound attachment, and to lay my respect at the feet of his most Christian Majesty.

"LE DUC D'ALAMÉDA."

Aramis had then performed more than he had promised; it remained to be known how the king, M. Colbert, and D'Artagnan would be faithful to one another. In the spring, as Colbert had predicted, the land army entered on its campaign. It preceded, in magnificent order, the court of Louis XIV., who, setting out on horseback, surrounded by carriages filled with ladies and courtiers, conducted the *élite* of his kingdom to this sanguinary *fête*. The officers of the army, it is true, had no other music than the artillery of the Dutch forts; but it was enough for a great number, who found in this war honours, advancement, fortune, or death.

M. d'Artagnan set out commanding a body of twelve thousand men, cavalry and infantry, with which he was ordered to take the different places which form the knots of that strategic network which is called La Frise. Never was an army conducted more gallantly to an expedition. The officers knew that their leader, prudent and skilful as he was brave, would not sacrifice a single man, nor yield an inch of ground, without necessity. He had the old habits of war,—to live upon the country, keep his soldiers singing

The Death of D'Artagnan

and the enemy weeping. The captain of the king's musketeers put his effort into showing that he knew his business. Never were opportunities better chosen, *coups de main* better supported, or better advantage taken of errors on the part of the besieged. The army commanded by D'Artagnan took twelve small places within a month. He was engaged in besieging the thirteenth, which had held out five days. D'Artagnan caused the trenches to be opened without appearing to suppose that these people would ever allow themselves to be taken. In the army of this man the pioneers and labourers were a body full of emulation, ideas, and zeal, because he treated them like soldiers, knew how to render their work glorious, and never allowed them to be killed if he could prevent it. It should have been seen then with what eagerness the marshy glebes of Holland were turned over. Those turf heaps, those mounds of potter's clay, melted at the words of the soldiers like butter in the vast frying-pans of the Friesland housewives.

M. d'Artagnan despatched a courier to the king to give him an account of the last successes, which redoubled the good-humour of his Majesty and his inclination to amuse the ladies. These victories of M. d'Artagnan gave so much majesty to the prince that Madame de Montespan no longer called him anything but Louis the Invincible. So that Mademoiselle de la Vallière, who only called the king Louis the Victorious, lost much of his Majesty's favour. Besides, her eyes were frequently red, and for an Invincible nothing is more disagreeable than a mistress who weeps while everything is smiling around her. The star of Mademoiselle de la Vallière was being drowned in the horizon in clouds and tears. But the gaiety of Madame de Montespan redoubled with the successes of the king, and consoled him for every other unpleasant circumstance. It was to D'Artagnan the king owed this; and his Majesty was anxious to acknowledge these services. He wrote to M. Colbert:—

"M. COLBERT,—We have a promise to fulfil with M. d'Artagnan, who so well keeps his. This is to inform you that the time is come for performing it. All provisions for this purpose you shall be furnished with in due time.   LOUIS."

In consequence of this, Colbert, who detained the envoy of D'Artagnan, placed in the hands of that messenger a letter from himself for D'Artagnan and a small coffer of ebony inlaid with gold, which, without doubt, was very heavy, as a guard of five men was given to the messenger to assist him in carrying it. These persons arrived before the place which D'Artagnan was besieging, towards day-break, and presented themselves at the lodgings of the general. They were told that M. d'Artagnan, annoyed by a sortie which the governor, an artful man, had made the evening before, and in which the works had been destroyed, seventy-seven men killed, and the reparation of the breaches begun, had just gone with ten companies of grenadiers to reconstruct the works.

M. Colbert's envoy had orders to go and seek M. d'Artagnan wherever he might be, or at whatever hour of the day or night. He directed his course, therefore, towards the trenches, followed by his escort, all on horseback. They perceived M. d'Artagnan in the open plain, with his gold-laced hat, his long cane, and his large gilded cuffs. He was biting his white moustache, and shaking off with his left hand the dust which the passing balls threw up from the ground they ploughed near him. They also saw, amid this terrible fire which filled the air with its hissing whistle, officers handling the shovel, soldiers rolling barrows, and vast *fascines,* carried or dragged by from ten to twenty men, covering the front of the trench, reopened to the centre by this extraordinary effort of the general animating his soldiers. In three hours all had been re-instated. D'Artagnan began to speak more mildly; and he became quite calm when the captain of the pioneers approached him, hat in hand, to tell him that the trench was again in condition for occu-pancy. This man had scarcely finished speaking when a ball took off one of his legs, and he fell into the arms of D'Artagnan. The latter lifted up his soldier, and quietly, with soothing words, carried him into the trench amid the enthusiastic applause of the regiments. From that time it was no longer ardour; it was delirium. Two companies stole away up to the advanced posts, which they destroyed instantly.

When their comrades, restrained with great difficulty by D'Artagnan, saw them lodged upon the bastions, they rushed forward likewise, and soon a furious assault was made upon the counterscarp, upon which depended the safety of the place. D'Artagnan perceived there was only one means left of stopping his army, and that was to lodge it in the place. He directed all his force to two breaches, which the besieged were busy in repairing. The shock

The Death of D'Artagnan

was terrible; eighteen companies took part in it, and D'Artagnan went with the rest within half-cannon-shot of the place, to support the attack by *échelons*. The cries of the Dutch, who were being poniarded upon their guns by D'Artagnan's grenadiers, were distinctly audible. The struggle grew fiercer with the despair of the governor, who disputed his position foot by foot. D'Artagnan, to put an end to the affair and silence the fire, which was unceasing, sent a fresh column, which penetrated like a wimble through the gates that remained solid; and he soon perceived upon the ramparts, through the fire, the terrified flight of the besieged pursued by the besiegers.

It was at this moment that the general, breathing freely and full of joy, heard a voice behind him saying, "Monsieur, if you please, —from M. Colbert." He broke the seal of a letter, which contained these words:—

"M. D'ARTAGNAN,—The king commands me to inform you that he has nominated you Marshal of France, as a reward for your good services and the honour you do to his arms. The king is highly pleased, Monsieur, with the captures you have made; he commands you in particular to finish the siege you have begun, with good fortune to you and success for him."

D'Artagnan was standing with a heated countenance and a sparkling eye. He looked up to watch the progress of his troops upon the walls, still enveloped in red and black volumes of smoke. "I have finished," replied he to the messenger; "the city will have surrendered in a quarter of an hour." He then resumed his reading:

"The coffer, M. d'Artagnan, is my own present. You will not be sorry to see that while you warriors are drawing the sword to defend the king, I am animating the pacific arts to adorn you with rewards that are worthy of you. I commend myself to your friendship, Monsieur the Marshal, and beg you to believe in all mine.
"COLBERT."

D'Artagnan, intoxicated with joy, made a sign to the messenger, who approached with his coffer in his hands. But at the moment the marshal was going to look at it, a loud explosion resounded from the ramparts and called his attention towards the city. "It is strange," said D'Artagnan, "that I don't yet see the king's flag upon the walls, or hear the drums beat for a parley." He launched three hundred fresh men under a high-spirited officer, and ordered another breach to be beaten. Then, being more tranquil, he turned towards the coffer which Colbert's envoy held out to him. It was his treasure,—he had won it.

D'Artagnan was holding out his hand to open the coffer, when a ball from the city crushed it in the arms of the officer, struck D'Artagnan full in the chest, and knocked him down upon a sloping heap of earth, while the *fleurdelisé* bâton, escaping from the broken sides of the box, came rolling under the powerless hand of the marshal. D'Artagnan endeavoured to raise himself. It was thought he had been knocked down without being wounded. A terrible cry broke from the group of his frightened officers. The marshal was covered with blood; the paleness of death ascended slowly to his noble countenance. Leaning upon the arms which were held out on all sides to receive him, he was able once more to turn his eyes towards the place, and to distinguish the white flag at the crest of the principal bastion; his ears, already deaf to the sounds of life, caught feebly the rolling of the drum which announced the victory. Then, clasping in his nerveless hand the bâton, ornamented with its *fleurs-de-lis,* he cast down upon it his eyes, which had no longer the power of looking upwards towards heaven, and fell back murmuring these strange words, which appeared to the surprised soldiers cabalistic words,—words which had formerly represented so many things upon earth, and which none but the dying man longer comprehended,—"Athos, Porthos, *au revoir!* Aramis, adieu for ever!"

Of the four valiant men whose history we have related, there now remained but one single body; God had taken back the souls.

THE END

GREAT ILLUSTRATED CLASSICS

Adam Bede—*Eliot*
The Arabian Nights
Around the World in 80 Days—*Verne*
Autobiography of Benjamin Franklin
Ben-Hur—*Wallace*
The Black Arrow—*Stevenson*
Black Beauty—*Sewell*
The Call of the Wild—*London*
Captains Courageous—*Kipling*
Christmas Tales—*Dickens*
The Cloister and the Hearth—*Reade*
A Connecticut Yankee in King Arthur's Court—*Clemens*
The Cruise of the Cachalot—*Bullen*
David Copperfield—*Dickens*
The Deerslayer—*Cooper*
Dr. Jekyll and Mr. Hyde—*Stevenson*
Emma—*Austen*
Famous Tales of Sherlock Holmes—*Doyle*
From the Earth to the Moon—*Verne*
Great Expectations—*Dickens*
Green Mansions—*Hudson*
Gulliver's Travels—*Swift*
Hawthorne's Short Stories—*Hawthorne*
Henry Esmond—*Thackeray*
The House of the 7 Gables—*Hawthorne*
Huckleberry Finn—*Clemens*
The Hunchback of Notre-Dame—*Hugo*
Ivanhoe—*Scott*
Jane Eyre—*Brontë*
A Journey to the Centre of the Earth—*Verne*
Kenilworth—*Scott*
Kidnapped—*Stevenson*
Kim—*Kipling*
King Arthur—*Malory*
Last Days of Pompeii—*Bulwer-Lytton*
The Last of the Mohicans—*Cooper*
Lord Jim—*Conrad*
Lorna Doone—*Blackmore*
The Luck of Roaring Camp—*Harte*
The Man in the Iron Mask—*Dumas*
The Mill on the Floss—*Eliot*
The Moonstone—*Collins*
The Mysterious Island—*Verne*
The Odyssey—*Homer*
The Old Curiosity Shop—*Dickens*

Oliver Twist—*Dickens*
The Oregon Trail—*Parkman*
The Pathfinder—*Cooper*
Père Goriot—*Balzac*
Pickwick Papers—*Dickens*
The Pilot—*Cooper*
The Pioneers—*Cooper*
The Prairie—*Cooper*
Pride and Prejudice—*Austen*
The Prince and the Pauper—*Clemens*
Quentin Durward—*Scott*
Quo Vadis—*Sienkiewicz*
The Red Badge of Courage—*Crane*
The Return of the Native—*Hardy*
The Rise of Silas Lapham—*Howells*
Robinson Crusoe—*Defoe*
The Scarlet Letter—*Hawthorne*
The Scarlet Pimpernel—*Orczy*
Sense and Sensibility—*Austen*
Silas Marner—*Eliot*
The Sketch Book—*Irving*
The Spy—*Cooper*
A Tale of Two Cities—*Dickens*
Tales—*Poe*
The Talisman—*Scott*
Tess of the D'Urbervilles—*Hardy*
The Three Musketeers—*Dumas*
Three Comedies: A Midsummer Night's Dream, The Merchant of Venice, As You Like It—*Shakespeare*
Three Histories: Henry IV, Part I; Henry IV, Part II; Henry V—*Shakespeare*
Three Tragedies: Julius Caesar, Hamlet, Macbeth—*Shakespeare*
Tom Sawyer—*Clemens*
Treasure Island—*Stevenson*
20,000 Leagues Under the Sea—*Verne*
Two Years Before the Mast—*Dana*
Typhoon—*Conrad*
Uncle Tom's Cabin—*Stowe*
Up From Slavery—*Washington*
Vanity Fair—*Thackeray*
Walden—*Thoreau*
The Way of All Flesh—*Butler*
The White Company—*Doyle*
White Fang and Other Stories—*London*
The Wreck of the Grosvenor—*Russell*
Wuthering Heights—*Brontë*

GREAT ILLUSTRATED CLASSICS—TITANS

Afloat and Ashore—*Cooper*
Anna Karenina—*Tolstoy*
Autobiography of Benvenuto Cellini
Barnaby Rudge—*Dickens*
Bleak House—*Dickens*
Crime and Punishment—*Dostoevsky*
Dombey & Son—*Dickens*
Don Quixote—*Cervantes*

Everybody's Plutarch
Little Dorrit—*Dickens*
Martin Chuzzlewit—*Dickens*
Nicholas Nickleby—*Dickens*
Our Mutual Friend—*Dickens*
Short Novels of Henry James—*James*
Twenty Years After—*Dumas*
Westward Ho!—*Kingsley*